man about town

ALSO BY MARK MERLIS

An Arrow's Flight
American Studies

man about town

MARK MERLIS

FOURTH ESTATE • *London* and *New York*

MAN ABOUT TOWN Copyright © 2003 by Mark Merlis.

Fourth Estate and HarperCollins books may be purchased for
educational, business, or sales promotional use. For information,
please write: Special Markets Department,
HarperCollins Publishers Inc., 10 East 53rd Street,
New York, NY 10022.

FIRST EDITION
Designed by Dinah Drazin
Printed on acid-free paper
Library of Congress Cataloging-in-Publication Data
Merlis, Mark.
Man about town/Mark Merlis.
p.cm

ISBN 0-00-715611-1

1.Gay men-Fiction. 2. Washington (D.C)-Fiction. I. Title.
PS3563.E7422 M3 2003   813'.54-dc21   2002019926

For Leslie Breed and always for Bob

one

It was almost six o'clock, so Joel Lingeman wanted a drink.

Senator Flanagan did, too, probably. He looked attentive enough. He had his head tilted more or less in the direction of Senator Harris, who was trying to explain something about Medicare hospital payments. Only the solitary, pudgy finger beating rhythmically on the arm of his chair betrayed that Flanagan's thoughts were the same as Joel's: they weren't going to finish that evening, there were about fifty more amendments, and the big ones late on the list. The Republic would not be imperiled if the Finance Committee recessed until tomorrow and everybody went off and had a drink.

Joel could almost hear Flanagan say it, the way he used to when he was chairman. "Let us recess until the morrow." How Flanagan used to love to say "the morrow," relishing and at the same time mocking its formality, drawing out the last syllable into a round mantra of transcendental self-esteem. Except he wasn't the chairman any more; a Republican was the chairman. So Flanagan didn't get to say when the committee would recess, no more than Joel did.

Flanagan gazed out at the room now, over half-moon glasses that somehow clung to the very tip of his prodigious whiskey nose. He scanned the little audience of staffers and Administration satraps gathered for the hearing, and his eyes met Joel's. Joel had worked on the Hill twenty years, Flanagan must have seen him a thousand times, but of course a senator wouldn't recognize Joel. Still, for a moment there passed between them a look such as might have been exchanged by the Sun King and a serving boy, each in his way held captive at some interminable dinner.

The committee had been marking up the chairman's Medicare proposals since about three—that was the phrase, *marking up*, as if each senator had come with his own little blue pencil. Three hours already, if you didn't count the long breaks when senators left for a floor vote, three hours of deliberation on gripping subjects like clinical laboratory reimbursement. Even a senator, whose entire job was just to keep his eyes open at sessions like this one, might have been forgiven if he had once or twice nodded off. But Flanagan dutifully turned back to Senator Harris, one eyebrow raised, his thin bluish lips curled in the little Buddha smile he always wore as he listened indulgently to a jerk.

Senator Harris was still expatiating about hospital payments in Montana. Joe Harris—that was how senators styled themselves now, Joe or Dick or Bob—had to be the most vacuous whore in the Senate. No one had ever heard a sensible word from him, nor detected a principle he would not abandon for a three-course lunch, unless making sure he never had a hair out of place was a principle. But he was kind of cute.

Joel had been noticing lately that there were a couple of cute senators. This was a function of his own aging, of course: when he had started in this job, all the senators were old men. Majestic, distant figures named Everett or Hubert who strode through the corridors talking gravely about matters of state. Some time when Joel wasn't looking, there had arrived these brisk, trim, thirty-something nonentities, each with his little White House dream.

Whereas Joel was forty-five and had arrived at his terminal placement. This didn't bother him especially; he didn't mind being forty-five, he didn't mind his placement. But it was eerie, sitting in a committee room in the Dirksen Senate Office Building and watching these juveniles acting like senators, as if they were in a high-school play. Joel's generation had taken over the world. The generation after Joel's really—in the person of moderately cute Joe Harris.

Harris looked even younger than most, with the faintly deranged perkiness of a Dan Quayle or a John Kasich. It was hard for him to look grown-up and serious as he presented some amendment he didn't understand to help some constituents he didn't care about. He was just finishing his prepared remarks about it, and he had the relieved look of a school kid who has delivered his book report without throwing up.

Senator Altman had a question. Senator Altman always came up with a question, just to show off, as if he were still the valedictorian at the High School of Science. Flanagan turned with histrionic ponderousness and looked at Altman with frustration and contempt—somehow conveying all this without breaking his smile. Nobody cared about the amendment, the chairman had already okayed it, it affected about three goddamn hospitals in Montana. They didn't have to take half an hour on it just so Altman could display his earnestness and intellect. Of course, Flanagan used to spend whole afternoons in similar self-display back when he was in charge. But he never ran over into the cocktail hour.

Harris couldn't answer the question. He raised his hand over his right shoulder, serenely confident that his legislative aide would already be hovering behind him with the relevant piece of paper. The LA, a tiny, harried-looking woman, was there.

3

Harris took the paper without looking at her or thanking her. They said he sometimes threw things at his aides. Papers, books, once a telephone. This primordial management technique evidently worked: the LA not only had the precise piece of paper he needed, but had a copy all ready for Altman.

Harris's paper was some sort of spreadsheet; Altman and Harris slogged through it together, column by column. They were, respectively, the junior Democrat and junior Republican on Finance, so they faced each other from the two extremities of the horseshoe-shaped committee desk at whose apex were the chairman and Flanagan.

Harris couldn't figure out what the different columns in his spreadsheet were. Altman peppered him with questions, and he was too proud to turn to his LA, who was literally kneeling behind him, for the answers. He stammered, got more and more confused, turned red with embarrassment and anger; this would be a phone-throwing night.

Flanagan stood up, exasperated, and darted out through the little door behind the dais. Headed for his hideaway, probably, and a shot or two of Irish whiskey. Senators could leave the room when they felt like it; Joel couldn't.

No, that wasn't right. Joel was a free adult, as free as Flanagan. He could have left if he'd wanted to, he wasn't strapped to his chair. Probably no one would have missed him if he had got up, like Flanagan, and had run off to his own hideaway—the Hill Club, just a few blocks away—for a quick one. Except then this would be the night, wouldn't it, when someone would have a question only he could answer. "What the hell happened to Lingeman? He was right here . . ."

What then? They wouldn't fire him. There were people in the Office of Legislative Analysis who had no apparent vital signs and who got merit increases every year. They wouldn't fire Joel Lingeman if he happened to disappear for twenty minutes, or thirty, tops, just a quick one and a couple of cigarettes. This anarchic thought scared him. It was so easy to move on to the next thought: go to the Hill Club and don't come back at all. And the next: don't show up for work at the OLA tomorrow morning. And the last, terrifying—leave it all. Job, apartment, even his lover Sam: ditch it all. Go somewhere and live on his 401(k) and . . . But there were penalties for drawing on your 401(k) when you were only forty-five. There were penalties for everything.

Joel slouched down in his seat and stared up at the ceiling. For some reason the ceiling in the Finance Committee room had plaster bas-reliefs of the signs of the zodiac. Whose whimsy had this been, to adorn a chamber in the Dirksen building with goats and crabs?

Harris's LA suddenly materialized to Joel's left, whispered urgently, "I can never figure out this payment stuff. What on earth is a 'Medicare-dependent hospital'?"

"Um," he said. A good thing he hadn't left. What was her name? Melanie something. Wearing an ill-chosen red suit with frogs of black braid, such as an organ grinder might have picked for his monkey. Practically a schoolgirl, like all the LAs. "It's, like, a little hospital that no one will go to if they can drive anywhere else. So all they get is old people on Medicare."

"Oh," Melanie said. "Are there a lot of those in Montana?"

"Beats me. Don't you know?"

"I've never even been there. I just started with the senator a few months ago."

"Right, I remember." They came and went so quickly, LAs: a year or two on the Hill, then off to be a lobbyist for a phar-maceutical company. This was just as well. If any of them had stayed long enough to learn their jobs they wouldn't have needed Joel, would they? "Anyway, these hospitals live on their Medicare money, so there are these special payment rules for them. First of all—"

Melanie shook her head; this was already too deep. "You'd better come up and explain to the senator."

Joel was startled: this happened once in a blue moon. Staffers hardly ever wanted him to talk to their members. Because of course they didn't want to admit that there were questions they couldn't answer.

Melanie led the way to the dais. Joel followed her without much trepidation. Senators were a little scarier than congressmen, even more prone to look at you as if you were some sort of lizard who had chanced to enter their field of vision. Still, all you had to do was remember that the instant you were out of sight they would forget they had ever encountered you. Forget that along with whatever bit of information you had tried to impart.

Joel and Melanie crouched behind Harris's seat and Joel—whispering and using very small words—explained the obscure payment rule Harris was proposing to amend. Harris sucked his lips in and tried to look comprehending. Joel was short of breath for some reason, maybe just thrilled with his own momentary importance. But he went on until Harris nodded and put a hand up. Meaning either that he understood or that he wasn't ever going to; either way, he'd heard enough.

Harris squinted at Melanie. "If you drafted this, why can't you explain it?"

"I didn't draft it. The state hospital association people gave it to you at that breakfast last week." Along with a check, probably.

"Oh, right." He turned back to Joel. "So, does this cost anything?"

"It's an asterisk," Joel said. Meaning a cost that rounded to less than a million.

"Fine." Harris smiled, actually thanked Joel, before turning to the microphone and playing back everything Joel had just told him. With surprising accuracy, but as if he had learned the words phonetically, like a foreign starlet making her Hollywood debut.

Altman, his tormentor, retreated. "Okay, I get it," he said.

Abruptly, because of course he didn't understand Medicare hospital payments any better than Harris. This had all taken a good fifteen minutes, for a lousy asterisk. The time they spent on things seemed to be in inverse proportion to their importance; billion-dollar items flew right by. Maybe this could all be expressed as some sort of equation. Where t is time and m is money, $t=1/m^n$. If he could just have figured out the formula, Joel might have computed exactly how long it would be before he could have a drink.

He was still feeling, as he headed back to his seat, that strange breathlessness. Not nerves, something almost sexual—as if a bubble of elation had arisen from somewhere and stuck in his throat.

Once in his seat he closed his eyes for a second and tried to imagine going to bed with Joe Harris. That is, he didn't spontaneously imagine it, he made himself imagine it as a sort of diagnostic test, to find the sore spot in him. Harris was undoubtedly straight, must have had the standard-issue buck-toothed wife and photogenic kids. So they didn't go to bed, exactly; Harris just unzipped his fly and brought forth his penis, the Member's member, for Joel to suck.

Impossible, there was nothing erotic about it at all. Joel didn't go for straight men. Well, as a practical matter, he didn't *go* for anyone; he and Sam had been monogamous for years and years. But he never even fantasized about straight men. Funny, when they were all he thought about as a kid. All those years before he came out, dreaming of something one-way with a fraternity jock or maybe a sailor. Trade, they used to call it. He hadn't heard that expression in years: I did him for trade.

Joel was quite sure he didn't want to *do* the junior senator from Montana. Whatever species of self-abasement those desires had involved, he had gotten over them. But if he didn't want sex with Harris, he wanted something. Something ancient and irrecoverable, something he'd wanted before he'd even known what sex was.

Joel looked up to find that Senator Altman's LA, a chubby and somnolent guy whose invariable blazer never quite covered his butt, was passing out a whole sheaf of new amendments. He handed a set to Joel, beaming as if it were a birthday present he had made himself. Which he had, sort of: that was pretty much what staffers did, labored all year so their members would have a few amendments. For a senator to come to a mark-up with no amendments at all would have been like showing up at a covered dish party without any potato salad.

Altman had brought plenty to the party: pages numbered Altman Amendment #1 through Altman Amendment #14. Even the chairman—who was either unflappable or brain-dead, it was hard to tell—looked a little dismayed as he riffled through the pages. "Are we going to need much time on these?" he asked.

"I wouldn't think," Altman said. "We've cleared most of them. Maybe we need to talk a little about number five. Oh, and number seven." Everyone flipped dutifully to Altman Amendment #5—sharing, perhaps, Joel's foreboding at the grim words "We need to talk a little."

Joel closed his eyes again. Something ancient, the thrill he'd felt while talking to Harris, that might not have been sexual, exactly, but was somewhere in the neighborhood. Joel expounding, the cute guy listening intently, Joel out of breath . . .

Alex.

In high school. They were in an empty classroom, side by side at two desks beneath the open windows. Joel was explaining the math problem. An October afternoon, classes over; outside some guys were playing touch football. Joel glanced at them, but Alex didn't, just looked steadily at Joel as they went over $t=1/m^n$. Joel's diaphragm tightened. Alex was looking straight at him—Alex, the golden lacrosse player, who, thirty years on, still sometimes made a cameo appearance in Joel's dreams.

Funny, he never dreamt of Sam.

Joel could not meet Alex's eyes, but Alex was *looking at Joel*. And Joel was tingling with excitement at the very fact that he had entered Alex's consciousness. Alex was listening to him. Alex was sitting next to him, so close that their thighs almost touched. Alex's thighs, slender and sturdy in the corduroy jeans the cool guys wore that year. Joel's thighs, in the shapeless flannel trousers his mother had bought at Robert Hall. Almost touching.

They didn't need to touch. Joel was sure of it, thinking back. He hadn't wanted to touch Alex. Not even touch, much less . . . no more than he wanted to kneel in front of Senator Harris. But he had all but exploded with happiness that afternoon in the classroom.

Now he was grown up and had other kinds of explosions; Sam knew where the detonator was and could hit it with gratifying precision. Gratifying, maybe a little monotonous. That was what grown-ups got, and it was plenty. Still, it was nothing like—this wasn't a matter of degree, but of kind—grown-up pleasures were nothing like the exhilaration, the almost harrowing joy of just *being there*, with Alex, being there in Alex's field of vision.

How much he had wanted to be seen in those years. Just seen, by Alex and his friends. As though, if they would only look at him, he would be alive, as they were.

Alive, those boys—what did their lives consist of? Going to practice, going out drinking Friday night after the game, making out on double dates, all the rest. Just what was natural to them. Yet their existence, the fact of them, was always on Joel's mind. Every moment in high school was colored by his continuous awareness of their lives, their instinctual being. The way they could do whatever they wanted to do and feel that it was right. Boys would be boys; whatever they did was, tautologically, what boys did. And they saw one another. They sat together in the lunch room, they joked together in the locker room, they shared cigarettes out on the parking lot, where you could smoke if you weren't failing anything. Which Alex was—that was why he and Joel were there together in that empty classroom.

They saw one another, when they wouldn't have seen Joel if he had shown up at assembly wearing a red suit with braided black frogs. But Alex was there with him. Maybe a little impressed that Joel could figure out what n was.

He wondered if he hadn't spent his whole life trying to impress jocks who couldn't pass high school algebra. All the years he had spent becoming, for Christ's sake, the world's authority on Medicare hospital reimbursement. So that he could for an instant enter the field of vision of pathetic Joe Harris.

Alex. Joel sat in the hearing room and almost spoke the name out loud.

Amendment # 7

Senator Altman

Medicare Restricted to United States Citizens

Section 1818(a)(3) of the Social Security Act (42 U.S.C. 1395i-2(a)(3)) is amended:

(a) by replacing the word "resident" with "citizen," and
(b) by striking the words "is either" and everything that follows.

"This changes Medicare for aliens," Altman said. Mumbled, rather, as if he were a little ashamed of himself. He went on: "Right now, a non-citizen can get Medicare if they're sixty-five and they've been here five years. This would eliminate that."

The chairman woke up. "We give Medicare to illegal aliens?"

"No, they're legally here. But they aren't citizens."

"What do you know," the chairman said.

"We let them get Medicare even though they may never have paid taxes."

"No kidding." The chairman turned to his chief of staff, frowning. Why had he never been told about this outrage, larcenous foreigners pouring off the ships just to get Medicare? Why wasn't *he* fixing it, instead of the junior member from the other party? The chief of staff avoided his gaze and turned to stare coldly at Altman.

"So this would put an end to that," Altman said.

Joel chuckled. Yes, indeed: some eighty-year-old immigrant would get her goddamn fingers out of the public purse. This had to take the prize for the stupidest and most malignant proposal, in a year when Congress had displayed an unprecedented degree of insouciance toward widows and orphans. And from Gerald Altman, no less, a Democrat who was for some reason regarded as a liberal. Maybe because he looked like a liberal—the UNICEF tie, the hair a hemisphere of tight silver curls—or maybe because everyone just assumed that a Jewish senator from a rustbelt state had to be a liberal.

Joel chuckled, partly because he couldn't stand up and scream, but also because his revulsion was not unmixed with a sort of simple, sporting pleasure. Was this corrupt, his almost aesthetic delight in the sheer sordidness of the spectacle? Was he altogether too inside-the-beltway, smirking as nineteen unprincipled men got ready to ambush some widow in a babushka who probably lived on cat food?

Because they would, surely, pass Altman Amendment #7. It was too beautiful to fail. Medicare on its way to bankruptcy, a bunch of parasites getting something for nothing. Usually you couldn't do anything to old people: swarms of Gray Panthers would show up armed with pitchforks and shuffleboard cues. But Senator Altman had found—eureka!—*old people who didn't vote*. Even the chairman was shaking his

11

head in frank admiration. Eighteen to one, easy, or eighteen to zero if Flanagan didn't stagger back from his hideaway in time to thunder what might be the only nay.

Joel found himself thinking once more about high school. Maybe because sitting in a closed hearing while Senator Altman demonstrated that he could name every goddamn subcategory of Persons Resident under Color of Law was not at all unlike being trapped in a classroom on a spring day.

He didn't just think about high school: he dove quite deliberately into the fantasy he sometimes had—who doesn't?—of going back and doing it right this time. Waking up one morning fourteen again and able to do it right. What would right have consisted of? Studying harder so he could have gone to Harvard instead of the ivy-deprived backup school he'd had to settle for? Coming out at about the same time as his first pubic hair, and then blowing every boy on the lacrosse team?

Usually these counterfactuals were good for a few minutes' entertainment as he waited for the Metro or stood in line alone at some movie Sam didn't want to see. Tonight he couldn't get into the game, for some reason. Even his favorite scene—the one where Alex put aside the algebra book and whispered that he had something momentous to reveal about himself, something Joel must never repeat to anyone—even conjuring that impossible instant left Joel feeling empty, empty and a little sour.

Pathetic, a forty-five-year-old man sitting in a closed hearing where weighty things were being decided, picking at scabs left over from high school. But maybe it was pathetic only if he called that part of his life "high school," those years of drama, ambition, burgeoning desire mockingly reduced to a situation comedy of phys ed, 45-records, and pimples. Those long years: whole lives, selves, tried on and abandoned in a single semester. Crushes—Alex only the most memorable in a continuous series, boys whose names he couldn't remember but whose faces, bodies were still quite vivid to him, those young bodies alive now only in Joel's memories. Oh, and vocations—lawyer, architect, actor, concert pianist.

Such plans: when he was older he would have a penthouse in New York and go out every night in black tie, like some guy in a magazine. Or, more domestically: smoke a pipe, wear tweeds, live in a house by Mies van der Rohe. Have strapping sons who played lacrosse and—this part of the picture, tellingly, always a little vague—a wife, wisecracking, petite, adoring. They would go to plays and fine dinners, they would go to Europe. They would somehow produce those sons.

Should it perhaps have been a clue for him, even at fourteen, that while other boys were keenly interested in the mechanics of production, wanted to *do it*—he just wanted *to have done it*? And, having done it, to lie with that terribly indistinct woman in their Mies bedroom, hold her and fall into sleep without thinking, not once, of Alex or Simon or . . .

So much that hadn't happened. Thank God: if he even tried to step into the dreams he had once dreamt so hard, he found them immeasurably tedious. A concert pianist—terrific. Whole days of practicing three measures over and over so he could stand in white tie and hear the ovation: "Good boy, haven't you practiced hard!" A Mies house, with the winter cold coming through all those windows and probably—art being one thing and shelter another—leaks in a million places. Mrs. Lingeman going through menopause by now, and those sons— those sons, what had he been thinking of?

He snorted; all too clear what he had been thinking of. A couple of captive boys, eternally sixteen, throwing the lacrosse ball back and forth on the lawn outside the plate-glass window. Even as a kid, years before he had uttered the word "gay" to himself, about himself, when he had tried to summon up a heterosexual future, he had peopled the conjugal dwelling with two hunks and, consigned to the shadows, the merely requisite Mrs. Lingeman.

He was gay, he couldn't ever have been anything else. That kid who had had other plans, he was just a laughable little chump. Whose very dreams were a tissue of self-deception and evasion. Except: how could someone lie to himself in his dreams?

Once you made up your mind, once you called yourself by name, then you had to whip the past into line. No unruly memories. But that little chump wanted what he wanted. And he was still crying for it. Sitting in a hearing room and looking at some moronic senator and crying out for it, whatever irrecoverable something he had wanted and never got.

A buzzer sounded, and a little light went on beneath the hearing-room clock. This was some kind of signal—one light for a quorum call, two for a vote, or vice versa. Joel had seen a card once with the code on it, but he could never remember. Though he did seem to recall that twelve buzzers was a nuclear attack. Whatever one buzzer meant, senators were standing up, wearily, like kids shuffling from history to algebra. Some were already heading toward the elevators and the new multi-million-dollar subway that would hurtle them the 400 yards from the Dirksen Building to the Senate side of the Capitol. The chairman was talking on the phone behind his chair. Joel was in suspense. The chairman could announce that they'd all come back and resume after the vote, or he could—

The chairman put the phone down, turned to the room, sighed. "I gather there are five or six votes. And people will probably want some dinner. So if there's no objection I think we'll recess until . . ." Joel's heart sank; he was going to say ten p.m. or something. "Until the call of the chair."

It was happy hour.

In the corridor the lobbyists cornered various staffers, trying to find out what had been going on. What had the committee done about home health payments? Had they gotten to Flanagan's amendment on teaching hospitals? One guy headed toward Joel, mouth already forming a question. Joel didn't recognize him; he must have been new, just homing in on anybody with an ID badge. Before he could speak, Joel put a hand up to stop him. "I'm from OLA," Joel said. Meaning that he wasn't allowed to talk about what he'd heard; a vow of silence was the price OLA people paid for the privilege of sitting in on exciting sessions like the one he'd just escaped.

Joel felt important: I know what happened to hospital payments in Montana and you don't. But the lobbyist said, "What's OLA?" and turned to pursue someone more helpful. Joel waved at a few people, veterans who had waited in this corridor year after year—the guy from the psychiatric hospitals, a couple of people from HMOs. They waved back but didn't interrupt their conversations with some of the more garrulous and indiscreet staffers.

Joel had made it through the crowd and was waiting for the elevator when Melanie caught him. "Do you understand this stuff about aliens?" she said.

"No," he lied. "Why don't you call me tomorrow morning when I've had a chance to check it out?"

She pouted. "All right. But I know the senator's going to want to know about this first thing."

"First thing."

It was only quarter of seven. Joel could make it to the Hill Club—on the House side, three or four blocks away—in ten minutes. And it was Thursday; Sam had evening hours Tuesdays and Thursdays. He wouldn't get off until nine or nine-thirty, so Joel could have just as protracted a happy hour as he wanted and still be home in time to fix a late supper. These late nights for Sam were a recent innovation, just the last few months. Sam said the office had to stay open, there were a million lawyers and people like that who wouldn't come in for physical therapy during the day, giving up a billable hour; if Sam's office couldn't accommodate them, somebody else would. Joel said it was a shame, though he was delighted that, two nights a week, he had a few hours of liberty.

It was warm out, the first really nice spring evening, or the first Joel had noticed; spring was so short in Washington, it was easy to let it slip right by. Joel even slowed down a little, strolled down First Street with the unhurried exuberance of a convict who has just been paroled. Free: free to toddle over to the Hill Club instead of having to rush home to Mrs. Lingeman and the two brats. He had been headed for the Hill Club his whole life.

Everything he had hoped for as a boy was silly. So why did he turn so often to the fantasy of going back and doing it over? It wasn't about finding and correcting some actual slippage from the course that would have led him to a fuller life. He couldn't imagine a fuller life. Or he could—not in a child-infested house but in that other fantasy domicile of his boyhood, he and Sam in that penthouse in New York, prepos-terously wealthy A-list faggots smiling for the photos in the parties-you-weren't-invited-to pages of the *Times*. But even these fantasies, which he visited regularly every Wednesday as he walked away from the liquor store with his two-dollar Powerball ticket, bored him after just a minute or two. For, if he could even conceive of being some other place right now, then he would also have had to be some other person. Still named Joel Lingeman, maybe, but somebody else. He could furnish the penthouse, but he could not think himself inside the richer, more successful, happier phantom who dwelt in it.

Who was to say, anyway, that Joel could have been any happier? He had a job that paid well and was intermittently satisfying. He'd had the same lover for going on fifteen years, a certifiable miracle for a gay man—people sometimes gasped when he said it. He had friends: losers and geeks, maybe, the grown-up versions of the marginal crowd he'd hung out with

16

in high school, while he dreamt of being Alex's pal. But probably about as much fun to drink with as, say, Hollywood stars or New York literati. If there were an Algonquin round table now, George and Dorothy and the rest would just talk about real estate, like everybody else.

He couldn't imagine another life, another way of being Joel. Sometimes, as tonight, he felt a little itch, but it was the itch an amputee feels in a phantom limb. There was no place to scratch, he had no wants that could be met through work or scheming or even the right Powerball ticket. Things were fine. It was spring, and things were as good as they were going to be.

The peace that came over him—of complacency or surrender, if the two are distinguishable—was broken by the homeless guy who sat on the low wall in front of the Madison Building. Joel had passed this guy a million times; he must have staked out his spot on that wall the day it was built. They always had the same colloquy. The man would say, almost inaudibly, "Spare any change." Not even asking—he knew the answer—but as if just feeding Joel a cue. Joel would say "Sorry," without looking at him. Always, ten or fifteen years now, and he felt a little guilty every time. But this guy was just the first in a gauntlet that started in front of the Madison Building and stretched down Pennsylvania Avenue all the way to Eighth Street. Blocks and blocks of them: why would Joel give his change to the first one he encountered? Or to the second, or the last? How was he supposed to pick, as if he were some capricious god singling out one mortal for his favors? Besides, who was to say this guy was really homeless? Maybe he lived somewhere and just came here every day, as if commuting to his job.

The man did his job. "Spare any change," he said, perhaps more loudly than usual. As Joel said his "Sorry," he was conscious of the jingling in his pocket. He blushed as he walked by. He had taken a few steps before the guy murmured, not

17

angrily, almost resigned, "Yeah, you're sorry, motherfucker." Joel glanced back, saw him maybe for the first time, or at least the first time in years. A black man, close to Joel's age, trim and dressed surprisingly neatly: clean flannel shirt, jeans, new-looking sneakers. His face had a sort of befogged nobility; once it was probably handsome. In some other world they might have fucked. In this world Joel was scared, suddenly; he turned away and practically ran the block or so to the Hill Club.

The Hill Club was nearly empty. That is, there were people eating at tables, but nobody at the bar, just one straight couple. And Walter, of course, the besotted old man who seemed to have been propped up at the corner of the bar every night as an admonition. The way, on the Oregon Trail, there'd be the occasional skull to let you know what fate might be yours if you continued on this route.

It used to be that Joel could come into the Hill Club at what they called happy hour—though they didn't do anything excessively happy, like reduce the prices or give away any food—and he could hardly make it to the bar for all the people. What had happened to everybody?

He ordered a Dewar's and water from the bartender—even the bartender was a stranger tonight, some substitute, or Joel wouldn't have had to say what he wanted—and looked around the room. All straight people, eating their burgers and the stuff the Hill Club called chili, a tomato puree you could have fed to a finicky baby. Several tables had, ominously, pitchers of beer. The one bar on the Hill that used to have a sort of gay tincture to it—never a majority of the customers, but a big enough constituency that the bartenders had to know how to make cosmos—seemed to be turning into the kind of place where annoying youths who thought they were still in school ordered pitchers of beer. Pretty soon the place would have a giant TV tuned to the sports network.

Well, it was past seven. If Joel had got there earlier, he

would probably have bumped into one or two friends; but they were a receding wave, a little contingent of survivors. That's what had happened to the Hill Club. Everybody had died; the straight people were just filling a vacuum. Everybody had died except, improbably, Walter, who was staring deep into his drink.

The couple on Joel's left were staffers, or at least the boy was. He was trying to impress the girl. The Congressman thinks this, the Congressman wants to do that. As if he were constantly having intimate policy discussions with the Congressman, when he probably spent his days answering constituent mail. Form-letter answers, mostly: "I want you to know how very much I appreciate hearing your views on _____." The kid would fill in the blank, print the letter out, run it through the signature machine. Which surely qualified him to expound, as he was now doing, on how to save Social Security.

Joel turned toward Walter and said "Hey." To no effect; Walter just went on gazing into his martini as if he expected to find an oracle there. Joel thought of trying to rouse him, but stopped himself. It was kind of pathetic, wasn't it, that he should even have attempted to strike up a conversation with Walter. Maybe it was time to find a new hang-out. Or maybe it was time to stop hanging out and go home at night like a grown-up.

Joel chugged the rest of his drink and was about to stand up when Walter said, "How are you this evening?" As if it had taken him a minute or two to process Joel's "Hey."

"Okay, how are you doing?"

"Not bad for an impoverished annuitant." Walter had a sort of trick: just when you thought he was comatose he could sober up sharply, just for a few minutes, and carry on a normal conversation. Joel thought about getting another drink. Except Walter would probably fade again before he was halfway through it.

"Kind of late for you, isn't it?" Walter said. It was hard to believe that Walter somehow kept track of people's usual timetables. Probably he just meant that it was kind of late for anybody. Happy hour was over, unless like Walter's your happy hour stretched around the clock.

"I had to work a little late."

"Uh-huh. What is it you do again?"

"I work at the Office of Legislative Analysis."

"Right," Walter said, as if Joel had made a lucky guess. "So you work for these Republicans."

"No, we kind of work for both sides. We're nonpartisan."

"Nonpartisan," Walter repeated. With a little edge, Joel thought, as if the very idea were preposterous.

Joel said, "So what did you used to do?"

"What?"

"You said you were an annuitant. So you used to work for the government?"

"Oh." Walter made a fluttering gesture; the subject wasn't worth talking about. "Whatever happened to your friend?"

"Who?"

"That friend of yours, the one you used to come in with."

"Oh, Sam."

"Sam, that's it. I haven't seen him in ages. You still together?"

"Sure, he just doesn't come in here any more."

"Oh." Walter's eyes wandered back to his martini. Probably he was going back into his trance again, as abruptly as he had emerged from it. Joel stood up, glad he hadn't ordered another drink. But Walter turned toward him again. "Let me ask you . . ."

"Uh-huh."

"Sit down, sit down a minute."

"I really have to run," Joel said. Nothing good ever happened when a drunk told him to sit down a minute.

"Sure," Walter said, as if he knew Joel had no place to go. "But let me just ask. You and—what's his name?"

"Sam."

"Sam. You've been together a long time."

"Fifteen years."

20

"No shit," Walter said, unimpressed. "Do you still have sex?"

"What?"

"Sex. Do you and . . . what's his name . . . still do it?"

Joel was aware that the couple next to him had stopped talking and were unabashedly eavesdropping. He wasn't embarrassed about it, exactly, but aware. "Um . . ." There was no reason he had to submit to an inquisition from some senescent drunk whose own sexuality was indeterminate—and, at this point in the slide to the grave, probably academic. But if he didn't answer, that would be an answer. "Sure," he said.

Sure, they still did it. Not every night, of course, that must have lasted only a little while; he couldn't remember. Nor was he certain just when they had drifted down to once a week, after Sunday brunch, or when even this observance became optional. They had never stopped enjoying it, not entirely; if they rarely saw stars, at least they knew what buttons to push. Sex was like . . . Communion, maybe. He imagined that people who partook of that strange ritual might have felt the same way about it. A routine most Sundays, maybe a few times a year a brief sensation that something faintly miraculous was going on. Except at least he and Sam had the weekly—or nearly so—miracle of, after the act, cuddling, dozing.

Joel said, with some trepidation, but he couldn't help it: "Why do you ask?"

Walter looked vaguely thoughtful. Probably he wasn't often asked why he said something; usually the accurate answer would simply have been that the spirits moved him. "Why did I? I guess I wondered why you didn't go home."

"I'm just going home."

"Because if I had someone at home, I'd be there."

If Walter had someone at home, the guy would have to be drugged or manacled or bewitched. Joel didn't say this, nor did he explain that he was out because Sam was working late. Which would have been a lie: he would have been out even if Sam hadn't been working late.

What he couldn't explain to Walter—as if Walter even deserved an explanation—was that you could have a perfectly happy home and not be in any rush to get there.

He hailed a cab. This was a pointless extravagance. Two hours at least before Sam would be home, nothing to do in the interval except maybe watch the Senate on C-SPAN engaging in their simulated debate and taking their five or six votes— the outcome of each predetermined, the roll calls meant only to get everybody on the record, for or against flag burning, for or against teenage pregnancy. He might as well have taken the Metro and saved a few bucks. But the sunset was spectacular: Washington was made for sunset, its monuments built low to the ground, leaving an open western sky. He wasn't ready to scuttle down into some tunnel and wait for a train.

He had asked to be taken to the Safeway on Seventeenth Street so he could pick up something for Sam's dinner. Funny, he thought of it that way—Sam's dinner—when he was the only one who cared very much whether they ate real food or energy bars. He even said it sometimes, "Got to get home and fix Sam's dinner." It was only an expression, maybe half a joke. Just because he did all the cooking didn't mean he had somehow turned into the little woman, rushing to get something on the stove for her caveman. He cooked and Sam fixed things; they just did what they were good at, everybody wore the pants in their family.

The cab was on Massachusetts Avenue, just ready to turn north, when Joel said no, he didn't want to go to the Safeway, he wanted to go to P Street west of Dupont Circle. The driver uttered a brief expletive in some West African language but complied. As Joel got out he penitently overtipped the driver, then stood looking at the entrance to Zippers with some bewilderment. What had made him come here?

He hadn't been to Zippers in years. It hadn't changed at all:

22

the place still smelled of spilled beer no one ever mopped up, the ceiling over the oval bar was so mantled in tobacco resin it might have been mahogany. There was no place to dance, no one could really talk over the music, the drinks were minuscule and watery, the bartenders inattentive or surly. But the place was jammed, at seven-thirty on a Thursday night. People came to Zippers, as they always had, because they could be sure anyone they encountered there had come on exactly the same mission. That Joel had even walked into the place was a sort of imposture really. To be in Zippers with no carnal agenda was to violate an unspoken contract.

For he surely had no intention of being picked up. He and Sam hadn't fooled around in years and years. Fidelity had probably been—he couldn't remember, but it must have been—Sam's suggestion. Joel had agreed eagerly enough. There was AIDS, of course, whose modes of transmission had only just been identified. There was his relative contentment with their—back then at least semiweekly—lovemaking. There was the fact that tricking had always been a lot of work for Joel, and why would he go to the 7-Eleven in the rain when he had a cow at home?

He had agreed, and he had kept his part of the bargain for—what?—twelve years, maybe, so long that the very idea of straying was outlandish and foreign to him. He could no more trick out than he could fly. What had brought him here? Some itch, after the hearing, after the Hill Club. Not an itch for sex, just some need to witness, to take in the smoky air of, a place where everybody was gay and did what gay people did. As if, far as he and Sam had soared away from this life, he needed every so often to touch down here. As if this, and not the apartment where he cooked and Sam fixed things, were home ground.

It took him a good five minutes to edge his way to the bar and order a scotch and water—generic, no one specified a brand in Zippers. He turned and was scouting for someplace he could stand that was as far from the jukebox as possible when, right where Joel was, a guy got off his barstool and started fighting his way to the door. Joel sat down without even checking, as he once would have, just whom he was sitting next to. Another sign that he was definitely not cruising.

Well, maybe a little. First ruling out the guy to his right, who looked uncannily like Peter Lorre, then canvassing the rest of the bar. Straight ahead, a guy wearing a tank top that not only displayed his arduously sculpted shoulders but also disclosed that they were covered with curly black hair. At three o'clock a thirty-something with thinning red hair and a face that was one continuous freckle—not Joel's type at all, if Joel could still be said to have a type—but slender and with some flicker of intelligence in his gray eyes. At ten o'clock a man at least Joel's age directing some sort of futile monologue at a sleepy-looking kid who couldn't have been more than twenty-three and who wasn't even pretending to listen.

Joel turned back to the redhead, looked at him pretty steadily until the guy happened to glance Joel's way and then instantly turned his head. Not peekaboo—first in the series of quick glances that would culminate in a connection—but a decisive and immediate "No way, sucker." In his real cruising days an abrupt rejection like that would have left Joel shattered; how many nights he had gone home alone because he couldn't shrug off one disdainful scowl from a stranger. Now he thought: it doesn't matter what you think of me, buddy, I've got mine. You may see before you an unaccompanied faggot on the prowl, but I'm not, I've got Sam. This was not, he supposed, mere complacency. It was the whole point of their endurance and their fidelity, that Joel could be sitting there alone and still have Sam invisibly at his side.

Still, it would have been nice if the guy had looked back, or even hit on him. So that he could have smiled regretfully and said sorry, he was seeing someone. He just would have liked to have had some signal, only for a minute, that a moderately desirable man might have seen some possibility in him.

The old guy to Joel's right departed, and somebody else immediately slipped into the seat. Joel glanced at him, too briefly even to form an impression beyond registering that he was an improvement over Peter Lorre, then turned away at once. If he didn't look, he wouldn't risk being shot down twice in sixty seconds.

Maybe his glance hadn't been as discreet as he had intended, because the newcomer instantly said, "Hi, how are you doing?"

Joel turned as if he were only just now noticing his neighbor. "Fine, how about you?"

The guy wasn't exactly Joel's type either, but—well, for someone sitting next to Joel in Zippers and actually initiating a conversation—not bad. Maybe pushing forty, but still slim. A couple of days' stubble; Joel sometimes wondered how people managed this trick of always looking as if they'd shaved the day before yesterday. His jeans were torn at the knees. Maybe he was a little old for that particular fashion gesture. Though it was, actually, kind of hot.

"Great," the guy said. "You live around here?"

He might have been asking if Joel lived near Zippers. But, even if the guy meant to pick him up, in the standard course of things this would be the next-to-last question, followed at once by, "You want to go there?" It wasn't the very first question you asked. So he must have meant, was Joel from Washington?

"I didn't grow up here, but I've lived here about twenty years." Joel at once regretted supplying the chronological detail.

"No shit," the guy said, as if it were remarkable to live in Washington. Or to live anywhere for twenty years. "I just got here."

"Oh, yeah? From where?"

"North Carolina."

"Oh."

There was a little pause, during which Joel debated whether

his next line was "Where in North Carolina?" or, *molto accelerando*, "Where are you staying?" Before Joel could resolve this, he recalled that he didn't have a next line, much less anything to accelerate, as of course nothing was going to come of this.

"I was in LA for a few years and then—last six months or so I was staying with my family. But I . . . I had to get out. So I thought I'd see what Washington's like."

"What's it like?"

"Expensive."

"I guess," Joel said. "So are you planning to live here, or just visiting, or . . ."

"I'm not sure." This was astonishing. At forty, or whatever age he was, not to be sure even of where you lived; there was something at once thrilling and scary about it. Scary, mostly; the guy was looking down at the bar, brow furrowed, as if he had to decide his future right then.

Joel, for his part, was looking at the guy's knee, which peeked out through the tear in his jeans. Joel had never thought of the knee as an especially rousing body part. Now, after a few seconds, he had to make himself look up. To find the guy smiling at him and holding out a hand.

"My name's Paul."

"Joel." They shook.

"Nice to meet you, Joel." He chugged the rest of his beer; this was a goodbye, not a hello. Another rejection, and this time not a little bruise. Joel felt a sudden wave of disproportionate sadness and longing. As though, if Paul had been willing, something might actually have happened. Was this possible? It must have been: how else to account for Joel's elation when, a second later, Paul said, "Can I get you a drink?"

How many years since Joel had been granted the elemental pleasure of *scoring*: the affirmation of his value, the warmth in his groin.

Now he really needed to say, "No, I just stopped in for one

drink. I've got to be getting home and starting dinner for my lover . . ." He had had his little rush of self-esteem, what he must have come to Zippers for; only a louse would play games with this nice guy. This lonesome, affable guy whose naked knee was making Joel a little dizzy.

"Sure," Joel said. "A scotch and water, please."

Sam hadn't, now that Joel thought back, suggested monogamy. Sam had announced it; that was how he and Joel reached agreements. Sam would say, "I'm giving up smoking," and Joel would say, "Me, too." Sam would say, "I'm not going to see anybody else any more," and Joel would say, "Me either." Nobody made Joel say, "Me either." Sam was only talking about what *he* was doing, not commanding. Though it sort of went without saying that he couldn't stop smoking in a smoke-filled apartment, or be faithful to a slut.

On those occasions when Joel treated one of Sam's announcements as the unilateral resolution it was—as, for example, when Sam said he wasn't going to the Hill Club any more and Joel kept going—the silent reproach that greeted Joel when he got home was two-pronged. Not just, you went and got plastered again, you boring cretin. But also, I am strong and you are weak. If Joel did something Sam didn't approve of but for which Sam had no predilection, like buying too many books, Sam would shake his head but it wouldn't be a big deal. A big deal was when Joel did something that Sam was nobly refraining from.

It would be a very big deal indeed if Joel were to fall off the wagon they'd ridden for twelve years and pick somebody up at Zippers. Of course he would have to tell about it. One of their rules, in the three or so years they had been together before monogamy set in, was that they always told about it.

This seemed, suddenly, an especially silly rule. Why should Joel have to tell about something that was none of Sam's business? A little excursion that had nothing to do with Joel and

Sam, that wouldn't constitute a betrayal any more than it was a betrayal if Joel thought about someone other than Sam when he jerked off. What possible good could come from telling about it? An hour or so with this nice guy, one explosion—Joel wasn't nineteen any more—one explosion and it would be over. Sam would be mad, coming home and finding no dinner. One night of sulking and it would blow over: by tomorrow morning life would be the same as it had been this morning.

Except that Joel would have a secret, an exciting, dirty, glorious secret—one little part of his life that was not transparent to Sam or anyone else. A little pocket in time that he could enter in memory whenever he liked and that, even as he sensibly, happily, returned to forever with Sam, would make being with Sam a choice, not a default. He would come back to Sam as somebody who had a life and not just a collection of habits.

"So, um . . ."

"Paul."

"Paul, sorry. Where are you staying while you're in town?"

"Place called the Hotel Latham."

"Where's that?"

"Over on H Street. It's a real dump, but it's all I can afford right now."

"Oh."

"They got, you know, this weekly rate."

A single-room occupancy hotel, then, or practically. The poor guy must really have stretched to buy Joel's scotch. Joel hadn't, picturing the unencumbered life of someone who was undecided about where he was living next week, figured that the choice was among a variety of different SROs. Nor had he figured that he himself would shortly be visiting one. If they even allowed visitors. Maybe they could get a room somewhere else; where did guys take tricks if neither one could go home? What had been a sudden impulse, a momentary and refreshing detour from everyday life, was already something else. Arrangements would have to be made, practical details attended to. The place would have to have a shower, for example; Joel couldn't just go home later without a shower.

If a guy lived in an SRO, what were the odds that he had crabs? How could Joel, in a million years, account to Sam for an infestation of crabs? Or—he felt like Rip van Winkle—of course, now there were worse things to worry about than crabs.

How could Joel be sure that his little secret wouldn't somehow corrode everything? Or that, having spent an hour or two with someone other than Sam, he might not find life with Sam insupportable? Might not find himself hurtling back into that world he had so luckily left behind, those pathetic nights of dashing himself against strangers as unyielding as rocks, waiting for last call, settling for whatever he could get in those frenzied last minutes when the lights were turned up and the room was alive with connections and rejections?

Paul said, "Where do you live, near here?"

"Yeah, a few blocks. But I can't . . ."

What he could do, just for a minute, was touch Paul's bare knee. Paul put a hand over Joel's, held it in place.

Joel said, "Do you think we can go to your hotel?" He didn't need to say more, the guy would understand that he was in some sort of *situation*, he didn't have to say how deeply situated he was. Or had been, until tonight. "I mean, will they have a problem if you bring someone in?"

"Shit, that dump? There are so many people coming and going you'd think it was an all night supermarket."

Supermarket, Joel had been headed to the supermarket. Sam would come in—eight-thirty now, Sam could be home in an hour, sooner if there weren't many patients—and find no dinner, no Joel. After waiting a while he would dig through the icebox, eat something, go to bed, turning off all the lights in the apartment as a sign of his disappointment and contempt. There would be hell to pay, and he was going to pay it. Because

Paul had brought Joel back to the world after his and Sam's protracted sabbatical.

"Listen," Joel said. "Maybe we should stop and get a bite somewhere. I'm kind of hungry."

"Me, too. I didn't eat today." Paul looked shyly down at the bar. Maybe he held Joel's hand a little tighter as he said, "You know, I'm real broke."

Joel knew the guy was broke, he didn't have to be told. Of course he intended to pay for dinner, but he was chilled by the simple sentence, "I didn't eat today." Which was one thing if uttered by some pubescent House staffer who was bragging about how many important meetings he'd been to, but quite another when said literally by a man who had nothing and—as if making some terrible gamble—had, instead of getting a Big Mac, spent his last couple of bucks buying Joel a drink.

Not a gamble, an investment. They would eat, Paul would take Joel back to the Hotel Latham, and at the end Paul would say, "Hey, you think you could help me out?" Or wouldn't have to say it; how would Joel be able to walk away from that tiny barren room and not help him out?

Joel would never know, not now, if Paul had even the tiniest bit of interest in him, or if he had merely looked like an easy touch. Or if both were true: it was possible that Paul was honestly attracted to him and was—also, not instead—in need of a little help.

"I—" Joel began. "Listen, I better go home." He didn't offer any explanation.

Paul supplied one. "To your lover."

"Yeah."

Paul nodded firmly. "You really should." He eased his knee away from Joel's grasp and turned to scan the bar; he was already hunting for his next prospect. "How long you been together?"

"A few years."

"That's nice."

"Listen," Joel said. "I want to help you out." He took out his wallet.

"No, jeez," Paul said.

"I want to." There were two twenties. He pulled one out, because he needed the other for the Safeway. He pulled the other out; he could go to the bank machine.

Paul didn't protest again. Joel gave him the forty. While with one hand he pocketed the bills he put the other hand on Joel's shoulder in silent gratitude, then their faces were so close, then they kissed. The guy pulled Joel closer, their tongues met, jousted for . . . how long? Long enough for Joel to think, we'd better stop. Long enough after that for Joel to wonder how he was going to get through life, the rest of his mostly wonderful life with Sam, and never feel this again.

Joel pulled away. Paul smiled, a little one-sidedly—as if to say, you liked that, didn't you?

"I better get home," Joel said.

"Okay. I might stay here and have a couple more drinks."

Instead of hurrying out and getting something to eat, he who hadn't eaten all day. So that part wasn't true. He was going to stay at Zippers and look for another Joel. So he could be with someone, or so he could score another forty, or both. There would never be any way of knowing.

There was still a chance he could beat Sam home. He went to the nearest bank machine—not his own, that would have meant a detour of a couple of blocks. When the monitor declared that he would be charged a fee and asked if he wished to proceed he punched the YES button, feeling like one of those big spenders in the movies who lights a cigar with a fiver. A buck for this bank and a buck for his own, just so he could save five minutes. Not twenty feet away, bedded down on newspapers in a doorway, was a guy who could have used two bucks.

As he hurried down Q Street to the Safeway, Joel saw everything. He saw the pictures on the walls of living rooms with uncurtained windows, and the fireplaces and the bookshelves. He saw the parked cars, each radiantly distinct under the street-lights, each with a Chinese take-out menu tenderly placed under its left windshield wiper. He saw the young couple who passed him without, of course, seeing him: but he saw them, heads lowered in earnest conversation, one chuckling now at a joke Joel couldn't hear.

He couldn't remember when he had felt so alive. As if, all these years, he had been under a spell that could be broken only by a forty-dollar kiss. He wasn't too exhilarated to remember that the forty dollars had preceded the kiss. But he didn't forget the kiss either. Something had happened. Not a tryst. Not even the ugly little ego boost he had planned on— just the opposite, really. But even the opposite was something after so long. Time had started again.

In the Safeway he got ground turkey, imitation cheese slices made from some petroleum byproduct, hamburger buns, and a can of baked beans. A little Independence Day picnic, but not too unhealthy. When he cooked real food—a couple of nice lamb shanks, say, or just once last year a duck—Sam would act as if Joel were injecting fat into his arteries with a hypodermic needle. He would clean his plate, but sullenly. Tonight he would have nothing to reproach Joel for. Not if he knew everything. Just a kiss, people kissed all the time.

Maybe Joel would even tell Sam about it. Leaving out the Latham and the forty dollars. Just that a cute guy had been trying to pick him up and he hadn't gone. Yes, a good story to tell, illustrating Joel's fidelity and at the same time remind-ing Sam that he shouldn't take Joel for granted. Or no, not a good story, as it would have to begin with some recitation of just what Joel had been doing in Zippers.

Joel looked over at the guy waiting in the next check-out line. Maybe a couple years younger than Joel, too old anyway to be wearing a baseball cap, but still kind of cute. The guy looked back only for a second before he turned away and scanned the tabloids lined up next to the register. Then he turned toward Joel again. Joel at once focused on the tabloids in his own aisle.

He didn't know anything about the people in the tabloids. He saw the same names in the headlines every time he went to the store, but—except for Princess Di, about whom each paper carried a weekly shocker—he had no idea who they were or why they were celebrated. Who was Kathie Lee, and why was she always furious? And Demi: he had a vague idea she was married to somebody famous, but to whom? He might as well have been in the magazine store up on Connecticut reading the headlines on the foreign newspapers. The tabloids were from a country he didn't live in. Of course, their readers would have been just as baffled if they were to come across *The Hill* or the *Congressional Weekly*, with their captivating accounts of the goings-on at the Commerce Committee. People Joel thought of as suns and moons were invisible to the rest of the country. So which was the real country, or was there no paper about the real country?

The guy in the next aisle had paid, gathered up his bags; on his way to the door, he gave Joel one last glance, then he was gone. Would he linger outside?

The woman ahead of Joel in line was paying with food stamps. This always took forever: the change from her big food stamp, with which she had purchased a cornucopia of junk food, had to be in the form of lesser food stamps, lest this parasite somehow get her hands on actual currency. Joel got agitated—the guy in the baseball cap would be gone—then he took a couple of breaths. Obviously he didn't mean to do anything with the guy in the baseball cap; he was categorically going straight home and making turkey burgers.

It was enough that the guy had looked at him three times. Just because someone who was probably hustling had lit on him at Zippers didn't mean that he was of interest only to hustlers. Any more than being bitten by a mosquito meant that you were put on earth to be mosquito chow.

This formulation was less reassuring than he had meant it to be. What else was he on earth for?

Sam wasn't home yet, thank God. Joel could have just one more drink. He could cook dinner without Sam leaning over the damn counter scrutinizing everything: that's cooking too fast; you'll burn it; jeez, you shouldn't cook when you've been . . .

Sam wasn't home, Joel hadn't been caught. If he had opened the door and found Sam sitting there, waiting, then he would somehow have been guilty, as much as if Sam had found him with his pants down at the Hotel Latham. Not that Sam would have suspected anything; Joel could just have said he had lingered too long at the Hill Club and Sam would have believed him. But this way he didn't even have to tell a lie. His trivial transgression had not occurred at all. He was exactly where he was supposed to be, and nothing had happened at all.

He got his drink and turned on the radio. It took a second to warm up, then hip-hop exploded from it—as if he were a passenger in one of those cars that goes by late at night, its stereo turned so high that you hear the bass from blocks away, thudding toward you like Godzilla. He almost spilled his drink before he recovered enough to change to the classics station. Some pianist—probably one of those interchangeable young Russian athletes—was in the middle of Liszt's *Funérailles*. He had always thought of that as violent music; after the hip-hop it was about as threatening as the tinkling of a music box.

Not hip-hop, maybe, maybe it was house music. Joel had never been too clear on which was which. Sam always kept up. He was a couple of years older than Joel, approaching fifty asymptotically, but he knew what the kids were listening to. Sometimes Joel thought this was kind of pathetic, the way the forty-year-old in the grocery store with the baseball cap was kind of pathetic. Other times Joel wondered if he himself was prematurely dead.

The pianist was doing the rumbling triplet figure, all octaves, in the middle section with about as much feeling as if he were doing a set of chin-ups. It was the only hard part of *Funérailles*. Joel had always promised himself that some day he would practice those few bars for an hour or two, he was sure he could get them down. Then he'd be able to play *Funérailles* all the way through. But for whom? Once or twice he had played for Sam. That is, he wasn't just making noise while Sam did something in the next room; he had sat Sam down and implored him to listen. Then he played badly: the shanghaied audience of one made him as nervous as if he were at Carnegie Hall. At the end Sam went, "Wow, great," with his patented mixture of affects: the voice warm and enthusiastic, the eyes wandering. He never asked for an encore. When they'd moved to this apartment there hadn't been room for the piano. Though there was somehow room for Sam's rusting exercise machine.

Joel had always thought it would be nice to have a lover who would play duets with him. Instead of just making the beast with two backs, they could also have made the creature with four hands. The Schubert Fantasy, the Mozart symphonies. Surely there were couples who did that. And who probably had arguments about who got the top part and who the bottom. Nobody shared everything; he just sometimes wished he and Sam shared a little more. Oh, and Sam probably wished he had a lover who knew the difference between house and hip-hop. But he came home to Joel.

Except tonight he wasn't home yet, and it was past ten. Where the hell was he? Sam was never this late—or so seldom that, when he was, Joel's thoughts naturally ran to catastrophe. Maybe he's had an accident. Maybe he's dead. Joel didn't, when these conventional, spousely thoughts came to him, tremble. Instead he found himself imagining how things would be. Dealing with Sam's family, then with the lawyers. Finding a smaller place he could afford by himself. Maybe quitting his job, going off to Provincetown, getting a piano again, practicing Liszt or, more probably, drinking himself to death. He could spin out a future without Sam and not focus at all on the words *without Sam.* Just construct sentences in which "Sam" did not appear.

Sam was leaving the office, the yellow flash of a cab, a crowd gathered around him.

Instantly Joel would rebuke himself. This wasn't the future he wanted. He never thought of leaving Sam. Even when they were fighting and he would list to himself, dared not recite aloud, the thousand ways Sam had destroyed his life, even then he never thought of breaking up. Just once in a while there came, unbidden, these visions of disaster. The call from the airline, the cop at the door. Some act of God that wouldn't hurt Sam—he never wanted Sam hurt—but simply make Sam disappear, expunge him from the text of Joel's life. Only when he imagined this, and confronted his own astounding equanimity in the face of it, did he ever wonder if perhaps he really wanted Sam gone.

When Sam would at last arrive—there had been an extra patient, he'd had trouble finding a cab—Joel's relief and disappointment and contrition would all swell up at once. Joel could never be sure, in this chorus of emotions, which one was singing the lead.

Just now he was contrite, and a little superstitious. He emptied the can of beans into a pan. He shaped the ground turkey into four patties, meticulously evening them out, so that no one could complain about getting the smaller portion. As if these simple acts would propitiate some deity, speed Sam home.

Sam just had to work late, that was all. When he got home he would be irritable. They would have one of those evenings when unspoken disapproval would color every word Sam said. Every vowel would be a nanosecond shorter than it should have been, as if he were saving his breath for some encyclopedic denunciation that was coming, any night now.

Except, of course, it wasn't coming. People didn't stay together fifteen years without learning a simple rule: complain about what he's doing right this instant and maybe he'll stop doing it. Complain about what he did last week and he won't even remember having done it.

The phone rang. Joel could tell somehow, from the ring, that it was Sam, not the police or some other harbinger of Sam's demise. He took a sip of his drink, let the phone ring again, at last picked it up with, perhaps, more than his usual ambivalence.

"Hello."

"Hi." Sam's voice was tired, yes, irritated, yes. They'd been together so long; how much Joel could hear in a single syllable.

"Where are you?" Joel said.

"With a friend."

An odd locution; he didn't have any friends Joel didn't know. Joel said, "Who?"

"Just a friend."

"Well, are you leaving soon? Dinner's practically on the table." This was true. Turkey burgers were practically on the table if you'd bought the turkey.

"Joel," Sam said. Any sentence that started with "Joel" ended in some kind of rebuke. Sam paused long enough for Joel to wonder what he could possibly have done wrong. No, he didn't wonder; he knew all his transgressions. He only wondered which one Sam was about to point out. "Joel," Sam said again. "I . . ." A long pause.

"Yeah?"

Sam said, almost blurted, "I'm not coming home."

"What?"

"Joel, I'm with this friend and I'm—I'm not sure if I'm coming home." His voice filled with sorrow and apprehension, as if he were lost. Or as if he had been kidnapped.

When in fact he had escaped.

two

When Joel got to the office there were already four voice-mail messages. Two were his favorite kind: a forlorn, anonymous sigh followed by a hang-up.

The third identified the sigher: "Joel, this is Melanie, with Senator Harris. I've been trying to get you all morning." It wasn't even nine. "The senator wants a briefing about aliens and . . . some other stuff, but mostly about this aliens thing. He's free at two o'clock. If you can't do that, he's got stuff until seven, but he could do it then. Let me know."

Joel hung up before he could listen to the fourth message. Seven at night, for God's sake, didn't these people have a life? Or maybe they did, maybe being a senator—or even a lowly LA—for sixteen or seventeen hours a day, every day, was a life. Maybe this was enviable. Joel's work was just a scar in his days, and his nights consisted of being not-at-work: happy hour, happy second hour, dinner, trying to read while Sam watched the Sci-Fi network. The whole routine suffused with a numb dread, as if some part of him never forgot that tomorrow he would be in the office again. Maybe it was better to be in the office every waking hour.

He should do the briefing at seven instead of two. That way he could postpone as long as possible the hour when he would go home and find Sam either there or not.

He hadn't slept much. After Sam's call he had poured himself another scotch, made his turkey burgers. He watched C-SPAN while he ate them. The House was voting on Mr. DiBrezze's appeal of the ruling of the chair that Mr. Hadley's amendment was out of order. While the members voted, by sticking a card in a slot as if they were using an ATM, C-SPAN played Vivaldi. They never carried the sound from the floor during a roll call, maybe because the nation didn't need to hear what the members said to each other as they stood in line to vote, gossiping and nudging one another like schoolkids waiting to get into the cafeteria. In two corners of the screen the tally of the yeas and nays mounted—the vote very close, Joel wondered which side he should be rooting for. Probably some of the members wondered, too. More than once Joel had got a panicky early morning call from a staffer whose member wasn't sure just what he had voted on the night before.

He finished his second turkey burger, mushing the last couple of bites around on the plate to soak up the puddle of syrup from the baked beans. It was time for a cigarette, except he didn't want to go all the way downstairs and out into the cold. Then it occurred to him that he might, just once, violate Sam's rule about smoking in the apartment. Perhaps it would not be the largest transgression committed that evening.

He lit his cigarette and made himself think about Sam. Not that Sam hadn't been on his mind in the half hour or so since the call. But he hadn't *thought* anything, had gone through his routine of cooking and eating almost unperturbed, the echo of Sam's last words just a sort of background hum. Actually, he couldn't recall ever having been so upset by something that he couldn't eat. Or sleep, for that matter: he could just as easily have gone to bed right then. Instead of, dutifully, trying to focus on Sam, on those words.

"I'm not sure if I'm coming home." A rather intriguing utterance, really, susceptible of any number of interpretations. The "not sure," first of all. Which could have meant that he hadn't made up his mind or that his mind wasn't a player, he was helplessly being carried along and couldn't predict what might happen next. Then the "coming home": it cried out for a modifier. Just now, for a while, tonight, ever.

There wasn't any ashtray, there probably wasn't one left in the apartment. There used to be ashtrays everywhere. On every table in every restaurant. In the arm of your seat on the plane or the train or the Trailways bus. In college classrooms and conference rooms and theater lobbies and . . .

He stubbed out his cigarette in the bean juice on his plate. Tonight, probably; Sam wasn't sure if he was coming home that night.

That is: he had a trick, but he couldn't be sure yet whether it would be the kind where you found your clothes in the dark and crept out, praying that some cab was still cruising at three in the morning. Or the kind where you lay together until daybreak and then had a rematch. In which case there wasn't much point in Joel's waiting up.

He did wait up, even microwaved the coffee Sam had been in too big a hurry to drink that morning. For Joel, having coffee so late in the evening was about as daring as, say, tricking out. But he needed to stay up: Sam would open the door, expecting darkness, and there would be Joel sitting in the living room: quiet, dignified, ready for a calm discussion. He knew he ought to prepare. He needed to adopt a position, formulate a few key talking points on the issue of Sam's truancy.

Every time he tried to focus on the issue he found himself

instead trying to picture what was happening at that moment: Sam somewhere in the city, with someone. Doing something. Joel couldn't picture the partner, just Sam, naked, some shadowy figure in his arms. And he couldn't, really, imagine what they might be doing. The same things Sam and Joel did? Just the same insertions in the same orifices but with a different set of parts? Or something entirely different, something Sam and Joel had never done? There were things Joel wanted to do and could never have done with Sam, things one could do only with a stranger. Perhaps Sam had a list of his own; and he was with a stranger.

At that very moment. In real time, that was the phrase computer people used. What was unreal time? Their last twelve years, probably; Joel thought it had been that long since Sam's unilateral declaration of monogamy. This was the real time, the hour or so now since Sam's call, and all those years were the unreal time. Joel had, more sharply, the sensation he had felt—only a few hours ago!—as he had sat with Paul at Zippers. The thisness, the presentness; the clock of his life had been restarted. He had a present tense, a future tense, a future conditional: possibility, uncertainty . . .

None of which would be very much diminished by a calm discussion between a coffee-enhanced drunk and someone who, if he came home at all, would be about as alert as a lion after the meat course. Joel went to bed, leaving one light on in the living room. Which was more than Sam would have done for him.

He woke up at around three. He didn't even have to raise his head to look at the glowing numbers on the clock radio. If he woke up in the middle of the night it was always three.

Sam wasn't in bed, and there wasn't any light from the bathroom. So Joel figured he must have been snoring: sometimes, when nudges, admonitions, actual rearrangement of Joel's sleeping body had no effect, Sam would go to the guest room. The first few times he did this, Joel would discover it in the morning and protest. Sam should make Joel go to the guest room. No, no, Sam would say; it wasn't Joel's fault he snored. Meaning that it was. Sam scored points under so many different categories in this argument that Joel lost count. Finally he concluded that *it wasn't his fault he snored.* This might have been the biggest victory over guilt in his entire adult life. If he woke up and Sam wasn't there he would just roll over and return to a no-fault sleep.

As he was just about to do when he remembered that Sam hadn't gone to bed with him, and why. Maybe Sam had come home and gone directly to the guest room, rather than risk waking Joel and having to discuss things. If Joel had been the one, if he'd crept home in the middle of the night, he wouldn't have wanted to discuss things either. Not because the discussion would have been so inherently painful: what had happened had happened, they were going to deal with it. But not that night, no; if it had been Joel, he would have gone straight to the guest room and drifted off to sleep. That's where Sam was, maybe, with the faint scent of what had happened clinging to his body.

Sam hadn't come home at all. How did Joel know this? Or rather, how would he have known the reverse, what would have told him Sam was in the guest room? After all, Sam didn't snore. But Joel could feel it: Sam wasn't in the apartment. He supposed he ought to get up and check, but he couldn't move.

He picked up the phone to get his last voice-mail message. Except the mechanical voice-mail hostess now intoned that he had two unopened messages. Someone must have called while he was listening to the others.

The first was Melanie again. "Joel, listen, seven o'clock is out, so we're going to have to do two. Please, please, please get back to me as soon as you can and—" He pushed 3.

"Message deleted," Ms. Voicemail said. "Press one to hear

your next message, four to return to the main menu, or nine to exit the voice messaging service."

It would only be Melanie again, unless . . .

Ms. Voicemail, with her inexhaustible patience, repeated, "Press one to hear your next message, four to—"

He pressed 1, as if hitting a detonator button.

"Hi, I came over to pick up some stuff, and you're not here. I thought I might catch you before you left for work, but I didn't. So . . . I picked up some stuff. Talk to you."

"Talk to you," Sam's customary sign-off, had always been not a promise but a confident prediction, almost a statement of the obvious. Of course they would be talking, they would be talking together until the end of time.

Joel wondered what stuff Sam had picked up. All thirty-eight of his—to Joel—indistinguishable sweaters? The VCR? Joel's mother's sterling? They had a lot of stuff. Early on, when they had first moved in together, each of them had his own stuff. It was possible to say this is Sam's loveseat, these are Joel's bookshelves. Even: those are Sam's candlesticks, Joel's colander, Sam's screwdriver, Joel's toilet brush. Since then, though, every household acquisition had been a joint one. The living-room rug might have gone on Sam's Visa or Joel's MasterCard, but it was their rug. How would they ever divide such things? With scissors?

A premature question. Surely, Sam meant only that he had come to get fresh clothes, whatever else he needed for the office. They weren't at the point of flipping a coin for the china.

He called Sam's office. The receptionist said, "Georgetown Sports Medicine." Hitting every consonant squarely; Sam had reported how she'd spent half a morning practicing, sitting at the front desk and murmuring the words, oblivious to the stares from the wounded gladiators in the waiting room. Pretty, they must have thought, but not much of a conversationalist.

"Hi," Joel said. "I want to make an appointment."

"What is your name?"

"Um . . . Joe Harris." The senator's name was the first that came to his mind. An errant choice, but there wasn't much chance the receptionist knew there was a Senator Joe Harris. Possibly she didn't know there were senators.

There was a long pause while she called his name up on her terminal or, rather, failed to. "You're a new patient?" she asked. Sounding a little irritated, perhaps because new patients involved work, challenging tasks like entering their address and phone number.

"Yes."

"Who referred you?"

"Doctor . . . uh . . . Jung."

"Doctor Young?"

"Right."

"And when did you want to come in?"

"I was hoping maybe Tuesday evening."

"Evening? Tuesday evening?"

"Right."

"We don't have any evening hours. What about next Friday at—"

"Never mind," Joel said. "Uh . . . bye-bye."

Joel played solitaire on his computer for the rest of the morning. Occasionally a staffer would call and ask him to explain Medicare and aliens. It was amazing how fast a silly proposal could become the issue of the day; another couple of days and no one would even remember it. After about the third call he had developed a canned recitation about the matter, one he could deliver without even ceasing to play solitaire. "What's that clicking noise?" one staffer asked. Joel shifted a little in his seat, so the mouthpiece of the phone would be a little farther from the mouse. "Beats me," he said, as he resumed clicking at the cards on the screen.

The nice thing about solitaire was that, while it required no intellection, it took just enough attention that you couldn't think coherently about anything else. He had a vague sensation of indignation and loss, that something terrible had happened, but he couldn't focus on it, it was all less immediate than the present task of putting the black eight on the red nine.

When the computer said that he had lost $10,000 at solitaire, he took this as a sign to go and get lunch. What he really wanted to do was go to one of the darker bars on Pennsylvania Avenue and have about five beers and an enormous non-turkey cheeseburger. But he had the briefing with Harris at two. While he could probably have met any intellectual challenge Joe Harris could throw at him if he were comatose, he couldn't stagger into a senator's office smelling like a frat boy on a Sunday morning. So he went to Le Dôme, a costly bistro that used to be jammed with lobbyists and their prey. The lobbyist's menu showed prices; the member's did not.

Today the place was practically empty. The rules had changed during one of Congress's occasional ethical seizures: members and staffers couldn't accept a lunch that cost more than a McDonald's happy meal. Possibly the committee that set a five-dollar limit hadn't meant to suggest that a member's soul could be had for five and a quarter. Anyway, Le Dôme was on its last legs. Few staffers, and no members, would reach into their own wallets for a thirty-five-dollar lunch. Joel was shown to the best two-top, the one that used to be Rostenkowski's, by the window with its view of the eponymous dome.

He sipped a single, prudent glass of merlot, looked out at the Capitol, and let himself think everything from which solitaire had distracted him.

Two months, closer to three: almost three months since Sam had announced his new evening duty. Just told Joel about it, matter-of-fact. Yes, now that Joel looked back, Sam hadn't been especially aggrieved, had made no show of dismay that two nights a week would be ruined.

So he had been seeing his new friend for three months. And

hadn't just stolen moments with him: had built him into his schedule. As on the calendar on Joel's computer you could make an appointment recurring. Every Tuesday and Thursday, 6–9:30: go and fuck with whoever. Once you'd done that, if you scrolled down you could see the same appointment months ahead, years. Unless you set an end date, it would go on as far into the future as the computer could see.

Sam had also, of course, built into his schedule the recurring lie. Not a complicated one. He came home with perfect regularity, and the most Joel would ask him when he got home was, "How was work?" The most he'd answer was, "Okay." He would look tired. Sometimes his hair would be damp. Joel would imagine he must have run water through it before leaving the office, because Sam was the kind of guy who had to look perfect before he'd step outside and hail a cab.

Not a demanding arrangement at all: Sam could have kept it up indefinitely. He and . . . whoever, they would have had to be careful where they went, but not very. Joel's Washington was a very small town, there were whole quadrants he never penetrated. And of course they had to part at nine-thirty; Sam had faithfully observed this rule. Maybe it was the other guy's rule. But Joel fancied it was Sam's—Sam had set the boundaries on his own adventure, and had for almost three months gotten up from the bed, showered, come home to Joel.

Until last night. Last night he had, for whatever reason, lingered an extra half hour, then an hour. Then he had picked up the phone, maybe even as he picked it up still meaning to say, "Hey, we had a couple extra patients, I'm leaving now." Then hearing Joel's voice, looking across at his . . . lover and hearing Joel say, "Dinner's practically on the table." Those harmless words somehow the last straw. Perhaps he had even visualized the turkey burgers and the canned beans. And then saw himself and his lover going out for a bite somewhere, someplace lively, talking and laughing together and then on the street, Sam not hailing a taxi to go home but the two of them going back to the lover's apartment; if it was dark enough, maybe even holding hands as they walked.

It was almost Joel's fault. If he hadn't said those terrible words.

The waiter brought Joel's foie gras en brioche, sauce framboise, and plopped it down before him as unceremoniously as if it were a liverwurst sandwich. Joel took a taste. It was, perhaps, better than a liverwurst sandwich. Not fifteen times as good, or whatever the price ratio should have dictated. And at least a liverwurst sandwich wouldn't have had raspberry sauce. He didn't mind the money; he had come here to treat himself. Post-trauma treat: as when he was little, stung by a bee once, and his mother took him for an ice cream cone. He hadn't understood that there wasn't much comfort in buying yourself an ice cream cone.

Harris's office was in the Hart Building, the new one built in the seventies that looked like one of the white cardboard office blocks you pass on the way to an airport. This was a mark of his juniority; longer-serving senators were in the Dirksen Building, dreary but less obviously prefabricated. The truly senescent hunkered down in the Russell Building, a Beaux Arts monolith. If you looked at the Russell Building you could imagine that senators were inside it. If you looked at the Hart Building, you were more likely to picture people in cubicles processing mortgage applications.

Joel always got lost in the Hart Building. The offices were grouped around a multistory atrium; no matter which elevator you took, the office you wanted was always on the other side of this chasm. By the time Joel could snake his way around to Harris's he was a couple of minutes late and almost out of breath. He could barely gasp his name to the receptionist, a beefy youth who didn't even bother to put down his cold-cut sub when Joel approached. The kid just nodded Joel toward one of the chairs in the anteroom and took a couple more bites before calling Melanie.

Joel sat a long while. He needn't have risked a heart attack trying to be on time for a meeting with a senator. Sometimes he would wait an hour or more, only to learn that the senator was backed up and would have to reschedule, or that someone had screwed up and the meeting had never been on the calendar at all. He hadn't brought anything to read, and the table next to him offered only such dispiriting stuff as *Montana Monthly*, *U.S. News and World Report*, and, perhaps for the more youthful lobbyists, a Donald Duck comic book. Joel just sat.

One wall of the anteroom was covered with a huge Montana flag. It said "MONTANA" in big gold letters, like the pennants Joel had in his room as a boy, the ones that blazoned the names of colleges he didn't get into. On the other wall were the inevitable pictures: Harris with George Bush, with Gerald Ford, with Charlton Heston. Harris with assorted Montana luminaries, gaunt men whose suits had Western features: waist-length jackets, or pockets whose openings made little smiles, like the ones on a Gene Autry shirt. In the center of the wall, the sun of this Republican solar system, Harris with Reagan. Harris in profile, trying both to grin and to look adoringly; Reagan looking straight out, of course, oblivious to anything but the camera.

Joel was about to nod off—either from a night without sleep or because he had, what the hell, had a second merlot—when Melanie appeared. She looked down at him but didn't speak for a minute. Possibly she was noticing that Joel hadn't shaved this morning. And had he, he wondered, put on that tie with the gravy spot? He didn't verify this, just drew himself to his feet.

"Thanks for coming," Melanie said, in the grave murmur a camerlengo might use before ushering you in to see the Pope. "The senator's just on his way back from the floor. Did Rob offer you some coffee?" On hearing this, the kid behind the reception desk stood up, disclosing the kind of body you see in half-hour infomercials for exercise machines. Joel thought about dispatching him for coffee, just to humiliate him. But if Joel went into the sanctum with coffee in one hand and a notebook in the other, this would be that rare day when a senator wanted to shake hands.

It was enough of a putdown just to ignore Rob. He turned to Melanie. "You said he might have some questions other than aliens?"

"I think so, some other health stuff. But we haven't connected all day, so I'm not sure." She cocked her head. "Oh, I guess he's in his office." Joel was always amazed at the way staffers could divine their member's whereabouts. Maybe if your boss threw things at you, you could sense somehow when he was in his lair.

Harris was on the phone. He must have seen Melanie and Joel come in, but he gave no sign of it, just went on talking. Listening, rather: he frowned and periodically went "Right, right." His mahogany desk, the size of a Volvo, held no papers at all, just the phone, a nameplate, and a silver scale model of a warplane shaped like some voracious moth. Did they build planes in Montana? Well, they must have built planes everywhere; probably they made one part in each district, so that every member had a little stake.

Harris hung up the phone, but still did not acknowledge Joel and Melanie, who stood worshipfully ten feet from his desk. He stood up and took off his jacket, draped it rather prissily on the back of his swivel chair, faced them again and turned himself on. Smiled as brightly as if Joel had arrived bearing a large check, came out from behind the desk, and held out a hand. "Joe Harris."

"Joel Lingeman." They had met the night before. Was it possible? So much had happened. Just the night before and the man didn't remember him at all.

Harris didn't exactly shake; instead he offered his hand, flat and firm as a spade, for Joel to grasp. "Really appreciate your coming over," he said, as if Joel had had some choice.

Harris gestured toward his standard-issue informal area: two wing chairs facing a loveseat. Joel seized one of the wing chairs. He had learned over the years not to sit in the loveseat. If you did, you wound up with two interlocutors, member and staffer, talking down at you from their chairs. Plus you couldn't sit normally in the loveseat: you had to resist the impulse to cross your legs, and wound up with your knees touching and your hands in your lap, like a maiden lady. Harris took the other chair, leaving tiny Melanie to sink into the loveseat.

Harris looked at Joel for some seconds with an expression of pleasant interest. Then he must have realized that he had asked for the briefing and ought to pose some question or other. He couldn't remember what the subject was; he turned toward Melanie.

She said, "Oh. Um . . . we wanted Joel to come over to talk about aliens and Medicare."

"Right," Harris said, as if he had just been testing her. He faced Joel, drew himself up and gripped the arms of his wing chair—a posture of dutiful attention.

"Right," Joel repeated. "Actually, Senator Altman pretty much summed it up. If you're over sixty-five and you've been legally resident here for five years, you can get Medicare by paying a premium."

"A premium," Harris said slowly, as if the word were new to him.

"Yes. A monthly . . ." Joel couldn't think of another word. "Premium."

"Uh-huh. So they're paying for their own costs."

"Yes," Joel said enthusiastically, as if Harris were a bright student. "Well, except . . ." He could have left it at "Yes." They're paying for it, it's no problem, why don't you just leave these poor old exiles alone? But someone else would explain it to Harris, sooner or later, if Joel didn't. "Well, they don't really pay all their costs. First, if they're poor, the states have to pay their premium. And second—"

"The states, yeah, someone this morning said that. What about the states?"

"If somebody's below the federal poverty level, then—"

"What's that?"

"Sir?"

"The federal poverty level."

"Well, it's this figure that's put out by . . . I guess the Census Bureau every year. It started out—this is interesting—they started out taking the cost of what they called the 'thrifty food plan,' and then they just multiplied that by three and said that's what someone needed to subsist on. And since then—"

Joel was wrong; this wasn't interesting. "No, no, no," Harris practically shouted. "How much is it?"

"Oh." Joel had no idea. "I think it's like . . . seven thousand or something for one person."

"Seven thousand!" Harris seemed amazed.

"Yeah, it's really not very much."

Joel had misstepped again. "Seven thousand," Harris said. "There are lots of people in Montana getting by on a lot less than seven thousand. And they don't come crying to the government for help."

"Um, right. But it's kind of a national average, you know? I mean, if you lived in New York, say, or here in DC, seven thousand wouldn't get you very far."

"Nobody says people have to live in New York."

"No, sir," Joel said, miserably. Five minutes into the briefing and he had Harris thinking he was some kind of communist. You had to be so careful with these guys, the new Republicans who had descended on the Capitol like blow-dried Martians. You could tell them the earth was round and they'd turn on you, snarling that this was just the kind of confused, outmoded thinking they'd been sent to Washington to straighten out.

"Anyway," Harris said, with a little wave of his hand, concili-
atory now that he had made his point. "Anyway, aliens below
this . . . 'poverty level' get Medicare and they don't have to
pay anything, the states pay for it."

"Well, it's not just aliens. It's anybody below that level.
Citizens, too."

"Fine, fine, but we're talking about the aliens. What are
they doing here?"

"Doing here?" How should Joel know what they were doing
here? Maybe they all crept across the border to get free heart
transplants. "Well, they were admitted here . . . you know,
refugees from somewhere or, I don't know, somebody's mother,
whatever."

"So why don't they become citizens? They could become
citizens."

"Um . . . I guess maybe they can't pass the test. You know,
they may not have learned English all that well, so they can't
pass the test." He would have liked to see Harris pass the citi-
zenship test. He would also have liked to see Harris subsist for
a week on the thrifty food plan.

Rob the receptionist appeared in the doorway. "Senator, excuse
me, it's . . . it's those people you were expecting. From——"

Harris cut him off. "Right, right." He turned to Joel. "This'll
just be a few minutes, if you can stick around. I think we had
some other stuff we wanted to go through."

"Sure," Joel said.

When Harris had gone, Joel said to Melanie, "I guess I put
my foot in it."

"Better you than me." Melanie giggled. "I loved that. There
are people in Montana living on nuts and berries!"

"Yeah. Proud and self-sufficient."

"Real Americans." She shook a fist in the air.

"Anyway, you'd think I'd know better, just keep my mouth
shut."

Melanie shrugged. "It's kind of . . . I'm never quite sure

what will set him off. You know, he's not— He's more complicated than you think. He really does care about people."

"Uh-huh."

"Look, just that he wanted to know more about this—at
least he's thinking about it, trying to think about it."

"I guess."

"I try to nudge him along. And then every so often he bites
my head off."

"Yeah, I hear he's a bear," Joel said.

"Oh, that's talk, mostly. Honestly, I never saw him throw
anything. You just have to know when to ease off."

"Well, I'm sure easing off. Just the facts, sir. That's if he
ever comes back."

"He'll be back in a few minutes, he's just meeting with—
He'll be back unless something happens on the floor. But do
you mind if I go make a couple of calls?"

"No."

"You sure we can't get you coffee or something?"

"Yeah, coffee would be good."

Joel stayed in his wing chair for a minute, looking over at
Harris's huge barren desk and the high-backed leather chair
on which Harris had draped his jacket. It was just a jacket on
the back of a chair; why should the sight of it have left Joel
suddenly desolate?

Well, it was half of a thousand-dollar suit, for one thing—
distinctly unMontanan; no pockets with openings like smiles.
But Joel could probably have paid for a thousand-dollar suit,
if he would ever have thought of such an extravagance, about
as readily as Harris. Senators didn't make so much, really; after
they paid for two houses and sent their kids to St. Alban's or
wherever, they probably weren't much better off than Joel was.
Except for the ones—more and more of them lately—who
had made their fortune someplace else and then bought their

53

way into office. Becoming senators as a sort of hobby after retirement, the way rich guys used to become yachtsmen. But Harris wasn't one of those.

The jacket wasn't, whatever its price tag, an impressive object. Just a jacket, which Harris put on when he went to the floor and took off when he got back to his office. Harris had got up this morning—early probably, around the time when Joel was just realizing that Sam might be gone for good— Harris had got up, showered and shaved. Put on his pants, as they say, one leg at a time, and then the jacket. Walked out of his tract house somewhere in Virginia. Got into his car and idled through the same gridlock as everybody else, to arrive at the Hart Senate Office Building and begin his humdrum day. Draping his jacket on the back of his chair, already a little tired: a day ahead of floor votes on vital issues like flag-burning, punctuated by briefings and little side-meetings like the one he'd run out to now, where he was almost surely begging someone for money.

Tonight he would drive to the airport, leave his car in the special members' lot that the newspapers lately had turned into some kind of symbol of how privileged senators were, how isolated from ordinary life. Catch a late flight to Montana—several flights, probably, it must have been hard to get to Montana—several legs, riding in coach, because he wasn't one of the rich senators. Then a weekend of flying around the state on puddle-jumpers and nodding thoughtfully as sheep ranchers bleated their grievances.

Who could have wanted such a life, why should Joel have been filled with sadness and self-reproach that he wasn't a senator and Joe Harris was? A pretty obscure senator, to be sure, who probably didn't have to worry that anyone would recognize him on the airplane. But still a somebody, his jacket draped on a senator's chair. While Joel, a nobody, sat in a senator's office with, yes, now that he looked, gravy on his tie.

It was about Sam, Sam and the jacket had got all mixed up.

As if somehow Joel had chosen between life as a senator and life with Sam, chosen irrevocably. Sam had cost him everything, and now Sam was gone.

The receptionist appeared, looking sullen. Here he had been a varsity—what?—wrestler, probably, who had graduated maybe a year ago from some school like Southwest Georgia Agriculture and Remedial Reading and had come to Washington planning to work at the White House. Instead he was bringing coffee, in a seldom-washed mug that read "Big Sky Country," to this geek with gravy on his tie.

"Thank you, Rob," Joel said.

Rob was a little startled to be called by name. "Uh . . . sure. Did you want cream or . . . whatever? Um . . ." He searched for the concept. "Sugar?"

"No, this is fine."

"Um . . . okay."

Joel regarded Rob's departing, varsity butt, his vast oxford-swathed back. So beautiful, so young, so dumb. And with infinitely more chance of becoming a senator than Joel had ever had.

Because he was a straight boy.

It wasn't Sam: being gay had cost Joel everything. Of course he would never have been a senator, not if he'd been as straight as a two-dollar bill. Perhaps there were some other, more plausible vocations that had been closed to him—or had seemed closed—in the early seventies, those last years before the closet doors started to crack open. Law, for example, or the foreign service: he had actually gone to interview at the State Department before he learned that they were still giving polygraph tests to screen out deviants. So he was cruelly prevented from embarking on a career of processing visa applications in, say, Zambia.

The price he had paid for being gay didn't consist of these specific handicaps. There were other things he might have been, instead of nothing. But being gay had taken up his whole life. He had devoted the whole of his youth to it, had studied it year after year as intensively as if he had been training to be a neurosurgeon. There hadn't been time for anything else.

First, of course, the many years of being not-gay. Starting with being not-in-love-with-Alex. Or even earlier, maybe, when he turned a page in a magazine, saw an ad with a little picture of a guy in swimming trunks, and knew. Knew, with hot astonishment, and from that instant devoted himself to the great vocation of not-knowing.

He spent the next ten years of his life not knowing: denying, renouncing, forgetting, explaining. How he explained to himself in those years. Ockham's Razor, the principle that a scientist should prefer the simplest explanation that will account for the available facts, should have led him quickly enough to the correct hypothesis. However, as a creationist can disregard whole mountains of evidence, waving away every fossil and geologic formation, just as faithfully Joel had dismissed every sign of the simple truth about himself. Every sidewise glance in the locker room, every vision conjured up during his nightly self-abuse, the even more compelling testimony of his recusant dick when he tried to make it with women—nothing was persuasive enough. Not even several years of actual praxis—the twenty or so tricks scattered across his last year of college, the couple of years of graduate school, his first years at OLA. He could account for it all: annotate every feeling, explicate every incident, until he had compiled a veritable *summa theologica* of rationalization and denial.

He knew gay men who had got through all of this by the time they could tie their shoes, and others who had gone to their graves refusing the irrefutable. His decade of resistance was, perhaps, longer than average. Ending abruptly and rather anticlimactically one day when he was twenty-six. He said, "Okay." Pushed into it, finally, by the crushing burden of the evidence? He couldn't remember, but it probably wasn't that way: would one more fossil make a creationist drop his Bible? Just one day—more exhausted than exuberant—he murmured, "Okay." It was okay, and stayed okay.

Okay through the next couple of hundred tricks, over about four years. Once a week, then, on average, though an average would mask the dry spells, the bacchanalian intervals, the handful of micro-romances, the longest of which might have lasted about ten days. Once a week Joel summoned up the nerve to talk to a stranger in a bar and then follow him home. Or take him to Joel's own place, whose pestilential untidiness in those years might, Joel could see now, have contributed to the brevity of his affairs. And of course the nights he scored were outnumbered by the nights he stood forlornly at the margin of Zippers trying to decipher whether some guy was looking at him or through him.

Either kind of night followed by the mornings when he would drag into the office, sleepy or hung over or both, and try to focus on . . . whatever the hot issues were back in the seventies. They seemed as far away as his tricks. The Nixon national health insurance plan. David, who turned out to have a wife and a baby. The Carter national health insurance plan. Steven, who saw him for almost a week before asking if Joel would mind co-signing for a little loan. The Gephardt national health insurance plan. Keith, who flirted with him for most of 1979, finally went home with him, and turned out to be wearing a girdle.

By the time Sam came along, Joel was thirty. He had used up nearly half his life, all the years of saying "No" and then the equally taxing years of saying "My place or yours." How could he have accomplished anything? Gay had been his profession; everything else had been a sideline. Now he was forty-five, Sam was very possibly gone, and he had nothing, was nothing.

Harris returned. He looked dismayed to find Joel still there, but covered pretty quickly. "Um . . . I guess Melanie will be back in a minute. Why don't you just go on?"

Go on? What the hell had they been talking about? "Right. I guess . . . you were asking why these aliens didn't become citizens."

"Uh-huh," Harris said blandly. He had already lost interest in this question. "Listen, let's hold off on this till Melanie comes back. There was something else I wanted to ask about."

"Yes, sir."

"AIDS."

"AIDS?" Joel's voice cracked. It was just another health policy issue. Surely Harris just thought: here's a health guy, I can ask him my AIDS question. Yet Joel felt himself blushing, as if he had given himself away somehow.

"Yeah," Harris said. "I hear people with AIDS get Medicare."

"Oh. Some of them do, yes, sir."

"How come?"

"Because they . . . you know, if they get disabled and can't work, they can get Social Security. And then two years after that they get Medicare."

"They have to wait two years for Medicare?"

"Right."

Harris was, astonishingly, taking notes. "Then after that they have it until . . ."

"Until they . . ." Joel repeated. It was creepy, joining Harris in saying "they." They were *they*, people with AIDS: to Harris they must have seemed as far away as Eskimos, and as unimportant. But they were *they* to Joel as well. Joel and Sam were negative. So were most of the people they knew, those who were still around by 1995. The epidemic had about finished with Joel's generation and had moved on to kids, with whom he felt only a tepid kinship.

"So how do they get disability? Just call in and say, 'Oh, I don't feel up to teasing anybody's hair today?'" Harris smiled.

Joel was supposed to smile, too. He was not supposed to say, "We don't all do hair." He didn't, but at least he didn't smile.

Mr. Integrity. "I . . . you know, I don't do Social Security, but I think you're automatically disabled if you actually have AIDS. If you have HIV but don't have AIDS yet, there's a list of, like, symptoms, conditions."

Harris sighed. Joel had no sense of humor. Joel was boring. "So they . . . get something on that list and then two years after that they get Medicare."

"Twenty-nine months, actually. I mean, they have to wait five months for their Social Security and then two years after that for the Medicare to kick in."

"Twenty-nine months. I guess not everybody . . . makes it."

"No, sir."

"So what do they do in the meanwhile? Buy their own insurance?"

"Well, they can't do that, usually. You know, insurance companies don't want them." Joel was encouraged to describe all the insurance problems of people with HIV. COBRA coverage they couldn't pay for. Limited drug benefits. State programs that required them to impoverish themselves. Probably he went on too long, but Harris listened with surprising attentiveness. Funny that a guy from a rural state should be interested in AIDS. Maybe Melanie was right, maybe the guy really did care about people.

When Joel ran out of steam, Harris shook his head and said, "My." He looked off into space for a second. "Anyway, the ones on Medicare. They're all on disability, none of them are over sixty-five?"

"Oh, I guess some are. You know, if they got it through a transfusion or something like that."

"Uh-huh. But those people just . . . got it, they didn't do anything."

Joel drew in his breath. It had been some time—the late eighties, maybe—since he had heard anyone distinguish between the innocent victims and the guilty. He was wondering if he might dare to point out, gently, that everybody just got it, it was sort of a no-fault microorganism, when Melanie came in.

"Sorry," she said. "Where are we?"

"Oh, Josh and I were just chatting," Harris said.

"Joel," Joel said.

"Right," Harris said, unapologetically. "Why don't we get back to aliens? How many aliens have Medicare?"

"About a million."

"A million! Gosh." Harris wrote down "1 MIL" in giant letters. He looked over at Melanie and intoned: "Young American families are paying for free care for a million foreigners."

Amazing. The man actually spoke in sound bites. "It's not the whole million," Joel said. "I mean, most of them——"

A buzzer sounded. Buzzers haunted these guys everywhere. There even used to be a couple of nearby bars linked up to the signal system, so a truant member could stagger back to the Capitol and vote.

"Shoot," Harris said. "Got to get to the floor." He stood up, put on his jacket one arm at a time, then came over and shook Joel's hand, actually grasping it this time. "Josh, I really appreciate your coming over on such short notice. It's been very helpful." He repeated, "Very helpful, very helpful," as he left the room.

Joel said to Melanie, "I shouldn't have told him a million. I mean, there are a million aliens, but most of them just get Medicare like anybody else—they worked, they earned it. I think there's only a few who are targeted by this Altman amendment."

"Shit," Melanie said. "Once he gets a number in his head it's there for good. How many is it really?"

"I don't know. I was trying to pin down the number this morning, but I don't have it yet." Inasmuch as the number didn't magically appear on the solitaire screen. "Not very many."

"Well, keep trying. I don't want him going around saying a million."

"Right."

"What did you all talk about while I was out?"

"Um . . . AIDS mostly."

"AIDS? I didn't know he was interested in AIDS." She frowned: now she would have to get up to speed on yet another issue.

"I wouldn't worry," Joel said. "He wasn't that interested."

"No, he has kind of a short attention span. He jumps around a lot."

"Don't they all?"

Joel trudged back to his office, a couple of blocks from the Capitol, in what had once been a tacky apartment building. Now the building housed OLA, along with minority staff from especially obscure House committees. He had to pass through a metal detector and let the guard x-ray his briefcase. This nonsense had started just a few weeks earlier, after the Oklahoma City bombing in April—as if, with all the possible targets in Washington, a terrorist would home right in on House Annex 2A, the very nerve center of American democracy.

He crept by his boss's office. Herb was on the phone, as always, and with his back turned to the door; he was looking out the window his exalted position had secured him, so Joel didn't have to stop and report how the briefing had gone. In his own office, a windowless cell that must once have been a supply closet, Joel reached for the political almanac to look up Harris. Usually he did this before a briefing, so he would know better than to babble about poor people to some raving Social Darwinist, but he had been too busy all morning.

In the almanac, a Harris campaign photo—shirtsleeves rolled up, no thousand-dollar suit in evidence—and the terse bio:

Raymond J. (Joe) Harris, Jr. (R-MT) b. 1961, Billings, MT. B.S., U. of Montana (Geology), 1983. Employmt., Big Sky Waste Management, 1983–7. Billings Bd. of Educ.,

61

1985–7. State Assembly, 1987–91. State Senate, 1991–4, Maj. Whip, 1994. Elected U.S. Sen. 1994. Harris 119,351 (44%); Freeman, Dem., 111,207 (41%); Kraus, Reform, 36,950 (14%); deBoer, Natural Law, 1,427 (1%). Committees: Finance, Natural Resources. Residence: Billings, MT. Wife: Trudi. Children: Raymond III, Jennifer, Scott. Ratings: National Rifle Association, 100; League of Conservation Voters, 5; Citizens for Responsible Tax Policy, 86.

Politics was all he had ever done, then; if he were ever defeated he'd have to go back to the nothing job in waste management. And he could be defeated: winning so narrowly in the year of the Republican sweep, all those mercurial Reform voters who might go for the Democrat next time. Ray Three would be—what? Twelve or thirteen, maybe. Likely to come home with some body part pierced any day now, and with college application forms not too long after that. So Harris had better stay a senator if he was going to put all those kids through school and get Trudi the Viking range. No wonder he was ready for a little alien-bashing. Safe enough in a state with no ethnic voters: probably the last aliens Montana ever saw were Japanese people in relocation camps.

Yet, he seemed to care about AIDS. Not enough to do anything, surely, but there was a little spark of humanity under that smooth Republican carapace.

Joel thought for an instant of going to work for him. Joel had never once considered becoming a staffer. Working those endless days, having to adjust to every change of mood or party line or purchaser, no life at all. Perhaps the idea came to him this particular afternoon because he wasn't sure what life he had. In any case, he let himself spin out the fantasy.

Supplanting Melanie first, then becoming indispensable, Harris's shadow. Slowly educating him, finding his best instincts, turning him into . . . some kind of moderate. Of course he would be immovable on some things: gun control, probably the environment. But on other stuff he could be— what was Melanie's word?—nudged. They would sit together on the two wing chairs in his office, Harris thoughtful and troubled, Joel explaining the world to him. Guiding him, step by simple step. Over time Harris would just naturally turn to Joel, as to a big brother. Joel would move to Virginia, they would drive in together in the mornings. Trudi and the kids would get used to his being around, he would become Uncle Joel . . .

Herb appeared in the doorway, briefcase in hand. "Hey, Joel, how'd the briefing go?"

"Okay. He wasn't quite as stupid as I thought."

Herb looked up and down the hall, afraid someone might have heard. Everyone at OLA agreed that the collective IQ of the 104th Congress rivaled that of an ant farm, but it was not usual to say so aloud. "What did you all talk about?"

"The aliens thing. And then AIDS, a little."

"AIDS." Herb frowned. "Did you bring that up?"

"No. I don't just . . . bring that up." What did Herb think— that because Joel was gay he went out to senators' offices and preached sermons? Well, he had preached a little.

"Why would a member from Montana care about AIDS?"

"Beats me."

"Anyway, I've got a meeting to get to," Herb said. He hoisted his probably empty briefcase as evidence that he was not actually sneaking off at four o'clock on a Friday afternoon.

"See you," Joel said. He needed to give Herb about a five-minute head start, then he could sneak out too.

Of course he wanted to rush home, ascertain just what *stuff* Sam had picked up. It would be a sort of measure of where they were: the volume of space left vacant by the items Sam had removed would correlate with the expected duration of his absence. Joel had a comical vision of the place denuded, then a much less risible vision of the place just as it was, only

Sam missing. Or, even worse, Sam present. There to tell Joel his future, how things were going to be now. Like a fortune-teller, except one who doesn't just predict the future but designs it. Sam would decide how things were going to be, and they would begin their new life, apart or tenuously together. If together, then with conditions Sam would specify.

He picked up his briefcase, put it down again: no sense in everybody toting an empty briefcase home.

When Joel let himself into the apartment, there were lights on. He called out, "Yoo-hoo." There was no answer; Sam must have left the lights on when he came for his stuff. Joel didn't bother to inventory what Sam had removed, just went straight to the kitchen and made himself a drink.

In the living room he sat, not in his chair, but in Sam's. The chairs were identical, there wasn't any reason Sam's should have felt any different from his own. Except the view was different: he saw the room from a slightly different angle, everything familiar shifted. In this shared space they had had territories, views of their own, places where they intersected and places where they avoided bumping into one another. Their relative positions were fixed. Sam sat in the left-hand chair, slept on the left-hand side of the bed. On the vanity in the bathroom, his gear was to the left. Joel had never inhabited the entire apartment; there were spaces that were Sam's. When Sam was away for a night, Joel never slept on Sam's side of the bed, or even in the middle. Even now, in Sam's chair, Joel felt as though he were sitting on the lap of a ghost.

He got up, meaning to move to his own chair, but instead he went to the bathroom to find that, yes, most of the toiletries were gone from Sam's side of the vanity. Not all: Sam had left behind about half his library of colognes. *Feral. Wall Street. Urge.* Which ones had he taken? Joel had never paid attention to Sam's colognes, unless he wore too much. This morning Sam had stood here and picked among them. Deciding how he wanted to smell for somebody who, maybe, did pay attention.

That he had left any of the bottles was sort of offensive. He hadn't just cleared out, he had prioritized, and left Joel with his trash. Joel didn't even have to go to Sam's closet to know that it would be full of pants he never wore and shirts that were out of fashion. Nor to his bureau to know that he had bequeathed Joel all the unmated socks. He had pruned, he was going to start his new life unencumbered by anything that was less than perfect.

Two or three months. Were they still in that early phase of courtship when you pretend to be perfect, watch every word, brush your teeth seven times a day, and try not to fart? That would end soon enough. But for a while Sam would be new, as if he had molted, leaving Joel with the bruised and blemished old hide and bestowing on Joel's successor a young, fresh skin.

They had tried to molt together sometimes, Sam and Joel. After a vacation, usually; after a few days in a strange place, at close quarters, every routine abandoned, and with it every chance of doing the routinely annoying things. They might even make love in a new position. And, for a while after coming home, they would be especially careful and solicitous. Sam wouldn't watch TV as Joel cooked but would sit in the kitchen talking. Joel would put his shoes away, hang up his towel. In the morning they would make the bed together instead of just leaving it in a tangle they would have to straighten up at bedtime. They would make love in the middle of the week, they would try that new position again, but it seemed awkward, here in their own bed.

They shifted to their customary postures. Later, Sam shook Joel awake; Joel was snoring. "You didn't snore the whole time away," Sam said. "I don't know," Joel said. "Ocean air or something." They couldn't bring the ocean air back; in a week it was as if they had never been away.

Joel had thought this cycle could be repeated indefinitely. He even thought it was salutary. They had already blocked out time in June; that was when they liked Provincetown, before it got too crowded. Joel had booked the tickets. Could Sam possibly have let him do this when he knew they weren't going anywhere in June? No, he was too frugal. If he had been planning ahead, he could have come up with some plausible reason they shouldn't book for June. He wouldn't have let Joel waste the money. So he must not have had even a premonition, not until last night.

Once he had decided, though, so quickly: a few hours later he was able to come here and systematically pick which colognes to take. He wasn't the least bit agitated, didn't, in a daze, hurl a few things into a bag.

Joel wasn't angry about whoever it was. He wasn't angry that Sam lied. He wasn't angry that Sam left if he had to go. Joel was furious that Sam could be so businesslike. He wanted to sweep all the rejected colognes off the vanity. Except the room would stink for weeks.

He looked at himself in the mirror. He saw a bright fourteen-year-old, ready for life. He had never stopped seeing that boy. He knew there was a middle-aged man named Joel, but he couldn't make himself see that geezer. His few remaining strings of graying hair, he saw those. He saw the bags under his eyes, the burst capillaries on the sides of his nose that might have suggested he drank a little too much. But it was as if this were a mask he had put on: from beneath it his eyes looked out as they always had, unblinking and brave and young. He had never believed anything he saw in the mirror, except his eyes.

He knew Sam didn't look at him and see a kid. Sam must have seen the comical mask that he had donned for life. Gradually, or all at once? That is: did Sam's love decline on a steady curve, shrinking with each recession of Joel's hairline or each increment in his girth, 33, 34, 35 and counting?

Or did he just look at Joel one day and think, Who the hell is this? How did I get stuck with this?

As Joel had looked at him sometimes. Not with revulsion, just wonderment. How did it happen that he was bound to this person, what were they doing in the same apartment? Joel was happy enough to be there, but there was something unreal about it. As if Sam's presence were just a continuing accident: Joel might at any moment blink and he'd be gone. Maybe it was the same for Sam. Maybe he didn't look at Joel one morning and see a monster, a drab, flabby, sexless lump holding him in thrall. Maybe he just looked and saw a stranger. One for whom he felt perhaps some mysterious affinity, but still a stranger, no one to him.

If they could have married? The idea had always made Joel snicker. The happy couples he saw in the gay paper—usually an accountant and a church organist—attending their commitment ceremony in matching gray tuxes. They had always been together about six months, and they had a damp, earnest look about them. But if they could have, Joel and Sam? So that they could have filed a joint tax return and suffered the marriage penalty? So that the impending decision, about whether they were going to split the matching pair of club chairs or let them stay together as a set in one abode or the other, could be made by a judge? A piece of paper, a legal document that would have said what all legal documents really boil down to: sooner or later some lawyers are going to get some money. It wouldn't have held Sam there one extra minute.

People lived—straight and gay, now—in a world of perfect freedom. The unhallowed contract between Joel and Sam had been as strong as any, good just as long as they both said it was. So no contract at all. Joel-and-Sam had never existed.

Hadn't Sam, at least, made an irrevocable promise not to hurt Joel? But how could Joel say that Sam was hurting him? How had Sam's departure injured him? He was deprived, yes. Deprived of Sam's conjugal services, as they said in lawsuits. But only in the same way that he was deprived when some hunk in a video didn't step off the screen and into his arms.

Only in the sense of not having what he wanted, and what Sam had no obligation to give him.

Love had no privilege; his being in love conferred no obligation on Sam. Sam was innocent, just innocently gone.

Joel went back to the kitchen, poured himself another drink, went to his own club chair this time, not Sam's.

He intended to cry. He could feel that he was pretty close to crying, maybe he could.

He waited.

Nothing. He tried to focus: say aloud, and simply, what had happened. "Sam has left me." He could see that this was pretty sad. If it were true—and as he said it a second time he was pretty sure it was true, all the evasions and maybes of the last twenty-four hours blown away, it was true—his life had changed immeasurably, everything he had taken for granted was gone. Like one of those people you saw on the news after a brush fire or a flood, standing and looking at the empty place where their house used to be. They didn't cry either, those people, at least not in front of the camera. Maybe later, but while the camera was there they just stood in disbelief.

Not disbelief, post-belief. They had supposed they had a home, but they had been suffering under a misapprehension. Mother Nature had gently pointed out their error: they had never had a home, just a pile of sticks or rocks, a little detritus in one spot on the surface of an indifferent earth. So they couldn't cry for something that had never existed, as Joel-and-Sam had never existed.

Too glib. Something inside him actually uttered this, critiquing his little effort to make sense of his feelings, as if grading a hastily written term paper. Too glib, too evasive. He couldn't cry because he had never felt anything, not really. He had not emerged from belief; he had never believed. He had never been in love with Sam, or with anyone.

He had cried at movies, but never at a funeral. He did not

cry for his parents, or for the friends who had been picked off one by one. He had cried for Yul Brynner in *The King and I.* Olivia de Havilland in *Gone with the Wind.* Even Old Yeller, a dog in some bathetic Disney movie. He could suspend disbelief at the movies, weep fluently as some actor collapsed to the floor of a soundstage. He could not suspend disbelief in the reality of his own life.

That was it, yes. How he had wept for Riff, the winsome Jet who was stabbed during the rumble in *West Side Story.* He was eleven or twelve then: he mourned for days, disconsolately listening to the record, looking at that young, doomed face on the album cover. And now he couldn't muster so much as a lump in his throat for the real man who had filled his life for fifteen years.

The tears came. Not for Sam. Perhaps more like the tears that flow in a psychiatrist's office, tears of sublime self-pity and self-absorption. He was some kind of monster, who could not know grief, who had never known love. What is missing, oh, what is missing, doctor? These first tears dried up pretty fast: even being a heartless monster was a pose, after all. What could be more narcissistic than to diagnose your own narcissistic disorder?

There were two ground turkey patties left in the icebox, and half a can of beans. He would need to start cooking for one. What had he eaten, back in his bachelor days? Carryout, mostly. Sandwiches. A couple specialties of the house. Spread a can of Hormel chili over slices of bread. Add a lot of Tabasco, cover with slices of Velveeta, nuke till Velveeta bubbles. He was in his twenties then, he could eat that stuff. If he were to eat that way now, he'd turn into Sydney Greenstreet. And who would notice? Sam was gone, Joel couldn't even really miss him, Joel didn't care if he ever met another man.

He turned on the TV while he ate his turkey burgers.

Congress had gone home, C-SPAN was rebroadcasting a press conference at the Department of Transportation. He flipped through the channels and found a show where male lifeguards with abdomens like relief maps of the Andes cavorted with female lifeguards whose bathing suits somehow stayed wet whether they went in the water or not.

He thought about the tickets to Provincetown. Non-refundable. Maybe Sam would get over . . . whoever it was, and be back in time for the trip. Or Joel could go himself, no sense wasting both tickets. Go by himself, all by himself.

When he and Sam had gone, he had sometimes met a man their age, or a little older, in a bar. They would chat, the guy would say he was staying a week, had a room in one of the tonier guesthouses. Joel would think: you pathetic, deluded geek, what could have brought you, all by your senescent self, to a town where boys in their twenties stroll down the streets in their underwear? You might as well have blown the money on a fun-filled week in Davenport, Iowa.

He lit a cigarette. When he felt himself crying again, he knew he was crying for Riff. *When you're a Jet . . .* He never got to be a Jet. He never danced down the streets of the West Side in rhythm with Riff, never hung out with him outside the candy store.

He never got to be with Alex, never again after that one day helping him with his algebra. Never cruised with him to the drive-in on a Friday night. Never sat with him watching TV. Never heard him say Joel was his best friend.

He never got to step inside that picture in a magazine, where a young man in swimming trunks had something to tell him.

He had lived a possible life. Being gay was what was possible. He had come out into the world and there were these choices: he could be straight or he could be gay. So of course he picked gay, and then there were some further choices, submenus: postures in and out of bed, attitudes, costumes.

None of it was what he'd wanted. It was what was possible;

he couldn't be a Jet, so he donned the gang colors of a faggot; All these years, played this game that had nothing to do with what he wanted. Sam had ended the game, which he had meant to play forever, or until the game was called on account of death. Sam had overturned the board, leaving Joel past the middle of his life, never having had what he needed.

As if Sam, and not the world, had stood in the way of what Joel had needed.

Innocently, Sam had held him, they had held one another. Innocently, Sam had left. Probably looking for something he had always wanted and never got. If Joel had been more noble, he might have wished Sam could find it. Maybe if he had ever really loved Sam he would have wished Sam could find it, whatever it was. Instead, he wished Sam were there with him, holding him.

So he was, finally, crying about Sam. He was supposed to stay there for a lifetime, comforting Joel for the irrevocable loss of Riff or Alex or . . . Joel wondered if Sam knew. He could not possibly have known.

When Joel went to bed, he put a drop of cologne on Sam's pillow.

three

Monday, getting on noon. Joel almost didn't pick up the phone, because it might be some staffer who needed the history of health care in the Western world before lunch. But he was pretty sure it was Sam.

"Joel Lingeman."

"Hi." Softly, the voice pitched low. The way you might murmur "Hi" to a friend you bumped into at a funeral.

Joel said "Hi" and waited. A long time; could Sam really have made this call without thinking even of a first sentence?

"I've been trying to get you all weekend."

"I was in and out a lot," Joel said. Out, mostly; he was still kind of hung over. "Anyway, you never left a number."

"Oh. Oh, I thought I did."

He had, Joel just wouldn't dial it. Not to hear the phone picked up by a stranger. Not to have to ask, "Is Sam there?" And hear a stranger say, "Who's calling?"

Sam coughed. "I . . . um, I wanted to tell you what happened."

"Uh-huh."

"I, you know, I met somebody. Actually, it's been a while, I met him a while ago."

"Couple of months," Joel said.

"About. What, have you known all along?"

"I wasn't completely sure." Better than saying no, he didn't know anything, he was a blinkered idiot. It struck him that he was calculating what to say to a man he had spent most of his adult life with. It struck him that he had always calculated what to say to Sam.

"I—maybe I should have told you what was going on. I thought it might go away, you know? I thought it might just be a thing."

"Just one of those crazy flings."

"What?"

Joel had spent most of his adult life with a man who didn't know Cole Porter. "But it didn't go away."

"No. And finally he said, you know, I had to choose."

He, the mysterious he, had issued an ultimatum. In bed, turning away from Sam, sullenly. Or over dinner, looking down at his plate, then up again, gravely, sincerely: "You have to choose."

"So you did," Joel said.

"It was hard. I had to think about it."

He could picture Sam thinking about it, the deliberate way Sam worked things out. The vertical line on the sheet of paper, the columns headed *Joel* and *X*. He would dutifully have filled the Joel column, maybe halfway down, with all Joel's good points. Here fifteen years. Cooks. Pays rent on time. Then he got to X's column and there was nothing to write down. He was in love, the name at the top of the column was so reverberant there was nothing else to write down.

"What's this guy's name?" Joel said.

"Kevin."

Would Joel have felt the same chill if the name had been

Fred? Or Seymour? Kevin was cool, acute, slender and sharp-featured. Hair dark-brown and cut close to the head.

"Tell me about him."

"I don't know what to tell. He's . . ." Sam cleared his throat. "He's twenty-three."

Of course, that's all he had to write in the column headed *Kevin*: twenty-three.

"But he's, you know, real mature."

Mature enough to sit across from a man who was pushing fifty and tell him, "You have to choose." Only a twenty-three-year-old could have been so dramatic. Only a forty-seven-year-old who was head over heels would have thought he really did have to choose. Poor Sam: how long did he think he was going to hang on to Kevin, twenty-three?

"So, um, anyway." Sam paused, then said, enunciating carefully: "I'm leaving you, Joel."

A senator who has flown to New Hampshire every weekend for two years schedules a press conference. Unless you've just flown in from Mars you know what he's going to announce, and still you might shiver a little when the clown finally says, "I am a candidate for the office of President of the United States."

So Joel was thrilled at the sheer expectedness of the words. *I'm leaving you;* he must always have been waiting to hear those words. Hadn't wanted to, perhaps. If he had made a list of the pros and cons, two columns, he would surely have concluded that it would be better to grow old with Sam. Wind up with Sam in the Lambda Continuing Care Community, rocking side by side and whistling at the cute orderly, if either of them could whistle. There must never have been a chance: that Joel had even imagined their breakup must have made it inevitable.

Like some virtuoso of the anticlimax, Sam now produced: "I want you to know that I . . . I'll always think of you as my best friend."

Joel was thunderstruck. Of course, if he had ever imagined

the scene any farther than that ringing line, *I'm leaving you*, these would have been the next words. But he hadn't imagined one instant past that line. He would spend the rest of his life on the other side of that line, starting with Sam's repeating: "You're my best friend."

Joel must have answered, the conversation must have gone on. Yet after Sam's usual "Talk to you" and the click of the phone he couldn't have repeated any of it.

You're my best friend: it was something a ten-year-old might say. And it might have gratified Joel if he had heard it when he was ten. If he had heard it from the right boy—from Alex, say, or from some ten-year-old imago of Senator Harris. Instead of the asthmatic losers who actually tended to say it to him, letting him know that he too was a loser.

Sam was his best friend, who else could possibly qualify? Joel had been thinking, the other night, of everything they hadn't shared. Piano duets. *Middlemarch*. But they had shared so much: Sam's hernia operation, Joel's periodontal work, all the vacations, all the people they'd buried. They were best friends.

Maybe that was better. Maybe they would actually mean more to one another if, say, they had dinner every couple of weeks, with something to talk about, stuff to catch up on, instead of dinner every night, with the only sound the intermittent clack of silverware on plates. Maybe they could simply love one another, now that sex was out of the way.

They had known such couples. Guys who had broken up and then become best buddies. Maybe this was how they could be. Sam and Joel: the exes. Maybe they could even use the nonrefundable tickets! What did you do for vacation? Oh, I went to Provincetown with my ex.

Sam and Joel, the Jets. Womb to tomb, sperm to worm. Just as soon as sex was out of the way.

A couple of days later Joel took a long lunch, mostly just strolling around the Hill, then spent the rest of the afternoon catching up on the *Congressional Record*. There was a whole week of issues he hadn't been through. Lots of great stuff. Last Wednesday Senator Byrd had inserted one of his thirty-page term papers, explaining how the line-item veto had brought an end to the Roman republic. Also there was one of those nifty eruptions of gang warfare in the House. Some Republican called the President a liar; some Democrat demanded that the member's words be taken down, whatever that meant; then rulings from the chair, votes; all told, at least an hour of carrying-on, two gangs of apes screeching and mooning each other. On Thursday there were the mysterious House roll calls he had watched while waiting for Sam. Friday the House passed the Commerce, Justice, State, and Judiciary appropriations, a hundred pages of fine print that Joel read with the greatest care, looking for the little poison pills that would make the President veto it. Tuesday there were about a hundred new bills introduced.

Senator Altman's aliens amendment had inspired the usual torrent of copycat bills. The less imaginative members had simply copied the proposal verbatim and introduced it under their own names. Others had grasped the underlying principle—that you could express your disdain for despised populations and at the same time save taxpayers money by cutting off Medicare for:

H. 2419, persons convicted of drug offenses;
H. 2471, flag burners;
H. 2502 and S. 978, simultaneously introduced in both houses, child molesters; and
S. 993, draft evaders amnestied by President Carter.

Joel wondered how many veterans of the Spanish Civil War were still doddering around. The Abraham Lincoln Brigade, if any were left, had better start hunting for health insurance.

Reading the *Record* these days was like reading about a snuff movie. Not seeing one, no one had ever attested to having seen a real snuff movie. There was just a flurry of articles about them some years ago, rumors that connoisseurs could buy videos in which women were killed right in front of the camera. Even if such a movie existed, the most attentive viewer would be unable to say if he had witnessed an actual murder or just special effects, ketchup and maybe, if the budget allowed, some chitterlings. The whole thrill was simply in what was alleged about the movie, and you already had this thrill just reading the articles that purported to condemn it. The frisson was in the concept, there was no need to execute it: just to say the words "snuff movie" made a world in which every woman was a little more at risk of starring in one.

So with all of these bills. Even if any of them passed, the President might veto them, depending on what his pollsters told him that day. And they were probably unconstitutional, *ex post facto* laws. None of these proposals would ever take effect, but they had already done their work. Simply by introducing them, their authors had conjured up a parallel nation in which old people were left to die in the streets in retribution for ancient transgressions. A nation in which everyone, really, was an alien, to whom benefits might be given or taken away by a bunch of white guys with bad comb-overs, voting silently in the middle of the night while C-SPAN played Vivaldi.

By the time Joel had worked through the pile of *Record*s, it was almost six, quitting time.

At the Hill Club a few of his friends were huddled in the queer corner of the bar, that shrinking space they clung to like penguins on an ice floe. Charles, who curated colonial furniture for the Smithsonian and whose raincoat was draped over his nondrinking arm, lining out, so everyone would see it was a Burberry. Albert, who had been chief of staff for a Senate committee until the Republicans lost the Senate in '86.

When they took it again in '94, he had just assumed he could go back to his old job. Not understanding that he should have filled the eight-year hole in his résumé with something other than: at Hill Club. Francis, who had been booted out of the seminary and had *then* become celibate—maybe from sheer exhaustion. Joel supposed you had to be pretty frisky if even a seminary couldn't overlook it. Buck, a paperhanger whose real name was Edward but who was called Buck because sometimes he worked in the nude. Tucked into the farthest stool, old Walter, who had possibly not moved since last week.

His friends. They were chattering away, only Charles pausing to say, "Hey, Joel, what's new?" Expecting Joel to answer, "Not much." Nothing had been new in years: same job, same lover. Joel was a consumer of news, not a producer. Until now. As the ads in the back pages of comic books used to say: "Amaze your friends!" He could already see the looks on their faces as he told them . . .

Until that instant, he truly had not comprehended that his predicament was a shameful one. Why? No one ever called a gay man a cuckold: infidelity was the norm, it was no reflection on you if your lover occasionally partook of strange meat. Here at the Hill Club, his friends, those who were coupled at all, routinely and unabashedly related their partners' latest escapades. They would cluck affectionately, like a doting mother reciting the hijinks of an errant son. Why couldn't Joel do that? Just make light of it? Wait till you hear what Sam has gone and done, the rascal!

Because they had been not a couple, but a sermon. Their loyalty a standing reproach to all the doubters who insisted it was impossible, no faggots could live like Joel and Sam forever. He had never, he thought, rubbed it in. On the contrary, he had always been half-apologetic about their deviant behavior. As if fidelity were a little idiosyncrasy of theirs. As if it hadn't cost them anything.

He could already see the faces. After the moment of astonishment, how Charles and Francis and Buck would marshal their faces, each of them striving to craft the appropriate mask of consternation and empathy. He had done it so often himself. He knew just how the muscles in your face tensed as you concealed your simple delight in unearthing a large uncut gem of misery. He knew how it felt to look straight in someone's eyes when you wanted to turn away with disdain for his fatuity and richly deserved ill-fortune.

All of these ordinary human sensations would be sweetened in this instance by a special triumph: they had been right all along, it was never possible to be Joel and Sam. If Icarus had pals like Joel's, they must have had to struggle just so, holding their frowns in place to hide their natural jubilation as he fell to earth.

Oh, and how would they ever keep a straight face when Joel said the most hilarious thing of all? We're still going to be friends.

"Nothing much," Joel said. "Um . . . listen, I just stopped in to say hi. I've got to get going."

"You're not even going to have one drink?" Charles asked. With honest amazement, as if Joel had announced he was giving up oxygen.

"No, I'm late for something."

Twelve years late, he thought, as he got into the cab and said, "P and Nineteenth." Twelve years since he'd been with anybody but Sam. Maybe that guy from last week would show up at Zippers again, or maybe . . . He found that he was—right there in a taxicab—getting aroused, just thinking of that guy, remembering their kiss. He could almost feel its traces on his lips. The thought of simply repeating that kiss made him short of breath, he didn't have to think beyond it to what would happen when they got to . . . the apartment. Not some hotel; they could go to the apartment. All the better if, improbably, Sam were there when they came in, picking up more stuff. You see, you're not the only one who . . .

Sam's catch, his Kevin, was twenty-three. And cared for Sam, didn't give up a kiss because he'd just been handed forty bucks. So what? It wasn't a contest. The issue was whether Joel was going to have a good time. But he couldn't help feeling Sam watching, judging. Even if he weren't literally present when Joel brought home his damaged goods, Sam would be there somehow. Like an angel: Joel had a sudden picture of him, his face floating near the ceiling in a corner of the bedroom. Just his face, like one of those grotesque putti who show up in Mannerist paintings, a head with wings sprouting from behind the ears.

Would he be there always, that accusatory angel? Maybe so, maybe this was what it meant to have an ex. A Sam in his head, murmuring: Joel, Joel, how could you do something so stupid and degrading?

Joel answered. Because it is my body now, and my money, and my dignity. All of these things were yours and you left them behind and I own them again. I can do anything I want.

Of course, the corollary to this triumphant riposte was that he would need to figure out what he wanted. No sweat. He wanted another kiss. Except that it was one thing to buy a secret kiss while your lover was working late, and another thing to have no lover and buy a kiss.

As it was one thing to sneak into Zippers while your lover was working late, just to see if anybody might look at you, and another thing to sit in Zippers having one drink after another while you waited to see if anybody might look at you. Past eight on a weeknight, lots to do tomorrow, he should just amble out, pick up a little food, go on home and . . .

Zippers had been almost empty when Joel came in, but it was starting to fill up now. Guys who had finished their errands or their naps, one or two of whom Joel wouldn't have thrown out of bed in a blizzard. He sat up, sucked in his stomach, wondered if he was holding his cigarette like the Marlboro man or if, come to think of it, maybe his cigarette was a turn-off now as it hadn't been fifteen years ago.

He knew it was crazy. Sitting here and feeling that he absolutely had to meet somebody; it was practically a guarantee that he would go home alone. But if he left now, he would go home alone anyway. So he might as well have just one more drink. He wasn't hunting, he was merely . . . available. That was how he should feel. No special urgency. He had simply been unavailable for many years, and now he was available, like an out-of-print book that has been reissued.

As the bartender, a kid with a shaved head and a black goatee, refilled Joel's glass he said, "You just visiting DC?"

"Me?" Joel said. "No, I'm from here. I just don't go out much."

"I didn't think I'd seen you."

"No." The bartender must have been about the age of Sam's Kevin; Joel found himself momentarily entranced by the kid's Adam's apple.

"Well, it's nice to see you now. What's your name?"

"Joel."

"I'm Scott. It's nice to meet you, Joel." He gave Joel a genuine and quite charming smile. "Excuse me, I'll be back in a second."

Joel waited many seconds for Scott to come back before he recalled that a smile from a cute bartender was not a token of incipient devotion. Cute bartenders smiled at older guys because older guys tipped. Joel was an older guy. Of course he knew that, he received a telegram on the subject every time he bent over to pick something up. But he had not been an older guy hanging out in a gay bar. One of those gray objects his eyes used to just automatically pass over, fifteen years ago, when he scanned the bar. Missing from the picture, like a disgraced commissar airbrushed out of a photo of the Supreme Soviet.

He made himself smile. Years ago someone had told him he frowned too much, he needed to smile more. He sat up and sucked in his belly and smiled. He could do it for only a few seconds before he felt like an idiot. Sitting there at the bar grinning at nothing.

He had meant to leave himself casually open to chance, a calm harbor if the wind should happen to blow a vessel his way. But already he was cruising again, he had fallen back into it as quickly as that. Alive again, as he had wanted, every nerve awake, his peripheral vision lit up by every shift in the crowd around him, every momentary turn of a face. His back feeling each tiny draft that meant someone had just come in, and should he turn now to look?

As if he had never been away at all. If he had not met Sam or any Sam, he might have kept coming here, 33, 34, 35 . . .

The life here had gone on all these years waiting for him to resume it. And it wasn't as though he and Sam had been in a foreign country and he was now returning to find his native land surprisingly unchanged. It was as though a parallel Joel had persisted in this world from which he had absented himself, and now the two had converged, they were in the same place now, $Joel_1$ and $Joel_2$.

He had arrived exactly where he would have been if there had been no Sam: just Joel coming into the bar. Still coming into the bar.

As was, uh-oh, Ron. Joel suddenly spotted him, leaning against the wall next to the exit. Part of the Hill Club gang, who hadn't been there this evening because, undoubtedly, he had taken a nap before changing into his cruising ensemble and coming here. He might as well have come straight from work in his K-Street-lawyer ensemble instead of putting on jeans that were a tad too small, so that his polo-shirted gut stuck out as if it were cantilevered.

Ron was panning the room, his head slowly turning like the security camera in a bank. When he saw Joel, he did a little double take, the head continuing its rotation and snapping back. He did it again, to make Joel smile, and Joel did.

But he was staring at Joel rather sternly, as if he had caught Joel somewhere he wasn't supposed to be.

Joel should have figured Ron would show up. The only guy in their circle who still had the energy, or the doggedness, to go out cruising four or five nights a week. Even though he was—what?—pushing sixty, anyway. Still casting his net out, night after night. As he had been doing since, Joel guessed, late in the Eisenhower administration. He had already been a fixture at Zippers, as much a part of the décor as the jukebox or the smoke-stained ceiling, when Joel started showing up. Late in the Ford administration.

Ron used to be good. He used to scan the room, register whatever new face had innocently manifested itself in Zippers—not uncommonly someone Joel had already fixed on—then just lean back against the wall, expressionless, and suck on his beer. A minute or two later he would be standing next to the guy, already in earnest conversation. Joel never actually saw him cross the room, it was as if he beamed himself over. Sometimes, just before he steered the fresh meat out the front door, he would catch Joel's eye and shrug. As if to say: it's tiresome, but somebody had to rope in the little maverick.

Joel wasn't even jealous, more nearly awestruck. What did Ron say to them? What had he said to Joel, Joel's first or second time there, when he swooped down and led Joel off for an encounter of which Joel could recall not the slightest detail? Joel could remember all of his good tricks and most of his truly horrible ones, so Ron must have been in that instantly forgettable midrange: both finished somehow, shooting stars were not witnessed, the one who wasn't home went home at three in the morning.

When they had started running into each other at the Hill Club a year or two later, they had, of course, not alluded to their prior encounter. Two men who had been naked together and had done . . . whatever they had done, and in all this time neither had ever mentioned it. Because it wasn't a big thing, not back in those years; whatever they had done had been about as weighty as shaking hands.

Joel was glad he couldn't remember what they'd done, but he did wish he could remember what Ron had said, what incantation he had uttered that let him carry Joel off, carry off all the boys so effortlessly it was if he were just entitled, exercised a sort of *droit de seigneur* with every newcomer.

Probably it didn't work any more. Twenty years ago he was nondescript but in possession of some magic words. Now he was a ruin, no longer a troller but a simple troll. He still talked about going out, but Joel couldn't remember the last time he had bragged about scoring.

Oh, Joel was jealous, after all. The ugliest part of him thought: Ron shouldn't still be here, not after a million tricks. He should have paid a price for having been endowed with those magic words.

Ron materialized next to Joel; once again Joel hadn't seen him cross the room. "Why, look what blew in!" Ron said. "You cruising or just drinking?"

"I don't know. How about you?"

"You don't know? You ought to at least know which it is you're doing." He thought about that a second. "Yes, I think you ought to at least know if you're cruising or drinking." Ron chuckled. "Not to say that you can't start out doing one and wind up doing the other."

"Yeah, I think I'm just at that segue," Joel said.

"So you *were* cruising. I thought you and the hubby didn't . . ."

"Um . . ." Joel was distracted by the annoying "hubby"; for a moment he couldn't think what to say. But there was nothing to say. Here he was, Sam was his ex, everyone was going to know sooner or later. "We kind of changed the rules."

"I wish I'd been a fly on the wall at that discussion."

"We didn't, uh, have a discussion. It was more a fait accompli."

"Ah. And which of you accomplied the fait?"

"Which do you think?"

Ron closed his eyes, just for an instant, before pronouncing: "Sam."

"How did you know?"

"Because, if it was you, you would have said so."

"I guess."

"And because I've seen him around."

"You have? Jesus. You never said anything."

Ron shrugged. Of course he hadn't. What was he supposed to say? Hey, Joel, guess where I saw your hubby?

"So how's the new arrangement working?"

"It's—" Joel swallowed. "It's not a new arrangement. He's gone."

"He's . . . Sam left you?"

"For some kid."

"Uh-huh." Ron looked away. "Name of Kevin?"

Joel felt himself blushing. Sam hadn't even been hiding it, probably the whole city had been laughing at Joel for months.

Ron must have understood; he shook his head. "I just bumped into them this one time, over at Gentry. Sam said it was a kid from his office, someone he was training, and they were going to have dinner. I didn't think anything about it."

"Oh."

"I didn't tell anybody."

"Might as well now," Joel said. "What's he like?"

"Kevin? I don't know. Young."

"Cute?"

"Oh, sort of." From which Joel understood that Kevin was a knock-out. He sighed. Ron said, "Nothing that special."

"Sam must think so."

"Maybe. Maybe he was just ready."

For the first thing that came along, Ron meant. Joel preferred to think that Kevin was a knock-out. That Sam couldn't have left him for anything less than a knock-out.

"Can I get you another drink?" Joel said.

"I better slow down. You better slow down."

"What for?"

"What for? My dear, you are back on the rack." No note of triumph, not even a suppressed one, nor of sympathy. Just matter of fact: Joel was back on the rack. People left the rack, people returned to the rack; it didn't matter if they were gone fifteen hours or fifteen years.

"I think I'll get back on the rack some other night."

"Why? Sam's getting his."

"I don't . . . I don't know if I even want mine."

"You don't?"

"I mean, it's not like I'm horny, especially. I'm just here because . . ."

"You're just here because Sam is getting his."

"I guess. Which is stupid. I should just toddle home."

"Hey, might as well find your own little belly-warmer."

What an ugly phrase. But what else was Joel looking for? Surely he wasn't here screening candidates for the next fifteen-year hitch. Just some trick, as in the old days, just take someone home and— What was the despair that gripped Joel as he conjured this . . . warming scene? That it probably wasn't going to happen, not tonight? Or that, if it did, he would be back here tomorrow night, smiling and sucking in his gut?

Joel called out to the bartender: "Scott!"

"Oh, you've met Scott. He's pretty cute."

"No kidding."

"There you go. Take Scott home."

"Right."

Scott refilled Joel's glass, took his money from the little stack of bills that Joel had meant for a tip. Maybe Joel would replenish it, even though Scott had forgotten to smile this time.

"Scott's a little out of my league."

"You don't know your league till you try out."

"I'm not sure I remember how," Joel said. "You know, I was never very good at this."

"No, you weren't."

Joel was stung, the way you are stung when you feign humility and are told that your estimate of yourself is right on the number.

Ron went on: "I used to watch you sometimes. You'd stare at the same guy for about five hours, you'd work up some line to say to him. Do you know, your lips would move while you rehearsed?"

It was all true, he had been such a jerk in those days. How awful that anyone remembered. It was like running into someone from high school who remembers you only as the guy with pimples. Ron must have recalled it every time they met at the Hill Club. Here comes Joel the jerk.

"It was kind of funny," Ron said. "Especially when you were so hot. Do you know that?"

"Was I? I never thought so."

"I know you didn't."

"If only I'd known." If only he had. Then maybe he would have had a thousand tricks, instead of a couple of hundred. In which case he'd probably be dead. Or alive and with a thousand tricks behind him.

Ron said, "The guys who are really hot are the ones who don't know they are." He looked around the room, possibly trying to spot one who didn't know. He spotted something, at any rate. He was gone, as abruptly as he'd arrived at Joel's side. This wasn't rude: if two hawks are flying side by side and one sees a rabbit far below, he doesn't pause to bid the other adieu. He swoops.

Joel craned his neck to see if he could spot Ron's prey. But Ron was already deep in the crowd somewhere, Joel couldn't find him.

Sunday night—his fifth straight night of striking out at Zippers—Joel stopped on the way home for carryout. A super combo platter from El Toro, with (1 ea.) burrito, enchilada, taco. Also rice, refried beans, chips, salsa (add guacamole and sour cream 50¢ ea.). As he walked home he held the foam carton straight out before him, keeping it level so everything wouldn't smoosh together. He felt silly and conspicuous. Passersby must have been thinking: look how that funny old guy holds his carryout, like Jeeves bringing in high tea. Look at that tacky old jacket he's wearing. And where did he get those shoes, Thom McAn?

Dupont Circle wasn't a true ghetto—it wasn't the Castro, or West Hollywood. For every guy carrying a gym bag or walking a small, skittish dog, there was a guy pushing a stroller. Or a young woman like Melanie, going home with her carryout on yet another dateless night and mourning that there seemed to be only two kinds of guys in Washington, the ones with gym bags and the ones pushing strollers.

Still, Joel did, on his little journey with the combo platter, pass many many many gay men. Of course, this had always been so; it was what made Dupont feel like home, a little village whose townspeople happened to have shaved heads and tattoos. But he had never really felt that he was one of them. He had been the star of his own life, and all the other gay men he passed on the street had been mere supernumeraries, faceless choristers in the opera of Joel and Sam.

Now they were fiercely particular. Men just heading out to the bars, others hurrying home to their lovers. Others shuffling along, having just struck out at one bar and debating whether they should try someplace else or just . . . Now that Joel had been demoted to the chorus, he could see that every one of them had a face. He looked at them, they looked back.

They looked away.

"Georgetown Sports Medicine," the receptionist said.

"This is Joel, is Sam around?" He had said those very words a million times. At first stammering, feeling that he was saying, "This is Sam's homosexual lover." After a while realizing that she had no opinion, that he was just a call to be put through. Or, even if she had an opinion, she still had to put the call through. This small epiphany had been something of a milestone on Joel's long reluctant crawl out of the closet.

Today she had an opinion: she drew in her breath sharply before saying, "Uh, I—let me see."

If even she thought it was a bad idea for Joel to call, maybe it was a bad idea. It hadn't occurred to Joel that Sam would have told everybody in his office what had happened. Of course, he had to: his home number had changed, they had to know where to reach him. Still, he could have just said, "Here's my new home number," he didn't have to explain. But he must have: one by one or collectively they must all have heard, in the couple of weeks since the break-up, that Sam had left Joel and embarked on a new life. How had he put it, Joel wondered. Had he been mournful or jubilant, had he catalogued Joel's deficiencies or just said softly that things weren't working out? It was eerie, knowing that you were a character in a story being told to strangers.

All strangers. Joel had never once been to Sam's office, or met any of the people Sam worked with. His only experience of Georgetown Sports Medicine was the practiced greeting of the receptionist. Sam had told stories, about some doctor's divorce or the funny thing that had happened to the nurse's son-in-law. But Joel couldn't really picture any of these people. He couldn't even keep their names straight, any more than Sam could follow Joel's stories from work. Though Joel's stories were studded with bigger names, they were still just work gossip. A lover was obliged to listen politely, but couldn't be expected to recall, from one time to the next, the difference between Congressman Miller and Senator Muller.

Georgetown Sports Medicine: Joel couldn't help conjuring a white-tiled locker room, radiant young athletes frowning stoically as the healers kneaded their wracked bodies. And perhaps Sam's daily schedule of middle-aged lawyers with tennis elbows and jogger's knees was indeed punctuated by the occasional golden youth. The lacrosse player would strip down to his briefs, Sam would give him his physical therapy—whatever the hell that consisted of; in fifteen years Joel had never quite pictured what exactly Sam did. Then Sam would come home and find . . . Joel. Maybe it was a wonder he hadn't drifted off years before.

"Joel," Sam said flatly when he came on the line.

"Hi. How are you doing?"

"Okay." There was a pause, during which Sam did not say, "And you?" He was just waiting for Joel to state his business. All right, maybe he was with a patient. But it wasn't as if he'd been in the middle of brain surgery.

Joel said, "You know, it's the third of the month."

"So?"

"The rent is due."

"The—? Oh." There was a pause, during which Joel actually imagined that Sam was debating whether to mail his half or bring it by in person. "Joel, I can't keep paying for half of an apartment I don't even live in. I mean—you know, I can't keep staying with Kevin, so I'm going to have to get a place of my own, and . . ."

Curiosity momentarily outweighed indignation: "Why can't you stay with Kevin?"

"Are you kidding? He has one little room in a slum off Logan Circle with about thirty-seven roommates."

Well, of course he did: if you chose to start over with a twenty-three-year-old, that's what you got. "How is that my problem?"

"How is your rent my problem?"

"You're on the lease. A lot of your stuff is still there."

"I'll be getting it out. Look, you know you can afford that apartment."

"That's not the point." Even as he said this, Joel wondered what the point was. He could afford the apartment; with twelve years' tenure under rent control, they were getting two bedrooms at the going rate for a walk-in closet. So it wasn't the money Joel wanted. He wanted the check, the physical object, like a little affidavit declaring that some connection was still there. A postcard from Sam's new world: Having wonderful time. Coming home soon.

Sam said, helpfully, "Maybe you need to get a roommate."

A roommate! The only worse thing Joel could imagine would be having to go through eighth grade again. A perfect stranger, haunting the living room, using the shower. Cooking in Joel's kitchen.

"I guess you're mad," Sam said.

Joel considered this. Of course he was furious. But he had somehow lost the right to be furious. It used to be, if one or the other of them got mad, then it had to be dealt with: nobody was going anywhere, it had to be worked out. Now, if Joel was mad, it wasn't Sam's problem, any more than if Joel had a rash. There it was: anger now would just be a condition Joel had, an itch Sam had no obligation to scratch. So he said, "No. No, I'm not mad."

"That's good."

"I'm not, you know, mad about any of it. I want you to know that. I mean, if this thing doesn't work out for you, I . . ." Joel stopped; he despised himself for having said so much. He had meant it, the door was always open, it had seemed important that Sam know. But just saying it, feeling so pathetic, like a dog that has been kicked by its master and raises a forepaw in submission—something in Joel rebelled. He had thought he would do anything to go back to the life that had been ruptured two weeks ago, yet some mutinous voice inside was protesting. He suppressed the voice, resumed: "If it doesn't work out, you know—"

Sam cut him off. "Joel, I didn't leave you for this kid."

"Huh?"

"I left you. And there was this kid. I was going to leave you if there wasn't this kid."

"You keep calling him a kid." Joel wasn't changing the subject, or failing to get what Sam had said. Joel got it fine: it seemed as though he could feel the blood jetting through every inch of his skin, as if he were blushing with his whole body.

"He is a kid. I'm . . . we have a good time, but I'm not fooling myself. I know I'll never have what I had with you."

"You still have it. Any time." Mouthing those words, but already scarcely able to conceive of what *it* could possibly consist of.

Sam said, "I can't pay the price any more."

Joel had to keep from laughing. Not just because Sam had thrown at him, with perfect gravity, a line that might have come from some fifties teleplay, but because he was actually living, here and now, in the scene from which that line had been stolen. He felt the strangest elation: drama, however hackneyed, had reentered his life, after so many years of contented oblivion. *Playhouse 90*. He said his line with a gravity to match Sam's. "What price?"

"I can't explain it. I can, I don't want to. You'll have to figure it out." Then, on cue, Sam hung up. Without his customary valediction: "Talk to you."

"Can you believe it?" Joel said. "The price!"

Francis, the ex-seminarian, intoned, "The price," in his deepest basso, and chortled.

It was funny: two weeks earlier Joel had dreaded telling the gang at the Hill Club what had happened. Of course, Ron had saved him the trouble; by the next time he came in everybody knew. And, so quickly, it had just become a fact about him. Joel works at OLA, he lives up near Dupont, he used to have a lover but now he doesn't. Already Joel was casually retailing stories about his ex, and enjoying it when Francis chortled with him.

"So I asked him, and he said, 'You'll have to figure it out.' Like I'm supposed to embark on a course of healthy self-criticism."

Francis opened his mouth, as if getting ready to recite a few of Joel's deficiencies, just to give Joel a little head start. Then he frowned, as if the project of enumerating Joel's faults were too daunting, and muttered, "Well, who knows what he meant."

Well, who did know? What was Joel supposed to do now, stew about it until he could assess the awful price Sam had somehow been paying? As if only Sam had paid anything.

Sam had never heard himself sigh, one of those long sighs that could fill the whole living room on a Sunday morning, squeezing the sunlight out and forcing Joel to put down his bagel and contemplate the abyss. Sam had never, on more jovial Sundays, gone shopping with Sam, those interminable excursions that left Joel feeling he had committed some misdemeanor and been sentenced to thirty days in the mall. Sam had never waited for Sam to get dressed, or sat cringing while Sam sent food back in a diner, for Christ's sake, or watched as Sam swirled wine from an eight-dollar bottle around his mouth and spat it back into the glass.

Everything Joel had loathed and had overlooked, gritting his teeth, just to keep it going. Love had never blinded him, he had never come to regard Sam's flaws as endearing idiosyncrasies. On the contrary, the years had magnified them, until even Sam's most innocuous habits loomed as felonies; a day with him could seem like a crime wave. Joel would have to tell himself, over and over, this is trivial, you mustn't focus on this when we have it so good.

Until perhaps the main thing they had, that was so good, was their very persistence. Some nights, when they went to bed angry, Joel would lie awake next to Sam, seething, and then recollect that he was lying next to Sam. Next to someone, on this cold night, when at that very moment at Zippers guys were darting around frantically, looking for any kind of connection before last call. This thought had been almost enough, even if it occasionally occurred to Joel that there wasn't, from this perspective, a great deal of difference between Sam and an electric blanket. Except that an electric blanket didn't pay half the rent.

Sam must have thought the same thing. He even talked about it. He was the one who would sometimes, just out of the blue, remark wonderingly that they were still a couple. When Peter and Hugh had broken up, Glen and Phillip had lasted—what?—not six months, poor James had never found anybody at all. Joel didn't bring this up; it almost seemed like bad luck. Sam did, counting aloud their years together, as if the very number—thirteen, fourteen, at last fifteen—had some weight. But numbers didn't weigh anything.

"You know," Francis said.

"What?"

"You have kind of . . . let yourself go."

This from some eunuch who was so fat he couldn't even pull his stool up to the bar. But Joel had asked for it: no one had made him tell his story to the eunuch. Who was undoubtedly compiling a mental list of all those to whom he could repeat it.

"Married life," Joel said.

"Uh-huh."

"We both let ourselves go." Just saying it made Joel realize that it wasn't true. He and Sam might have grown matching paunches over the years, but Joel's was definitely bigger. And Sam was, perhaps, a little more assiduous about little details like getting his hair cut or making sure both his socks were the same color.

Was this obvious to everyone? If even Francis thought so, maybe everybody thought, had been thinking for God knows how long: why is Sam sticking with this frump?

"Do you think that was it?" Joel said. "He could at least have warned me."

"You mean like: 'Honey, gain five more pounds and I'm out of here'?"

"Yeah."

"Maybe he didn't know the magic number till you went over it."

"Maybe not."

Francis shrugged. "What do I know? The only long-term relationship I ever had was with a teddy bear."

"I wasn't going to say that." Or point out that Francis probably hadn't even been laid since . . .

"At least I still have the teddy bear."

Well, yes, you do, you asshole. And at least I *had*—

Charles ambled over. The curator: today he was wearing a linen suit—he was meticulous about not bringing out the linen suit until after Memorial Day—and a suspiciously perfect bow tie. "What are we talking about?"

"Stuffed animals," Francis chortled.

"We were talking about why Sam left," Joel said.

"Oh." Charles rolled his eyes. "I thought it was something interesting."

"Sorry. I sort of find it interesting."

"Why? What are you going to do about it now?" A sound question. "Anyway, I thought he left for this little cutie."

"But Sam said it wasn't the kid, he would have left anyway."

"Hmm."

"Francis says I . . . let myself go." Joel smiled, as if this theory were absurd, though he was afraid Charles would second it. Let himself go: an odd phrase, if you thought about it. As if you held your self a prisoner but could commute the sentence any time. Freeing your self to become a frump.

"Oh, I don't think so," Charles said. It wasn't clear if he meant that Joel hadn't let himself go or only that this wasn't Sam's reason. He scratched his head. "Maybe it was the drinking."

Charles was clutching what had to be his third cosmopolitan. They might as well have strapped a nipple on the vodka bottle and handed it to him. "Sam drinks," Joel said.

"Well, that's true." Charles was expressionless. "Beats me,

then. Excuse me." He went over to talk with Walter. If he was going to try to wake up old, pickled Walter, he must have found the topic of Joel-and-Sam immeasurably tedious.

It was, wasn't it? Who but Joel could possibly have wished to unravel the mystery of Sam's departure? Even Joel was, he found, suddenly tired of the subject. He didn't want to know, didn't ever.

He thought, just then, that maybe he didn't ever want to talk to Sam again. Not just because Sam had been such a prick on the phone; Sam had always been kind of a prick. But because, if they didn't talk again, he would never have to hear—he didn't know how he could possibly bear to hear—that Sam knew everything about him, everything he knew about himself.

A day or two later, Joel had a six o'clock meeting at Senator Harris's office. Rob the varsity receptionist ushered Joel into a conference room, explaining that Melanie would be a little late—as if six o'clock weren't late enough. The room was decorated in the usual way: on the shelves a never-consulted set of the United States Code, on the wall a map of Montana and a blown-up photograph of the senator, on two-thirds of the conference table stacks of newsletters headed *Capitol Update* and bearing the same photograph. At the cleared space at one end of the table sat a man about Joel's age or a little younger, his jacket off. Blue suspenders marked the boundaries between his powerful shoulders and arms and his perfectly proportioned chest. Above this intimidating vista floated a gentle, spectacled face; chestnut hair.

The hunk stood up and said, "Andrew Crawford, leg counsel's office." Leg—pronounced "ledge"—counsel were the people who drafted bills, translating members' ideas into language so majestic and impenetrable that only a few initiates could detect just how bad the ideas really were.

"Joel Lingeman, OLA." As they shook hands, Joel's radar

registered the tiniest blip. A man who called himself Andrew instead of Andy, the obvious hours at the gym. A definite maybe. They sat opposite each other, saving the head of the table for Melanie. "So we're here to draft something?"

Andrew gave Joel a one-sided smile and said, "Oh, we've already drafted something. We're here to perfect it."

The pages he slid across the table were a dummy bill; leg counsel could print bills out now so they looked just like the real thing.

104TH CONGRESS
1ST SESSION

S. _____

To amend the Social Security Act to provide incentives for
personal responsibility.

IN THE SENATE OF THE UNITED STATES
_____, 19__

Mr. HARRIS introduced the following bill; which was read twice and
referred to the Committee on Finance.

A BILL

To amend the Social Security Act to restrict Medicare
payments for certain services, and for other purposes.

1   *Be it enacted by the Senate and House of Representatives*
2   *of the United States of America in Congress assembled,*

3 **SECTION 1. SHORT TITLE**

4 This Act may be cited as the "Personal Responsibility

5 Act of 19__."

6

7 **SEC. 2. RESTRICTION OF MEDICARE**

8 **PAYMENT FOR SERVICES RELATED TO A**

9 **DIAGNOSIS OF INFECTION WITH THE**

10 **HUMAN IMMUNODEFICIENCY VIRUS**

11 **RESULTING FROM HIGH-RISK BEHAVIOR**

12 (a) IN GENERAL.—Section 1862(a) of the Social

13 Security Act (42 USC 1395y), relating to exclusions from

14 coverage, is amended—

15 (1) In subclause (15)(B), by striking the word "or",

16 (2) At the end of subsection (16) by striking the period

17 and inserting "; or", and

18 (3) By inserting after subsection (16) the following

19 new subsection:

20 "(17)(A) where such expenses are for the treatment of

21 illnesses or conditions related to a diagnosis of acquired

22 immunodeficiency syndrome (AIDS) or infection with the

23 human immunodeficiency virus (HIV), and

24 "(B) the individual is determined, on or after January

25 1, ____, to have engaged in one or more of the high-risk

26 behaviors described in section 1861(oo)."

27 (b) DEFINITION OF HIGH-RISK BEHAVIORS.—Section

28 1861 of the Social Security Act (42 USC 1395x) is amended

29 by inserting after subsection (nn) the following new sub-

30 section:

31 "High-Risk Behaviors

32 "(oo) The term "high-risk behaviors" means any act or

33 pattern of acts performed voluntarily by an individual and

34 determined by the Secretary to increase the likelihood that

35 such individual will become infected with the human immuno-

36 deficiency virus (HIV)."

37 (c) LIST OF HIGH-RISK BEHAVIORS.—No later than 90

38 days after the effective date of this Act, the Secretary

39 shall cause to be published in the Federal Register a list

40 of the behaviors determined by the Secretary to be high-

41 risk behaviors for the purposes of this Act.

42 **SEC. 3. EFFECTIVE DATE**

43 The amendments made by this Act shall be effective

44 for services furnished to an individual on or after

45 January 1, ____.

"Jeez," Joel said, when he'd finished scanning it. "They want to cut off Medicare to people who . . ." He almost used a graphic expression, but he wasn't sure enough about Andrew. "People who have unsafe sex."

"You got it. Or, you know, needles, whatever."

The gleaming viciousness of this idea didn't even surprise Joel, really. It was a wonder no one had thought of it before, Helms or Inhofe or Lott. But he had had the silly misapprehension that Harris was educable.

He hazarded: "I don't guess this will have much effect in Montana."

"Nope." Andrew grinned. "I don't think you can get AIDS from fucking sheep."

They laughed. Joel was pretty sure about him now, and he must have reached his conclusions about Joel as well. Joel laughed a little too long; Andrew was looking at him.

"Anyway," Joel said. "I think I see a couple little drafting questions right away."

Andrew got serious, took up a pen.

"First, in section seventeen B . . ."

"Uh-huh."

"You can't really tell if it's the determining that happens on or after January 1 or if it's the engaging in high-risk behaviors."

"Oh. Oh, I see."

"So if it's the determining you'd move 'on or after' to the start. Or else you'd put 'on or after' right after 'engaged.'"

"Right," Andrew said, a little shortly. It was, after all, his handicraft Joel was picking at. "Well, I don't know which it is. We'll have to ask Melanie."

"Okay. And then there's this bigger thing. You're making it apply to services furnished on or after the effective date, but the Secretary doesn't even come up with his list of behaviors until 90 days after that. So, you know, a doctor wouldn't know if he was going to get paid until after he furnished the service."

This was an obvious blunder on Andrew's part, so he got even more defensive. "I think a doctor could pretty well guess what's going to be on the list."

"Sure. But you probably shouldn't make it effective until the list comes out."

He shrugged. "That's Melanie's call. Anything else?"

"Not that I see right away, no." To appease him Joel said, "Other than those couple of things, it's done just right."

Just right. Once he and Andrew had fixed those little things, the incendiary being hurled straight at them would be perfectly crafted. Here: let us help you with that fuse. Except the bomb wasn't really being thrown at Joel. After all, it didn't seem likely that he would engage in high-risk behaviors on or after any date they filled into the blank in the bill. Any solidarity he might have felt with the targets was abstract, a dull sense of insult rather than threat.

Joel said, "You're new at leg counsel?"

"Uh-huh."

Leg counsel on the Senate side were usually fresh out of school; it was just a line in their résumés before they went off to the big law firm. So Joel wondered why a guy—well, almost Joel's age—would take the job.

He supplied the answer without Joel's asking. "I was with McCutcheon and Halsey." One of the biggest firms, named for a couple of New Deal brains trusters who had gone on pulling strings straight into the nineties—theirs and the century's. "But I never made partner because . . . you can guess why."

"Oh."

"And I— I don't know, my . . . uh . . . friend died a couple years ago." Joel wondered if he should say he was sorry, but Andrew went right on. "And I just, I don't know, I just got tired. I don't want to work so hard."

"You came to the right place, I guess. You'll pull a few all-nighters in the fall, when they're scrambling to get stuff passed."

101

"Right."

"But, you know, the House guys draft most of the stuff. You can just copy their work."

That was a joke, but Andrew bristled. "I'm sure I can do my own, once I get the hang of it."

"Oh, sure, I was just kidding."

Joel thought about Andrew's being tired; did that mean he was sick? Like, presumably, his late . . . uh . . . friend. Making it, perhaps, a little more remarkable that he could, like Joel, just do his job on a bill like the one that lay festering on the table between them.

"Anyway," Joel said. "Except for the fall, all you mostly do is wait around for meetings that never get started."

"Like this one. I guess it makes her feel important."

"Oh, staffers have lots of ways of feeling important."

Of course Melanie arrived at that moment. If she had heard Joel, she didn't show it. Nor did she apologize for being late. She was like some of the guys Joel dated in his pre-Sam years, twinks whose paper-thin gold watches were just jewelry, never consulted. Waltzing into a bar an hour after they were supposed to meet him and never explaining.

"Joel, you've seen this?" Melanie said.

"Uh-huh."

She looked at him blandly. Probably she knew he was gay. He didn't wear a pink triangle, or even an ear-stud, but she must have known. She was waiting for him to denounce her.

"Yeah," Joel said. "I had a couple little technical things."

They went over them; Melanie handled them. She didn't need to talk to her boss; minutiae like the effective date of a law were beneath him.

"Anything else?" she said.

It was almost seven: any other time Joel would have been itching to get his liver out of there and down to the Hill Club. But he had just realized why her nasty little bill wouldn't work. Sometimes he kept quiet about those things, happy to let the staffer and her boss look like morons. This time, maybe, he wanted to impress Andrew with his bravery and acumen.

"How's anybody supposed to know who's done something unsafe and who hasn't?" Melanie's eyes narrowed, but Joel went on. "When somebody shows up for a service, how's the doctor or whoever supposed to find out if they did something unsafe months, years before that?"

Joel thought he was doing her a favor, actually imagined she would be grateful that he had pointed out this problem before somebody else did. Melanie was not grateful. Maybe because she worked for a senator who threw phones. If she told him he had a bad idea, who knew what he might throw at her?

Melanie said, coolly, "That's interesting. I might have to think some more about that." Meaning that the meeting was now adjourned.

Andrew didn't get it. "He's right," he said. "You'd have to, I don't know, you'd have to have some process for determining that . . ." He trailed off. "I just don't see how it would work."

Melanie gazed for a while, as if for inspiration, at the portrait of Harris. "Well, you know, if you have AIDS, you must have done something."

Joel began, "Unless you had a transfusion or you're a little baby or—"

"Do babies get Medicare?"

"No."

"And transfusions, people aren't still getting it from transfusions. If you didn't do anything wrong, you can get a letter or something. Otherwise I think you can kind of assume . . ." She turned away from Harris's picture and said to Andrew, "We'll figure it out. For now, let's just leave it the way it is." Forever, she meant. This proposal wasn't going anywhere, the bill was merely the physical embodiment of some random firing of neurons in her boss's perfectly coiffed skull. She didn't need to work one more minute of overtime perfecting it. "We want to introduce by Thursday." She stood up. "Joel,

I'm going to need some help with the floor statement."

"Okay."

"We want to emphasize, you know, this isn't about punishing anybody. It's, like we say, it's about rewarding personal responsibility."

"Right."

"So you'll have something tomorrow morning?"

"Um . . . sure. *Late* morning."

"With numbers. Some kind of numbers." She meant that literally, just any numbers at all. Harris was one of those members who liked to have an easel on the Senate floor and point to numbers on a big chart. Maybe in the hope that channel surfers would pause a moment at C-SPAN if they saw a chart and not just some guy in a thousand-dollar suit. It didn't matter much what the numbers showed.

"Numbers," Joel promised.

In the hall, he said to Andrew, just to say something: "You got all those changes?"

Andrew nodded, and Joel tried to think of something else, to hold him there a minute. Maybe some pretext for meeting with him. Just to sit across a table from him again. Joel couldn't think of anything—didn't try, really. Instead he was already rebuking himself for imagining it when he heard Andrew say, "You got time for a drink?"

Joel couldn't believe his ears. Not just because, for a few more minutes with Andrew, he had time to walk across hot coals. But also because he couldn't remember anyone ever having said that at the end of a meeting. In movies, as meetings broke up, people said, "Got time for a drink?" In real life people had to go pick up their kids, or they had to get to the gym, or it was just the nineties and they didn't drink.

So it was with a sense of unreality that he strolled with Andrew the couple of blocks to Union Station, neither of them saying a word, and sat down with him at the semicircular bar in the Great Hall. Past seven: the commuters were mostly gone.

At the bar just a scattering of travelers, their garment bags leaning drunkenly on the floor beside them, and at one end a few regulars who were leaning a little themselves.

Andrew ordered a beer, so Joel did too, much as he hated beer. Andrew began, "Back there . . ."

"Yeah?"

"I guess I'm new to this. I mean, we told her the bill wasn't going to work, and she didn't care, she just wants to go ahead."

"That's right."

"But, you know . . . if it became a law, it would just be unenforceable."

"It's not going to become a law. They don't even want it to." Joel could never resist a chance to be wise and superior, even though he had learned in about first grade that it wasn't the best way of making new friends. "He's going to introduce it, and then maybe later on he'll move to attach it to some bill that's certain to go through. Just to get a vote on it, you know. It'll pass the Senate, and then when they go into conference with the House the thing will just be quietly dropped."

"So it's just some kind of gesture."

"It's a way to make everybody go on record as being for or against decency. They do this three or four times a year. The vote's always about 96 to 4."

"Four, that's all the friends we've got?" Andrew said. The "we," so quickly, was unusual on the Hill. You could work with somebody for years, with a tacit understanding that both of you were gay, without any direct reference to it. This hasty disclosure led Joel to suppose, only for a second, that they might not just be having a beer. He knew this was farfetched and tried to suppress it. This was never easy: once the hound inside believed it had caught the scent of possibility, he couldn't persuade it otherwise. It just went on sniffing until Joel made a fool of himself.

"Uh . . ." Joel said. What had Andrew asked? "Four is about the number of members whose seats are so safe they don't

105

have to worry about a thirty-second ad that says they support sodomy."

"Well, here's to them," Andrew said. They clicked their bottles, then Andrew looked around. "You know, the last time I was here I was with Kenyon."

"Kenyon. Your friend."

"Uh-huh."

"Kenyon, um . . . he had . . ."

"No," a little too emphatically. "I'm sorry. I mean, everybody just assumes that. He had a heart attack."

"Oh. I'm sorry."

"Just wham, at the office."

They were getting on—Andrew, Joel, everybody. Those who escaped the plague were starting to go wham at the office. Some of the guys who were cut down early would, if they had lived, be going wham at the office by now.

"What did he do?"

"Do? He just, I mean, fell over."

"No, for a living."

"Oh. He was at Labor." Andrew added, "A Deputy Assistant Secretary." Proudly, as if these were less common than pigeons.

"Public Affairs?"

"How did you know?"

"Just guessed." If a gay man reached that exalted height he was always the press officer. Since they didn't have deputy assistant secretaries for window treatments.

"Anyway, he just went. Nobody even called me. I mean, he wasn't out, you know, at the office, nobody knew to call me, nobody knew there *was* a me. I just got home and he wasn't there, and then for hours he wasn't there, and I started calling hospitals."

Joel remembered the night he was waiting for Sam—the last night he would ever wait for Sam—and thinking Sam might be dead. Would that have been worse? At least if Sam had been dead, it would have been no reflection on Joel.

106

"He was already talking retirement. I mean, we were both negative, we thought we had years."

It was a little gratuitous, wasn't it, this mention of his antibody status? As if he wanted Joel to have this information. The hound stirred.

Andrew sighed. "So anyway, I'm by myself."

"Me, too."

"Yeah?" This said with no apparent interest. The hound dozed. "Did you ever have a lover?"

"Until a few weeks ago."

"What?"

"He left me. I mean, he just up and left a few weeks ago."

"No kidding. How long were you two together?"

"Fifteen years." That weightless number.

"Had you been . . . what, you hadn't been getting along?"

"I thought we were. He was seeing somebody."

"Oh."

Joel realized, too late, that this made him sound like a loser. He shrugged. "So I guess we're in the same boat."

Andrew looked over but didn't answer. From which Joel deduced that, in his view, being widowed and being dumped were not at all the same boat. Maybe they weren't, though half the bed was empty either way.

Joel changed the subject. "Where do you live?"

"A little house we fixed up on H Street southeast. You know, down near the Marine barracks?"

"Uh-huh. Isn't it a little scary down there?"

"It's not too bad. We did have a drive-by shooting once."

"Really?"

"Yeah. But I mean, we're almost twenty years into the mortgage, my monthly payment wouldn't rent me a studio now. It's a nice place. Kind of damp."

"Built on a swamp."

"Isn't every place? Sometimes on real rainy days these slugs will come inside, they crawl right up the kitchen wall."

"Ugh."

"Yeah, Kenyon used to always run to the front of the house, like slugs could catch him. So I had to take care of them—you know, I'm the country boy. Kenyon would stay out in the living room and make jokes about whether we should bake them in puff pastry or just serve them naked with a dab of garlic butter."

Joel forced a little laugh. Andrew was opening up a little, Joel wanted him to keep talking. Even if his only subject was Kenyon. "So Kenyon was the cook?"

"Oh, God, yeah. I can barely make toast."

Joel could hardly breathe. This had to be the sexiest thing he had ever heard a man say. The soft voice, the broad shoulders under his pinstripe suit, the old-fashioned aw-shucks masculinity: Joel might have been sitting next to Gary Cooper. "So what do you eat?" Joel said.

"TV dinners."

Poor baby. Joel almost said, "I should cook for you some time." Which would have been only a little less brazen than suggesting that they head to the men's room for a quickie. But he could say: "I was going to maybe get a bite here before I head home."

"Oh," Andrew said. "I wish I could join you."

"Why don't you?"

"I've got to . . . I can have maybe one more and then I need to head home." Joel was afraid he'd go on to say "to feed the cats," replacing Gary Cooper with Franklin Pangborn. Instead he added: "Kenyon's parents are going to be calling."

"Oh, yeah? You're still in touch with them?"

"Uh-huh," Andrew said, tight-lipped; then he was lost in thought a second.

Joel had met Sam's parents just once, for dinner when they were passing through town. He wasn't sure they understood who he was. Sam had met Joel's mother a few times before she died. That was it, they never became part of each other's families. Joel wondered what that was like. Actually, the thought made him a little queasy, the way he got queasy when some queen brought his mother into a gay bar.

Andrew snapped out of whatever reverie he had been in, signaled the bartender for two more beers. "So where do you live?" he said.

"Up near Dupont. We have this two-bedroom. I have."

"Are you going to stay there?"

"I guess. But, you know, he's not going to be paying. He thinks I ought to get a roommate." Joel had a momentary flash of Andrew in the apartment.

"I've thought about that," Andrew said. "Just to have some-body around." Now Joel was on H Street. He would cook; Andrew would kill slugs. "But, I mean, when I think about it, I wouldn't want to keep running into some stranger. Someone just living there."

"Me either," Joel said. "You'll—I guess you'll meet some-body."

"I haven't even been looking."

"No? You never . . . you haven't . . ."

Andrew shrugged. "No, I just haven't felt like it. Not since Kenyon."

Two years seemed a little long to Joel. He had known guys who were, in their lover's last months, dating the successor. One even brought the heir apparent to the apartment, while his blind lover called out, "Who's that with you?" Even leaving these miscreants aside, he really couldn't think of anyone who had stayed in widow's weeds as long as two years.

Joel said, "He'd probably want you to . . ." Joel was too disgusted with himself to finish the sentence. Yes, indeed, your dead lover is looking down on us and wishing you'd take me right back to the bed you shared on H Street.

Andrew shook his head patiently. Not angry at the sugges-tion, almost apologetic, as if he knew he was being a little obstinate. "He probably would. I'm just not ready yet."

109

The "yet" was like a rain check. Sooner or later he'd be ready.

"Listen," Andrew said. "We better get the tab."

"Oh. Oh, I'll take care of these. You run along if you have to."

"No, I . . . well, thanks. I'm sorry I couldn't stay for dinner."

"Maybe some other time."

"Great." They shook hands; with his left hand Andrew grasped Joel's shoulder, and he smiled broadly for the first time all evening—a big, affectionate smile. "I'm glad we did this," Andrew said. "I mean, sometimes I get up from my desk at the end of the day and I don't know where to go."

Me too, Joel wanted to say. Except he had already been warned against comparing their predicaments.

As Andrew walked away, he turned and smiled once again.

When Andrew was out of sight, Joel traded in his untouched second beer for a scotch.

How many times, before Sam, he had felt this very glow, this sensation of being at the beginning of something. How many times he had been mistaken. The guys who smiled and kissed him goodbye in the morning, after scribbling what turned out to be the phone number of Kim's Korean Bar-B-Q or Murray's Car Wash. The guys who made dates and didn't show up or, worse, the ones who did show up. So many times: the hope should have been burned out of him. Maybe it was built in, maybe the brain released some enzyme, Possibilitase, that induced this state of fatuous optimism for the hours until it wore off. Maybe the scotch kind of helped it along.

A rain check, for God's sake. As if, whenever Andrew was ready, he would be ready for Joel. Probably Andrew was just this affable with everybody, probably he clutched everybody's shoulder when he shook hands. Falling for him was as silly as falling for a movie star or a picture in a magazine.

Eight o'clock now; the bar was empty, all the commuters were gone, the huge main concourse was traversed by a few serious-looking people waiting for trains that would get them home very late, a few tourists who wandered among the shops, having found nowhere better to go in Washington on a June evening. Senator Biden passed by at a half trot—he went home to Wilmington every night and was just about to miss the Metroliner—but only Joel recognized him. A forgotten nebbish who seriously thought for a little while he might be president. What was it like, to have had that dream obliterated, so long ago, and then go on living? Did he sometimes fall into it again, a little spurt of Possibilitase tricking him into imagining that maybe next year he would . . .

Joel hoped so.

four

Joel pressed Talk on the intercom, said "Hello," then pressed
Listen. He caught Sam in midsentence. ". . . kind of awkward,
but . . . Hello? Joel? It's Sam."

Sam had brought somebody. He was coming to pick up a
few things, he didn't say what. Joel was surprised, as he inven-
toried the apartment, just how many of Sam's things were still
around, things Joel looked at every day.

Sam had brought Kevin, surely. That was why he buzzed,
even though he still had a key. So Joel would have a minute
to get ready. Joel had no use for the minute. He'd already
straightened up, made fresh coffee. He had even run down the
street for bagels and Sam's favorite cream cheese (a particular
sacrifice, as it contained raisins). The bagels were set out
discreetly in the kitchen as if they just happened to be there
and Sam could pick one up if he liked. Which he would: Sam
picked up things. If he visited someone's house he wouldn't
just look at the photos on the piano or the Staffordshire dogs

on the mantel, he'd pick them up. So maybe Joel ought to have expected that he would eventually pick up one of the cuties to whom he was always drawing Joel's attention.

Now one was in the elevator. Joel couldn't decide if he should stand in the little foyer like Perle Mesta or be somewhere else in the apartment—make Sam use his own key and be somewhere else, busy. He wound up in the foyer, the door wide open. The elevator came, there was giggling, then a "Sshh" from Sam. Sam appeared, came in and stepped aside like a footman to reveal, framed in the doorway: a juvenile.

Joel had understood in the abstract that Sam had snared a genuine kid, but he somehow hadn't expected one in full regalia: the voluminous black T-shirt, the baggy pants with five hundred pockets, the baseball cap, the little ring through the eyebrow that made Joel itch just looking at it. Whatever else might be said about this get-up, whatever it was all supposed to signify, it was certainly uninformative. Joel was left to guess about the body, deduce what he could from the only exposed parts, neck and forearms, as our ancestors were once inflamed by the glimpse of a lady's ankle. The kid's neck and forearms were slender and graceful and so terribly young. He had a scab on one arm, probably from tumbling off a skateboard.

"This is Kevin," Sam said superfluously. The kid stepped forward. His hand was extended, but not in such a way that Joel could shake it; rather it was configured for some alternate greeting ritual Joel knew nothing about. Joel ignored it, put his hand on the boy's bony shoulder for a second, and looked beyond him to Sam.

Was Joel imagining that Sam was a little abashed? That he himself knew this kid wasn't exactly a trophy bride? No, he was the other kind of abashed: I'm too lucky, I'm afraid of showing off. And maybe he was lucky if he thought he was.

"Come on and get some coffee," Joel said.

"Um," Kevin said.

Sam translated as he led the way into the kitchen. "Kevin

only drinks tea. Oh, look, bagels. Do you want a bagel, honey?" Kevin shrugged, meaning apparently that he wouldn't object to a bagel. Luckily, Joel had three; he had been planning to have the spare with liverwurst later on.

Honey. Joel and Sam used to call each other that. So automatically that Sam would forget and say it in the wrong places. At the discount mall in deepest Virginia, he would say, "This sweater would look good on you, honey," and rednecks would gawk at them. Joel was stung that Sam had transferred the endearment to Kevin. Not that Sam spoke affectionately: Joel didn't mind so much sharing Sam's store of affection, meager as it was. But that Sam had said it automatically, as they used to do.

"Where do we keep the tea?" Sam said. "Is it still . . . ?" He went to the right cabinet, found the canister where they saved miscellaneous teabags for visitors eccentric enough to want tea. He rummaged through it. "We've got something called Orange Delight, and Peppermint, and a lot of Tetley. Jeez, how long have we had this?"

"Peppermint," Kevin said. Joel wondered if he had heard Sam saying "we." Busy in the kitchen of Joel-and-Sam, saying "we."

Sam was washing out the teapot, last used some time in the Reagan administration. "Do you want your bagel toasted?"

"Okay," Kevin said graciously. Having completed his order, he went out to the living room.

When the bagels were ready, Sam smeared his and Joel's with the raisin-infested cream cheese. Kevin's he laid out on a plate with a dollop of cream cheese alongside and a fresh knife. Joel wondered if he was going to add a bud vase with a single rose. Sam had never waited on Joel this way, not even in their first weeks. He wasn't just being nice to the kid, who repaid him with grunts and shrugs; it was some sort of expression of power.

Kevin was sitting in Joel's chair as they came out. Sam started for his old chair, then swerved to the couch, at least thoughtful enough not to subject Joel to a tableau of the new couple in what had been Joel's and Sam's matching chairs. Joel joined him on the couch, so they wound up facing Kevin like a panel of judges, or like doting godparents. Or like a couple themselves. Kevin was spreading cream cheese on his bagel with great care, trying not to get any over the hole, but he kept glancing up at Sam and Joel. He was trying to imagine them.

Sam had made a mistake, maybe, bringing him. Because what he must have seen, looking over at them, was two old men, more like each other than not.

Everyone ate in silence. Kevin rhythmically devoured his bagel: bite, sip of tea, bite. Joel got through his almost as fast, while Sam was taking little nibbles. He always ate as much as Joel did, but in microscopic nibbles. Sometimes in a restaurant Joel would sit for what seemed an hour while Sam consumed a salad, so slowly he might have been eroding it rather than eating it. Anyway, the kid and Joel were through with their bagels. Somebody would have to talk now.

Joel began. "So, Kevin, you're . . . in school?"

"Uh-huh. I'll be a sophomore." Joel must have signaled somehow that he thought Kevin was a little old to be a sophomore. Kevin explained without being asked: "I was in the army, so I just started last year."

"You were in the army?" Joel failed to keep the incredulity out of his voice.

"Yeah." Kevin grinned; he was accustomed to incredulity.

How different Kevin looked, transformed in Joel's eyes by this single disclosure. Joel was of the draft-dodging generation—scared not so much of dying in some rice paddy as of succumbing during basic training, which he imagined as a sort of infinitely protracted gym class, weeks of twenty-four-hour-a-day humiliation. That Kevin, this slight creature, had got through didn't suggest to Joel that he had exaggerated the rigors of military life; instead the news turned Kevin into a

115

little he-man, an abbreviated Schwarzenegger.

Kevin added, "I was in the Persian Gulf."

"No kidding."

"I didn't see any combat. Just a lot of sand."

"I bet." The casual, "I didn't see any combat," was unspeakably hot. Joel found himself trying to conjecture exactly what lay concealed in Kevin's voluminous trousers. Then he looked up, embarrassed. Kevin had caught him, wore a tiny and ambiguous smirk.

Sam was still intently pecking at his bagel, leaving Joel to keep the conversation going. Joel thought they'd better get off the subject of Kevin's war record before he bounded toward Kevin on all fours. "So what are you studying?" Joel said.

"Food service management."

Joel was relieved. He had expected something like astrophysics.

Kevin went on: "But Sam thinks I might be good at physical therapy."

Sam jumped up and went to the bookshelves, perhaps to deflect Joel from asking what particular aptitudes Kevin had displayed. He began scanning each shelf systematically, running a finger from left to right, even though all Sam's books were in the spare bedroom. It was, perhaps, snobbery that made Joel insist that Sam's sci-fi be segregated from his own shelves of unread landmarks of the Western canon. He was pretty sure Sam wasn't going to find *Legends of the Galactic Bandits* or whatever the hell he was looking for. This was a charade, to let Joel and Kevin keep talking. Maybe the whole visit had been conjured up for that purpose, so they could get to know each other. Did he suppose that they would all be buddies, start having brunch together and then going to sci-fi movies? Or was this some sort of therapy? Maybe Sam thought Joel's healing could be accelerated if he just understood that Kevin was actual.

Kevin obviously wasn't going to talk unless Joel asked him

a question. Joel didn't have any more; he didn't care if Kevin was from Oshkosh or if he had any siblings, or hobbies, or undisclosed tattoos. The only thing Joel wanted to know was: what has Sam said about me?

"Do you want some more tea?" Joel said.

Before Kevin could answer, or even shrug, Sam said, "No, we better be going pretty soon. Let me just get a couple things." He went back to the bedroom.

The minute he was out of sight, Kevin whispered, "I'm real sorry."

Joel shook his head, Kevin had nothing to be sorry about. He meant that; he realized that he had never blamed Kevin for an instant, not even before meeting him. What could Joel blame him for? Being twenty-three, being wherever he was the night Sam stumbled upon him?

"Sam really likes you," Kevin said. Innocently: he couldn't have thought how offended Joel would be, to hear from him what Sam liked. At least he hadn't used the past tense.

All Joel could answer was, "Sam likes you, too. I can tell." Kevin stared at him, properly thinking this was an idiotic thing to say.

Then Kevin managed, "I hope . . . you know, you guys ought to go on being friends." This, too, was well-intentioned, but outrageous in so many ways that Joel just nodded, got up, and went to see what Sam was up to.

Sam was making the bed. That is, he had pulled off the old sheets—which, admittedly, hadn't been changed since his elopement—and was contentedly making hospital corners with the new set. He glanced up as Joel came in and shook his head grimly.

"Maybe I ought to get you to come in once a week," Joel said.

"Or somebody. This is disgusting."

"It's not disgusting." The sheets had been there maybe six weeks; this wasn't unprecedented even when Mr. Clean was in residence. Not to mention that nothing of consequence had been spilled on them. "Did you find everything you were looking for?"

"Uh-huh." Sam gestured with his head toward the little pile on the dresser: one sweater Joel couldn't recall ever having seen him in; a fantasy novel Joel knew he'd finished; a pair of sunglasses. So the visit had been a contrivance after all.

Sam picked up one end of the comforter and looked to Joel to pick up the other. Joel did, they flung it over the bed, Sam smoothed it and tugged at it as always, to make sure it was even on both sides, no one got more than his share. Then he tossed Joel a pillow and a pillowcase. He was slipping a case on the other pillow, but Joel just let his own fall to the ground. Joel wasn't going to play anymore. He left the room before Sam could ask him what he thought about Kevin; he knew Sam was just about to ask that.

Kevin was looking at the pictures from the surprise party Sam had thrown Joel for his fortieth birthday. There was Joel, laughing a lot, all the friends Kevin didn't know. All the old men, and among them Sam and Joel laughing, hugging.

What could Kevin see in Sam? This might possibly have been the first, the primordial human question, voiced long before anyone thought to wonder why the sun came up or the rain came down. What does Mng see in Thrng? Joel didn't even know what he himself had seen in Sam, just that he had fallen somehow for the way Sam smiled peacefully when he made hospital corners with the sheets. Maybe Kevin had fallen for the very same reason, or maybe he had found out other things about Sam to love, things Joel had never been aware of. Either possibility was nearly unendurable, but especially the former, that this callow student of food service management had the very same aperture in his heart that Joel did, that Sam had walked in through the very same door.

Sam came out from the bedroom, Kevin turned and realized that Joel had been looking at him. He looked back, again a tiny smirk forming on his face. He thought Joel wanted him. He thought everything was that simple: Sam had got him and Joel wanted what Sam had got. Joel, for his part, wasn't sure which he wanted, Sam or Kevin.

The two of them were standing very close together: Joel could see that Sam had to keep himself from putting an arm around Kevin's hard little shoulders.

"We better get going," Sam said.

Kevin nodded. "It was nice meeting you, Joel. I hope we can get together again." Quite a protracted utterance; perhaps he had composed it while Joel and Sam were in the bedroom. He held out his hand; this time Joel grasped it and found that it was damp. Warm and sticky as a child's hand.

He went to the foyer, leaving Sam and Joel facing each other in the living room. Neither knew what to do. Shake hands? Hug? Sam must have been discovering the same thing Joel was. They were indissoluble, and at the same time there was nothing between them, nothing left at all.

Kevin was still in the foyer, stamping his foot a little, like a dog who needs to be let out. Sam went to him, they escaped together.

"A roommate!" Charles was incredulous. Of course, Charles had a whole townhouse to himself on the best street in Capitol Hill; he had one entire room that contained only a colonial highboy that was worth about as much as Joel's life savings. All this money came from a string of car dealerships in suburban Virginia. The handful of Hill Club regulars who had actually grown up around Washington had spent their childhoods watching Charles's father on TV, dressed as a clown and screaming about deals! deals! deals! That everyone knew where his money came from did nothing to diminish Charles's hauteur. "How could you *possibly* . . . ?"

"I was just thinking about it." Joel had been thinking about it since Sam and Kevin's visit. The first time in weeks there had been another soul in the apartment. He hadn't felt very lonesome until their visit; once they'd gone he'd felt the emptiness for the rest of the day.

He was poring through the Housing Wanted columns of the gay paper as Charles looked on. "You know, I've got this extra bedroom." What he and Sam had sometimes called the exercise room, because the two of them for a few months had religiously pretended to go cross-country skiing on a piece of equipment that had stood in the room as a quiet reproach ever since. "They all seem to be students."

"What did you think?" Charles said. "People our age aren't putting ads in the paper looking for a room."

"I guess not." Unless maybe they were refugees like Sam. "A student wouldn't be so bad."

"Are you kidding? Living in the next room, playing hippity-hop in the middle of the night?"

Even Joel knew it wasn't called hippity-hop. Past that, he really had no idea what kids were listening to; the first time he learned the names of current idols was when they killed themselves. Sam knew. Sam could distinguish hip-hop from gangstah from house. And he knew all about the Web and stuff, and what people watched on TV, and who those one-named celebs in the tabloids were—everything Joel didn't keep up with. He must have felt sometimes, coming home to Joel, as if he were entering one of those period rooms in a museum, with the rope across the doorway. Was that the price he couldn't pay any more, living a life that amounted to a perpetual reminder that they weren't twenty-three any more? Did he think he could become twenty-three again if he were only freed of the bourgeois accretions—the club chairs from Crate and Barrel, the Mission-like dining room set—that had pinned him to the earth?

Any of the kids in the Housing Wanted section would have been happy enough to come to earth in Joel's apartment, with one-and-a-half baths and a washer/dryer and a roof deck Joel never visited and only sporadic guest appearances of vermin. He could probably pick any one of them, call, and have a roommate tomorrow. A live-in Kevin, but wearing a Don't Touch sign.

"It might not be so bad," Joel said.

"As if any of these children could afford half your rent."

"Well, maybe they wouldn't have to pay half."

"Ah." Charles snorted. "Don't worry about the rent this month, dearie. Just step on back into Uncle Joel's bedroom."

Pointless to explain that he was thinking about something entirely different, a chaste, almost paternal relationship with some kid. Some youth he could gently guide and who would in turn make him young again. Make him young the first time.

Through some impecunious guy with an entry-level job he would live that first youth he had squandered in those years when he was afraid of himself. The roommate wouldn't be afraid of himself: he would be okay about everything, the way kids were now. Okay with being gay, hopeful about his place in the burgeoning global economy, going to the gym uncomplainingly, thinking of a latte as a stimulating beverage, now and then spiriting some mate into the second bedroom. And in the morning seeking Joel's counsel: about where to put his 401(k), about which health plan he should choose, about whether it was a good idea to keep seeing somebody who wanted to be tied up.

"If I had your house, I'd fill it with a whole fraternity," Joel said. "Lambda Lambda Lambda."

"Can you imagine! Flinging beer cans at the highboy. Throwing up on the Kirman." Charles snatched the paper away. "Let's give up on the Lingeman Memorial Shelter for Wayward Youth and find you some true love." He turned to the Men4Men section. "We've got, let's see, Glimpses, Relationships, Dates, Friends, Situations, Masseurs, and Escorts."

Joel knew what they had. Glimpses, of course, were those

optimistic, almost delusional misreadings of some momentary flicker of interest from a stranger: *Foggy Bottom Metro, 6/14. You: baseball cap. Me: black T-shirt. You looked my way. Java?* Relationships were people who wanted a long-term deal and didn't say what they did in bed, except sometimes that they liked to cuddle. Dates were people who didn't want an LTR and said exactly what they did in bed. Friends were people who voiced no romantic or sexual inclinations but merely wanted someone to join them in a healthful activity, like bicycling; oddly, they tended to specify what this companion should look like. Situations were extremely successful and youthful-looking professional people who could offer an appropriate young person opportunities for foreign travel and other broadening experiences. Masseurs, of course, used their hands, while Escorts used other parts.

All of this used to be a joke. Something Joel might page through as he sat in the living room waiting for Sam to pick what sweater to wear. Discovering in the packed columns a whole metropolis of yearning of which he was luckily not a citizen. No, never entirely a joke. Even in the days when he was certain that he and Sam would be parted by death, not some accursed Kevin, he couldn't help imagining how he might fare if he were hurled back into that world.

He would fold up the paper so Sam wouldn't know what section he'd been reading—as if there were anything else to read in the gay paper, with its riveting accounts of activists' meetings with city councilpersons and the latest Toys-for-Tots drive by fat guys wearing leather hoods. He just didn't want Sam to think he was shopping. He would set the paper on top of the recyclable stack, or sometimes bury it beneath a day or two of the *Times*. But he would know it was there, the chronicle of a whole world that was humming along in perfect oblivion of Sam's and Joel's oh-so-fortunate pairing.

A scary world; he must always have wanted to know how he might fare out there. Like any armchair traveler, wondering if he could survive in the Arctic. Grateful to be in his warm apartment but knowing he had never truly been tested, never had a chance to find out if he had the right stuff.

"So you want a Date or a Relationship?" Charles said.

"I don't know. How about a Date?"

"Hmm." Charles ran his finger down the column. "Hmm. Maybe we should go straight to Masseurs."

"Nothing?"

"Not unless you can pass for thirty-five. It's amazing, every blessed one of these queens says that's the absolute cut-off. I personally have had some entirely satisfactory dates with more mature gentlemen."

"How about Relationships?"

"They do appear to be somewhat more accessible. Do you enjoy going to sporting events and working out?"

"No."

"Do you want someone discreet?"

"You mean closeted?"

"How about 'tired of bar scene?' There's lots of those."

"I bet." Joel was certainly tired of bar scene. Who wasn't, except the indefatigable Ron? But there was something off-putting about a guy who said it in an ad. Tired of human condition.

"Here's someone witty. Witty is good."

"Absolutely nobody who says he's witty."

"Well, you are one extremely picky faggot. I wash my hands of you." He folded the paper and gestured to the bartender for another negroni.

Joel took the paper back and flipped idly to Situations. "Here we go." He read aloud. "Enterprising young man seeks mentor."

"Right," Charles said. "Lazy, grasping little brat seeks sucker to pay for his college tuition in return for four years of continually postponed access to his charms."

"Probably," Joel said.

Alex, turning to him for help with the algebra problem.

Except a little gay Alex this time, so that there would be at least a chance that their growing closeness would culminate in the day the kid turned, looked at Joel, realized he was in love. Why did Joel resist acknowledging this, why should he have insisted to himself that it wasn't about sex? When what he was picturing, undeniably, was some shapely youth in a towel, padding from the bathroom to the second bedroom, one night turning to Joel's bedroom instead.

All right, of course he was picturing that. Why should a lonesome man with an extra room not have peopled it, in his mind, with some hot little roommate? He wasn't denying that, he just felt that he wanted two different things. To be with the boy, brother father friend, and also to lay him. Two different things that were hard to sort out now, after so many years of living out the possible, performing the acts that are possible for two bodies in a world of matter. So much easier to suppose that there had only ever been the one thing, that helping Alex with the algebra problem was just a pathetic substitute for giving him a blow job. But he was sure of it: he had wanted, still wanted, two different things—neither anterior to the other, not one chaste and one sullied. Just one possible and one not.

Richard had said, when they set up the date, "I'll be wearing a navy polo shirt." So Joel already had the premonition, as he walked into the Trattoria Basilico, that Richard would be, if not queeny, a little too precise. The kind of guy who knew what color he'd be wearing two days ahead. The kind who said "navy" instead of just "blue."

Anyway, there he was at the bar, his back to the door. The bar faced the wood-fired pizza oven. Which was better than if it faced a mirror: Joel could approach him without his knowing, or fail to approach him and get the hell out of there. Joel didn't know how he would bear the flicker of disappointment that was sure to cross Richard's face when he slid onto the adjacent stool. Joel hadn't misrepresented himself; nor, from what he could see, had Richard. But each of them must have had some frail hope that the other was being too modest.

Richard greeted Joel, when he sat down at last, with a big smile, a warm handshake, a rush of friendly words: Joel looked just the way he'd described himself, Richard knew the navy polo thing was corny but he was so nondescript he had to pick something Joel could identify him by. If he'd known it was so hot, sitting practically inside the pizza oven, he would have worn a tank top. From what Joel could make out, this would have been unwise. Still, Joel was taken with him, started babbling right back. The bartender had to get Joel's attention, an almost unprecedented reversal.

In the moment it took Joel to order—several moments, Joel was torn between a scotch and some citrus drink like the one Richard had before him—in the moment before Joel turned to look at him again everything cooled down. Just a little. Richard was nice-looking: that was the exact phrase, he looked nice.

"Should we get a table?" Joel said.

"Sure. Let me take care of these."

"Thanks."

While Richard paid, Joel looked at the guy who made pizzas. A young Latino with a baseball cap, strewing the toppings on a disk of dough and sliding it into the oven with his paddle almost in one continuous movement, already glancing at the next order slip. Moving very fast, yet with a calm and gravity that made Joel think of somewhere far away, El Salvador maybe, wherever the boy or his people had come from. Joel felt colorless. They were all colorless, Joel, Richard, everybody eating. They might all have been a haze to this dark, graceful boy, a blur of white faces that streamed by while he worked, so quietly. He took off his cap for a second and wiped the sweat from his forehead with a slender brown arm.

Richard must have been watching Joel for a second, watching Joel watch the pizza guy. "All set," he said. Joel followed him to the headwaiter's station. Joel couldn't help noticing that Richard's khaki-swathed butt was . . . rather broad.

Richard ordered a pizza. Joel for some reason didn't want to be an order slip for the kid to glance at, so he got some kind of pasta with about thirty ingredients. Then, while they waited, they exchanged data. Richard was a librarian in the DC public system. This seemed—Joel didn't say it—very sad. The one time he'd been to the main library he had counted more bums than books. To be a librarian there must have been like being a lifeguard in the Gobi desert. Joel explained his own job, they established that Richard was from Ohio and had gone to Bucknell and then University of Maryland library school and . . . here he was.

Joel found himself, uncomfortably, able to see Richard's entire life, every step on the way to here-he-was. The closeted years at Bucknell, coming out in DC, partying in the seventies, shivering through the eighties and then finding himself, inexplicably, still alive, still here. Across from another middle-aged guy who was also here; however differently they had lived, they were both here.

So this was a date! Not a Date, Richard was from the Relationships column, but this was how a date worked. Joel had never been on a date. People used to ask how he and Sam had met, and Joel would say, rather proudly, "At the baths." Proudly because, while it sounded so unromantic, meeting at the baths, it was really the most romantic possible start. Something out of a fairy tale, that two people could bump into each other in the half-light and then make a life together.

If he and Richard were going to make it through the next half-hour, Joel would need to say something. Well, a librarian, he could ask who Richard's favorite writers were. Richard promptly mentioned Anne Rice. Joel said, "Oh, uh-huh," perhaps failing to conceal his dismay. What a fool he was, now Richard was sure to ask who *his* favorite writers were, and what was he going to say? All he read any more was the

Congressional Record and the occasional underwear catalogue.

He was spared: their food came. By the time the waiter had done the peppermill thing and the cheese-grater thing Richard had forgotten the subject. He delicately ambushed his pizza with a knife and fork.

Some while later, Richard coughed. Joel wondered how long he had been staring at the pizza boy. "Um . . . this is so good," Joel said, gesturing with his fork at his gummy pasta. "How's yours?"

"All right." Richard formed his mouth into a small, mildly off-putting pout. Joel tried to imagine kissing him, and then . . .

Would he do? As, in the old days, at the bars, when last call came, you stopped grading people, stopped handing out A minuses and C pluses, and shifted to a pass/fail system. Is this one better than sleeping alone?

Joel's standards had gone up since those days. In all the years with Sam the only people he'd concretely imagined going to bed with were in porn. So the curve on his pass/fail system had skewed sharply. If Richard had popped up on a video, Joel would definitely have hit the fast-forward button. But this wasn't a video. If Joel was hoping ever again to date someone other than his fist, he'd better relax his standards.

The waiter cleared their plates. No, no dessert. Nor coffee; if Richard had a sip after noon, he'd be up half the night. So he wasn't, anyway, planning to be up half the night. Joel wanted another drink, but Richard might find it odd to order a cocktail right after dinner. Joel didn't want him to think there was some kind of problem.

It was only eight o'clock. Still light out. They hadn't timed this at all well.

Richard was looking steadily at Joel. To avoid his eyes, Joel craned around the room, as if trying to find out where the waiter was with the check.

Richard was looking at Joel and trying to decide. Grading

Joel according to his own pass/fail system. Joel wanted to pass. It was more important, really, than what he thought about Richard. His difficulty in imagining what they could possibly do together, Joel and this . . . nice man, didn't matter. He just didn't want to flunk on the first date of his life.

Richard insisted on paying, the waiter brought their change fast, because the place was filling up and he wanted their table. So they were hurled out onto the sidewalk, in the bright light. They faced each other: two middle-aged men gazing reciprocally at the possible.

No. Joel could see the No gathering in Richard's throat and, to forestall it, he said, "Well, it was nice meeting you," and stuck out his hand.

Richard was aghast. He had thought they were going home.

Was it too late for an amendment? Just kidding, my place or yours. It was too late. Already Richard was shaking Joel's hand and saying, with a cold smile, "Nice meeting you, too." Then he rushed down the street.

Luckily, Joel was only a block from the video store. Maybe one of those tapes with the cute Latino boys.

The phone rang. Joel ignored it and went on playing solitaire on the office computer. If he didn't answer after four rings, the system sent the caller to voice mail. Unless he was pretty sure who it was, he always let this happen. He felt guilty, but it was better than picking up and having to deal with whatever surprise was on the other end: a staffer with a self-declared crisis; his boss, Herb; a former lover. You couldn't pick up and hear people leaving their voice mail. You had to wait until they were finished and the message light on the phone started flashing. Joel would feel, in the minute or two this took, like a deaf man who can't read lips, as he helplessly watches someone try to tell him something.

The light came on. The message was from Stanley Hirsch,

who covered health stuff for the *Post*. "Mister . . . uh . . . Lingeman," he said, reading from a Rolodex card. "I had a couple of questions about Medicare. I'll be around here for a half hour or so."

Not asking, commanding. Who would fail to return a call from the *Post*? Still, it was always flattering to get a call from Stanley Hirsch, to know that one was in his Rolodex of experts. Joel called back right away, and of course got Hirsch's voice mail. They played tag most of the day. Finally the phone rang just as Joel was turning off his computer and heading out for happy hour. He hesitated: it might be Stanley Hirsch or it might be some staffer with an emergency that would keep Joel there half the evening.

"Joel Lingeman."

"Yeah, Stanley Hirsch. Listen, you got a minute to talk about this AIDS thing?"

"What AIDS thing?"

"This bill Senator Harris dropped today." That was the usual word, dropped. Perhaps new bills really were still dropped into some actual container, but the word always made Joel think of a dog, dropping a couple of bills, kicking some leaves over them, moving insouciantly on.

"Oh, so he finally introduced it? I hadn't heard." It had been a couple of weeks since Joel had supplied the numbers for the senator's floor statement. Melanie had been frantic, Harris had to introduce it the very next day, and then it had just vanished. This was the way things worked: matters of great urgency suddenly disappeared, then became urgent again weeks later, as if governed by phases of the moon.

"You knew about it, then," Hirsch said.

Oops. This was a serious breach: people at OLA weren't supposed to say what they'd been working on. "No, I . . . maybe I heard somebody talk about it. What does it do, exactly?"

"It looks like it cuts off Medicaid for people who—"

"Medicaid? Are you sure?"

"Oh, no, right. Medicare, I meant Medicare."

How could somebody who'd covered health stuff since about the Truman administration be unable to distinguish between Medicare and Medicaid? Joel sometimes wondered if there was a Stanley Hirsch on every beat—he could spot the mistakes in the health stories, but could it be that every story in the papers was equally misinformed?

Hirsch went on: "It cuts off Medicare for people who've done something . . . I guess risky."

"Uh-huh."

"So what do you think about that?"

"I . . ." Joel sighed nonpartisanly. "I think it sounds like it might be kind of hard to enforce."

"Right. But if they could, would this save a lot of money?"

Joel had given Melanie some numbers, but he couldn't remember them. "I don't know. Did they put out any numbers?"

"Yeah, their press release says Medicare spends about a billion dollars a year for AIDS."

"That sounds right."

"So that's what they'd save?"

"No. They . . . oh, we're on background, right?" He was supposed to say this at the start of the call, he always forgot. If you didn't say it you could find your name in the paper, along with a misquotation. Herb didn't like seeing Joel's name in the paper. Herb's boss liked it even less.

"Right, sure, background," Hirsch said dismissively. He had had no intention of making Joel famous.

"Okay. First of all, they're just guessing what Medicare spends, because doctors' bills don't come in with 'AIDS' written all over them. And second, there are these offsets."

"Offsets."

"Offsets. If you save money in one program, you may wind up spending it somewhere else." Joel launched—partly as an experiment, to see how many things Hirsch could get wrong the next morning, partly just showing off—into a discourse peppered with arcana like SSI and spenddown and the FMAP.

Hirsch pretended to take it all in, even made Joel repeat some of it. At the end he said, "So you think maybe they wouldn't save a billion?"

Joel sighed. "That's right. I think, with the offsets and the enforcement problems and all, maybe . . ." Joel's message light flashed on, someone else had called. "Maybe a hundred million."

"That's all?"

"I'm still on background. And, you know, I don't do these estimates, the budget office does. But I'd bet they score this at about a hundred million."

"Maybe I should call them."

"Maybe so."

"You got a name I can call?"

He gave Hirsch a couple of names at the Congressional Budget Office. They wouldn't talk to Hirsch even on background.

When he was through with Hirsch, he got his new message. "Hey, Joel, it's Andrew. From leg counsel?" As if Joel wouldn't remember. "Listen, I wasn't up to anything, and I thought I'd see if you'd like to have a drink. But it's . . . about six-twenty, I guess you're gone. I'll catch you again. Enjoy your evening."

Now it was past six-thirty, Andrew had to be gone. Joel almost didn't call, thinking that the sound of Andrew's extension ringing, ringing, would make him even more lonesome than if he didn't try.

Andrew was already at a table, at the outdoor bistro on Massachusetts Avenue where they might have dinner if they felt like it. He was deeply tanned, when a few weeks ago he'd been as pale as Joel was. His brown hair was bleached almost blond; even his eyebrows had little flecks of red-gold in them.

The sleeves of his crisp white shirt were rolled up; his fore-arms, sinewy and dark, were also lightly strewn with gold. When Joel got to his table he stood up. As at their last meeting, he smiled hugely and grasped Joel's shoulder as they shook hands.

"You got some sun," Joel said, fatuously.

"Yeah, I was off all last week."

"Where'd you go?"

"My backyard, mostly. I spent a couple days down with Kenyon's parents, but then I mostly just hung out."

"Where are they?"

"Florida. You know Silver Haven? It's on the Gulf Coast."

"Uh-huh." Joel didn't know Silver Haven, but it had to be dreary. Andrew was an angel to go waste part of his vacation visiting these people.

"What have you been up to?"

"Just work," Joel said. "Oh, Harris put his bill in."

"I know. Melanie had me make the last changes a couple days ago."

"Yeah?" Joel was a little hurt that he hadn't been consulted. Why, to help perfect a nasty little bill that wasn't going anywhere? Maybe he just didn't like it that Andrew was already in on something he wasn't. Last time they'd met, Joel had played the insider. Already the balance between them had minutely shifted.

The waiter came. Andrew ordered a real drink, so Joel could too. No, they weren't sure yet if they needed to see menus. Joel was sure.

When the waiter had gone, Andrew said, "So how's your love life?"

Joel was startled. "Um. I— I was dating this guy, a librarian. A nice guy, but . . ." That just came out. A harmless fib, but he felt awful. Partly because it was crummy to have walked away from Richard and then invoke him. Partly because, if he hadn't walked away, they might in fact have dated for a while;

he would have had a little something instead of nothing. Mostly because he was already lying, just so Andrew wouldn't think he was a loser.

What, after all, was wrong with lying? He and Sam wouldn't have got through fifteen years on sodium Pentothal. But he was in effect saying: if you knew about me you'd think me pathetic and unworthy. I have to be somebody else to be worthy of you, while you can just be your dazzling, deeply tanned self. "We . . . actually we just saw each other a couple times." This was only off by one time, better than the higher if indefinite number implied by "dating."

Andrew nodded understandingly. Joel wondered what he understood. That is: he had formed some picture of things. Whatever image the word "librarian" conjured for him, then that image conjoined with Joel's in whatever scenario "dating" would mean, and then whatever revisions he adopted when Joel added "a couple of times." Not that Andrew was sitting there writing a screenplay, just that a few words from Joel must have left him with some fleeting impression. Every word Joel uttered must have made these pictures in other people's heads; the people who seemed to know him really knew this movie they ran inside their heads and that had about as much relation to his real life as a Hollywood biopic.

"And how's your love life?" Joel said.

Andrew shrugged. "Still hibernating. But lately I, uh . . ." He grinned. "I think about it. I mean, I look sometimes and I . . . think about it."

Joel smiled, too. "Think about it."

"Yeah. One-handed."

"Oh. I take two."

"Right."

The waiter came, sans drinks. "Excuse me, is one of you Mr. Crawford?"

"That's me," Andrew said.

"There's a call for you inside."

"Oh." He said to Joel, "I've got to take this, sorry. I should just be a couple minutes."

He scurried inside, leaving Joel wondering who he could have given the number to. Andrew wasn't a surgeon or a deputy assistant secretary; there wasn't any reason he'd tell people where he was going to be.

Did he think of Joel, now that he was thinking? Enough to have called, anyway. There wasn't much chance that, when he thought about it with one hand, the vision that came to his mind was of Joel. Still, he'd brought the subject up, all by himself. So it didn't seem inconceivable that, when he was ready to emerge from his hibernation, he would . . .

The waiter came with the drinks, finally. Joel nursed his, he didn't want to get too far ahead, and watched the people go by on Massachusetts Avenue. Staffers in their twenties, lawyers in their thirties, a couple guys Joel's age—with the fanatical parts in their hair that betrayed them as fellows at the mammoth conservative think tank down the street. Those who had worked late were still in their suits or their Elizabeth Dole dresses; others had gone home and changed into the late June evening unisex costume of polo shirt, khaki shorts or the occasional atavistic madras, loafers worn without socks. As if it were 1964. This had to be the whitest few blocks in the city, or at least the whitest east of Rock Creek; Joel never went west of Rock Creek. These people saw only one another and thought they were America. Even the scattering of gay couples who passed by had a Republican look to them. Their legs, between the shorts and the loafers, so white.

Andrew came out and strolled toward their table. Trim and bronze. Joel thought, a little chilled: he's working on his tan because he's planning to go out this summer.

"Sorry." Andrew frowned. "Kenyon's parents."

"They called you here? Is something going on?"

"Not really. They're a little worried about this one hospital bill their HMO isn't paying. See . . . um, Kenyon's dad had

134

this fall, and he went to the ER and it turned out everything was OK, and now the HMO says it wasn't an emergency and they're not going to pay for it."

"Oh. I thought it might be something urgent."

"No. They get upset if they can't get hold of me. So I usually—I mean if I'm going to be gone more than a couple hours, whatever, I let them know where they can reach me."

"Uh-huh."

"I should get a cell phone."

"Maybe so," Joel said. They were quiet a minute. Joel couldn't think of any way of steering the conversation back to the exciting subject of Andrew's hand and the object of its attentions. So he said, "You're very close to Kenyon's parents."

Andrew nodded. "We used to go down to Silver Haven alternate holidays, Kenyon and I. I mean, Kenyon went every holiday, he even went home for Easter, but sometimes I had to go to my own family. But I'd be at Kenyon's either for Thanksgiving or Christmas, it would just be the four of us, Kenyon and me and his parents."

"That's kind of neat. Like you're family."

"Yeah, it's funny. I mean, Kenyon and I were together for years before I even met them. You know, he'd never actually had *the discussion* with them. They knew they had a forty-year-old son who had never so much as mentioned a girl. They knew I sometimes answered the phone when they called Kenyon—which was a couple times a night, they've always been this way. If we ever went out there'd be this worried message on the answering machine, he should call whenever he got in, no matter how late, just so they'd know he was okay.

"They knew I answered the phone, but it was just, 'Let me get Kenyon,' or 'He's out for a second, he'll call you right back.' They had to know what I was doing there, but it was a whole nother thing for me to just show up there in Silver Haven, Exhibit A. I didn't want to go at all. And when we got off the plane, when we got off the ramp thing and there they were,

I just felt naked. Like, look, here's the man your son has sex with. Why don't we give you a little demonstration right here in the airport?

"They hugged Kenyon and shook my hand, like I was just someone who happened to have been next to Kenyon on the plane, and we went to the car. And the whole way to their place they talked like I wasn't there—about their ailments and Kenyon's father's golf game and the problem with the roof and the news about somebody Kenyon had gone to school with. No, not like I wasn't there, they'd pause a second to explain who Mabel was, like that. They were just perfectly natural, just catching up with Kenyon about things. And they went on talking that way straight through dinner. Maybe they asked me one or two things about my job, whatever, or if my parents didn't mind my being away for the holidays. I said we were a big family, they'd probably lose count. And they said, 'Well, we just have Kenyon,' and then turned back to him, to tell him something else that had gone on in Silver Haven or, before that, Buffalo, where he grew up: 'Remember the time we . . .'

"Then Kenyon and his father and me went to watch TV in the family room while his mother did the dishes. We didn't say anything at all, just watched some cop show. When it was over, his father stood up, turned off the TV, and said, 'You boys must be tired. You'd better be getting to bed.' Just as casual as that, 'you boys.'

"Well, this was the big moment: where were they going to have us sleep? Kenyon got our bags from the front hall and led the way upstairs and into his room. There were twin beds, each with one corner of the covers turned down. Now, there were lots of rooms upstairs. I mean, I could see there was a guest room right down the hall. Kenyon said, whispered, 'They just put these beds in.' I whispered back, 'What?' And he said, 'I always had a double bed in here. They must have just gone out this week and put these beds in.'

"And I figured out how they'd been treating me: like a

sleepover, like some friend of Kenyon's from junior high who had come for dinner and was spending the night. That was how they'd decided to handle the fact of me.

"It was the kind of house where somebody in the basement could hear somebody fart on the second floor. So we couldn't put the beds together, too much noise. And Kenyon was a big guy, there was no way we were going to squeeze into one twin bed. So we slept apart, the two boys. The next time we went, we did work up the nerve to move the beds together. But we'd get up and move them back before breakfast."

He chuckled. "We'd move them back and go downstairs and his mother would say, 'I hope you boys are hungry.'"

Joel said, "So they never did have *the discussion*."

"I guess they didn't need to. They were just happy Kenyon had somebody."

"Well, that's nice. And you've gone on seeing them. Since . . ."

Andrew took a fairly big slug of his drink. "When Kenyon died, we had a service up here. You know, all his friends were here, the people we worked with. I arranged a service here and they didn't come, his mom was having some kind of problem, I can't remember what it was, probably her arthritis. I wound up flying down there with his ashes. I stepped off the plane and there they were in the waiting area, greeting me alone this time. They hugged me, not all teary or anything, just like, 'Good to see you.' In the car they talked about the usual stuff, the house and golf and stuff. Nothing about Kenyon. And when we got to the house, Kenyon's father said, 'Why don't you take your bags up to your room?'" He shook his head. "I had his ashes in one of those bags."

"Do they . . . they don't think you're . . ."

"They're not senile or anything, or crazy. They just— I mean, Kenyon let them, his whole life he let them rely on him for every little thing. Should we have the roof fixed? Should we let our T-bill roll over? He never let a night go by without their hearing from him, they could call him about anything. They just depended on him, you know."

"So now they call you."

"It's like when he was gone they just . . . I don't know, transferred it."

"And you let them," Joel said. Neutrally, he hoped, though there was really no way of pitching those words without at least hinting that Andrew was a spineless schnook.

"What can I do? They're pushing eighty. I can't just cut them off."

Sure he could, Joel thought. He could get an unlisted phone number. In which case they'd probably have the police hunt him down. "Huh. I guess it's hard."

"I'm trying to . . . you know, wean them a little? Not cut them off but ease them down a little."

"Like by telling them you were coming here?"

"Well, they're upset today. You know, this thing about the bill."

"Uh-huh."

"Hey, you know a lot about health care. Maybe you could help them."

"Um." Right. As if Joel were going to get involved with these loonies. Next thing, he'd be going down for holidays. He and Andrew would get the twin beds. "Why don't you get the details from them and then maybe I could help you out?"

"Great."

"They . . . it's a Medicare HMO, right? They can appeal it, they have federal appeal rights. I can call around, find out what you need to do."

"Okay. Thanks."

The waiter came by with menus. "No, just the check, please," Andrew said. Then to Joel: "I'm sorry, but I really better get home and call them. You know, let them know I'm going to try to take care of it."

"Sure," Joel said. "Maybe another time."

138

"Absolutely." He looked out at the street, then back at Joel. He said, very softly, "One of the reasons I've been kind of taking my time—about going out again? I know I need to fix this. I mean, I know I can't expect . . . if I start seeing somebody, I know I probably can't expect them to deal with this."

Joel might have answered: I could deal with it. Applying for the hypothetical future job vacancy for a *somebody*. Maybe the application was even being solicited, maybe Andrew understood their aborted dinner-if-they-felt-like-it to be the first in a possible chain of encounters that might eventually add up to *seeing* Joel.

On the sidewalk, people were moving more briskly. It was dark, everybody had to scurry home to their townhouses and turn on their alarm systems. These streets belonged to them only until it got dark.

Under the streetlight Andrew's brown face and gold-flecked hair glowed above his starkly white shirt. He and Joel shook hands; Joel was a little bereft that, this time, Andrew did not grasp his shoulder. They parted, Joel toward the Union Station Metro stop, Andrew to wherever he had left his car. So he could rush home to call these crazy people who had somehow conscripted him.

"I could deal with it," Joel might have said, if only Andrew had posed the question clearly enough. He might have said that, and it would have been a lie. He already felt himself pulling back. Andrew's story was weird; he had to be a little fucked up to have let this happen to him. Okay, he hadn't volunteered, he had been drafted, and Joel could see that it might be hard to cut those poor people off. To tell them they didn't have a son any more, Kenyon was gone and they would need to get through the business of dying all by themselves. Maybe Joel was the weird one, he who would have changed his phone number.

Andrew was just a decent guy who . . . had volunteered, Joel was sure of it. Had—not spinelessly but gratefully—allowed a *must* to enter his life. He must get home so Kenyon's parents wouldn't worry. Maybe he needed a must, some reason to get home after Kenyon stopped being the reason.

Joel had no reason to get home. No one wondered where he was, no one would have missed him if he had spontaneously combusted. On the other hand, he found suddenly that he had a very good reason—one so compelling he took a cab instead of the Metro—to get to Zippers.

Tonight he wasn't just going to lower his standards: no, he was going to institute an open admission policy. First applicant gets the slot. Having been left alone on the sidewalk by a very decent guy, decent to the point of lunacy, he wanted just the opposite. An impersonal and mildly degrading encounter with some loser he would never see again. Just to get on with it. Sex was a bodily function, for God's sake, not some kind of holy grail. Anybody would do, just any live body at all.

Of course this resolution collapsed the minute he walked in and sat down. Not-a-chance to the left of him, out-of-the-question to the right of him, straight ahead not-if-you-were-the-last-man-on-earth. He wasn't expecting somebody out of *Men's Health*, but really . . .

Really, what if that guy straight ahead, the fifty-five-year-old church organist with freckles and two spreading seas of dampness under his arms, had been the last man on earth? Presumably he had all the standard accessories, was equipped to perform any act in Joel's limited repertory. Wouldn't Joel, after some period of combing the depopulated planet for any alternative, have turned to him sooner or later? As a Hasid on the brink of starvation would, at long last, try just a taste of the shrimp salad? Sooner or later: why not now?

The organist, or vice-principal, or whatever he was, smiled at Joel. Joel looked away, swallowed, looked back. It was just for tonight, he wasn't going to marry the guy, he could just close his eyes and . . . Not if he were the last man on earth.

On his way out Joel got the gay paper again. At home he skipped the non-mercantile categories of longing and went straight to Escorts. Not seriously considering it, not after one more dead night at Zippers, just curious about what could be had if he should ever be in the market.

On the shelves just then were Ivy League, drill instructor, Euroboy. Some would share unspecified toys, others had repertories that were summarized in acronyms. Most of these indecipherable to Joel, but he could pretty well bet that activities involving acronyms were going to hurt. A few supplied grainy and ill-lit pictures of their torsos, never faces. The bodies were more or less interchangeable: arms with veins that looked like they were about to pop, abdomens formed into so many little quadrilaterals they might have been turned out at a quilting bee. About as erotic as a perfect SAT score. And who knew if the advertisers really used their own pictures? What if a guy showed up at the door and turned out to be . . . ?

All right, he was seriously considering it. If he couldn't bring himself to go home with the goddamn organist, or with Richard the librarian, ·or with anybody in his league; if he wasn't going to settle for that, he was sooner or later going to have to take something out of his wallet. Besides the condom he had begun superstitiously carrying there. He could be one of those gentlemen who hung out at the guppy bar, Gentry, in search of a presentable young man whom they could take to dinner and who might eventually show some tepid appreciation for the occasional gift of a wristwatch or a fine briefcase. Or he could just cut to the chase—more accurately, cut to after the chase—and call up an escort. Money was what he had, not youth or muscles or any other currency. What was reprehensible about spending what he had?

One or two of the advertisers cited credentials. Rick Harding reported that he was in the July issue of *Baskets*, while Tony Silva was the superstar of *Latino Latrine*. Each would be in town next week; there was a number to call for an appointment.

Imagine: you called up, and at a specified hour there would appear at your door the guy from the magazine, the guy from the video. Magically endowed with a third dimension.

Oh, they should always have had this service. What would life have been like if Joel could just have called up Stephen Boyd from *Ben Hur*? Or Riff from *West Side Story*. Or the guy in that swimsuit ad in *man about town* thirty years ago. What was the company? Something of New Mexico.

These people existed. They had three dimensions. They and Joel walked the same planet. Once he had read in some gee-whiz science article that every time he inhaled he took in some number of oxygen molecules that had also passed through the lungs of Leonardo da Vinci. Golly. And maybe the water he drank was also the sweat on Stephen Boyd's shoulders, the air he breathed was once a zephyr tickling the ineffable midriff of the New Mexico boy.

Joel hadn't seen that advertisement in thirty years, yet he remembered the boy more clearly than, say, his college roommate. He had been—what?—fourteen when he discovered the little ad tucked in the very back of the magazine, hidden in the crowd of cut-rate, back-of-the-book ads for memory improvement programs, hair-loss cures, elevator shoes. A young man wore white swimming trunks—not a bikini, but very abbreviated boxers—that stopped well below his navel. Low enough that you could see his hipbones. His dirty blond hair was a little longer than a crew cut. He looked straight at the camera and smiled.

Joel had seen that picture and, after an instant, snapped the magazine shut, buried it about midway up the permanent stack of junk—books, LPs, sweaters from his aunt still in their gift boxes—in the corner by his dresser. He didn't hide it: the spine, with the familiar **man about town**, was perfectly visible. It was okay for him to read *man about town*; it wasn't as racy as *Esquire*, even. His parents couldn't possibly tell,

142

from a single exposed edge, that this one issue concealed—

An opening. Three column inches in the back of the book, a fuzzy black-and-white rotogravure the size of Joel's thumb: it blew a hole in the wall. In the cluttered bedroom of a fourteen-year-old who was lucky the word *nerd* hadn't yet been coined, who knew nothing about the world and less about himself, there was suddenly this aperture, through which he could see everything. He wasn't sure just what he was seeing, but he knew he had stumbled on a great secret. He felt enormously powerful and blessed, just to be in possession of the picture and know he could look at it again.

For a week or two, every time he was sure he was alone, he would grab the magazine, flip to that back page, glance for just a second or two before stuffing it away, as if someone might break in on him at any moment. He knew it was a crime, looking at that picture, even having it in the room. Not just the obvious crime. Perhaps he already had some vague intuition that a good boy wasn't supposed to be quite so profoundly interested in a picture of a handsome guy in swimming trunks. But there was something else about the picture, something seismically subversive.

It didn't seem to Joel that he had been captivated by the body itself. He couldn't even remember it really, just the smile and the swimming trunks, nothing in between. What was in between was probably fine—the guy was in a swimsuit ad, after all—but he had no recollection of wanting to touch it, nor of even the slightest curiosity about what was under the swimming trunks.

Something else about the picture: he couldn't remember. Just that, after one look at it, he had never been a good boy again.

For $150 in/$200 out, he could be a bad boy this very evening. Did he want to? Not any of the guys with pictures. Maybe Marco, hot Latin, hardbody? Except that particular adjective suggested that making love to him would be like humping a lamp-pole. Fred, perhaps—there was a wholesome, unthreatening name. Into most scenes. Older guys okay. Here was a wrinkle Joel hadn't thought about. Did this mean older guys weren't okay with Fred's competitors? In which case who the hell were their clients? And was forty-five older? To be rejected by a hustler while Sam was banging a twenty-three-year-old Gulf War veteran . . . Fred, then, best to settle on nondiscriminatory Fred. Besides, Fred was into most scenes. Maybe including Joel's.

Why shouldn't he call Fred? He had friends who unabashedly used these guys. Charles would talk about it as casually as he would about the new sweater he got at Nieman Marcus. More casually: finding cashmere in just the right shade at Needless Markup was a bigger event than an encounter, at roughly the same price, with a hustler. It wasn't like the old days, midnight cowboys smashing in the teeth of pathetic old cocksuckers in fleabag hotels. Escorts were just part of the booming global service economy. Patronizing them was no more shameful or dangerous than—going to a tanning salon, say. Very like going to a tanning salon: it might not be the real sun, but your skin didn't know any better. And Joel's body would not recoil from whatever friction he and Fred contracted for, his body would not wonder whether it was true love. Not so long as Fred did his job and got hard.

Really, how did Joel ever surmise that his passion was requited? The other guy got hard. Fred would get hard, and they would . . .

Joel knew what they would do. He didn't have a couple of months of pent-up longings, a couple of months since the last time with Sam. He had a lifetime of desires he had never satisfied. Because there were things he wasn't ready to do before he met Sam, he hadn't been far enough out to do them. And of course he couldn't do them with Sam: there were things you couldn't possibly do with someone who was going to be there the next day, and the next.

Scenes. A whole repertory of sacrileges and indignities that he could inflict or endure. He had his hand on the phone, he was about to pick up the receiver and dial.

"What are you into?" Fred would say. Expecting an acronym. Probably there was one. Joel would start to explain: first you do this, then I . . . Fred would say, "Oh, QZ. That's cool, we can do that. But, hey, QZ will run you another fifty."

Or if, improbably, Joel was the only man on earth who had ever conceived of his particular scene—so that he would have to detail for an astonished but complaisant Fred the script he had been revising and polishing so many years—how could he put out of his mind that Fred was enacting it pursuant to his instructions? First you Q, then we Z, and then I . . . How could he possibly forget that it was only a scene?

He could forget. His hand was still resting on the phone. He could call Fred right this instant, it was what he wanted, why shouldn't he have it? Because he could have it. And, having had it, would—he could already see the end of it, was filled with premonitory despair as he pictured Fred gathering up his jock strap and his twenties and heading out the door—would only discover that it wasn't what he wanted.

No? He had been practically squirming just now, imagining his *scene*, the hand that wasn't on the phone had left the crotch of his khakis grimy with newspaper ink. Why should he keep insisting to himself that he required anything more ethereal than a little QZ? Fred was real, and procurable; Joel could dial the phone right now and have his wish, in three dimensions, in real time.

Or he could call Andrew—and get a busy signal because Andrew was talking to his demented auxiliary parents. He could call Sam, who would be short with him. Or Alex Rivers. "Hey, guess who this is?" Click.

He wished—like a child for a moment he wished he had a magic phone, so he could call New Mexico.

five

In the Yellow Pages there were two listings under Magazines—Back Number. One was an 800 number, someplace you could call and order a search. Right: please find me an issue of *man about town* from 1964. I can't remember just which month, but way in the back it has this picture . . . The other listing was right in town. The Past Recaptured—Vintage Records, Magazines, Collectibles. 2317 Monroe Street, NW. While the name was promising, Joel suspected that he would find only old issues of *Life* or *National Geographic*, Chubby Checker albums, and maybe some Beatles posters. But it was only a couple of blocks from where the Coen brothers retrospective was playing, and there was nothing going on at the office. He thought he might just take the afternoon off and check the place out.

It wasn't there. He got to the 2300 block of Monroe and could see right away that there were no businesses at all, just a church and its appended school on one side and a block of uniform gray stone townhouses on the other. The address was a misprint, or he had written it down wrong, or, most likely, The Past Recaptured had sunk again into oblivion. These junk shops came and went so quickly: one more old queen's dream of retiring as an *antiquaire* gone, along with all the money from his 401(k). He almost turned away, thinking now he'd have time for a wine before the movie, but he could at least take one look at the townhouses. 2317 was no different from the others: five door-bells by the door, each labeled with an ordinary surname; beneath the front stairs, the entrance to a basement apartment. He stepped down, found a door with a frosted glass panel. Taped to the inner surface of the glass, so that it was utterly illegible from outside, was a card that had three words written on it. These might or might not have been, "The Past Recaptured."

Joel rang the bell.

The door was flung open by a stupendously fat man who wore suspenders and a necktie that reached only part of the way down the vast expanse of his shirt. "It says, 'Open by Appointment.' Can't you read?"

"Sorry," Joel said. "I'm sorry. Is this The Past Recaptured?"

"That's right."

"Well . . . could I make an appointment?"

"What are you looking for?"

"I'm not sure."

The man said, "If you don't know what you're looking for, you'll never find it." Still, he stepped aside—or as far aside as he could manage in the little vestibule—opening the narrowest of channels through which Joel could see a tiny, fluorescent-lit shop with knotty-pine walls. "Look around," the man said. "But don't be too long, I got places I have to go."

The shop was as Joel had feared. Movie posters, Hopalong Cassidy lunchboxes, Mondale-Ferraro buttons. Newspapers in plastic sheaths with headlines about moon landings and assassinations. A few stacks of *Time* and *Reader's Digest.* A book-shelf full of the Hardy Boys, Nancy Drew. *Tom Corbett, Space*

Cadet: Stand By for Mars! This last aroused a faint erotic tingle; something that went on at the space academy must have stirred Joel as a boy. Maybe he would leave with this book if nothing else. He opened it and found that the man wanted thirty dollars for it, for Christ's sake. For that he could buy a whole batch of current periodicals that would give him more than a faint tingle.

The man called out, "You got any questions?"

"Um, no. I mean, you don't have any . . ." Joel was, for some reason, ashamed to ask for *man about town.* As if an interest in that were somehow less elevated than a desire for a Hopalong Cassidy lunchbox. "Any other old magazines?"

"In the basement." Joel had thought he *was* in the basement. He had a vision, out of Gustave Doré, of endless descending levels. "Through the curtain."

What the man called the basement, beyond the curtain of plastic beads, was only two steps further down, but unfinished, with asbestos-wrapped pipes and a furnace so old it probably burned peat. Magazines were piled floor to ceiling in long arrays, with aisles between defined only by the absence of magazines. A temporary situation: vagrant magazines were spilling into the aisles like sand obliterating a desert highway.

Or a cemetery: looking over the stacks was like reading the names on gravestones. *Collier's. The Reporter. Look. Coronet. The Saturday Evening Post. Show. man about town.*

Two piles of *man about town*, each about four feet high. The nearer pile so placed that if he worked his way into the narrow fjord between *man about town* and *Holiday* and squatted, he could just make out the dates on the spines. They weren't in order, of course. January 1951 sat on top of October 1938 on top of April 1973. That would have been about the year of the magazine's demise, Joel thought: the world it had depicted utterly blown away, even the possibilities of nostalgia and self-parody exhausted.

Nothing from 1964. He tried to slide the whole first stack

out of the way so he could look at the one behind it, but the bottom issues were mildewed and disintegrating. He had to move the magazines a few at a time, making a new stack. When he crawled into the space he had cleared and squatted again to study the exposed spines of the second pile, something popped in his right knee. He tottered, fell over onto his side. He could feel the damp concrete through his pants; probably he would emerge from the basement looking as though he had been mud-wrestling—and without any prize. As he righted himself he saw, midway down the stack, like a neon sign: **may 1964**.

To get at it he had to move all the copies above it, making yet another stack. Then he reached for it, hand shaking. On the cover, Sean Connery in a white dinner jacket, holding a martini. Familiar, he seemed to recall this image, but there must have been a million such pictures in those years. He flipped to the back. Not on the last page, not on the two preceding, or the two before those. Before them was all text: the ghetto of cheap ads at the back of the book was just five pages. He took a breath and turned through them again, more slowly, though he couldn't possibly have missed—

He had missed it. And he had the name wrong. "Simms of Santa Fe," above a little, rather fuzzy picture of a boy in white trunks, his head no bigger than a fingernail. Joel's memory of him had been life-sized, as if Joel had actually known him, seen him. But there had been only this, so tiny, like someone seen from very far away. Or like a miniature that he might have worn hidden in a pendant close to his heart.

Joel was moving into the light to see better when the proprietor loomed up in the doorway. Joel snapped the magazine shut, afraid the man had seen, afraid the man knew he had been crawling amid the mildew and the dust to recapture a tiny photo of a boy in a swimming suit.

The man surveyed all of Joel's little stacks, pouted. "I hope you're going to put things back where you found them."

"Yes, I was going to."

"Did you find what you wanted?"

"Yes," Joel said. "This is what I wanted."

At the Hill Club he bumped into Ron. There was no one else around; they decided to sit and have a bite together.

"So how you been making out?" Ron said.

"You mean . . ."

"I didn't mean at the racetrack."

"I'm not."

"Oh. Well, God knows I've had the occasional dry spell."

"I'm not even trying," Joel said. "I don't know, it's all . . . undignified."

"Undignified? You want it dignified?" Ron stuck his nose in the air. "Mr. Joel Lingeman requests the pleasure of your company sitting on his face."

This rather loudly; Joel glanced around the room. "No, I mean . . . You must know what I mean. I—anywhere else I go, I'm a person. A solid, middle-class adult, with a decent job and money in my pocket. I go into a store and they're happy to see me, I go to a meeting and people want to hear what I have to say. I walk into Zippers, and I feel like some homeless guy who hasn't been taking his Thorazine and hasn't had a bath since October."

Ron sighed.

Joel added: "Or like the Ancient Mariner."

"How do you think I feel?" Ron said. "What are you, forty-seven, forty-eight?"

"Forty-five."

"Jeez, at your age I hadn't even come out."

"You hadn't? I thought you came out in kindergarten."

"I was married for twenty-one years."

"Married?"

"Straight out of school. I didn't come out till I was—what? Forty-six."

150

"Really." Joel did the math: they'd met, probably, seventeen or eighteen years ago. Ron had to be sixty-four at least. He looked pretty good for sixty-four. "Did your wife know, all those years?"

"Oh, I suppose. She must have suspected. But she must have thought: we got this far, maybe it just wasn't ever going to come up. Hell, I thought it wasn't ever going to come up. Just the peeps, and then going home to Helen, and then the old folks' home." He shook his head. "God, was she mad when I told her. She threw stuff."

"She threw stuff?"

"Like in a movie," Ron said. "She started throwing crockery."

"Why would she have been so mad if she suspected?"

"It was. . . like we had some kind of understanding, even though we never said a word about it. Or that was the understanding, that we wouldn't say it."

"Did you . . . I mean, did you know when you married her?"

"We got married in—what?—1956. The only gay man in the world was Liberace. I knew I was awfully fond of my roommate in law school. I knew I wasn't Liberace. And . . . I loved Helen, I kind of still do. I thought I could just put the other thing aside."

"But . . ." Joel said.

"But."

Their food came. Ron had a burger and a stupendous bucket of onion rings. Joel had the fried shrimp special. He hadn't realized shrimp were an endangered species; there were apparently only four left on the planet.

Joel said, "So you must have been just coming out when we met."

"I was, I think."

"You seemed a lot more experienced than me."

"Did I?"

"Well, more at ease with it. I mean, the way you could just walk up to anybody."

"I was in a hurry. I'd lost all those years, I couldn't . . . wallow in my own insufficiencies."

Joel said, "Like me, you mean."

"Did I say that?"

"I always wondered what your secret was. Like, it wasn't just that you could walk up to people. But it seemed like you scored every time. I was always amazed."

"Ah." Ron chuckled. "You want to hear my secret?"

"Sure."

Ron looked around, then stage-whispered: "I didn't score every time. Maybe you only noticed the times I scored."

"Oh. Maybe."

"I must have batted, I don't know, two hundred back then. And now, jeez, I'm probably batting point oh-oh-five."

"But you still go out."

"I'm not dead. When I'm batting zero I'll stop going out."

Joel didn't say anything, concentrated on cutting his very last shrimp into many little morsels. Ron said, "You think that's pathetic."

"I think it's hard."

"What else are you going to do? You're just going to jerk off the rest of your life?"

"I don't know."

"Well, there's always hustlers," Ron said. "Or the peeps."

"Jesus."

"Oh, you're too fine for the peeps? You remember being too fine for the peeps. You're barely up to standard."

Joel dropped his fork.

"I'm kidding," Ron said. "No, I'm not. Look at you. You're not taking care of yourself at all."

"Somebody else said that."

"You ought to listen. Go to the gym. Get some clothes. And God, where do you get your hair cut?"

"House barber shop. It's a bargain."

"I bet." Ron shrugged. "I'm sorry. Look, it's your business."

"No, no, I'm sure you're right," Joel said. He wasn't irritated, exactly, just tired. Suffering that deep weariness that can overcome you when you receive advice that you know is right, all but irrefutable, and that you know you aren't going to take. Go to the gym, Jesus. Even the thought of finding a new barber made Joel tired.

Joel's plate was empty. He said, "Do you mind if I smoke while you eat?"

"No, go right ahead. Unless you want some of these onion rings?"

"I guess I shouldn't."

"Oh, have some. Pull yourself together tomorrow."

Joel had some and looked around. The place was almost empty. One gay couple and two straight families of identical demographics: youngish Mommy and Daddy, infant in high chair. One infant playing with a strand of spaghetti, the other screaming to be let down. Probably in a few minutes they would reverse these roles.

"You and your wife," Joel said. "Did you have kids?"

"Uh-huh, two. All grown up now."

"Do they know about you?"

"Oh, Helen made sure of it. 'Your daddy's leaving the house because he's a fairy.'"

"Jeez."

"Hell, she even called my mother. My mother must have been eighty, and Helen just calls her out of the blue and tells her that her Ronald is *funny*."

"That was sweet."

"Oh, she got hers. My mother just snapped right back that if Helen had been any kind of woman I'd still be there."

"Good for her."

"It wasn't fair," Ron said. "But yeah, good for her."

"How did your kids handle it?"

"Learning I was gay? My daughter was okay about it, right from the start. Ron Junior . . ."

"You named your son Ron Junior?"

"What? Anyway, he doesn't . . . we hardly ever see each other. I thought he could handle it. I mean, when it happened I tried, you know, to talk to him about it. He'd just kind of hear me out, politely, and when I asked him how he felt he just shrugged. Like it was no big deal."

"But it was a big deal."

"I don't know. Whether it was that in particular or my breaking up the house or . . . I guess there can be a lot of reasons sons don't talk to their fathers."

This was certainly true. What amazed Joel were sons who did talk to their fathers. "I wonder sometimes, what it's like," Joel said. "Having kids."

"Expensive. By the time I finished paying off Helen and putting them through school—well, I'll be lucky if I retire before I'm ninety."

"But worth it?"

"I don't know. It's not like a deal you make. It just happens. You screw, you pay."

"I never did."

"You mean with a woman. Not once?"

"I tried a few times, I just couldn't."

Ron smiled. "You should have done what I did. Closed your eyes and thought about your roommate."

"Is that really what you did?"

"No. Did you want to get dessert?"

"How about you?"

"Just coffee, probably. I need to get home and make myself beautiful."

"You're going out?"

"It's like they say on the lottery ads," Ron said. "You gotta play to win."

Joel ascended from the Metro and made his way home through streets clogged with men who had made themselves beautiful and were just on their way out to party.

He could go to the gym. He could get a new haircut, new wardrobe. Facelift, tummy tuck, liposuction. He had even read somewhere that guys were getting abdomen implants—some kind of plastic six-pack actually inserted under the skin, substituting for a million crunches. Easier to sneer at the manic and grotesque than face up to the simple fact: he could go to the gym.

Joel's living room looked enormous when he walked in, big as an armory. It took him a second to register that there was only one club chair. Sam had come with no notice at all and taken away the Sam chair. He had a right to one of the chairs; they'd split the bill fifty-fifty. But he could have called; this way it was as though he had stolen it. As he had stolen everything else.

The May 1964 *man about town* was on the coffee table where Joel had left it before heading out to the Hill Club. It was open; somebody had been looking at it. Probably not Sam; Sam would have put it back exactly as he'd found it. Kevin, then, along to help. Sam went to use the bathroom, Kevin picked up the magazine, leafed through it. He must have wondered why Sam's ex had this old magazine from before he was even born. Kevin was of the generation that scarcely believed the world had existed before they were born.

Joel sat down in the remaining club chair, lit a cigarette, and started to read the magazine. He didn't turn at once to the back, even though now he could look at the picture indefinitely without fear of discovery. He meant to read the magazine as carefully as he had when he was fourteen. Page by page, trying to put out of mind what was on the penultimate page. As if he could make it catch him by surprise again, that surprise from which he had never recovered.

The magazine was huge. Some time around 1970 they changed the postal regulations and it became prohibitively expensive to mail the giant magazines: *Esquire, Holiday, man about town.* They all shrank to the size of *Time* or *Newsweek*, and something was lost. They had been like monthly presents, celebratory albums, with their dramatic graphics, their glossy photo spreads by Avedon or Penn. Their lavishness was really their entire content: it said money, sophistication, money, elegance, money.

On the cover, Sean Connery, in *Goldfinger* that year. The top of his head obscured part of the logo, so that it read **man ab t town**™. Always the same, for the forty years or so the magazine ran, always in a jaunty, mid-century lower case. As in *archy and mehitabel*, the epic typed by a cockroach who couldn't manage the shift key. Or e. e. cummings, the lower-case modernist who was still presented as the dernier cri when Joel was in high school, forty years after his efflorescence. That, too, would have been 1964, when Joel first read "anyone lived in a pretty how town . . . he sang his didn't he danced his did," and thought he had discovered something daring and new. Those years when Joel awoke to the world were, maybe, closer to the twenties than to the seventies: the end of something, not consciously the beginning. When the new world came along, it swept *man about town* away with it.

How Joel had loved *man about town*, waited for it every month. Most boys he knew preferred the other men's magazines, *Esquire* or *Playboy. Playboy* for the obvious reason, *Esquire* because it was then, as now, targeted at bright but randy adolescents. *man about town* was less leering, more self-consciously elegant and arty. Its implied reader was the man of its title, a wealthy bachelor who dined at fine restaurants, went to Broadway first nights and gallery openings, and still found time to keep up with Sartre and Bellow and Kubrick.

At the front, before the featured articles, were what would be called now the lifestyle columns. A cookery piece featuring a menu for two to be whipped up by a guy who couldn't boil water: a can of crabmeat and one of cream of mushroom soup, a jar of pimentos, sherry. Pour into chafing dish, stir. Serve over toast. A travel piece about where to stay in Venice if you could afford a staggering $100 a night. All punctuated with ads for jet travel, stereophonic high-fidelity systems, and, above all, liquor and cigarettes. The romance of liquor and cigarettes, the delusion Joel had never entirely outgrown.

How cheap and smarmy it all seemed now, *man about town*'s vision of sophistication, of manhood itself. A whole world of consumption that was, for the intended reader, nothing but a prelude to getting laid.

But of course the intended reader did not exist, there were no such men. The real readers must have been gay men, or boys like Joel who were drawn to the life depicted in *man about town* for reasons they didn't yet understand. The editors must have known it: column after column was peppered with assurances that elegance was masculine, that you were cooking a seductive dinner for your lady friend, that you cared about clothes because the fairer sex wanted to see you looking your best. The anxious tone made Joel think of Fred Astaire or Cary Grant, men who had gone just exactly, to the micrometer, as far as a man could go without being called a pansy. That was the razor's edge on which *man about town* skated, only the Santa Fe boy buried in the back of the book hinting at the great deception.

Joel got to the fashion pages. Gray suits and golfing outfits. With the peacock look and Nehru jackets still a year or two away, how ever did they fill the clothing section month after month? Perhaps with oddities like the feature in this issue, a long, precious article on the glories of the seersucker suit. "Surely its foremost proponent was the memorably dapper Damon Runyon, who once said [continued 174] . . ."

He never had found out what Damon Runyon once said. Nor did he now. This was how it happened. Joel sitting in his room, a child reading an article about Damon Runyon's seersucker suits. Flipping as instructed to page 174, and never a child again.

He closed his eyes, opened them. He had never, he supposed, looked at the picture for more than a few stolen seconds at a time. Thirty years ago, guiltily peeking at it maybe a score of times in the few weeks before the magazine vanished, victim of one of his mother's cleaning frenzies. He waited for the June issue, but the ad wasn't there, nor in July, nor ever again.

Even at the time Joel had suspected that *man about town* had decided not to carry any more ads from Simms of Santa Fe, as if that little box of innocent flesh somehow sullied the last pages of the magazine. He was sure of it now, having read through this issue: someone was distressed about what the ad implied about the typical reader and excised it. Just as, a few years ago, the management at *GQ* suddenly realized who was buying their swimsuit issue and remade the whole magazine to drive the faggots away.

So Joel had seen the Santa Fe boy for, cumulatively, a minute or two three decades earlier. He remembered the smile and the swimming trunks. He had not remembered the body.

Joel was inured now to the sight of men's bodies. In the underwear and perfume ads, in the videos and the magazines, everywhere now images of stupefyingly perfect men. It was hard to recover what he must have felt, encountering the Santa Fe boy so long ago. Really, the boy wasn't, by current standards, remarkable. His was not, like the bodies in the underwear ads, a wrought thing, end product of presses and crunches and steroids. The belly was flat, but not a washboard; the chest and shoulders and arms were powerful but not enormous. The front of his trunks was flat, without today's obligatory bulge, natural or enhanced.

The body was not perfect, it was merely beautiful. Which must have been enough to astonish Joel back then. He mustn't, until he turned to page 174, have known there was even such a thing as a beautiful man. There were handsome men, tall, strong, with cleft chins and broad shoulders. But the sultry open grace of the Santa Fe boy defied everything a man was supposed to be like, and opened to Joel's vision everything a man wasn't supposed to see. Joel hadn't just stumbled upon something he in particular wasn't supposed to see, wasn't supposed to know about. He had happened on what no one was ever supposed to know: no one was supposed to know that a man could be so vulnerably lovely, that his full arms could hang so loosely, candidly, that his pelvis could tilt just so, that a man could have a body every inch of which was an invitation.

An invitation, most basely, to kiss, to lick, to bury your face in those hips. All of those ways into it foredoomed: the touch of lips or flesh to flesh would only remind you that you were two different people, sealed in your separate sarcophaguses of skin, impermeable carapaces through which a soul could not pass. What he had wanted—wanted and would never get, he had known that even as a kid—was somehow to pass into those hips, enter through that intraversable route, and inhabit the body of the Santa Fe boy. Be at home in that body and smile the smile of the Santa Fe boy.

He could go to the gym. He could have gone to the gym at fourteen, or at twenty-four, he could go tomorrow morning and possibly—even at his age, with a patient trainer and hefty doses of testosterone, conceivably forge some passable facsimile of the body in the picture. But he would never stand the way the Santa Fe boy did, so proud, so innocent, never smile so broadly. As if his body were a gift he was giving. Here it is, that smile said, and isn't it something? He looked straight out at Joel, from a world where a body was a gift.

Joel must have known it was impossible the instant he first saw that picture. He had known what he would never get and had somehow understood—at fourteen, had seen so clearly— that nothing he could do or have or be would make up for that impossibility. And that he would never want anything else.

The boy had disappeared. Joel had been looking at him for so long he was just a bunch of black dots. Which was all he had ever been. Dots. Well, what was anybody? What was Sam, but a continuing series of sensory impressions, less orderly than the dots on this page, that Joel had somehow pieced together into a lover?

Just a picture, the boy was just a picture. A fragmentary image: you couldn't even see his knees, the likelihood that he had a back was an untestable hypothesis. Joel knew there was, or had once been, an actual Santa Fe boy. He stood in a room somewhere, under bright lights. The light bounced off him, through a lens, burned an image onto some film. Through some even less comprehensible process, the image was somehow turned into a pattern of dots, ink on a page. In Joel's very distant room, light hit the page and bounced into Joel's eyes. It was the white he saw. The black dots were the places from which no light was reflected. Absences: he conjured the Santa Fe boy from gaps in the light.

This was the kind of insight Joel had had the couple of times he dropped acid. Which was one of the reasons he only did acid a couple of times. The other being that the cheap hits he bought from the campus pusher were so laced with speed that he spent both trips racing along, about as paranoid as Richard Nixon. It was time for bed.

He glanced one more time at the picture. The smile wasn't quite as broad as he had thought. Maybe there was some sorrow, or at least tension, around the eyes—as if Joel could interpret the expression in eyes the size of a period. And maybe—you could hardly tell, but it was just possible—the boy wasn't looking straight out at the camera. No, he wasn't: he was looking off to one side, beyond the edge of the frame. As if he had been caught unaware; or as if he were receiving direction.

The boy was, yes, looking away. Smiling for the camera, but not looking at it. Only his body smiled straight at you.

Whether or not Joel was going to embark on the course of self-improvement Ron had mapped out for him, he could at least floss. Usually he flossed only in the last few days before a dentist's appointment. So when the dentist looked in his mouth and said reproachfully, "Have we been flossing?", he could answer, "Some."

He clicked on the TV in the bedroom and went to the bathroom to see if, through some oversight, Sam had left the floss behind. While he hunted through the jumble in the cabinet beneath the sink—Ajax, shoe polish, tanning lotion, abandoned stop-smoking programs, and a marital aid that he had never noticed before and that Sam certainly should have taken with him—he listened to the news. The local news, murders and fires and accidents and about ten minutes of weather.

There was some floss. Probably ten years old, but what could happen to floss? As he went back into the bedroom with it, the news broke for an ad.

A woman of about seventy put down her newspaper, looked at the screen, and shook her head. A kindly but puzzled smile on her echt-grandmother face. "Jim and I went through a lot. The depression, the war. Raising our kids. Good times and bad times, we worked hard and we stuck together. Jim's gone now, but he'd be so proud of the kids. The kids turned out fine, and my grandchildren! And one thing that really matters to me is that they don't have to worry about me, what would happen if I got sick. Because there's Medicare. It's not a giveaway, we earned it, all our working lives, and I've felt so secure. My kids, too, knowing they wouldn't have to worry about how they'd pay my bills."

She looked down at the newspaper, then up again. "But now I read that Medicare's in trouble. The way things are going, it might not be there for me. And one of the reasons is that it spends a billion dollars a year—one billion dollars!—paying for . . ." She glanced sideways, a little abashed. "Well, for young people who did dangerous things, when they ought to have known better. I'm awfully sorry if they're sick." Her brow furrowed; you could bet that, as soon as the ad was over, she

161

was going to pop right into the kitchen and make the poor young people some chicken soup. "But you know, it's not too much to ask that people take some responsibility for their lives. Jim and I always did, and we taught our children to live the same way." She shook her head again. "If they take Medicare away, we'll get by somehow, my kids will help out. But it isn't fair, when they've worked so hard, raising their own families. When they've done the right things all their lives. It just isn't right."

The screen went black. Then, in white letters: Citizens for Personal Responsibility. Whoever the hell they were. And an 800 number.

Joel had a late meeting at the Dirksen Building, with the Finance Committee chief of staff and a guy named Mullan from Senator Flanagan's office, who did health stuff for the minority. Joel was there on time, and Mullan, but the chief of staff was, they were told, in the conference room, just finishing up another meeting. They were left standing in the reception area, which deterred loitering by having no chairs, for ten or fifteen minutes.

Joel despised Mullan. The smart people on Flanagan's staff had decamped when the Republicans took the Senate and Flanagan lost the chairmanship. All that was left was Mullan, who was one of those managed-competition zealots. The kind who wanted to herd the elderly into private health plans. Once Joel had said, rather meekly, that it might be hard for old ladies with Alzheimer's to study a list of health plans and pick one. Mullan had just stared, trying to figure out if Joel was a socialist or an imbecile.

Today they didn't speak, just avoided each other—in a space the size of a powder room—as each tried to eavesdrop on the meeting that was ending. The conference room door was closed, all they could make out was murmuring and occasionally a sharp laugh from the chief of staff. This was reassuring: if you heard her swearing, business was still being transacted; if you heard laughter, the meeting was in the gossip stage, just about to break up.

Sure enough, the door opened and the chief of staff emerged, followed by no fewer than five pharmaceutical lobbyists. Joel knew all of them from their time on the Hill, and each said, "Hey, Joel," while filing past him. Nothing more; none paused to chat. They looked cowed; the meeting might have ended with laughter, but they hadn't got what they wanted.

The Ice Maiden, people called her, with her austere Shaker outfits and her hair in a bun. This was archaically sexist, Joel knew, but even senators called her the Ice Maiden. Even senators were a little afraid of her.

Cordelia, as senators called her to her face, looked over at Joel and Mullan, but didn't say hello. She was just registering that they were there, and that this meant she had a Medicare meeting she had forgotten about. "Oh," she said. She led them into the conference room and they waited while she riffled through her organizer, one of those complicated binders with a million to-do lists and project-tracking tables and little inserts with inspirational quotes on them:

The really efficient laborer will be found not to crowd his day with work, but will saunter to his task surrounded by a wide halo of ease and leisure.   *Henry David Thoreau*

While she tried to figure out their task—she couldn't just ask—Mullan said, "What was that about?"

"What?" she said.

"That meeting?"

She didn't answer, just looked at him with an expression that would have said to any sentient creature: If you were supposed to know what it was about, you would have been in the room, wouldn't you?

Mullan didn't read expressions. "All those drug people. Was this that tax credit?"

"No." She closed her binder.

"Because the senator was very interested in that . . ." Mullan looked over at Joel and finished, warily: "That thing we were talking about."

As if Joel cared about tax credits for pharmaceutical companies. Though Senator Flanagan, being from New Jersey, would care profoundly. All the signs you saw from the train while riding through New Jersey: it was like reading the labels in someone's medicine cabinet.

To assure Mullan that he hadn't been cut out of anything, Cordelia had to divulge, "It was about the child health plan. They're trying to kill it."

"The drug people?"

"Haven't they been talking to you?"

"Um . . . no."

"They will." Cordelia closed her binder triumphantly; she had figured out what they were there for. "Rural hospitals," she announced.

"Right," Mullan said, wearily.

"We need to go over all these technical amendments. Um . . . do you all have copies?"

"No."

"Oh. Me, either. I'll be right back."

She left to dig up her amendments. Mullan rolled his eyes, and even Joel kind of had to feel for him. What did he care about rural hospitals? There weren't any rural hospitals in New Jersey, because technically there weren't any rural areas in New Jersey. Somehow every place in New Jersey was a suburb of someplace else in New Jersey.

After they'd waited a couple of minutes, they could hear Cordelia's voice. She was back in her office, talking on the phone. Joel and Mullan shook their heads. She had gone to get the amendments and she had taken a goddamn phone call.

They might be on Medicare themselves before this meeting was concluded.

Mullan got the *Wall Street Journal* out of his briefcase. Joel hadn't brought anything to read. Well, last week's *The Nation*, but it wouldn't do for Mullan to see impartial, nonpartisan Joel reading a commie rag like *The Nation*.

Joel looked at the pictures of the chairman on the wall. It was interesting: his wig was of a different color in different pictures, but not in any clear chronological sequence. That is, it wasn't black during the Nixon years, salt-and-pepper during Reagan, gray during Bush. Instead, he seemed to grow older and younger at random. Possibly the black-hair periods coincided with his several rumored affairs. Joel found himself, queasily, visualizing the chairman *in flagrante*, when Mullan said, "Why would the drug companies care about the child health plan?"

Joel shrugged. He hadn't been following the child health plan, it wasn't his area. He just knew from the papers that the chairman, who apparently would think nothing of throwing an eighty-year-old Russian immigrant from a moving train, wanted to expand children's health insurance. You could say "child" to a politician with a heart as big as, say, Strom Thurmond's, and he'd just melt. In a budget plan that hacked away at every social program enacted since the Cleveland administration, the Republicans had set aside two billion to cover uninsured kids. Joel wondered when they'd get around to providing health insurance for transvestite prostitutes with a little heroin problem. Probably they'd give insurance to puppies first.

Joel had never liked children much. Well, he liked them okay until they were two or three and could begin to articulate their world views; after that he would have been happy if somebody froze them and thawed them out when they were hot eighteen-year-olds. He understood in the abstract that they mattered, that it was important to school them and make sure they got their shots and their Ritalin so they could grow up to be productive adults and keep the GDP humming along so maybe there would be a chance Joel could get his Social Security. He just didn't want to be anywhere near them. The most welcoming and cheering sign an establishment could have on its door was No Strollers.

It was fortunate, then, that he had never risen to those few occasions that might inadvertently have culminated in progeny. Nonetheless, he found himself more and more living in a paedocentric universe. Everywhere, he saw family restaurants, family entertainment, family communities. In Congress the word had become almost obligatory. Bills didn't have names like the Tax Cut for Major Contributors Act or the Pointless Subsidies for Superfluous Farmers Act anymore. Instead, they would have snappy titles like the Fair Shake for Working Families Act or the Family Farmers Emergency Protection Act. Joel would draft report language for some committee, and the staffer would cross out "people" every time it appeared and replace it with "families."

He knew he shouldn't take this personally. The word was merely a decorative flourish; only a few demagogues really wielded it like a knife, to divide the world into two classes, families-with-kids and deviants. Mostly the family-family-family was just nostalgia, or whistling in the dark, in an era when the average marriage went stale faster than the wedding cake—certainly faster than his and Sam's had. Still, whatever people meant by it, Joel got the message almost every waking hour: the whole point of human existence was to have children, make a family, pass your name on.

Maybe it was. Raymond J. (Joe) Harris, Jr., had sired Raymond III, not to mention Jennifer and Scott. Even Ron, before he escaped to Zippers, had dutifully produced the resentful and uncommunicative Ron Junior, who in turn would sooner or later overpopulate the back seat of his SUV. Raising his family, doing the right thing, as that grandmother on the

Citizens for Personal Responsibility ad had so sweetly put it. Something to show for his time on the planet, something to leave behind him besides a great many sweaters or the definitive collection of Deanna Durbin memorabilia. Some reason to have been here.

"Jeez, it's seven-thirty," Mullan said.

"Uh-huh. Can I borrow part of your paper?"

"No, look, I gotta go. Senator Flanagan doesn't care about all this rural shit, why don't you just tell her everything's okay with the minority?"

"You know, every dollar they give to a rural hospital comes from an urban hospital."

"What?" Mullan said.

"The way they do hospital payments is zero-sum. They give to Montana, they have to take from New Jersey."

"Oh." Mullan's eyes widened, possibly with a dawning understanding of how the American system of government worked. "Well, I have to leave anyway. I have to pick up my kids at my mother-in-law's. Tell her we'll just have to reschedule."

"You better tell her that," Joel said. "I've got no place I have to be."

Almost eight. Everybody would be gone from the Hill Club. Joel decided to stay over on the Senate side and get a bite at one of the joints on Massachusetts Avenue. He wound up at Corcoran's, the kind of bar that served buffalo wings and margaritas in ice-cream flavors and had junk hanging from the foam rafters—oars, photos of baseball teams with handlebar mustaches, war bond posters. Some queen must have assembled this stuff and sold it to bars by the wall-foot. Possibly the same source supplied the equally predictable bartender, a beefy straight boy in the uniform of pinstripe shirt, khakis, apron. The place wasn't crowded, but he found a million things to do before serving Joel: made a couple of blender drinks, rang up a check, changed the channel on the TV from the baseball game on ESPN to the baseball game on ESPN2, served somebody an order of nachos. All this probably took only a minute or two, but Joel felt himself flushing with anger, as if the guy were deliberately ignoring him. He made himself calm down; it wasn't as if he were going into the DTs. When at last the bartender appeared before him Joel asked very politely for a white wine. The bartender said, "Chardonnay?"

"Do you have anything else?"

"No."

Then why do you ask, Joel thought. He knew he was going to get his chardonnay from a two-gallon jug, but what did he expect, ordering wine in a prefabricated burger joint?

Actually, there was something he found soothing about places like Corcoran's, even though—or because—they operated with such utter indifference to his needs. He was about twenty years older than the target customer, he didn't drink beer, he didn't care which baseball game was on, as long as it wasn't so loud that he couldn't read the copy of *The Nation* he pulled out of his briefcase. No one would cruise him here— or rather, fail to; no one would even talk to him. He was just a faceless middle-aged man who would be having a few drinks and a burger.

After his second wine, he ordered what they called an elephant burger and went back to *The Nation*. Maybe he could be a responsible citizen without finishing yet another article on the International Monetary Fund. Or the next, an inspiring piece about how to mobilize labor and bridge the gap between workers and social activists. He lit a cigarette, sipped his wine, and watched as the bartender mobilized himself enough to bring Joel silverware, ketchup, salt and pepper.

Joel felt kind of sorry for him. Maybe he did okay on tips, but he didn't have health care, retirement, any of that. If he'd had any brains, he would have joined a union, but he probably didn't see himself as a worker, more as a kind of performer.

When he got a little older, he wouldn't be the hunky ex-jock the demographics of this place dictated, he would be a middle-aged bartender. They'd kick him down to the day shift, where he'd mostly bus sandwiches instead of pulling drafts. Or they'd just find some reason to fire him, some larceny they were ready enough to overlook when he was still pulling in the customers.

Joel didn't feel sorry for him at all, this was all a way of feeling superior to him. Joel's 401(k) versus the bartender's muscles. Joel was a member of the New Class, the little privileged crust that spent its days analyzing and communicating and making heaps of money while the mass of men brought the silverware and ketchup. Of course Joel deplored this arrangement—hell, he read *The Nation*, didn't he?—he knew he shouldn't be paid outrageous sums to sit around in meetings that never even started, while this sucker brought him ketchup. He didn't even want to imagine how the people who actually made the ketchup must have lived.

Still, if there was going to be a New Class, he was glad to be in it. Just barely in it, maybe, but he didn't have to worry for a nanosecond about paying another, for Christ's sake, dollar fifty to add bacon to the elephant burger. More: he was glad that he was in the New Class and the bartender wasn't. That the bartender's goddamn Simms of Santa Fe body was at Joel's service. As if that made up for anything, as if Joel wouldn't have given his 401(k) to be that bartender for one instant.

Someone sat down on the stool to Joel's right. Joel glanced over. It was Senator Harris. Joel stammered, "Hi." Harris nodded curtly and looked away, fixed his gaze on the bartender to keep Joel from saying more. Of course he had no idea who Joel was; probably he was approached by his share of loonies.

Harris raised a finger, as if that would bring the bartender over. The bartender was busy churning up margaritas. How democratic, that he should ignore a senator as blithely as he did Joel. Except of course he didn't know it was a senator. Even so deeply inside the Beltway as this, people went about their business oblivious to the great personages who deigned to walk among them. And if the bartender had recognized Joe Harris, he wouldn't have been impressed, not half so much as if some relief pitcher had walked in.

Only Joel was impressed. He didn't stare, he kept his eyes straight ahead and nibbled at his elephant burger, trying not to look like a pig. But he felt a faint glow to his right. As if Joe Harris, a mental midget from a nothing state, gave off light. Why should he have felt Harris's presence so intensely? Some atavistic reverence for senators that had somehow persisted after years of observing at close hand their deep mediocrity? Or just that faint sexual stirring he had felt at their first encounter, his nearsighted libido somehow mistaking the man for Alex Rivers? Perhaps the two sentiments were not in fact distinguishable.

He ought to have hated the man. Here the guy had introduced a bill whose basic premise was that faggots should die in the streets. Probably he was not unacquainted with whatever shadowy forces financed the Citizens for Personal Responsibility. Harris apparently hated Joel; why couldn't Joel hate back? Maybe because, after so many years on the Hill, he didn't connect people with the noxious things they said and did. There were people, and there were issues, and there was no connection at all.

In the minutes before a hearing started, senators would trudge into the room, chat with one another or just take their places at the table. This one was measuring Sweet'n'Lo into his coffee and stirring it with childish concentration; this one was reading his schedule for the afternoon, slowly shaking his head with weariness and dismay; this one was whispering with his kneeling LA, trying to figure out what the hearing was about. Once the hearing began, the one who had been stirring his coffee might say the most poisonous things: he might propose mandatory life sentences for flag burners, or wonder what was so wrong with toxic waste anyway. Still it seemed to

170

Joel as if the words just came out of the man, as if he were possessed like the little girl in *The Exorcist*. And in a way he was: merely the mouthpiece for the accumulated anger or thoughtless greed of the people who had sent him here. Once Joel had seen a senator stirring his coffee, it was impossible to view him as the embodiment of evil, or even as an independent actor. He was just a schmo trying to get through the long days in a place where nothing good could ever possibly happen.

The bartender came over, finally. Harris barked: "Absolut martini, up, and I'll see a menu." The bartender looked at him with mild disdain, strolled away, and began to wash a few glasses in order to illustrate that barking was not an effective motivational tool. Joel peeked at Harris. His face was clenched; it relaxed slowly as, perhaps, he reminded himself that the cosmos was not on his payroll.

Joel wouldn't have guessed the Absolut martini. Not that he had any idea what people drank in Montana, but it complicated Harris somehow.

"Hey, pal," Harris said, turning toward Joel. "What is that?"

Joel was almost too thrilled to speak. "It's the elephant burger. They also have a donkey burger."

"Sure. What's the difference?"

"The elephant burger has blue cheese and the donkey burger has Monterey jack."

"Uh-huh. And it comes with the fries?"

"Yes, sir." The "sir" just automatic, but it betrayed that Joel knew who Harris was.

Harris acknowledged this: "Well, I guess I'll cross party lines and have me a donkey burger."

Joel smiled vapidly at the little joke. Harris's martini arrived. "Donkey burger, medium rare," he said to the bartender. He turned back to Joel and raised his glass. "Thanks, pal."

Joel was emboldened to say, "I'm Joel Lingeman from OLA. I briefed you a couple months ago. About immigrants and Medicare?"

"Oh. Oh, sure," Harris said, certainly not recalling him. "That was very helpful, uh . . ."

"Joel."

"You're always, OLA, you're always very helpful. You know, some of this stuff is pretty complicated; I'm impressed you guys know so much."

Joel shrugged. "Well, you know, we specialize. You're the guys who have to know everything."

Harris nodded, frowning a little to suggest what a burden it was to have to know everything. It was impossible to overtax a senator's tolerance for sycophancy. "You know, I've got a Medicare bill in myself."

"Yes, sir. I . . . uh, I helped draft it."

"Oh, did you?"

"Well, I mean, Melanie drafted it, I just made a few comments."

"Sure. We appreciate your help."

"Yes, sir."

Harris glanced at the open magazine to the left of Joel's plate, squinted a little. Joel put his arm over it. Probably Harris already suspected that anyone working for OLA was an undercover leftist; he didn't need to see that Joel was reading *The Nation*.

"I was wondering," Joel said. "What got you interested in that issue?"

"Hm?"

"AIDS and all?"

"Oh. I was just—I read an article somewhere, about how they, you know, the gays, started doing stuff again. This article said they stopped for a while, but then they started again."

"I guess I heard that," Joel said. About them, the gays.

"So if they want to kill themselves, fine. But I don't see why families should have to pay for it."

If they had been in Harris's office, Joel would have nodded. But they were in a bar, they were talking to each other like normal people. "Well, you know, here I am having this glass of wine, and for all I know I might get cirrhosis some day."

"What? Oh, I see."

"I mean, I guess we all do some risky things. And they might cost Medicare money sooner or later."

Harris nodded. "I see what you're saying. That's interesting." Joel was elated and amazed. Maybe Harris really was, as Melanie had said, educable. Joel was about to lead him gently into Lesson Two when his donkey burger came.

"Gosh, look at the size of that thing," Harris said. Joel wondered if he naturally said "Gosh" or if he monitored himself all the time, even here where no one could hear him. No one who counted.

"Probably full of cholesterol," Joel said. "Sooner or later Medicare will pay for that."

Harris didn't answer, didn't even look at Joel, just frowned a little as he poured ketchup on his fries. It was just a joke, Joel wanted to say, but he knew he had gone too far. The senator would decide when jokes were to be made. Still not looking at Joel, he said, "There's a difference between eating a burger and . . . doing the things they do." He lifted his burger, but didn't bite into it at once, just looked at it for a few seconds, puzzled.

Joel was through with his own burger, and he had recovered from the momentary delusion that he could single-handedly transform this moronic bigot. Eight-thirty, and he had had only a few glasses of wine; a splendid night to head to Zippers and see if he could, at last, find somebody who wanted to do stuff. The stuff *they* had stopped doing and were now doing again. He signaled the bartender for the check.

Harris grunted. His mouth was full of donkey burger. When he had swallowed, he said, "Hey, stick around, let me get you another drink."

"Um . . . thanks." He couldn't say no; when in twenty years on the Hill had a senator offered to buy him a drink?

"The family's already in Montana for the summer, and I can't get out of here till the August recess."

"Right."

"So the house is empty."

"Uh-huh." This was, Joel knew, an insufficient response to this sudden, almost embarrassing intimacy. My house is empty, too, he might have said; I'm lonesome, too.

Harris took another enormous bite of his burger. While he chewed he peeked at Joel, looked away again. Peeked: as men peeked at Zippers, the series of millisecond glances that preceded a pick-up.

Could he possibly have been gay? Or at least on the edge? God knows it wasn't unprecedented for a closet queen to compensate by publicly attacking homosexuals. Roy Cohn. J. Edgar Hoover. Robert Bauman, the congressman who had practically invented the use of "family" as a weapon. Until it was revealed that, after a hard day of fag-baiting, he would go and get drunk at the Chesapeake House while feeling up the go-go boys. Maybe it was even a rule: maybe if a politician spent his time lashing out at queers, he was declaring himself.

"Do you mind if I smoke?" Joel said.

"No, no, go right ahead."

No way: Harris raised not the tiniest blip on Joel's radar. All of those others—once you found out, you could see it. The fussiness, the languor, the effortful heartiness; you should have known all along. Harris was just a straight guy whose family was gone, whose empty house was way the hell out in Virginia, who was amusing himself talking to a pushy nonentity in a theme bar.

Harris said, "I don't know if you should get Medicare."

Joel was alarmed; it took him a second to realize Harris was talking about the smoking. Echoing Joel's own little joke.

"Oh," Joel said. "Actually, I'm saving you money."

"How's that?"

"Somebody figured this out: smokers cost more for medical

care, but they don't live long enough to take out of Social Security everything they paid in."

"No kidding."

"It's probably true about people with AIDS, too." This was about as close as Joel had ever come to calling a senator an idiot to his face. And he wasn't sure it was so. What if Harris called tomorrow and wanted the numbers? Memo to himself: do not have three glasses of wine and chat with a redneck senator about AIDS.

Harris, though, seemed to be thinking. He gobbled a few fries, shook his head, and said, "It doesn't matter, it isn't the money."

A chance to hedge. "I wasn't sure about the money anyway."

Harris waved the money away. "I don't care about the money. It's just . . . I don't know, maybe they're born that way, maybe they can't help it. I don't want to put them in prison or anything. I just don't think they deserve anything special. Like we don't have to give them some kind of prize. You understand?"

Joel said, quietly, but he could not keep from saying: "Giving people health care when they're dying isn't exactly a prize." A career-ending remark. While he waited for the explosion, he wondered when he had last updated his résumé.

Amazingly, Harris just shrugged. "You're entitled to your opinion."

"I'm sorry. I'm not supposed to have an opinion."

"Hey, you can't help but have an opinion. Listen, we're just in a bar, talking. It's okay. I guess we'll find out what the American people think."

After they had seen the ads. Harris must have known who was paying for them, who the Citizens for Personal Responsibility were. If he hadn't shot off his mouth he might have gotten Harris to tell him.

"I think I'm going to get some coffee," Harris said. "You?"

"I can't drink coffee this late. Anyway, I need to be getting home."

175

Harris nodded. "You got kids?"

"No."

Now Harris turned to look straight at him. "You married?"

"Um . . ." This was when Joel was supposed to strike a blow for honesty and understanding. Look, I'm gay, he was supposed to say, and we just had a normal conversation. If that's what they'd had. See, we're not like you think. "Divorced," Joel said.

"Oh. Well, then, what's your hurry? This was interesting."

"I . . . I've got sort of a date."

"Ah." Harris winked. "Then you'd better be shoving off."

"Yes, sir. It was good talking to you, sir."

"You, too. Don't do anything I wouldn't do."

Joel weighed the chances that if he went to Zippers, he would be presented with an opportunity to do something Harris wouldn't do. They were slim, and he was tired. Maybe he would just rent a video Harris wouldn't rent. Or that Harris would rent: how was Joel to know? Maybe the man was passing after all, maybe he had even been trying—as hard as he could, without blowing his cover—to pick Joel up. If you looked closely enough, you could find the signs in anyone. Weren't Harris's suits a little too flashy for a straight boy from Montana, wasn't his hair just too perfect? But if these things spelled g-a-y, how come Joel was such a slob?

Joel wanted Harris to be gay because that would account for his animus, his nasty bill: all about self-hatred. All about punishing people who did what he couldn't do, because he couldn't face himself or because he had made a calculated decision to live a lie so he could be a senator. This was a satisfying way of explaining the world. There were others: Harris was jealous because gay people didn't have kids and could party without looking for a babysitter. Modern straight men were uncertain of their masculinity and were threatened by gay men. It was all Cardinal so-and-so's fault, because he failed to speak out against gay-bashing and so fomented an atmosphere of . . .

There had to be a reason, some pathology. It couldn't be that happy and well-adjusted straight people were just plain bewildered by Joel Lingeman, bewildered and disgusted. To admit that would be to say that he was still bewildered and disgusted by himself.

Which he was, maybe. He knew it: some part of him had never really gotten over it, had never expelled the poison that had been fed to him—that he had swallowed eagerly enough—when he was a kid. He didn't believe anymore in the tooth fairy or the dangers of touching doorknobs, he still believed the ugly things he had been taught about himself. And if he still felt in his gut that being gay was wrong and sick, how could he expect vacuous Joe Harris to have heroically thought his way through to some other conclusion?

Twenty years out of that morass and he was sinking into it again. Because he wasn't getting any. This was why he had been chewing so much on his boyhood lately. Trying to imagine that there had been something else he wanted, something more elevated than sucking and fucking and whatever other stuff Harris had heard *"they"* were doing again. Something transcendent. Just because he was alone, Sam was gone and he wasn't getting his rocks off. Telling himself again, the way he used to when he struck out twenty years ago, that he didn't belong in the gay world, that he wasn't anything like those creepy faggots who had turned up their faggoty noses at him.

He needed to get over this. He needed to do whatever had to be done—even find a new barber—and get over it.

Yet: before he went to bed, Joel looked at the Santa Fe boy. He had taken to doing this, the last few nights. He looked at the Santa Fe boy before he turned out the light, the way other people said prayers.

177

There was a text, to which he hadn't paid much attention.

NEW! LO-RISE RACING TRUNKS.
Swim, lounge, or cruise. Quick-
drying nylon, dashing contour fit.
Colors: white, gold, aqua, loden,
contrasting stripe. S-M-L. 6.99
plus 50¢ shipping per order.

SIMMS OF SANTA FE. P.O. Box
5743, Santa Fe 2, New Mex. Phone
orders: LLoyd 5-1719.

Of course at fourteen he wouldn't have understood the code word "cruise." Probably he must have wondered just exactly where someone would keep a boat in Santa Fe, New Mexico. For he was always quite sure the boy actually lived in New Mexico. That if he went to Santa Fe, the boy would be there, hanging out at the back of the Simms store, or maybe in the parking lot washing his Mustang or his Corvette. He was a creature whose only function in life was to be beautiful in New Mexico—to swim, lounge, and somehow cruise. Somewhere nearby was Mr. Simms. Just outside the picture frame: maybe it was Simms the boy was looking at, instead of straight at the camera.

On the block where Joel grew up there was for a little while a man who owned a Rolls-Royce. Joel's neighborhood was solidly middle class, not wealthy; it was remarkable that there should have been a Rolls-Royce parked right down the street. Joel never, not that he could recall, saw the man who owned it, a Mr. Ryder. But he did sometimes see a boy washing and polishing it, or two boys. In their late teens, probably—they would have seemed like grown-ups to Joel—and hoody: duck-tail haircuts, cigarette packs in the rolled-up sleeves of their T-shirts. He spoke to them only once. They let him sit in the back seat of the Rolls-Royce, open the little bar, wonder at the burled wood and the leather. They told him that they lived in the house with Mr. Ryder. No, he was not their father, not their uncle.

When Joel got home he told his mother all about it; she said that he must never go anywhere near those boys again. A few months later Mr. Ryder, his car, and the boys who lived with him were gone. Joel was well into adulthood before it dawned on him exactly why two delinquent-looking youths should have lived with a man to whom they were not related and who had a Rolls-Royce. But he knew, just from the vehemence with which his mother warned him away, that there was something special about that ménage, something scary and alluring. Even after Mr. Ryder had moved away and a . . . normal family had moved in, the house always seemed haunted to Joel. He wished to heaven he had ignored his mother and gone inside. He wished it even now. How different his life might have been if, at eight or nine or whatever he was, he had gone into that house and learned everything.

This must have been in his mind when he looked at the Santa Fe boy and thought about Mr. Simms. He could not have formed the concept that the boy was being kept. But he knew that something forbidden and exciting was going on in New Mexico. Something hinted at by those few words accompanying the picture. A message from a mysterious place where beautiful men wore tiny garments, lo-rise and with a dashing contour fit, and lounged in the sun under the protective eye of Mr. Simms. There was another place.

The true prince has been sequestered in the tower; the gruff but kindly guard brings lunch. When the prince cuts into his blackbird tart he finds . . . a note! *Do not despair.* That is all it says: nothing about how he will be rescued, or by whom. Only that there is a world outside the walls and that someone out there is already planning his escape.

The *Today* show was on while Joel shaved. He heard the weatherman—he couldn't tell by listening if it was the fat white guy or the fat black guy—say that everyone should count their blessings and send their prayers to the Lord on behalf of the good people of Okumchee. The fat white guy, then, always a moment of piety before he started the commercial. Where was Okumchee, and how had the Lord made known His displeasure with its people? Tornadoes, locusts, drought?

Count his blessings. He made a lot of money, some multiple of what the hunky bartender at Corcoran's made. He was healthy, if pudgy. He had a roof over his head. He—

Maybe it was just too abstract. At the Thanksgiving table, when the same injunction was issued, you could at least survey the hypertrophied bird and its attendant vegetables and literally count the dishes, the rich harvest bestowed on you by the god Safeway that you were going to eat up this very minute. While the blessings Joel was counting up now were ongoing states of being. Or negative states, really: he was not homeless. He never got AIDS. He wasn't blind or lame or certifiably crazy. Of course, if you went on in this way, there would be no end of blessings to count. Hurray, I'm not in Bangladesh, or even Okumchee! Lookit, four, count them, four limbs!

After the commercial, they had the Vice President on, describing a bunch of initiatives. Lately the White House had been trotting out the Vice President every time they wanted to announce a piece of pork, so that people would remember him as Santa Claus when it came his turn to run. Disaster relief for Okumchee. Toxic waste treatment for Nevada. As if all these things were his idea. He wound up talking about something so wacky it could very well have been his idea. Biotechnology innovation zones. Companies would get some kind of tax credit if they did biotech research and manufacturing in places like Newark.

Right. All those unemployed biochemists loitering on street corners would drop their quart bottles of Colt 45, troop into the shiny new labs, and start collecting stock options while they combined snake and human genes so people with psoriasis could shed their skins. Katie Couric listened with undisguised boredom and then asked him about his cat.

Oh. This was that . . . that *thing* Mullan and the chief of staff were mentioning, the break for the pharmaceutical companies that Joel wasn't supposed to hear about. All wrapped up as some kind of welfare-to-work proposal. The companies would build something in the ghetto or the barrio they were going to build anyway. The workers would come in on the train, they'd be met at the station by an armored car labeled Merck or Glaxo, they'd toil away in the bunkers, they'd scurry home to the suburbs at night and the drug companies would get to write off all their profits. Nifty.

Joel was always stupidly thrilled when the news covered something he already knew about. He would say to Sam: "That bill they're talking about. I worked on that." Sam would say, "Uh-huh," strangely unimpressed, wait politely until the story was over, and then turn the channel.

The Vice President's cat had had kittens. Great. Maybe they'd be eligible for the child health insurance plan.

Huzzah, he thought, as he walked down Q Street to the Metro. I have four limbs and lunch money. I sit in important meetings and am privy to the innermost workings of the corporate welfare system. The fog is burning off and it's going to be a beautiful day.

All of this was true. In the immeasurable ocean of suffering that was the world, how tiny Joel's complaints were. He ought to have been ashamed of himself, he ought to have practically danced down Q Street on his way to the Metro every morning. And the homeless guys he stepped over ought to have been happy they weren't in Calcutta.

He knew that his discontent—and that of all the fat, desolate Americans around him—had something or other to do with their loss of faith. But he couldn't just turn into . . . Willard, that was the weatherman's name, beaming pious

Willard, who knew the world was wonderful and people were wonderful and God was in Heaven and one day Willard would be up there giving the unchanging celestial weather report.

Here was the truth: because Joel did not believe in Paradise, an eternal life, he was left believing in New Mexico. To be there with the Santa Fe boy, swimming, lounging, cruising forever. Just dwelling with him, as so many people have dreamt of a timeless dwelling with the altogether less attractive and unsmiling deity they have conjured up. Joel at least had incontrovertible evidence that the Santa Fe boy existed. Or that he had existed once. More than anyone could say about Jesus.

For an eternity they would wash his Mustang, each of them wearing his little lo-rise trunks, then take a dip in the pool to cool off, pop a couple of brews and lie in the sun. They wouldn't touch. But he would look over at Joel from his chaise longue, raise his hips and adjust his wet trunks, lie back. Still looking at Joel, that sad impenetrable smile dawning on his face. Joel would smile back. They would not touch. For ever, Joel would live in that moment that was so much more intense than mere touching, that instant when you knew you were going to touch.

Through aeons he would be with Him in Santa Fe and would be about to touch Him.

Santa Fe. Holy faith.

six

Ron was a lawyer, so Joel thought he'd know the name of a detective.

"What's up?" Ron said. "You're going to have Sam followed?"

Joel glanced around. No one at the Hill Club seemed to have heard. "Of course not. There's just someone I'm trying to locate."

"Who?"

"I— Well, you know, I'm still trying to settle my mother's estate. And there was this one kind of personal thing she wanted to leave to an old friend. So I'm trying to track down this person."

"Isn't there a lawyer handling all this?"

"Yeah, but this—it wasn't something in the will, it was something my mother told me."

Joel waited for a bolt of lightning. None came; most of civilization consists of lies about the dead.

"So, anyway, you know any detectives?"

"Um, a few. Let me . . ." There was a silence while, presumably, Ron flipped through his mental Rolodex. "Why don't you try this guy named Bate. Gordon Bate. I think that'd be the best one for you."

"He's good, huh?"

"He's . . . a little less like a detective. Call me tomorrow, I'll get you his number. Or he must be in the book."

"Okay. Are these guys expensive?"

"Relative to what?"

Relative to just taking the picture out one more time, gazing at it for a minute, and tearing it up. "I mean, do they charge by the hour or . . ."

Ron wasn't listening, he was staring over Joel's shoulder. Joel turned to see what might have transfixed him. Sure enough, a boy of stupefying beauty had inexplicably stumbled into the Hill Club. He sat alone at a table and read the specials on the blackboard, his lips moving only a little. Joel thought: five, maybe ten minutes, and Ron would be sitting at that table. Or, more probably, Ron would be told to scram; the guy might as well have had "straight" tattooed on his forehead. But Ron would at least try, while Joel sighed and made a beeline for the only vacant stool at the bar.

"Hello, hello, hello." Francis, the ex-seminarian, was especially manic this evening, as if he had skipped a dose of whatever kept him out of St. Elizabeth's. Joel thought of escaping, but a stool was a stool. "What's new?" Francis said, with an urgency that meant he had some terrific news of his own to spill.

"Not much," Joel said. Then, just to get it over with, "What's new with you?"

"We-e-e-ll. I've been— Mercy!"

"What?"

"There is a positive angel at that table by the window."

"Uh-huh."

Francis went on looking for a few seconds, then shook his head and turned away. Frowning, as if beauty made him angry.

Well, beauty made Joel angry sometimes. He thought again of destroying the picture, and felt a brief homicidal thrill. Some part of Joel did want to annihilate the Santa Fe boy. The way he smiled, smiled with his whole body: who would not wish to obliterate such a smile, shred the little swatch of paper that was the only evidence of his mocking existence? And why shouldn't Francis, biting his lip and staring at the bar, savor a momentary vision of, say, hurling a firebomb at that table by the window? Where a creature whose very existence was somehow a reproach sat innocently, trying to decide between a burger and a cheese steak.

"So," Francis said. "Are you in touch with Sam at all?"

"I hear from him once in a while." This wasn't so, Sam hadn't called in weeks. Possibly because of an annoying habit Joel seemed to have developed, of crying over the phone.

"Is he still with that kid?"

"Kevin. I guess." Speaking of candidates for annihilation.

Francis leaned in so close Joel could see the veins in his eyes. "They say he beats Sam up."

"What?"

"That's what I heard from somebody. I don't know."

Should Joel credit this not altogether ungratifying bit of intelligence? Amplified, probably, in its transit on the wires of rumor, so that what might have been one spontaneous blow became the ongoing "beats Sam up." He couldn't, really, picture it happening even once. Trying, he got only a cartoon: Kevin's skinny arm thrust forward, Sam reeling and bouncing back like an inflatable punch-me doll. Kevin was expressionless, not angry; Sam was wide-eyed but kept bouncing back.

"Sam wouldn't let somebody beat him up," Joel said. "I mean, he'd leave."

"Maybe so."

Joel had no idea if it was so. Fifteen years with somebody,

185

you ought to know everything about them. But hitting Sam was an experiment Joel had never conducted. Maybe Sam just took it, accepted the occasional—slap? punch?—as the price of Kevin. Affordable, unlike whatever price he couldn't go on paying for Joel.

Or maybe it was part of what Sam wanted: not a bad habit offset by the kid's many virtues, but an integral part of Kevin's appeal. Under the languor and the childlike freshness Joel had seen the day they visited, some ferocity. Joel could understand, in the abstract, that it would be exciting to be with a man who could potentially hit you. But only if it were merely potential. And even then: to spend your time avoiding any word or deed that could provoke it—it would be the same as being hit all the time.

Could this be what Sam had always wanted? Not to be hit, necessarily. But to be with someone so aware of him, someone who felt the frictions and snags of being with him so intensely as to have to strike out. Someone who paid that much attention to him. Instead of, say, blithely going on for months unaware that he was cheating.

Joel didn't think people could get through fifteen years paying that kind of attention, caring that much.

"Look who's sitting with that boy," Francis said.

On his way out, Joel picked up the gay paper to do his weekly scan of the ads. He skimmed through them on the Metro and was done by the second or third stop. Practically all repeats this week, and none of the handful of new contestants in the Win-a-Night-with-Joel competition had submitted the winning jingle.

He flipped to the front part of the paper. He usually skipped this section, all the solemn stories about which candidate the Eleanor Roosevelt New Democrats were endorsing for Registrar of Wills, or the latest standings in the Mid-Atlantic lesbian shot-put tournament. This week, though, they had a big headline: WHO IS CPR? Followed by an article that was mostly a list of all the people who might have known but who hadn't returned the reporter's calls by press time.

The ad Joel had seen had aired a few more times, in DC, a few other markets. And another ad Joel hadn't seen, apparently the obverse of the first: a young couple worried about Mom. These little dramas were the only traces of the mysterious Citizens for Personal Responsibility. The paper assumed that it was some kind of religious right group, like the Family Research Council or the Traditional Values Coalition. But there was something funny about it. No spokesman, for one thing: usually these groups were fronted by eerily juvenile-looking men with waxy complexions and prominent eyelashes. CPR was faceless, and—even more suspicious—it wasn't raising any money. What kind of organization never passed the plate and could afford ads that were a full sixty seconds long? An organization whose members also belonged to the Fortune 500. But which industry cared about . . . ?

In a sidebar, there were statements by famous gay leaders. Famous in the sense that, when Joel saw their names, he recalled having seen their names before: Geoff Pfeiffer, Adrienne Broom. They were the people who were called when statements were needed. Some were attached to organizations; Adrienne Broom, for example, was the public affairs director of the Association for Lesbian and Gay Advancement and Education. ALGAE: wasn't that the group that kept pushing for hate crimes reporting, on the theory that if you counted something it would go away? Or were they the people who thought that, when lesbians broke up, courts should arrange joint custody of the cats? Geoff Pfeiffer, on the other hand, was identified merely as "activist." Suggesting that he got out of bed every morning and embarked on a day of furious, purposeful activity. Joel supposed that made him a passivist.

Geoff thought gays, lesbians, transgendered and transfigured persons should boycott the TV stations that had aired the ads. Adrienne thought her organization might run counter-ads, and offered an address to which concerned readers could mail their checks. Claude pointed out that gay people were often quite close to their mothers and cared as much about preserving Medicare as anybody else. Absolutely, Joel thought. They ought to get Andrew as poster boy: he was so fond of old people he had acquired a second set.

The spokespersons speculated about CPR, they wondered what might have motivated an apparently affable man like Harris to introduce his awful bill. No one offered the simple explanation. That it was about personal responsibility. That, to a man from Montana, where people got by on nuts and berries, there was honestly something disturbing about the spectacle of people partying—pumping themselves up, dropping a few chemicals, getting it on in open defiance of every recommended precaution—and then handing Uncle Sam the bill.

The leaders didn't talk about this. They didn't even allude to those kids who were reckless and self-destructive—some of them even trying to get sick, as if seropositivity were a Boy Scout merit badge. Nor did they offer the argument Joel had tried on Harris the other night. That once you started down this line, there was no end to it: smokers, drinkers, eaters of elephant or donkey burgers, the sedentary, the choleric. All kinds of weak people, giving in to temptations and incurring future bills. The leaders must have known what the answer would be when they lobbied the congressmen who were willing to talk to them, the answer that would show up in CPR's counter-counter-ad. "There's a difference between eating a burger and . . . doing the things they do." The twisted diseased things they did, all those beautiful boys on the—what did they call it? The circuit, as if they were vaudevillians doing the round of the Orpheum theaters.

Joel didn't know anybody who went to circuit parties, he had only read about them. Wistfully: what must it have been like to be young and buffed and flying off every weekend to whatever city was hosting the white party or the black party or the masque-of-the-red-death party? He would have gone. The only reason he wasn't having unsafe sex was because he wasn't having any sex at all. And if he did, if he got his rocks off and then paid the viral price? He was forty-five. He could go wham at the office any day now. Or he could, if infected, live something close to a normal life span, whatever the actuaries would say was normal for a man with his many unhealthy proclivities.

Joel wasn't any more responsible than anybody else. Why should he be: to whom was he responsible, what was he here for? The only responsible person he knew was poor Andrew Crawford, rushing home to take the calls from a couple of people with incipient senile dementia who probably thought he was their sainted son. Only Andrew thought he knew what he was here for.

Did you have to be invited to circuit parties or did you just sort of show up?

Joel did not destroy the picture. He carried it in an envelope in his inside coat pocket as, at lunch hour, he went to meet Bate.

Bate was expensive. They had established this over the phone. He cost, per diem, about what Joel might have had to spend to get an escort to stay with him per noctem. Which would have been crazy, but more rational than hiring a detective to find the Santa Fe boy.

He was doing something crazy. After so many years of being balanced, like a checkbook whose stubs add up. He went to work and pretty much did his job, he paid his rent, if he talked to himself on a public thoroughfare he did so in a low, conversational tone that bothered hardly anyone. Now he found himself doing something demented. He didn't feel high or agitated, he just felt that he was doing the next thing. Today it's a little chilly and I should zip the liner into my raincoat.

Today I should do something about that CD that's about to roll over. Today I should find a detective who will help me locate the Santa Fe boy. He giggled. People on the Metro looked at him.

Back before Sam, Joel used to get up some mornings, serve a trick coffee, get him out the door, and then *go to work*. He didn't know which seemed more implausible now: having tricks or being able to get up after about ninety minutes' sleep and go to the office. Anyway, he'd arrive at the office and get on the elevator and look around at the gray faces and think: I have a secret. I have this whole other life you know nothing about and that would shock you to your bones.

He had forgotten this. Of course it was better to be out, he had not forgotten the grind of dissimulation, evading match-makers, feigning interest in women he and a straight friend passed on the street, eschewing pink shirts, and trying not to hold his cigarette funny. But there had been, he remembered now, the compensatory thrill of having the great secret and knowing that it made him a million times more real and alive than anyone else in the building.

He smiled at the people on the Metro. You wouldn't believe what I'm on my way to do.

Bate was in one of those L Street office buildings from the sixties whose style would probably be classed in the architectural histories as Parsimonious. Every feature, from the ceiling height to the light fixtures to the printed wood-pattern plastic on the elevator doors, was dictated by cost-per-square-foot calculations. The directory behind the unguarded front desk was the typical mix of periodontists and obscure lobbying groups—the Farmgrown Catfish Association, that sort of thing. Bate was in 526.

A small gold-look plate said Bate Agency and, in slightly larger letters, Please Knock. Joel did, and a voice he recognized as Bate's called, "Just a minute." He didn't have a receptionist, so he had to be pretty small-time. Could he find a missing person? Well, how hard could it be to find somebody in this world where merchants and hospitals and banks and political parties exchanged enormous dossiers on each of us? Joel felt as though it were all but done, they had practically found the boy already.

Bate looked as though he himself were in the process of disappearing. He was tiny, wearing a gray suit he might have bought in the boys' department, and bald.

"Mr. Lingeman?" he said.

"Uh-huh."

"You're a little early."

This wasn't so. Joel had walked around the block three times to avoid being early. But he said, "Oh. Should I come back?"

"No, no. If you don't mind watching me eat." Bate stood aside and admitted Joel to a one-room office that looked as though Bate's tenancy had begun twenty minutes earlier. There was nothing on the walls, nothing on the desk but a telephone and lunch, which consisted of a few tatters of lettuce in a plastic container and a bottle of water. At a right angle to the desk was a typing table with a Hermes portable identical to the one Joel had taken to college.

They sat down, Joel in the little visitor's chair, Bate in a grandiose vinyl executive throne that made him seem even smaller than he was. Joel could barely see around it to the window, which looked directly into an upper level of an open parking garage; he could almost have touched the cars.

"So," Bate said. He fussed at his salad with a plastic fork— didn't actually eat anything, just shuffled the leaves around, as if hunting for a prize. Finally he shoved the container aside and produced from a desk drawer a yellow legal pad and a ballpoint pen. He wrote Joel Lingeman and August 5 in a hand so large that he had already used half the page. "So. You're looking for somebody."

"Uh-huh."

A car with its headlights on careened around a corner in the garage, it looked as though it were about to plow into the office. In the glare Joel discovered that Bate was not in fact bald; he had a corona of preternaturally fine blond hair that seemed to float, like cloud cover, half an inch above his baby pink skull.

Bate waited, pen poised, for a name, or "my wife," something like that. Joel could only pull out the envelope, extract the little picture, mutely hand it over. Bate held it daintily, thumb and forefinger at the top, as if afraid of touching the almost naked body. "And who is this?" he said.

Joel almost said, the Santa Fe boy. Instead he gave the accurate answer: "I don't know."

Bate placed the picture on his desk. Which now contained, in a perfectly straight line, picture, pad, pen, salad, water bottle, and telephone. He regarded Joel for a while. Joel felt like an idiot. A deviant idiot, at that. But Bate didn't look at Joel as if he thought Joel was stupid or crazy or perverted. Rather as if Joel had told him something very sad. He made Joel sad, just for a second.

He folded his tiny hands on the desk and said, "This is an advertisement."

"That's right. I'm trying to find the person in the advertisement."

"Oh. Oh, I see. And where did this appear?"

"In *man about town.* May 1964."

"*man about town.* Do they even print that any more?"

"No."

"No, I didn't think I'd seen it." Bate put a hand over the picture, almost casually. "You don't know anything else about him?"

"Sorry."

Bate let the faint pencil line of his mouth droop into a frown. "Thirty years is a long time."

"So you think he's not going to be easy to find?"

"No, I'd guess it will be either easy or impossible. No, what

I meant was . . ." He bit his lip. "You know the man in this picture doesn't exist any more?"

"I'm sure he's changed," Joel said, quickly. Though of course that wasn't what Bate had said. "So, um, will you take the case?"

Another car squealed by. Bate shivered. "I need to— I'm sorry, you seem like an ordinary person, but this isn't a very ordinary request. So I have to ask: what are you going to do if I find him?"

"Nothing. Maybe just go see him. Once, I mean. I'm not going to stalk him or anything."

"Why do you want to see him?"

Joel couldn't explain, he couldn't explain it to himself. "I don't know. This is—" How could he have thought that he wouldn't be asked these questions? That he could just lay his money down and make his not very ordinary request and the man wouldn't wonder if he was a stalker or a murderer or . . . He should have thought of some answer. "I don't know, it seems silly. Maybe we should just forget the whole thing." He took the picture, started to slip it back into the envelope.

Bate watched him and must have concluded that, along with the picture, Joel was stuffing into the envelope a potentially large sum of money. "I'm going to need that," he said.

"Oh, of course." Joel had marred the picture, smeared the dots a little. Only on the torso, the face was still intact.

"If you want, we could go down to Kinko's and make a copy of it."

"That's okay." He would have liked a copy, but he didn't want Bate thinking he couldn't get through the days without looking at the Santa Fe boy.

Bate came out into the hall with him. As they were shaking hands, Joel saw under the fluorescent light that Bate had a mustache, almost white gold against his pale skin.

As he walked through the lobby, Joel heard again: "Thirty years is a long time." The walls were of that pocked pink-gray

193

stone they used in lobbies thirty years ago instead of the marble of today, a laser-cut veneer not as thick as the butter on Joel's morning toast. It occurred to him that the building must have been about coeval with the Santa Fe boy—that is, with the photograph, they were artifacts of the same era. He looked up at the building as he stepped outside. Yes, the milky blue glass and the brushed aluminum mullions, it might very well have been 1964. Architecture for the great society. A long time ago.

The interview with Bate had been so brief. If Joel got on the Metro right away, he could be back in the office without having been gone much more than an hour. Or he could stop and get a sandwich and be more emphatically late. No one in the office cared. August recess was just about to start, nothing was happening. Only his own compulsiveness made him feel guilty if he took sixty-one minutes for lunch.

He felt exponentially guilty as, already tardy, he ordered a full-sized cheese steak sub with everything on it. In one ear Sam was telling him he was getting too fat, in the other his mother was telling him he was late for the office; if he had had more ears there would have been one to hear—from whom?—that his pursuit of the Santa Fe boy was . . . breaking what rule? All the rules that had been beaten into him and that he violated, and he had no precept to cover this situation, except maybe a general guideline against doing things that were crazy. What he was doing was crazy but not wrong. There was no rule that said a man couldn't try to learn where another man was. If he actually knocked on the guy's door, that might be a minor trespass of some sort, a violation of some right the man had, to be whatever he was now instead of the Santa Fe boy. But Joel hadn't done anything wrong yet.

The Santa Fe boy didn't exist any more. Joel didn't believe that. He understood what Bate meant. If the boy lived, he was in his fifties. A shapeless nonentity or, maybe worse, one of those men who kept themselves trim, emblems of futility. Joel didn't care, really, it didn't matter what the man looked like now. Partly because Joel knew the boy persisted, perfect as ever, in some realm where Bate could not possibly track him down. Partly because . . . the only way he could learn why he had to see the man was to see him. He had meditated over that picture for hours, days. But he knew he'd never understand anything until they were face to face. The thrill and trepidation that filled him at the very thought of that encounter were, surely, the merest foretaste of how it would actually feel when he—

Accosted an aging stranger who would, after momentary bafflement, probably punch his lights out.

Mayonnaise dripped down onto his pants leg. It wouldn't ever come out, these pants were ruined. Sam and Joel's mother both scolded him.

Joel and Ron were going to meet at Gentry and then figure out some place to eat. Joel went straight from work, in the suit he had worn because he thought there was supposed to be a briefing for Congressman Patchen. But the briefing was put off for a day, and this was the only suit he could fit into, so he'd have to wear it again. He needed to try not to spill anything at dinner. And maybe he should eat light, so that in some indefinite future he could fit into another of his suits. This had never happened: his closet was filled with clothes he was going to wear again as soon as he took off just a few pounds. If he could have arranged them in order he would have had, not only a precise gauge of how his waistline had grown, but also a chronicle of men's fashions he looked stupid in. The Jordache look. The Miami Vice look. The L.L. Bean look.

His current look, bureaucratic nondescript, was not terribly out of place at Gentry. This was the bar where men came in suits. Mostly young men, Hill boys and PR types, in suits that were vaguely Milanese. A scattering of guys Joel's age, some of whom had failed to discern that Italian suits require that your shoulders be wider than your waist. Others, like Joel, in shapeless sacks, but with costlier haberdashery than Joel's: French cuffs, contrasting collars. The Orrin Hatch look.

The bar at Gentry must have been a hundred feet long. Almost deserted near the entrance—the guys who came to Gentry were out enough to go to a gay bar at happy hour, but not enough to display themselves in the front window—more crowded at the back. Joel was out enough to sit at the front, where sunlight fell on the magazine he planned to read while waiting for Ron. The bartender was so far away he might possibly have been in Maryland. Joel waved, not too frantically. The bartender didn't notice, but Joel attracted some attention from the throng at the far end. One of their number detached himself, ambled down toward Joel. As he got closer Joel could see that it was Andrew.

"Hey, Joel," he said. "I thought that might be you."

"Hi." They shook hands, Andrew grasping Joel's shoulder. Joel whispered, "Don't be alarmed, but you're in a gay bar."

Andrew mimed shock, but he also moved around to Joel's left, so his back was to the front window. "I just stopped by on my way home." Gentry was categorically not on his way home. He must have seen Joel thinking this; he added, "Well, I . . . actually, I've been going out a little."

"Oh, yeah?" Joel said, as casually as he could. Was the hibernation over?

"Yeah, once in a while. I mean, I'll come here after work, or I'll go to the Pledge some nights and have a beer or two."

"Uh-huh." The Pledge: Joel had stepped into the Pledge a few weeks earlier, didn't even stay for one drink. A sea of tank tops, pumped chests, meticulously sculpted arms.

"I haven't, you know, met anybody."

"It's hard," Joel said. Meaning: you may be in better shape than I am, but it's kind of uppity to think you could make it at the Pledge.

"I mean, I meet people, guys try to pick me up, but . . ."

Joel saw them: shadowy, slender figures standing next to Andrew as he had one or two beers, leaning toward him, smiling. Shadows moving in on him. "I don't know, it's been so long. I'm . . . ready. I mean, I get horny. But it's like, after a couple years—it's like I haven't met anybody who should be the very first one."

Joel thought, I should be the very first one, you twit. And maybe the last. Part of him was saying: if he's telling me these things, he just sees me as his confidant, I am not on his agenda. Part of him was conjuring up one of those movies in which the hero, having been dumped by the spoiled socialite, is dictating a memo, stops, suddenly realizes that his secretary would be beautiful if she took her glasses off.

"What have you been up to?" Andrew said.

"Me? I . . . you know, I go out. But—what's the old saying?— the screwing I get isn't worth the screwing I get." This was worse than, at their last meeting, inventing a fling with the librarian. Maybe Andrew would think he was trashy. Still, better trashy than Emily Dickinson.

"We ought to go out together some time," Andrew said. Uninterpretably. If he had accented the "we," or even the "out," he would have been asking for a date. If he had accented the "together," he would have meant that they should go out cruising together. Sisters. With the understanding that, if one of the sisters got lucky, the other sister got lost. But he hadn't, really, emphasized any one word.

Joel said, "Sure." Not so warmly as to commit himself to sisterhood, nor so coldly as to foreclose a date. Andrew looked a little puzzled. Good: why should Joel be the only one puzzled?

"You're not drinking?" Andrew said.

"Guy never came down here."

"Let me try, I'm going to have one more." Joel thought: really? Don't you have to rush home for the call from Kenyon's parents?

While Andrew sent semaphore signals to the impossibly

distant bartender he said, "So what else is up?"

"Nothing much," Joel said. "Oh, I ran into Senator Harris a couple weeks ago."

"Ran into him?"

"At—you know Corcoran's?"

"Uh-huh. You met Senator Harris in a bar? I would have thought he was a Mormon or something."

"If he is, he got some special dispensation to drink Absolut martinis."

"Well, I hope you told him he's a homophobic asshole."

"Practically. I told him too much, anyway."

Andrew did a take. "You came out to him in Corcoran's?"

"No, we just talked about his bill."

"Which is going into the chairman's package."

"What?" Joel was, again, dismayed that Andrew should be deeper in the loop than he was.

"I mean, they're going to put it in if it saves money. Which it doesn't so far; the budget people are scoring it at zero."

"That's what I thought." Give or take a hundred million.

"Melanie and I keep rewriting it. I mean, we must be on the thirtieth draft, but the budget people keep coming back and saying it's unenforceable. You can't get any saving unless you can show there are actually claims that won't be paid. And nobody ever sends a claim in with a diagnosis of AIDS."

"Right."

"At one point we had it so if a doctor sent in a bill, he had to check a little box. Like, 'Was this service HIV-related? Yes/no.' Melanie says the AMA people just went bonkers."

"No kidding," Joel said. "I can just see physicians checking a box that says, 'Please don't pay me for this service.'"

"Not to mention there are these, you know, patient rights issues. So that's dead."

"Maybe they'll just drop the whole thing."

"Well, like I said. They need the savings for something. I mean, there's something else they're trying to pay for."

"Isn't there always?" Joel said.

Ron came in, wearing jeans and a polo shirt. When he saw Joel's suit he said, "I thought we weren't going anywhere fancy."

"I just came from work," Joel said. "Ron, do you know Andrew?"

"Hi, Andrew. Don't let me interrupt you."

"We were just talking shop," Joel said.

"Oh, politics. What do you do, Andrew?"

Andrew murmured, "I, um . . . I work for Congress."

"Which office?"

"It doesn't matter."

"I hate politics," Ron said. "I used to be a junkie like everybody else, but I took the cure. Now the only thing I read in the paper is the funnies and Miss Manners."

"Probably better off," Andrew said. "Listen, I was talking to a guy down that way. I'll let you two guys catch up. Nice meeting you, Ron."

Ron watched him as he walked to the far end of the bar.

Joel said, "I guess he didn't want you to know where he worked."

"I guess not. He's a nice-looking man."

"You think?"

"I banged him once."

"What?"

"Years ago. It didn't look like he even remembered." Ron shrugged. "Where did you want to eat?"

"I don't care. We could just stay here."

They got a table not far from Andrew's end of the bar. Andrew saw them and waved, then went on talking to, Joel was happy to see, a fat guy who had to be seventy. So Joel wouldn't have to watch him leave with some cutie who had passed the entrance exam for *the very first one.*

Ron squinted at Andrew. "Maybe it wasn't him. It was a long time ago."

"You sure did get around."

"I sure did. Sometimes I walk into a place and it's like *This Is Your Life* with Ralph Edwards."

A guy emerged from the crowd at the bar and walked up to their table. A black man, maybe in his late twenties, with skin of an even cocoa and eyes that were . . . possibly what is called hazel, but they looked almost golden. He was wearing gabardine slacks with about a twenty-inch waist; the body above it, flaring to powerful shoulders, was swathed in the kind of shirt that made Daisy Buchanan swoon, the fabric somehow rich and ascetic at the same time. The open collar disclosed the hollow at the base of his neck, the hollow like a well, cocoa and hazel and golden.

"Hi, Ron," he said, very softly. "I didn't see you come in."

Ron didn't look at him. "Hello, Michael."

Michael turned toward Joel. Just looked at him, silently. Ron didn't say anything, and Joel offered, "I'm Joel."

"How are you, Joel?" Michael graced him with a meager smile.

"Uh . . ." Joel couldn't remember the answer to that question; he was looking at Michael's eyes. "Fine."

"That's good," Michael said. With a trace of condescension? No, patience: he must have been used to aging white boys who looked at him and forgot how to talk.

He said to Ron: "I've been trying to call you."

"I know," Ron said. He picked up his menu and tilted his head back, so he could study it through the lower part of his bifocals.

Michael blinked, his lips parted a little, at this studied rudeness. "I just thought if we talked, if we could just talk about it, maybe . . ." He ran down: he couldn't address this appeal to the back cover of a menu. He glanced at Joel, embarrassed. Joel frowned. He went on: "I don't know why you won't believe me."

"Okay," Ron said, without looking up from the menu. "I believe you."

"All right, then." Michael nodded gravely, as if those words were all he'd wanted. He turned back toward Joel. Michael's face was blank, there wasn't any reason for Joel to feel that he was being sized up. But their eyes locked for, Joel thought, a long time. He imagined there was some meaning in Michael's parting "Nice to meet you, Joel." If only because Michael had bothered to remember his name. He watched as Michael walked the length of the bar and out the front door. Michael's butt should have been designated as a national monument.

"What are you having?" Ron said.

"I haven't looked. Who was that?"

"Michael? Just someone I saw a few times."

"He's beautiful."

"You don't want to play with that."

The menu took about a paragraph to describe each dish. Salsas, infusions, reductions, essences. There was a meat loaf special, probably inserted over the chef's furious protests. They both ordered it, and a round of drinks, finally: Joel had been just about to go into withdrawal.

"The only tasty thing here is the waiters," Ron said.

"I don't know what it is about gay restaurants. They try so hard, and you wind up with . . ."

"Cafeteria food. Nobody comes here for the food, just the view."

"I guess. Why don't I want to play with that?"

"What? Oh, Michael. Do you want to play with Michael?"

Who wouldn't? But Joel said, "I'm just asking."

"It's a long story."

Joel shrugged; he wasn't going anywhere, not till his drink got there.

Ron began: "I got my Amex bill—oh, a couple months ago, and there were all these charges on it. Bloomingdale's at Tyson's Corner, about four hundred in men's clothing. You know, I never go out there. Couple of restaurants, Red Sage, Obelisk, places like that. Big bills. I thought, oh, it's some computer error. But, you know, they give you copies of the slips and there they were, the card was imprinted on them. And the same signature on every one. Nothing like mine, my name misspelled even. I guess they don't even try to match the signature any more, they just ring up the sale. So I looked in my wallet and, sure enough, the card was gone. I never missed it, I don't even use the thing, it's just for travel or some kind of emergency. I kept it in an inside pocket, there's no way it just fell out.

"So I knew: some trick took it. But I didn't know who, you know? Not that there's a stream of traffic through my apartment, but I'd been having . . . kind of a run of luck. Plus I use the card so little, it could have been months. Except I guess a guy wouldn't have just held on to it for months and then gone and started using it. Anyway, there were a fair number of suspects, and Michael wasn't even the main one. He seemed like a really sweet kid, we'd seen each other a few times, I was even thinking we were headed for something. There were a couple of other guys who were . . . kind of bottom of the barrel, you know. So I figured it was one of them. And what was I going to do about it? I didn't even know their last names.

"I called Amex, reported that my card was lost and there were all these charges that weren't mine. They wanted to know, had I lost my wallet? I said no, just the one card. They said, who would have had access to my wallet? And I felt like the criminal. What was I going to say, one of my tricks must have gotten hold of it? I mumbled something about how maybe I hadn't locked my locker at the gym one day. As if I went to the gym. I was sitting there, on the phone in my office, and I swear I was sweating, like it was Sergeant Friday on the other end and I was getting the third degree. Of course, they didn't care, it was just somebody filling out a form. They were going to send me a new card, I had to pay the first fifty dollars, that was it.

"A couple weeks later, I opened a book. It was something

I'd started and hadn't finished, it was already two or three down in the pile. I opened it and there was my card. God, I thought, it wasn't ever taken, I just misplaced it. Used it as a bookmark for some reason. So I don't need a new one, I ought to call and tell them. Then I realized: of course it was taken, you idiot, it was used. It hasn't been in this book all along, someone took it and used it and then brought it back.

"That kind of narrowed the list of suspects. I don't have that many repeat visitors, you know? I tried to think: who was over here before the card was used and after? There was just Michael and this one other guy, Bud. And—well, you don't need to hear about Bud. But there was no way Bud was dining at the Obelisk and handing them an American Express card. It had to be Michael. I felt awful: I really liked him."

"So what did you do?" Joel said.

"Nothing. What was I going to do? I just chalked it up to experience. But then a couple weeks ago he dropped by, out of the blue. You know, the front desk at my apartment called up and said there was a Michael Greeley. I was going to say, no, I don't want to see him. But I said okay. And then: it's funny, I was afraid to have him in the apartment. I went and stood by the elevator. The door opened, he stepped out. Grinning. I thought for a second: hey, what difference does it make? I'm horny. And I've paid a lot more than fifty dollars for worse times than I had with Michael. What the hell?

"But I was scared. I thought, if he'd do that, go through my wallet, who knew what he'd do? I didn't know him, who knew what he could do? We were just standing there, I guess he must have wondered why we're just standing there. So I told him all about the card. Of course he said no, he didn't do it. I said, yes, he did, it had to be him. And then, you know: he didn't shout at me or tell me I was crazy. He just said, 'Well, if that's what you think.' He pressed for the elevator, he was just shaking his head. He got on, turned around and looked at me. Just went on shaking his head, till the doors closed."

"Do you believe him?"

"I'm not sure. Oh, I am, it had to be him. And, you know, these people can just lie and they don't show a thing."

Joel knew what he meant by "these people," but he let it pass. Ron would just have said it didn't mean anything. Joel said, "It's funny, though. I mean, why would he bring it back and not just ditch it? Why would he keep trying to call you?"

Their meat loaf came. Joel testily reminded the waiter that he'd never brought their drinks. Ron asked for ketchup. After all these important transactions, it was almost natural for Ron to have forgotten Joel's questions and say, "I'm thinking of growing a beard."

Joel assented to the change of subject. "Oh, yeah?"

Ron must have caught Joel glancing at his hair, which was a moderately convincing dark brown. "I know it'll come in gray. I might just go gray all over." He chuckled. "I've got this friend Harvey, looks like Santa Claus, and he has to beat the boys away with sticks." They laughed. Ron said, "What's been happening with you?"

"Nothing."

"Still not scoring?"

"I don't even go out. I kind of lost interest."

"That's like saying you're kind of dead. In which case I'll finish your meat loaf. Anyway, seemed like you were pretty interested in Michael."

Joel blushed a little. "I was just curious."

"Or that guy you were talking to."

"Andrew? We just know each other from work. His lover died a couple of years ago and he hasn't, you know, he hasn't done anything. He's thinking he might be about ready to dive back in."

"And you'll be the pool."

"I doubt it," Joel said.

"There's the fighting spirit. Have you thought about asking him out?"

"Actually, I think he asked *me* out. I mean, just, 'We ought to get together some time.'"

"What are you waiting for him to do? Hire a skywriter?"

"It was sort of ambiguous."

Ron grunted. The waiter brought ketchup; Ron stirred about a pint into his mashed potatoes until they turned into a pink fluff, like cotton candy.

They ate in silence for a while. Then Ron said, "Oh, did you ever get in touch with Bate?"

"Uh-huh." Joel should have stopped with that; there wasn't any reason to blurt out the whole story.

When he had finished explaining, as best he could, Ron didn't point out that the Santa Fe boy didn't exist any more. Nor did he ask what the hell Joel thought he was going to do when he found the guy. Ron just said, "Well, I wish you luck."

"You don't think this is crazy?"

"Oh, of course I do. But for forty-six years I thought it was crazy to hope for the life I'm living now."

"I don't guess that's the same."

"I just mean, if you want something, it doesn't matter much if other people think you're crazy."

"Okay."

"What are you hoping for, that I'll somehow talk you out of it?"

"You could save me a lot of money."

"You want me to fail to," Ron said. "You want me to tell you this is stupid and you ought to get on with your real life. And then you'll walk away saying I couldn't understand, I didn't get it, it was all over my head."

"I don't know what I want you to tell me," Joel said. "I don't even know why I brought it up."

"Ron Junior, any time we had a fight he'd go into this dramatic wail about how nobody understood him. And it worked, it always made me feel bad; if I could possibly give in, I would. Because I knew he didn't mean that at all, what

205

he was really whining about was that he was understood all too clearly. And I knew just how maddening it was to be excessively understood. I went to a shrink . . . oh, twenty years ago, when it was clear that Helen and I weren't ever going to be a real couple again, but I couldn't see any other life. And about midway through the second hour, he said, 'You're gay.' And I said, 'It's not that simple.' Oh, don't you hate it when people go and-then-I-said, and-then-he-said. But he said, 'This is all pride. You're not here to get better, you're here to be admired for your courageous refusal to live.'"

"All right."

The waiter materialized with a vast dessert tray. "Just the check," Ron said, without asking Joel. Which was all right; dessert was the only vice Joel didn't have.

"Look, I'm not lecturing you. I'm just telling you I've been through it. I kept crazy resolutions for a long time, I went on demented quests for a long time. And I wouldn't be bitter about the years I wasted if I had ever really felt any of it. But I never did. I knew I was being arbitrary, that I had made up all the rules I lived by and could rewrite them any time. I was just playing a game I'd made up, and I was losing it.

"If you tell me that you're really not ready to deal with a live human being—it's too soon or you're too depressed or whatever—I could respect that. If you tell me that something deep within you needs to find the Elvis of El Paso boy or whatever, fine. But if you're just putting on a show, all I can tell you is that everybody is very, very busy with their own spectacular dramas."

Ron couldn't understand, he didn't get it, it was all over his head. They split the check. While they were waiting for the change, Joel suddenly said, "Is Bud black?"

"Bud? Oh, Bud. No." Ron looked puzzled.

Joel didn't say anything more. He decided he wasn't going to talk to Ron again. Because Ron was a racist, that's what he said to himself. But, of course, he had plenty of friends who were

racist, in varying degrees. Racist, sexist, every other bad thing.
If he started crossing them all off his list, who would be left?

He wasn't going to talk to Ron again because he had told
Ron something he should never have told anybody.

Joel was trying to figure out where the computer had stashed
the memo he'd been working on all morning. He almost didn't
answer the phone: he had the idea that, if he didn't track down
the file right away, it would disappear. But the ring sounded
urgent.

"Joel Lingeman."

"Mr. Lingeman." It was Bate. Joel felt the way he did when
he opened the paper to the page with the lottery numbers.
Bate was going to tell Joel that he'd found the boy, or that the
boy was dead. Joel discovered that some part of him hoped the
boy was dead.

"I found Simms of Santa Fe."

Oh. That was as far as he'd got? "Uh-huh. You went out
there?"

"What?"

"You've been to New Mexico?"

"No, no. They weren't ever in New Mexico. That was just
a post office box."

A whole world vanished, obliterated, irretrievable as the memo
in Joel's computer. The boy did not stand under a western sky
washing his Mustang, the ring of mountains over his shoulder.

"The company was actually Leonard Siperstein and Son."

"Was?"

"Was. In Baltimore. They went out of business twenty-eight
years ago."

"Oh."

"I gather 'and Son' didn't want to take it over. So when
Leonard Siperstein retired he just shut it down."

Over already, this little caprice of Joel's, or this spectacular drama; the trail was cold. Joel wondered what he had spent for this intelligence.

Bate went on. "Siperstein is still alive, rather surprisingly. Living in a place called . . . let me see. Pikesville."

"I know Pikesville." The Jewish suburb northwest of Baltimore. Joel had been there a couple times, visiting his college roommate. Steven, what had become of him? The college magazine was filled with news about classmates he had never encountered, while the people he wondered about just disappeared. Steven: the merry eyes and the perpetual half-smile; the hair, in the style of those years, a helmet of tight reddish-black curls in which he wore an Afro pick like a tiara; the compact, furry body.

" . . . didn't wish to talk to me," Bate finished.

"What do you mean? Did you go see him?"

"I called him. He didn't want to see me."

Joel was nonplused. Perhaps he'd seen too many detective shows, but he didn't have the idea that the shamus called ahead and asked for an appointment.

"But you could . . . you know, go there."

"And do what? Spring at him from behind a tree?"

"What if you had to . . . I don't know, give him a subpoena?"

"I am not a process server," Bate said. Joel imagined him, with offended dignity, drawing himself up to his full, if negligible, height. "In any case, it's one thing to give somebody something and quite another to get something from somebody. He most emphatically did not wish to discuss . . . the subject of our inquiry."

"You told him?"

"I told him. And he recalled the person."

He recalled the person! Not forty miles away there was a man who recalled the person. Who had seen him in the flesh. Like the last apostle, able to testify to what he had seen with his own eyes.

"What did he say about him?"

"He said—I am reading from my notes: 'I got nothing to tell you about that goddamn kid.' Then he hung up."

"So what are you going to do next?"

Bate sighed. "I attempted to find the proprietors of *man about town*, on the possibility that they might have some record of the agency that placed the advertisement."

"And?"

Bate recited, in a monotone. "*man about town* ceased publication in 1974. It was put out by a concern named Universal Periodicals, which continued to publish several other magazines, including *Crock Pot Cuisine* and *Modern Dry Cleaning*. Universal was subsequently acquired by Supreme Chemicals, which is now a division of National Products, formerly National Tobacco. My informant there demurred at the suggestion that they would have retained any thirty-year-old records from Universal."

"So that's it? You can't think of anything else?"

"I'm afraid I've explored every avenue. Short of just walking around and showing the picture to people."

"I could do that myself."

"I suppose so. You surely don't want to pay me to do it. So, unless you have any other suggestions, I believe I will prepare my invoice."

"Yeah, I guess you might as well."

"I'm sorry."

Joel said casually, "You know, I used to have a good friend in Pikesville. Where did you say this Siperstein guy lived exactly?"

The *Times* magazine had a cover story about the Harris bill. Written, of course, by Dennis Callahan, the official and ubiquitous thoughtful faggot. His take on the Harris bill was predictable enough. Gay people had to accept adult responsibility for their actions. Gay people wouldn't ever be tolerated until they married and lived in little cottages with two children per couple.

Joel knew a few of those couples, guys who had adopted. Little girls, of course, because you could buy them so cheaply from China. Not to mention that people weren't quite so spooked by the idea of faggots raising a little girl. If they were to acquire a little boy they would keep him home from Little League and make him rearrange furniture.

Joel didn't guess there was anything wrong with playing Mi-Lin has two daddies, if that's what people wanted to do. It was certainly more wholesome than whatever sort of parenting the daddies who advertised in the gay paper had in mind.

What if he and Sam had done it, would that have held them together? A baby girl with diapers to be changed. Throwing food, sometimes throwing up on one of Sam's sweaters. Yuck. Joel didn't have enough nurturing instinct to take care of a goldfish. It would probably just have been another thing for them to fight about. They had hardly been able to change a light bulb together; how could they have raised a child?

Joel went back to the Callahan article. The Harris bill, while misguided, was a reflection of the larger society's legitimate concern that extending basic rights to homosexuals not be construed as implying approval of immature and self-destructive patterns of rhubarb rhubarb . . . It wasn't the article that got to him, though he knew this was all the debate the *Times* would countenance on the subject, the designated homosexual having been heard from. What got to him were the illustrations. Pairs of men, under the glare of a streetlamp, their faces obscured in shadows. Planning to do something immature and self-destructive. The underworld.

He tossed the magazine aside and picked up the news section. The main headline was something about Syria, which he naturally skipped. He couldn't have cared if the very existence of Syria proved to be an extended practical joke by Rand McNally. Further down there was a piece about how civil rights leaders were objecting to the Vice President's proposal for biotechnology innovation zones. That silly thing about tax credits for research companies that relocated in the inner city.

It seemed that the residents of the potential zones weren't thrilled at the notion of biotechnology innovation going on right down the block. There were murmurings about the Tuskegee experiment, about toxic waste dumps, about how nobody seemed to want all these genomes and clones and stuff in Chevy Chase or Beverly Hills. The report ended with a gratuitous reference by the reporter—no one, apparently, had brought this up—to the persistent rumors that the government had created HIV in a lab and introduced it to the cities as a way of wiping out black people. Deadpan, but the point was clear: black people were irrational and paranoid, blaming mysterious forces for their own social pathologies and resisting every effort to help them restore the wasteland they had made of the cities.

The reporter didn't say that, Joel thought it all by himself. He caught himself, but he also thought it and wasn't even sure it was wrong. As he wasn't sure Ron was wrong. Somebody had used his American Express card. Why should Joel have returned a not guilty verdict just because that kid was cute? What was his name? Michael. Ron said "these people." He was an unrepentant racist, and he could also be, in this one instance, correct.

Well, and it was—wasn't it?—crazy of them to think that there was some secret committee working on the final solution for the Negro problem. Or that the Vice President's plan to give tax breaks to needy pharmaceutical companies was a plot to modify the DNA of innocent black children. Didn't these self-anointed black leaders have some real issues to deal with, instead of constantly stirring up this imaginary crap?

These people. Joel sort of wished no one had ever thought up races.

He was leaving the bagel shop and there was Sam. It wasn't a big neighborhood. Sooner or later, there had to be Sam. That they hadn't run into each other before suggested that Sam must have been avoiding it. Which should have been easy enough; Sam should have known better than to pass the bagel shop at nine on a Sunday morning.

Sam saw him at the same time. They both stopped, didn't speak for a minute. They were just there, on the sidewalk together. As if they had come to the shop together and Sam had been waiting outside for Joel to get the bagels.

"Hey," Sam said.

"Hey."

"I see you got bagels."

"Uh-huh." I see you're wearing sunglasses on a cloudy day. I see you have a goatee, which has come in partly gray, and a flat-top haircut.

The haircut was ill-advised; it turned Sam's already narrow and angular head into a perfect oblong. And the sunglasses: was he just trying to look cool, or was he hiding the evidence that Kevin beat him up?

"You want one?" Joel said.

"Um . . . sure."

"You want to come back to the apartment?"

"No," Sam said. A little alarmed, as if Joel could enchant him with a bagel and he'd never escape again. "Why don't we just sit in the Circle?"

"Okay. We better go back in and get knives and stuff. And did you want something to drink?"

They went to one of the long semicircular benches in the park at the center of Dupont Circle. The park was already busy: bums, people with dogs, across the circle a knot of ghoulish-looking kids who had probably been up all night raving, whatever the hell that was.

As Joel spread out their little picnic, he said, "I didn't get your kind of cream cheese."

"What did you get?"

"Scallion."

"Yuck. Well, I guess I can pick them out."

"Okay."

"I always tell you not to get scallion."

"I don't expect to be kissing anybody."

"No, but they get in your teeth, and you don't even see, and . . ."

Sunday morning. If they had been together, they would have finished their bagels, then Sam would have said Joel needed to brush his teeth. When he had complied, they would have gone back to bed together.

Joel said, "How's Kevin?"

"He's fine." Sam tilted his head. From which Joel understood that he was thinking: what have you heard about us? So, if Joel could read his mind, why couldn't Joel detect Kevin all those months before Sam left? Still, he was sure of it, Sam was afraid Joel had heard something. He wished Sam would take off the sunglasses. Not to reveal anything, just so he could look Sam in the eye as they talked.

"We're going to be moving," Sam said. "I'll have to give you my new number."

"Moving where?"

"I found a little studio near AU."

"Won't the two of you be pretty crowded?"

"Oh, no, Kevin's moving to College Park. You know, school's starting again pretty soon, he wanted to be closer."

"So you're not . . ."

"We're still seeing each other, but we couldn't take that group house any more. And we both, you know, needed our space."

"Uh-huh," Joel said. Sam wouldn't have used that phrase when they were together. He might have wanted to use it, but he would have known Joel would laugh at him. Now, apparently, he wasn't afraid of Joel's laughter. Joel, for his part, no longer found the phrase funny; he understood space now. He had too much of it, but he wouldn't have given it up—not an inch. Maybe not even if Sam were to occupy it.

On the grass a black man in sweatpants and a neon tank

top was practicing, in the slowest of motion, some ancient and exotic form of mayhem. Poised and controlled as a dancer, beautiful if you forgot that every time he extended his leg in a perfect arabesque he was picturing his pointed toes gouging out the eyes of some, probably, white guy. More bad thoughts about *those people*, so many on a single morning. Joel couldn't help it. He could imagine where the guy had acquired those astounding shoulders: at a gym where the membership was free and lasted five to ten.

Sam was saying, "Actually, we . . . we decided we could go out some."

"I'm sorry?"

"I mean with other people."

"Oh. And do you?"

"Yeah. You know, I meet guys. But they don't seem as mature as Kevin."

Where was he meeting these less mature guys, junior high school playgrounds?

It wasn't, objectively, worse to know that Sam was seeing multiple youths than to know that he had snagged Kevin. Well, yes, it was. Joel felt the way a Chinese peasant must feel when he sees a fat man. He pictured Sam and Andrew at the Pledge, each at his own end of the bar, flocks of young men gathered around each of them like iron filings.

"How about you?" Sam said. "You seeing anybody?"

Joel couldn't say he was seeing the librarian, whose name he had already forgotten. "No," he said. Sternly, as if he had made some sort of resolution, instead of just repeatedly striking out.

Sam sighed. "You should, Joel."

Joel said no again. Maybe he had made some sort of resolution.

The black guy had finished his ballet and was standing still, head bowed; evidently his particular school of self-defense entailed meditation. What did he think about? He looked up

214

to find that Joel was staring at him. He returned the stare, impassive; he couldn't come to work out in Dupont Circle and be outraged that fairies looked at him. He bowed his head again, his hands tightened into fists.

Sam was only on the second half of his bagel. He had spread cream cheese on it and was, as promised, picking out the scallions and flicking them down on the ground. Joel lit a cigarette.

"You're still smoking," Sam said. What did he think: he left and Joel was supposed to turn into someone else? Joel didn't answer. After a minute Sam said, "So how are things at work?"

If Sam asked him how things were at work, it meant that he had exhausted every other conceivable topic. "Okay. Things have kind of slowed down. You know, when the Republicans took over, they were going to remodel the universe in a hundred days. But they kind of ran out of steam."

"Uh-huh. Did you see they want to take away our health care?"

"You mean this Medicare thing?"

"Medicare?" Sam said. As if, in fifteen years with Joel, he had never heard the word. "I guess. It was something in the gay paper."

"I wouldn't worry about it. It's just a lot of hot air. They're not going to do anything."

"Oh." Sam finished his bagel, took a long swig from his bottle of iced tea flavored with apricot or something equally cloying. "About Kevin."

"Uh-huh?" Was he going to tell?

"Sometimes we don't get along. You know, we fight. It's funny, you and I never fought."

"No."

"We fight, and we couldn't stay in the same place, and . . ."

Serves you right, Joel thought. Then he thought it was too bad if Sam was unhappy. That, having lost what they'd had, not even one of them got to be happy. He was annoyed with himself. Wanting Sam to be happy was just a habit, from their years together: if Sam was happy, there was no bad weather in the apartment. Why should he care now?

Sam went on. "He looks up to me. Right from the start he looked up to me, that's what it was. Not the sex. It felt good."

"Uh-huh." Joel suppressed a little foul shudder of contempt. Vacant Kevin looking up to, of all people, Sam. Sam feeling big.

Sam spoke carefully. "I never felt that you looked up to me. I don't mean you should have, we were equals. But you looked down on me."

"No."

"You did. I know you loved me. But I always felt, like, I was just the best you could do." Some memory stirred; Joel couldn't catch it. Sam finished: "You never really thought I was good enough."

"God." Joel wanted to put his arm around Sam, but he couldn't, not in front of the martial artist. "I never felt that way."

Probably Sam was insulted by this pointless lie. But what else could Joel say? Yes: you were never good enough, I spent the whole time waiting for the goddamn Santa Fe boy. Had Sam known it, all those years? How it must have hurt. That was the price, then: all those years loving Joel enough to pay that price.

Defiantly, Joel put his arm around Sam. "I loved you as well as I could."

"I know you did."

"I do."

"I know," Sam said. "I still love you, too."

Sam stood up, slowly, and looked down at Joel. The way, a century ago, they might have been reading or watching TV in the living room. Sam would stand up, Joel would look up from the paper, Sam would have a tight but genuine smile on his face, and they would race down the hall to the bedroom.

Here they were, a couple of blocks from the bedroom.

They looked at each other for a long time. Perhaps they were both thinking the same thing, the way they used to think the same thing. They could go to Joel's place, Joel could brush his teeth, they could make love; if Joel was especially attentive and adept he might make Sam forget for a few seconds that he was merely the best Joel could do. Which he was: the dearest man Joel would ever know, and he had thrown him away.

Joel broke the look first. Sam understood. "I better get going," he said.

"Kevin will wonder where you are."

Sam smiled. "He doesn't wonder where I am much. He's got a pretty full calendar."

"Oh. I hope you're being safe."

"What? Oh, sure."

"Because some of these kids, you know, they're not very careful."

Sam shrugged. "Talk to you," he said.

The black guy had resumed his ballet. As he went through his motions, he occasionally glanced at Joel. Was this permissible? Wasn't he supposed to be concentrating? But he was showing off for Joel. Maybe that was why he came to this of all parks. So he could show off for Joel. Who imagined for a second what it would be like to bring back to his apartment this prepotent creature, who might kiss him or might kick his teeth in.

seven

On the train to Baltimore, Joel tried to read. But he kept coming back to the Simms boy—must he now call him the Siperstein boy? He had no landscape to put him in now. The vague, paradisiac vision of Santa Fe was dispelled, giving way to an image of his roommate's ranch house in Pikesville. With the kidney-shaped pool in the backyard: Steven was rich, his father was a tax lawyer. Joel tried to place the boy by that pool. He was on the lounge chair with the plastic webbing; behind him, on the patio, Steven's mother and her friends were playing mah-jongg. This ludicrous picture was not improved when Joel replaced Mrs. Rosoff with Leonard Siperstein. By the pool, some middle-aged garment manufacturer with a bald head and a cigar knelt in front of the boy, pulled down the quick-drying tank trunks. The boy looked off, with that sad fixed smile, into the middle distance.

Baltimore. Abandoned factories loomed to the left of the tracks. Joel could imagine, on one of them, the faded lettering:

Siperstein and Son. Swimwear. Foundation Garments. Then a tunnel, so they were almost at the station. Joel thought about just turning around and getting the next southbound train. He had plenty to do, this was pointless, he really ought to go back.

Outside, he gave a taxi driver the address. "That's in the county," the driver said. "I'm gonna have to charge you double."

"What's the county?"

"There's Baltimore City and there's Baltimore County. So I gotta charge for the return because, see, I can't pick up in the county."

"Can you wait and bring me back?"

"Yeah, that I can do, probably cost about the same. Except I gotta leave my meter running while I wait." After what Joel had already spent on Bate, this didn't seem like a big deal—until they pulled onto some kind of expressway. The cab groaned and clanked, they stayed in the slow lane, maybe going forty, but the meter turned over so fast Joel could hardly keep track. The meter was deep into four digits before they turned off onto something called Stevenson Lane.

Joel hadn't thought about what he was going to say. He would need to have some reason for wanting to find the boy. He's inherited a fortune. He's my long-lost half-brother. He's wanted for something. All silly: none of them explained why the only thing Joel knew about him was that he had been in that ad. Joel was going to have to tell the even sillier truth. Siperstein was going to laugh at him, or more probably turn away with bewilderment and disgust.

They passed a synagogue, an early-60s Quonset hut with soaring wings, manner of Eero Saarinen. Had he seen this place before, visiting Steven? So long ago—jeez, twenty-fifth reunion next year, was it conceivable that Steven would show up? An excellent reason not to go. There were plenty of reasons: that Joel wasn't rich or famous or even well-preserved. But he surely did not want to find himself having to talk to Steven. He had nothing to say to Steven, there had been nothing left to say after that last afternoon, by the kidney-shaped pool, when he had haltingly spilled out those things he had meant never to tell anyone.

The cab turned off onto a street lined with tall hedges. At the breaks for driveways Joel caught glimpses of enormous houses, mostly Georgian, with porte cocheres at their sides harboring large German cars. If Siperstein lived here, he must have done pretty well in the rag trade.

The driver slowed. "3568," he said. "What is that next one, 3546? It's gotta be right along here—yeah, right here."

"Don't turn in."

"What?"

"Wait here, I'm going to walk up. I'll be back in . . . ten minutes."

"Right. Why don't you leave me twice the meter so far, then I'll wait."

The driveway curved in front of a long brick wall. There was a roofline, this had to be the front of the house, but a good hundred feet of umber brick was punctuated only by a blank redwood door, next to it a single narrow panel of frosted glass. On the doorstep was a newspaper, still rolled up in its blue plastic wrapper. No one was home, and the meter was running.

Joel pressed the doorbell. He couldn't even hear, through the slab of redwood, if it rang. While he waited he was already thinking about the ride back, the memo he had to finish. Between him and the boy was a long brick wall with a door no one was going to open.

From around the far corner of the wall a man appeared, carrying a hose. He aimed it unsystematically at a shrub here, a patch of grass there, not so much watering as "watering," in the desultory and ironical way Joel used to do chores as a kid. Mrs. Siperstein had sent him out to do this, maybe just to get him a little sun. Siperstein was a sphere with no shirt on, shorts sagging so you could see a few inches below his navel.

He noticed Joel, shut off the hose, then just stood eyeing Joel, not speaking. Joel called out, "Hi." He didn't answer, so Joel had to tramp over the lawn to him. "Mr. Siperstein?"

"Who are you?" Not hostile, but not interested.

Joel looked fixedly at his face, rather than look at his teats with their shag of white hair, the white globe of his belly. He looked back at Joel through glasses with heavy black frames and the sort of lenses that are supposed to change color with the light but are always a jaundice yellow.

"Joel Lingeman. I rang, I didn't think anybody was home."

"I'm home. I'm always home."

"Uh-huh."

"Twenty years, I went to the club every day. I pretended to play golf, five or six holes, and then I went to the bar and had lunch with my buddies. But all my buddies are dead. So I stay home."

"Uh-huh. Um . . . It's a nice house." An inane thing to say about a brick wall.

"I hate this house. My second wife read some magazine, she had to have the most modern house in Pikesville. Can you guess what it costs to heat this house?"

"No, sir."

"So you're not a furnace salesman. What are you selling?"

"What? Oh, nothing."

"Did you want to state your business?"

Joel did not want to state his business. "I came to— I came to ask you something about Simms of Santa Fe."

Siperstein dropped the hose, turned and began walking away. He stopped after a few feet, but did not face Joel. "You're the guy on the phone. I told you, I don't want to talk about that model. I don't know anything about him."

"I'm not the guy on the phone. I'm his . . . he was just helping me. It's real important that I find that . . . model." Joel could barely shape the word. He had never thought of the boy as a model. How silly, a kid looking at a hired model in an ad and making up stories about how he came to be there. "Anything at all you could tell me."

"It's important why?"

"I . . . I can't really explain it."

"Ah." He turned around, squinted at Joel through the yellow lenses. "Come around back, I need to sit."

Around back were three huge Miesian pavilions of bronze and glass, forming a U the base of which was the blank wall out front. In the center, a slate terrace, from which a vaguely Asian garden, with artfully placed cypresses and stone lanterns, sloped down to a pool built to look like a natural pond. Beyond the pool, the green lawn on which Joel's strapping sons would have thrown the lacrosse ball back and forth, lazily. Leonard Siperstein and Joel Lingeman sat on matching teak chairs on the terrace of Joel's dream house. Joel's chair faced the center pavilion; behind the expanse of glass was a nine-foot Steinway.

Siperstein searched in the pocket of his commodious shorts and brought forth a half-smoked cigar and a book of matches. He lit the cigar, dropped the match on the slate terrace. "I can't offer you a cigar," he says. "This is it till my wife comes back with the car."

"That's okay," Joel said. "I've got cigarettes."

"You shouldn't smoke cigarettes."

"No." So he didn't.

Siperstein looked up in the sky and began. "I wasn't in swimwear. We made riding outfits, catalog business mostly. A lot of Western goods. You know, for wearing at the dude ranch. That's where the name came from; I didn't figure I'd sell a lot of riding outfits if I was Siperstein of Baltimore. So I rented this box in Santa Fe, and I contracted with a distributor out there to take phone orders. You know, so it would be a Santa Fe phone number. We advertised in *Town and Country*, sometimes *Holiday*. A very specialized business, outfitting debutantes with big tushes who rode horses. But there's a lot of those, or there was.

"So one day my brother-in-law Bernie comes to me and says he's bought an odd lot of swimming suits. In some bankruptcy. A terrific businessman, Bernie, he can't figure out that if a concern goes into chapter 7 maybe their goods were a little hard to move. Bernie was crazy, he got into one stupid deal after another, I must have had to bail him out a hundred times. Anyway, Bernie has a whole goddamn warehouse full of these swimming suits, he brings one to show me. It's a little schmatte, like skimpy underwear with a stripe down the side. 'See the stripe?' he tells me. The moron. He thinks I'm going to buy his swimming suits. So I tell him to go to hell, but my wife nudges and nudges, and finally I say I'll handle them on contingency. If they move, I'll pay him; if they don't, I won't.

"I talk to my agency, we agree that this garment ain't for the *Town and Country* set. They say we should try *man about town* and, for some reason, *Opera News*. So we take this little ad, just one time, and we sell a lot of suits. Do we ever sell a lot of swimming suits. And at six ninety-nine a pop. Bernie's strutting around like he's Bernard Baruch instead of Bernard Schlemiel. I tell him we need more suits and he says, well, the guy's bankrupt, there are no more suits. I have to explain to him that this guy was not the last person in the world with a sewing machine, it is possible to make more suits. I'm doing him this favor, I'm going to buy suits from him instead of just going out and finding my own supplier. So he goes off to dig up a supplier but—I don't remember, I don't think he ever followed through. And then I shut down just a few months later. So that was that."

He sat back, puffed on his cigar, looked at Joel as if he had said everything Joel could possibly want to know.

"About the model . . ." Joel said.

"The model, I don't know from that model. The agency got him. I guess in New York."

"What agency, do you remember?"

"Of course I remember," he said, as if Joel had just called

him senile. "Dinkeloo, who could forget a name like Dinkeloo?"

"D-i-n-k-e-l-o-o?"

"That's right." He chanted: "Dinkeloo and Dinkeloo."

"Are they still in business?"

"Beats me."

Joel recalled that he had a taxi with the meter running. "Listen, I better get going. Thank you so much for your time."

"What's your hurry? Your cab pulled away while we were out on the lawn."

"Son of a bitch."

"Don't worry, we'll go inside, I'll call you a cab. Unless you want to wait till my wife comes home, she might take you. Where you got to get?"

"The train station."

"In Baltimore? Forget it, I don't think my wife has been downtown since the last department store closed."

"How about you?"

He shrugged. "There isn't any Baltimore any more. Just a fancy stadium and a million schwarzes."

Siperstein stubbed out his cigar on the slate beneath his feet—carefully, so he could light it again. Joel followed him into the house. Siperstein's tennis shoes squeaked on the travertine floor in the living pavilion. While he called the cab, Joel looked at the Steinway. A couple of strings were broken, no one had played it in years. Maybe no one had ever played it, it was just the right thing to have in front of the plate glass window.

"Probably twenty minutes or so," Siperstein said. "We can wait in here, they'll honk."

"Thanks."

"I'm sorry I don't know anything about that boy. Except that he sure sold a lot of swimming suits."

"Did he?"

"My distributor, his phone just rang off the hook. Orders, and also . . ." He looked away from Joel for a second. "Also a lot of people who wanted to know where to find him."

"Oh."

Siperstein snorted. "There was this one guy, my distributor told me, he wanted the suit the boy was wearing. So my distributor says, you mean same size, same color? No, he wanted the actual suit, the particular suit that boy was wearing in the picture."

"Uh-huh." Joel felt himself blushing, for himself and all of his kind.

"So I say to my distributor, you get any more calls like that, tell him 'Yes, sir,' send him a suit and charge the schmuck fifty bucks."

"Uh-huh," Joel said. "Look, you've been real helpful. I guess I better wait outside."

"I'll go with you, finish my cigar. God forbid I should smoke a cigar in my own house." He smiled. "So some people fall in love with a picture, what do I care? I myself had a terrific crush on Myrna Loy."

"Oh, yeah?"

"I don't think I ever tried to buy any of her garments. Or went looking for her. She was just a picture."

Joel followed him back out, he lit his cigar. Now Joel did have a cigarette.

"Maybe we better wait out front," Siperstein said. "We might not hear the cab back here."

As they walked around the house, Siperstein suddenly put his arm around Joel's shoulder. "So, uh . . ."

"Joel."

"Joel, you're from where?"

"I grew up outside Philadelphia."

"Your parents are still there?"

"No. I mean . . ."

Siperstein squeezed Joel's shoulder in silent acknowledgment of his orphanhood. "Did they know about you?"

"About— Oh. My mother did."

"My son was a gay person. My wife—his mother, my first

225

wife—she didn't know. Or maybe she knew and didn't tell me, I sure didn't know. Just that I wanted him to go into the business and he wouldn't, he wanted to go to New York. He couldn't stay in Baltimore, he had to go to New York. So I fixed him up with a job at Dinkeloo and Dinkeloo and then I shut down. It broke my heart, he couldn't stay and he couldn't tell me why. I never figured it out, not until he came down with this AIDS."

"I'm sorry."

"Do you have the AIDS?"

"No, sir."

"That's good." They were in front of the house now. "So anyway, yes, they are."

"Sir?"

"Still in business. Dinkeloo and Dinkeloo. I forget where, Lexington Avenue I think."

The cab appeared. Siperstein père took his arm off Joel's shoulder. "Thank you," Joel said.

"I hope you find . . ." Perhaps Siperstein started to say he hoped Joel found the boy. He studied the end of his cigar. "I hope you find your way back okay."

Like and-Son Siperstein, Joel hadn't gone into the family business, having for some reason no passion for urology. And he hadn't gone into the family-business, the lifelong enterprise of raising Lingemans so there could be more Lingemans. The cycle of generation was broken: and-Son and Joel would pass nothing on. As their fathers had passed nothing on to them.

Unfair. Siperstein had tried to pass something on; and-Son had declined. Maybe it was the same way with Joel and his father. I can't, I won't: it must have seemed to Joel's father that Joel never said anything else. Over the years refusing every companionable, manly diversion his father proposed: camping, sailing, skiing. Joel preferred not to.

Joel tended, thinking about his father, to recall the few

226

occasions when the man hollered at him. But mostly in those years the poor guy must just have looked at Joel quietly—hurt, confused, at last resigned. Joel wasn't ever going to be what he wanted. Not even wanted, just expected: when he heard the words "It's a boy," he must have had an automatic vision of what lay ahead for the two of them. How could he have known that those words predicted nothing about his son except that the kid would pee standing up?

In the last couple of years before he died, he and Joel would play pinochle when Joel visited for Sunday dinner. Then Joel would go home and change for the bars. Once they were sitting on the couch together, watching something on TV while Joel's mother cooked. His father put an arm around him. Tentatively, but with clear premeditation. Joel didn't squirm away, just let the arm rest on his shoulder. Until his father coughed and removed it.

All the refusals. He had spent his life saying no, like a cross baby, even to what was good for him. No, you don't understand, I am special, I am different, my life isn't anything like yours. Joel's life was a spectacular drama that had culminated in a heroic quest for a swimwear model.

Why should it have bothered Joel so much to learn that thirty years ago some queen had tried to buy those lo-rise trunks, the very ones the boy had worn? Like the Shroud of Turin. So he could bury his face in them while he jerked off.

"Simms of Santa Fe. How can I help you?"

"Hello, I . . . uh . . . I saw your ad in *man about town* and I . . . I want to order the swim trunks."

"Uh-huh. Name?"

Siperstein's distributor got the particulars, wrote up the C.O.D. order. "You should have that in a week, ten days," he said.

"Great. Oh, I meant to ask. The guy in the ad looks exactly like this buddy I went to high school with. I wondered—I've kind of lost touch with this guy—I wonder if you know how I might get hold of him?"

So many of them. Call after call. Until:

"Size?"

"Um . . . I wonder . . . what size do you think the guy in the ad is wearing?"

"I don't know," the distributor said. "I'd guess maybe a medium."

"Okay. 'Cause you see, I'm just about the same built as that guy, so that's what would fit me."

"Fine. Medium. Color?"

"As a matter of fact, you know, if you . . . if you happened to have the pair the guy was wearing, I'm sure that would . . ." The caller's voice trailed off.

"What?"

"Aqua. I want the aqua."

How could Joel have supposed that he was the only one captivated by that picture? Obviously the ad had been targeted at gay men. The model—the boy was an anonymous model—had been carefully selected by Dinkeloo and Dinkeloo, because they figured they weren't just selling swimwear. The ad had been targeted at grown-up homosexuals who knew exactly what they wanted and had $6.99 to throw away, plus 50¢ shipping. One confused boy just happened to be caught in the cross-fire, as a bystander is hit in a drive-by shooting.

So what? Was a sunset any less beautiful because a lot of people enjoyed looking at it? Well, yes, as a matter of fact. Joel and Sam had been to Key West once, and had gone one evening to the pier where a crowd gathered to watch the sun sink into the Gulf. There were vendors selling jewelry and ice cream, clowns, a guy playing the trumpet. The sun went down on schedule, gorgeous as the guidebook promised. The tourists clapped. Joel and Sam, abashed, hurried down to La-Te-Da for the last of tea dance. The sun was the sun, billions of people looked at it every day. You had to have a mighty high opinion of yourself to think you saw anything other people couldn't see, felt anything other people couldn't feel.

To admit that other men might have felt as he did about that picture was pretty much the same as admitting that he felt *no more* than they did. That he might always have wanted nothing more than to bury his face in the crotch of those lo-rise trunks, sniffing for any trace of the boy who had worn them. Some religious experience.

Except really: what could possibly be more spiritual, more sacramental, than sniffing a pair of swimming trunks? Straining after the scent of God?

When he got back to the office, he learned that he had seventeen new voice-mail messages. It was the middle of August recess, and almost quitting time. None of these people could possibly have a problem that couldn't wait until the morning. So he might as well just head to the Hill Club—as soon as he called Bate.

He recited what he had learned, proud of his initiative and skill.

"Dinkeloo and Dinkeloo," Bate repeated, sounding rather cross. "Spell that, please."

Joel spelled it. He had thought Bate would be pleased that Joel had secured this important intelligence. Maybe Bate was jealous, that an amateur should have done his job better than he did. Or maybe he didn't want Joel to find the boy.

The last Wednesday in August, Joel had a meeting in the basement of the Cannon House Office Building. Congress was still in recess, but there were a few staffers already back in town. Just enough to have this meeting, called by Cordelia, the Finance chief of staff, and her opposite number from House Ways and Means—on the fantastical premise that they could reach agreement on various minor provisions before Congress came back. Work a few things out before the annual frenzy of trying to finish a budget bill by the end of the fiscal year on September 30. This was a delusion: there was no provision so minor that they could reach agreement on it before they absolutely had to, which would be just before the government shut down. Still, Joel and the rest were dutifully gathered in the House leg counsel's office to go over the Medicare amendments.

The health drafter for the House, Jerry Frankel, presided, sitting at his computer terminal; next to him was his Senate counterpart, Andrew. Around the table were Cordelia and a couple of people from Ways and Means, Mullan from Senator Flanagan's staff, Joel. They were going line by line through hospital payment rules. Every so often someone from Ways and Means spotted a problem, or Joel did. Jerry Frankel would come up with a fix and enter it into his computer. He would look at Andrew, who would just nod, that looks fine. They would print out the corrected page and give it to Mullan, who would say he wasn't sure the Senator could agree to it, they'd have to come back to it. Because he didn't understand it and wouldn't ask Joel to explain it to him, not in front of the House people. This had been going on for a couple of hours.

Andrew had apparently gone on sunning himself in his backyard all summer; he had reached the Al Jolson stage, startled white-boy eyes staring out from a mask of even mahogany. He looked stupid, in the languid sexy way of a pampered high school boy who didn't get a summer job and spent the endless afternoons at the swimming club. One of those guys who would show up in September and whose what-I-did-last-summer essays would consist of the single sentence, "Worked on my tan."

Andrew looked stupid, and Joel realized he hadn't contributed a thing all afternoon. He just agreed with every change Jerry Frankel typed in. "That's fine. That's fine." Joel wondered if he was distracted or maybe just not very good at it. Maybe he never made partner at McCutcheon and Halsey because he was, like, not very smart? But they wouldn't have kept him, even as an eternal associate. Distracted, then. Maybe by the renascence of his night life.

They had finished the hospital amendments. That is, they had reached agreement on none of them, and it was time to disagree on something else. Jerry Frankel said, "Should we work on this AIDS thing?"

One of the House people said, "Why bother? That's not going into the agreement."

Mullan said, "I'm not sure about that."

"Well, your guy isn't supporting it, is he?"

"He hasn't made up his mind."

This was pretty astonishing news. Matthew Flanagan, silver-haired patriarch of the neoliberals, might be supporting the Harris proposal? Well, he was from New Jersey, there probably wasn't a big gay vote there, or at least not an organized one. But Flanagan had always been pretty liberal on social issues: abortion funding, hate crimes, all of that. If even he might . . . For the first time it occurred to Joel—to everyone in the room—that Harris's gratuitous little sneer of a bill might become the law of the land.

"Then I guess maybe we better look at it," Jerry Frankel said. "There were . . . I saw a couple of problems."

Andrew looked attentive and eager. He and Melanie had been working all summer on this language, and now he had to pretend that his ego wasn't invested in it and he would be delighted to hear about any little problems.

Frankel ripped him apart. Andrew hadn't even fixed the mistakes Joel had pointed out in May, and since then he'd added a lot of new language Joel hadn't seen before—full of circular references, internal inconsistencies, undefined terms, even subsections without sections. Of course, Frankel had been working on this stuff forever; he could probably recite the Medicare statute in his sleep. But Andrew looked like a fool.

He took it all stoically. "Yes, I'm glad you caught that." Or, "Uh-huh, I was kind of concerned about that myself. What would you suggest?" No one in the room looked at him; everyone kept their eyes on the draft and penciled in the changes Frankel dictated.

Joel wanted to hold Andrew and go, "There, there. Poor baby." But he also felt a dawning disdain. Andrew might have made everyone else in the room look pasty and flabby, but he was way over his head. He should have studied the Social Security Act, those afternoons he had spent sautéing himself in his backyard.

Joel peeked up from the draft, met Andrew's eyes. Andrew was expressionless, and Joel didn't know what face to put on. He just stared, conscious that Andrew would read that stare as contempt. He looked back down at the paper, resumed marking up the corrections like everyone else at the table. This was just business; there wasn't any reason Joel should have felt that he was letting Andrew down. But the room now consisted of Andrew and everybody-else. Joel couldn't detach himself from everybody-else.

"Why don't we print it out and see what we've got now?" Frankel said.

"Um," Andrew said. "I'm a little late for another meeting. Is it okay if we go through this next time?"

It was almost six o'clock on a Wednesday at the end of August recess. He couldn't possibly have another meeting. Frankel began, "Well, if we could just . . ."

But Andrew had already gathered up his papers. "I'm really late, sorry," he said. "Next time." He glanced at Joel on his way out, but Joel still couldn't read his expression.

Frankel rolled his eyes. "I guess we'll come back to this. Should we move on to the claims processing rules, or do we need a break?"

"Let's just keep going," Mullan said.

Joel stood up. "I'll be back in a couple minutes." They didn't need Joel to help them make up rules about how hospital bills received in September should be paid in October, or how HMOs should get their October check September 30, thus moving expenditures from one fiscal year to another. Did the nation know that Congress met its deficit reduction targets by kiting checks?

"Joel's going to smoke," one of the House people said darkly. As if he were going to step out into the corridor and shoot heroin.

"Go on without me," Joel said. "I'll catch up."

They went on, perhaps not noticing that he had taken his briefcase with him.

Andrew was almost out of sight, past First Street and headed east. Bound for home, then, not back to his office. Joel ran; people looked at him, a man running, his tie flapping over his shoulder. When he had got within a hundred feet of Andrew he yelled, "Hey, wait up! Andrew!"

Andrew turned. Stood, looking faintly perplexed, waiting for Joel to traverse the great distance that had opened between them. Which Joel had to cross like a messenger boy about to deliver an unwelcome telegram. He hadn't thought what he should say. How ever had he concluded that this, of all moments, was the right time to make his move? He hadn't even thought about it, just knew somehow that if he let Andrew walk out of that meeting and away—that meeting where Joel hadn't helped, couldn't—he wouldn't get another shot.

He reached Andrew, panting a little, and said: "Hey, I was wondering if you wanted to have dinner?"

They were in front of the Madison Building. On the low wall before it sat the homeless guy who was always there— still, in the August heat, wearing the flannel shirt Joel had seen him in last May. The guy looked at Andrew and Joel but didn't bother to say, "Got a quarter?" Maybe it was just too hot; maybe he knew it wasn't worth the trouble.

"Don't you still have to be in that meeting?" Andrew said.

"It was just breaking up."

"Oh."

Andrew looked down at the ground. Joel repeated, "So how about dinner?" Hopelessly: he already knew the answer. Knew it because he himself heard the quaver in his voice as he uttered this innocent question. Andrew must have heard it, the mix of elation and terror and shame in Joel's voice, must have known what Joel was asking.

Once, in the year or so he'd pined after Alex Rivers, once he had worked up the nerve to ask Alex if he wanted to come over to Joel's house and work on his algebra. A natural question: Joel had helped him a couple of times, it would not have been a leap for him to come over for a little more tutoring. Alex considered it, looked at Joel and bit his lip. Joel held his breath, picturing the two of them in Joel's room, sitting on the bed maybe, the textbook between them. Alex looked at him, and Joel realized that Alex was forming exactly the same picture in his mind, and that it was distasteful to him.

Alex would not have put a name to his discomfort, would not have thought *homosexual*, any more than Joel would have used that word about himself. But there was something wrong with the picture; even if he could really use the help, Alex knew that somehow there would be a serpent in the room. So Joel knew the answer, even while Alex was still biting his lip and trying to think of some way to say no without hurting Joel's feelings. Joel had never loved Alex so desperately as in that instant: the sad look in his eyes as he hunted for some gentle way of explaining that what Joel wanted was impossible. The nameless thing Joel wanted was impossible, he would not have it in this world. "I can't," Alex said at last. He didn't invent an excuse and he didn't need to. He just couldn't.

Joel waited, knowing Andrew's answer. Not even sure if he cared, startled to find that he didn't care very much. Andrew

234

was cute, he was a nice guy. But he was also kind of dumb: Joel couldn't shake the disdain he had felt as Andrew stammered, back in the meeting room.

"I . . . Joel, I can't."

Joel looked away, embarrassed for both of them. The homeless man was watching with evident interest, as if he understood what was going on. Maybe it was obvious.

"I can't, Kenyon's parents might call, and . . ."

He should have left it at "I can't." It was insulting to hear an excuse; even Alex, a stupid jock, had known enough to spare Joel this insult.

"Okay," Joel said. "Another time." He tried to sound casual; he hoped Andrew hadn't heard that he could barely get the words out, his throat was so tight. He turned to head back to the meeting. If he walked fast, he'd be far away from Andrew before the tears came. About what? Andrew was stupid. And weak, or maybe a little demented, trapped in this weird deal with Kenyon's parents. Tears about what?

Andrew called after him. "No." Joel stopped. "Joel, I really like you. But I don't want to lead you on or anything."

Joel didn't turn around. "Okay," he said again.

"Listen to me a second. It's not you. It's nothing about you."

How many times had Joel heard this line? When he was young, he had never believed it; of course it was about him, what else could it be about? Now he was older, he ought to have been able to understand that there were a million other things it could be about. Of course it was about him.

Andrew went on. "You're a nice guy, you've got a nice smile, I really thought about it." This was, maybe, worse than hearing he had refused Joel spontaneously, out of simple revulsion. He had deliberated. "When I met Kenyon, I was young. We were both young. And over time we started to, I don't know, we both started to grow hair in our noses and ears, but he still looked young to me. I mean, he was always twenty-eight."

Joel thought: you son of a bitch. Did I need you to tell me

I'm not twenty-eight? He turned to face Andrew, finally, and managed to produce a nice smile. "I could trim my ear hair." This wasn't, come to think of it, a bad idea.

Andrew smiled back. "I'm trying to tell you, I can't start again. A relationship, I mean. I've . . . last month or so, I've been to bed with a few guys. But I can't get into anything serious."

Joel found himself deeply aware, suddenly, that the homeless man was still sitting there, taking all this in. What could he possibly think about it? Joel shrugged. "Who was talking about anything serious?"

Andrew opened his mouth but didn't speak right away. Who could blame him? This had to have been the clumsiest thing Joel had said in his entire life. After a second, Andrew said, gently as he could, "I don't think it's a good idea."

"No." More or less by definition: not if they were gravely discussing whether it was a good idea. For a minute they looked at each other, neither moving. It seemed to Joel that he had never looked at Andrew before. Andrew was handsome and sweet and Joel was about as eager to sleep with him as with . . . what was his name, that librarian? The incredible shrinking crush: Joel felt no desire at all, couldn't remember now if he ever had. "I'm still hungry," he said.

"I am, too, but I really have to get home." To call Kenyon's parents, the poor shit. "You going to be in the office tomorrow? I'll call you, maybe we'll have dinner this weekend. Or brunch or something."

"Okay."

"I'm . . . I'm kind of glad we got this over with."

"Me, too," Joel said. He sort of meant it, but as Andrew walked away he didn't feel glad for very long. It was true, the whole thing had never been real, he must just have fixed on Andrew as the appropriate man. Still, the deeply inappropriate man who was just turning the bend into Pennsylvania, who was already out of sight, had turned him down. In front of—

he was conscious of it, once again—the homeless man, who had sat unmoving through this whole little soap opera. He reached into his pocket, found a couple of crumpled dollar bills. Their hands touched, Joel felt the warmth of the man's hand.

"Bless you."

"Uh-huh."

"Your man sure go to a lot of trouble to look like a brother, don't he?"

They smiled at each other. "He sure does," Joel said.

Joel had been gone from the meeting how long, ten minutes? Too long for a cigarette. He was sweating a little, from running after Andrew; he had the odd notion that, if he went back to the meeting, they would know what had happened. He had chased Andrew, Andrew had escaped. Anyway, there was every chance the meeting had broken up by now. There wasn't much point in their running through a bunch of claims payment amendments just to hear Mullan say he wasn't sure about them.

He was just a block from the Hill Club, but he decided to go to Corcoran's, up on the Senate side. Confident that no one he knew would be there—not even Harris, home in Montana for the recess—and he could mope in peace. He walked up First Street, past the east front of the Capitol. There was some kind of concert, one of those summer things by the Marine Band. They were playing swooping arrangements of Rodgers and Hammerstein for a sparse crowd. Joel tried to conjure up some indignation, something about cuts in the National Endowment while there was unlimited funding for this crap. But he couldn't get worked up. There was a sort of innocence about the scene, a deep communion of futility. The musicians—hardened pros for whom the Marine Corps was just one extended gig— dutifully honking out the overture to *Carousel*, the audience of old people and a scattering of heat-whipped tourists with wandering brats clapping wearily. This event was not so much occurring as referring, to some never-was summer not even the old people had ever seen, a bandstand in the square of a town no one had ever dwelt in. That world wasn't gone, it had never existed.

Behind the band loomed the deserted Capitol. Maybe only Washington—only the Hill, really—could feel so empty in August, emptier than Paris. The offices didn't shut down any more, the way they used to before air conditioning. Not everyone went away, but those who remained moved through the heat with purposeless calm. Most of the year nothing was actually happening on the Hill, but it *could* happen: the general indolence could be broken by some sudden mysterious directive— "We will bring this to the floor Thursday . . ."—and there would be a sudden turmoil. So there was, in any other month, a waiting-for-the-shoe-to-drop feeling in the air. But in August the shoe could not possibly drop. Joel slowed down, strolled past the Supreme Court and the Methodist Building as if he were in no hurry to get anywhere, as if he had nothing special to do.

Inside Corcoran's, sunlight poured through the front window onto the ranks of empty tables; sugar bowls and ketchup bottles cast long shadows on the checkered vinyl tablecloths. The air conditioning battled the heat, but could not leach out all the dampness of August in the swamp capital. There were only two or three people at the bar. So the beefy bartender, whose eye Joel could never catch on an ordinary night, turned at once from his ball game and was elaborately polite. When Joel asked for white wine, he didn't just pour Joel the house swill but enthusiastically described their new pinot gris, which he said as "grease"; he wanted to give Joel a taste. Tonight the bartender's sleeves were rolled up to display his great golden-fleeced forearms; yet with what delicacy he reached above him for the glass, brought it down with the stem poised between two fingers. Joel tasted the pinot grease and said "Fine," though he knew it had to be two bucks more than the jug chardonnay. Because he wanted the bartender with the golden arms to think highly of him.

Only when this transaction was done did he realize that the black guy a few seats down from him was the one Ron had been seeing. Michael, that was it, wearing a suit, preternaturally crisp in defiance of the heat and damp, and drinking some kind of ice-cream confection. After a second, Michael saw Joel, but turned away with no sign of recognition. Instead he sat up straight and sipped his pastel cocktail with deliberate and unwelcoming dignity. Joel reached down for his briefcase, meaning to get out this week's *The Nation*, and found himself instead grabbing the briefcase and the pinot grease and moving to the seat next to Michael's.

Found himself: he didn't even begin to think about why until he was already sitting next to Michael and saying "Hi." Michael was startled but managed a rather dismissive "Hey."

Of course Joel imagined that, if Michael had dated Ron, he might not be altogether out of Joel's league. But this conjecture alone would not have driven Joel to the very daring gesture of changing seats in a bar. Something else: a gut lonesomeness that had to do not with Andrew but with the Marine band and its deflated listeners, and with this vacant theme bar whose replicas darkened the continent. A whole fraudulent nation, got up on purpose, as if someone had thrown a party and hadn't invited Joel—had in fact thrown the party expressly in order not to invite Joel. So maybe it was just that he thought they hadn't invited Michael, either. Sitting stiffly in his suit, in a bar that—in this part of the Hill—was about as integrated as a Birmingham lunch counter in the fifties.

Joel needed to say something. "Um . . . I think we met at Gentry."

"Yes."

"I was with Ron."

"I remember, Joel."

This was, perhaps, encouraging; but some people just remembered names more readily than others. Joel couldn't think what to say next. He came up with, "It's hot out."

Michael looked at him, perhaps with a flicker of pity, but didn't answer. Joel was trying to think of some equally snappy follow-up, perhaps about the humidity, when Michael said, "You know Ron long?"

"Yeah. Well, yes and no. I mean, I've known him for years, but we haven't really been friends. We just, lately we've had dinner a couple times."

"Uh-huh."

"You . . . I guess you dated him, huh?"

"Dated," Michael said, as if trying out how this euphemism felt on his tongue. "We saw each other a few times."

"That's what he said, yeah. But—I don't remember, it seems to me you had some kind of disagreement?"

Michael looked down at his ice-cream drink. "He didn't tell you about it?"

Joel wanted to say no, so he could hear the story directly, not as a refutation of Ron's. But he didn't dissemble very well; he would have given himself away somehow. "He said there'd been . . . some kind of misunderstanding about money."

"Yeah." Michael grimaced. "We misunderstood each other." He looked at himself in the mirror over the bar. Smoothed an eyebrow with a finger, a paleolithic swish gesture that didn't, when Michael performed it, seem effeminate. Just attentive: he was attentive to himself.

He swiveled a little on his stool—not actually turning his back on Joel, just shifting a degree or two, the way men did at Zippers when they wanted to let Joel know he shouldn't waste his breath. And why not? Joel might as well have said, "Hey, Ron told me you robbed him." He had killed it already.

Joel was already thinking about getting the check when Michael murmured, "We kind of misunderstood each other all along. You got another cigarette?"

"Sure." Joel held out the pack. Michael wrapped one hand around Joel's, while with the other he extracted the cigarette. His hand still rested on Joel's as he reached for Joel's lighter.

Joel glanced over at the bartender, who immediately turned to look up at the baseball game. Michael smiled at Joel's skittishness and removed his hand.

"It was only a couple weeks, we saw each other a couple weeks. But he must have thought all along that I was . . . there for his money. Like he even had any money, like I was too stupid to see how he was living. He must have thought I lived with rats and garbage on the floor and shit."

"He never went to your place."

"I don't take people to my place." This sounded mysterious and forbidding, though of course it was merely prudent; Joel had learned this rule in his tricking days. If you went to somebody else's place and he, say, killed you, he would at least have to go to the trouble of disposing of you. Whereas if you went to your own place he could do it and just walk away.

Michael went on: "The money thing—it was like it was the only way he could make sense of me. He's an old guy, and here somebody thirty years younger than he is wants to fuck him." This said quite loudly, Joel thought. Joel peeked again at the bartender. He looked back at Joel impassively, made no effort to pretend that he was watching his ball game. Joel was chagrined; Michael had blown his cover. As if he'd had any cover, as if he and Michael weren't quite plainly two gay men who had somehow popped up in a sports bar. Joel relaxed. Yes, they were, that was just what they were.

"I guess . . ." Michael said. "I guess he had to tell himself a story about it. Some guys—you know, they see a black face, there's only one story they can tell about it."

Some guys like me, Joel thought. He looked at Michael's beautiful eyes and felt that he could not imagine what was behind them. Or, rather, that he could, that some ineradicable core of viciousness that must have been imparted to him as a child was ready to tell the same story, to fill in the space behind those eyes with elemental Negro feelings. Resentment. Laziness. A propensity to steal people's money to buy drugs. All in a broth of indiscriminate, animal sexuality. Joel hated thinking these things, but they were there. Michael must have known they were there. What was it like, to go through life knowing that, to everyone you met, you were just a cartoon?

Joel was staring. Michael allowed him to, looked back calmly for a minute, then turned and called out to the bartender, with summoned-up brazenness, "Hey, honey, could you freshen me up? And get my friend one."

"That's okay," Joel said. "I . . ." He caught himself. Let Michael make his point, even if he couldn't afford it. And who said he couldn't afford it? He was wearing a suit, for Christ's sake. "Thanks."

What was Michael doing there, sitting in a suit in a straight bar on Capitol Hill? Joel had been so gratified to happen upon him that he hadn't even thought about this puzzle. He was about to ask—"What brings you to this neighborhood?"—when he realized that he would be as much as saying that Michael was in the wrong neighborhood. Instead he said, "I was thinking about getting something to eat."

"Oh. Me, too, I guess."

"You want to get a table?"

The two of them turned to look at the tables, bathed in fire from a Key West sunset. "Let's just stay at the bar," Michael said.

They studied the menus in silence. Joel wound up getting his usual elephant burger, Michael a caesar salad with grilled chicken.

"What were we talking about?" Michael said.

"About, I don't know, how Ron felt about you."

"He did tell you . . . the whole story?"

"Yes."

"Do you believe it?" Michael asked this neutrally, as if he were just taking a poll.

It wouldn't have cost Joel anything, or not very much, to say no. Of course not, how could I believe such a thing? But he felt

242

cornered by the question, summoned for jury duty in a case he knew nothing about. Maybe even conned somehow. A facile No would mark him as an easy touch, or at least as a man who would say what he needed to get into Michael's pants. "I don't know," he said.

"Well, how would you? You mind if I take just one more cigarette?" Joel slid the pack over, didn't offer his hand to be touched again. "So, Joel: tell me about you."

"Like what?"

"I don't know. You got a boyfriend?"

"No." Joel was almost prompted to tell his story, but caught himself. "Not just now."

"You live by yourself?"

"Yeah. Up near Dupont."

"Uh-huh. But you work around here, Joel?"

"Yes. How about you?"

"No," Michael said. "No, I don't work around here."

That studiedly uninformative response was not unusual in Washington. Even in the 1990s some gay men wouldn't say where they worked, as if their interlocutor might, next day, call their boss and unmask them. But it did raise again, in Joel's mind, the question: then what are you doing here? He had the momentary idea that Michael was trolling, had come here just to hook a Joel. This was silly: he could hardly have chosen a more barren fishing ground than Corcoran's. If he wanted to reel in a rich white guy, he would have been at Gentry. Where, come to think of it, Joel had first encountered him.

"What exactly do you do, Joel?"

The insistent use of his first name bothered Joel. It was a salesman's way of establishing intimacy. "I work for Congress."

"Oh." Michael nodded, his brow furrowed a little. Possibly he was speculating about whether people who worked for Congress made any money.

The elephant burger wasn't so enormous that Joel should have felt like Henry VIII, but he regretted ordering it. As if

243

his belly wouldn't have been obvious without the evidence of its cause, as if Michael wouldn't have noticed the smoke if he hadn't seen the fire. Still, it was impossible to eat an elephant burger without picking it up with both hands and burying your face in it. While Michael took birdlike pecks at his healthy little salad.

"How is that?" Michael said.

"Just, you know, a burger."

"Wish I could eat a burger. But I got to watch it."

"Oh, like you need to."

"Honey, I work out two, three hours a day."

Not a routine Joel thought of as compatible with continuous gainful employment. But he supposed some men managed it, at the cost of everything else. In any event, the results were evident.

"You should see my family," Michael said. "My mother, my sisters, they're all big as houses."

Joel nodded. He resisted the vision of Michael at home, surrounded by steatopygic black women. "I should start watching it myself."

"Come on, you're in good shape for your age."

Even with the qualifying phrase at the end, this wasn't so. Joel was conscious of being hustled. And maybe that was okay so long as he didn't kid himself. It would only be pathetic if he kidded himself.

"Your family," Joel said. "Are they . . . are you from around here?"

"New Jersey. Trenton."

"I've never been to Trenton."

"You're lucky."

"All I know is that big sign."

Michael recited: "Trenton Makes, the World Takes."

"That's the one."

"Trenton doesn't make anything any more."

Joel almost said, "It made you," but stopped himself. Not just because it was corny, but because it was pushy and lubricious. The kind of pick-up line an old man would use.

Trenton had made Michael. Joel pictured the blasted war zone Trenton must be now, and little Michael darting through the streets, dodging gang members, sidestepping abandoned needles, to get home to some hovel filled with his enormous mother and sisters, growing enormous somehow on food stamps. The thrifty food plan. Or maybe Michael's life had been nothing like this, maybe his mother was an overweight neurosurgeon. But Joel didn't think so. Michael had come from nothing and battled his way here, made the unimaginable journey here, where he sat in his crisp suit and ate rabbit food, holding his fork correctly. How, exactly, did Joel expect him to hold his fork?

The bartender cleared their plates and said, "Will there be anything else?" Michael looked over at Joel, as if he were supposed to answer for both of them. So he did: "No, I think that's it." And then, spontaneously but also feeling somehow steered to it, "I'll take our check."

Michael had done nothing to steer him to it.

Outside, Michael carried his jacket over one shoulder, hooked on his forefinger in that Sinatra way Joel had never been able to carry off, his other hand in his front pants pocket. Under the streetlight his white shirt glowed.

"Where are you headed?" Joel said.

"Home, I guess."

"Where's that?"

"Near Twelfth and T."

"Oh. We could share a cab."

"Great."

Joel waited for Michael to hail one. He sort of owed Joel, after dinner. Michael said, "A cab won't stop for me."

"You have a suit on."

"It doesn't matter."

Twelfth and T was closer than Joel's place. It should have been their first stop, but Michael insisted they should drop Joel off first. Maybe he didn't want Joel to see where he lived, or maybe he was planning to get out when Joel did.

The turbaned driver was talking over the two-way radio, in whatever language Sikhs spoke. He and the dispatcher were having some kind of argument; when it was the driver's turn to speak he became so impassioned that he almost brought the cab to a full stop. When he was listening, he drove with the speed of deliberation.

And what was Joel's hurry? If they had taken all night to get to Joel's place, that would scarcely have been long enough for Joel to decide what to do. When they finally arrived, though, there was nothing to decide. If he couldn't, under these extremely promising circumstances, manage a simple "Would you like to come up," he might as well have entered a convent.

"Would you like to come up?" Joel said. Realizing that the Sikh had ended his conversation; wondering if he would ever be far enough along not to care what a cabdriver thought about him.

"You bet," Michael said.

Not just "Okay," which would have left another bridge to cross up in the apartment, but the unequivocal "You bet." Unambiguous, maybe a little scary.

It used to be, before Sam, Joel would bring a trick home and they'd sit in the living room. Joel didn't even have the brains to buy a second-hand sofa; he had two Breuer chairs at the ends of the big table he used for a desk. He would sit down on one, as if he were about to type, and the trick would sit on the other, a good six feet away. They would supply the usual, instantly forgotten details about where they'd gone to school or what they did for a living. After some painful silence, Joel would at last say something lame like, "Can I show you the rest of the apartment?" And then they would go to the other room.

Later, some sleepless nights, Joel would lie next to Sam and think about how he might have done things differently in the pre-Sam years—about how he really should have bathed more in his early twenties, even if he was a bohemian; about how he couldn't have batted much worse if he had just walked right up to cute guys and gone "Hey," instead of mooning at them until someone else picked them off. When he rehearsed how he might have lived gay life more competently while he had the chance, he arrived at the conviction that he should have grabbed the trick the minute they got inside his apartment and he closed the door.

So this is what he did with Michael. Shut the door, grabbed him, tried to kiss him. Before Joel knew it, Michael was about fifteen feet away, arms in front of him in some sort of improvised martial arts pose. Joel felt like Senator Packwood.

Michael was almost as embarrassed as Joel was. "Sorry, I . . . uh, you kind of took me by surprise."

"I don't know what I was thinking."

"I know what you were thinking. I was, too, I just . . . Why don't you offer me a drink?"

"Michael, would you like a drink?"

"I'd love one, Joel. What do you have?"

"I don't know. Wine. Scotch. And—I think there's some beer in the icebox."

"The icebox?" Michael said. Joel felt a hundred years old. Even though he just said icebox because his mother did. "I'll take a beer if you find one."

Joel hobbled geriatrically to the kitchen. There was a beer. Neither Sam nor Joel had ever drunk beer, it must have been bought for some guest. They didn't have many guests their last couple of years together; the beer had to be getting kind of antique. Did beer stay okay? You never heard about auctions of 500-year-old cases of Löwenbräu. Now a glass. But all the glassware had been Sam's, Joel had six highballs he picked up at Woody's, and they were all in the dishwasher, unrun. Michael didn't need a glass, Joel could drink wine from the least besmirched highball.

What were they going to do, just . . . minutes from now?

Michael had been pretty clear about what he'd done with Ron; even the bartender at Corcoran's knew what Michael had done with Ron. But Joel and Sam hadn't done that for a long time, not since the time Sam threw his back out. Years. Joel wasn't sure he'd be able to handle it. He should have been practicing, maybe, with the marital aid Sam had left behind.

An opener. Joel fished through the utensil drawer, trying not to make a panicky clatter. There was a tea ball. There was a lemon zester, a melon baller. Every requisite for occasions that would never arise, but not for this occasion. Joel finally got the cap off the beer by sticking the point of a knife under the edges and prying it away crinkle by crinkle. When he brought their drinks out to the living room, feeling that he must have been in the kitchen half an hour, Michael was gone.

"Michael?"

No answer, but in a moment Michael emerged from the back of the apartment. "I had to pee like a racehorse," he said.

This simile alarmed Joel. He handed over the beer, then they were both aware that Joel had only the sibling-bereft club chair and the sofa. Michael took the club chair, a little smile on his face: he would teach Joel patience.

Patiently, Joel said from the sofa, "So what do you do?" Michael's mouth opened; he didn't speak. "I mean for a living."

"Oh. Right now I'm working at Hecht's."

"Oh, yeah? Which store?"

"Downtown. In men's wear."

"I go there sometimes."

"About every ten years?"

"I guess I'm not too into clothes."

"I'd like to dress you up," Michael said. Joel shrugged. "You'd feel better."

"Would I? I don't feel bad."

"Yes, you do."

Actually Joel had been feeling good, he thought this was how good felt. Attractive, something imminent.

"I can tell by the way you dress," Michael said.

Joel was irritated. Not that this was going to spoil anything, the way a trick used to be able to kill everything with a single fatuous word. Joel wouldn't have cared at this point if Michael had announced he was a member of the Nation of Islam, he had not made his last visit to the back of the apartment. But Joel disliked this facile assumption that Michael knew something about Joel and was called upon to share it, that this was somehow helpful. When really he was just a clothing salesman; if he were a car salesman he might have said Joel would feel better if he got an SUV.

All right, of course Joel had heard that depressed people let themselves go. But he had always been a slob, in good times and bad. It couldn't be that he'd been depressed his whole life.

It could be. "What should I wear?"

"I don't know. Stand up."

Joel stood up. Michael looked at him. He tried to put out of mind what an unprepossessing figure he must have cut. Michael had already seen him, and was here anyway. But Joel felt the special ungainliness he had always felt with clothing salesmen. He would come out of the cubicle wearing the suit, the unfinished pants legs gathered up above his shoes. The salesman would look at him, the way the coat barely buttoned over his belly, the lapels hovered over empty air where Joel was supposed to have a chest. The salesman would start talking alterations, and Joel would feel that it wasn't the suit that needed altering. He always had to leave when they started talking alterations, which was why he hadn't actually bought a new suit in ten years. Because he couldn't get it into his head that it was just a bit of cloth that could be unstitched and restitched; it was a template for the standard man he would never be.

Michael tilted his head, looked at Joel gravely. "You ought to get some better slacks. What are those, Dockers?"

"I guess."

"About a size . . ."

"I don't know. Thirty-four, I think." As if he could fool a clothing salesman.

"Uh-huh. You know, once the size gets up there . . . uh, gets a little larger, they start leaving a lot of room for . . . I mean, that's why they're kind of baggy at the crotch." Joel looked down. His pants were baggy at the crotch. There was a stain on the left leg. A forensic lab could probably have traced it to an elephant burger. "You shouldn't get these ready-made khakis, you need to get real slacks so they fit you."

"I guess I'm just cheap."

"You can afford real slacks," Michael said. Joel felt a little chill. How did they get into what Joel could afford? How did Michael know what Joel could afford? "And, I don't know, have you thought about changing your glasses?"

"I just did." Not four months ago, just before Sam went. Trifocals, for reading the *Congressional Record*, playing solitaire on the computer, and gazing listlessly into the distance.

"Take your glasses off."

Joel did. He was about to explain that there was no way in hell he was getting contacts when Michael was out of his chair, he was close to Joel, he brought his face into Joel's field of vision, and they kissed.

Joel woke up in the morning alone, on Sam's side of the bed.

After a minute he remembered: waking in the night, reaching an arm out to his own side of the bed, warm but empty. He looked up; by the ribbon of streetlight edging around the window shade he could just make out Michael—fully clothed, even his jacket on—standing, his back to Joel, before the dresser.

"Hey," Joel said. Michael turned, startled, then produced a smile Joel could see in the dark. The same smile he had worn all the time they were making love.

"Hey."

"You're leaving."

"I gotta. I got a staff meeting real early. And, I don't know, I don't sleep real good with strangers. I mean the first time."

"Oh." This was better than no excuse. But only a little: if it were true, he might have said it earlier, and he wouldn't have tried to sneak out while Joel dozed. Only when Joel had thought all this did he hear: the first time.

"I'm going to leave you my card. With my number at the store. Call me at . . . I guess eleven, it's real slow at eleven."

"Okay. Um . . . are you sure I should call you at work?"

"People call all the time. You know, is my suit ready, that kind of shit."

Joel got up, they kissed, Michael held him for a minute. Naked, in the arms of a man in a suit: a wonderful slutty feeling.

Michael pulled away. "Call at eleven, I'll be sure I'm on the floor. So we can figure out what to do tonight."

Joel lay in bed in the morning on Sam's side, remembering Michael's going, then remembering earlier. Michael had smiled the whole time, smiled and kept his eyes open. Sam was always serious: he clenched his eyes tight—was this only (and understandably) in their later years, or always?—and had the sort of frown a man wears when he is about to lift a heavy weight. Michael smiled the whole time.

Joel was touching himself, then he thought he'd better not, not if they were getting together again tonight. He got up and went to the dresser, picked up the card that was next to his wallet.

HECHT'S_____
Metro Center

Michael Greeley

Sales Associate

Men's Apparel   (202) 555-7914

About the size, if you turned it on end, of the ad in *man about town*. And as dense with meaning. Its bourgeois respectability, its square-edged whiteness, such an inconsonant thing, really, to have been left behind by the live brown creature who had warmed Joel's side of the bed for a while. The last name he had forgotten. Michael Greeley, Sales Associate. A whole life beyond this bedroom. Staff meetings, people calling to see if their pants were ready. The call at eleven.

It used to be, when the phone rang in a department store, it gave off a single clear tone: Ding. Ding. That was the sound of a department store when he was little, the dulcet intermittent bell, and he was quite grown before he realized that it *was* the phone and not some mysterious signal to the sales associates. Twelve dings for a nuclear attack.

Joel would call, Ding, and Michael wouldn't be there. Or he wouldn't recognize Joel's name. Or he would be astounded by Joel's naïveté and gall, calling him at work. What Joel held in his hand was no more consequential, made no more promises, than a salesman's business card.

For lunch Joel went to a place with a salad bar that was really about two or three little bins of wilted greens and then all kinds of Chinese stuff. His plastic tray had one big section and two smaller sections. He dutifully loaded salad into one of the smaller sections, filled the other with sparerib chunks, and packed the big section with kung pao chicken and sesame noodles. At the register he looked in his wallet and found three singles.

The night before he had paid his and Michael's check at Corcoran's, then the taxi, and, after getting his change and leaving the tip, he had put three singles back in his wallet. Next to a twenty. There had been a twenty left.

The bill compartment of his wallet was always filled with junk: ATM receipts, reminders of dental appointments, lots of paper. The twenty could have been buried. He hunted for it, conscious of the growing line of ravenous salad-eaters behind

252

him, and of the worried face of the cashier-matron. "Look," he said. "I, uh . . . can you hold on to my salad? I need to run to the bank machine."

As he waited at the bank machine, he saw himself quite clearly, sticking the three singles next to the twenty and even thinking, Good, I won't need money tomorrow, twenty will be enough for lunch and the Hill Club and I can stop at my bank when I get back to the Circle.

The cashier-matron looked as surprised to see his return as, say, Pat Robertson would be if there really were a Second Coming.

It was a million degrees out. He had meant to eat his nearly vegetation-free salad back at his desk, in the air conditioning. But he would have been interrupted, and he wanted to think hard about questions like: (1) when, exactly, Michael took the twenty; (2) what ineradicable germ of racism deep in his cortex made him think Michael took it; (3) whether someone who took the twenty would actually keep the dinner date they'd made when Joel called at eleven; (4) if he could have given all three twenties to the bartender and the shit just pocketed the excess; (5) where might be a good place to hide his money when he took Michael home and excused himself for a moment; (6) whether Michael was more likely to keep seeing him if maybe he failed to hide one twenty each time.

He sat on the low wall in front of the Madison Building, a good distance from his new pal the homeless guy. As he twirled sesame noodles around his little plastic fork, he watched the parade of staffers going to and from lunch. Serious young Republicans in their well-fitting khakis and blue shirts. If all the congressmen were straight, how come the staffers they picked were so uniformly cute, buffed and perky-looking, like the guys who won the scholar/athlete award in high school? Cute and malignant, working overtime to unravel the social safety net, going to their bars at the end of the day and bragging

253

over their nachos about how many people lost their food stamps today. But maybe it was only because life had never rubbed their perky little noses in any contrary idea. Sound bites ricocheted in their vacant skulls: there was still room for experience, some might graduate all the way to the summit of ambivalence and immobility Joel had reached long ago.

Joel tore himself away from the staffers and returned to the subject of Michael. Of course, unless you had the seven habits of highly credulous people, you didn't actually sit down and work through lists of numbered life-issues. He found instead that he was remembering their call that morning. The way Michael just took it for granted that they would meet that night, was even a little short with Joel on the phone—the way you can be short with somebody when everyone understands that you just have to get back to work. "Baby, I have to get off, I'll see you at seven," and he was off before Joel heard "Baby." Just a habit of speech; except Joel heard in it the smile Michael had worn all night.

Joel wasn't sure that smile had anything to do with him. He thought it was just about loving life, and then he thought at once that this, too, was a racist idea: that he was turning Michael into some sort of happy-go-lucky Negro. Only Michael did smile. In a here-we-are, grateful-for-the-moment sort of way that was not incompatible with, in the next moment, gratitude that Joel's wallet should contain a twenty. Joel pictured him, standing before Joel's dresser in the half light. Thumbing through the oddments of paper in Joel's wallet, feeling the distinct crispness of the buried twenty. Smiling.

The picture didn't displease Joel at all.

Joel looked up to see his boss Herb approaching. Wearing a jacket, despite the heat, which meant that someone had just taken him to lunch. He had a bow tie on today, so there was nothing to punctuate the tundra-like expanse of flimsy white shirt beneath it. Joel wished Herb would wear an undershirt;

it was disconcerting to see your boss's nipples.

Joel said, "Hey."

Herb said, "Joel, how's it going?" and sat next to him on the wall. This was an enormous incursion; Joel didn't want to talk to Herb in the middle of his lunch hour. Actually, he didn't want to talk to Herb ever.

Herb had been a GS-15 in the Social Security headquarters, having reached that eminence through longevity and a prodigious ability to kiss ass. After the Incident—whose details Joel had never quite been able to piece together, but which apparently involved a truly catastrophic misplacement of a decimal point, one that had darkened the golden years of many an annuitant—Herb had bid farewell to the executive branch and somehow found shelter as a Social Security analyst at OLA. There his gift for sycophancy had once again secured his promotion, so that he had become Joel's boss without the tiniest inkling of what exactly Joel did.

They only had two kinds of conversations. Ones in which Herb exhorted Joel to keep up the good work, whatever the hell that was. And ones in which Herb tried to assert himself, remind Joel who was boss by giving him some disastrously incorrect instructions. Joel would explain why he couldn't do what Herb wanted; Herb would smile indulgently, like a Mother Superior correcting an unruly but amusing novice; Joel would do what Herb wanted.

Herb had not interrupted Joel's lunch to present him with a meritorious service award. They were going to have the other kind of conversation.

"I just had lunch with Randy Craven," Herb said.

"Oh, yeah?" An old friend, with the Commerce Committee for years, then . . . Joel couldn't remember where he'd wound up. "What's he doing now?"

"He's with Hygeia."

"Right," Joel said. A pharmaceutical company. Where else? "So where'd he take you?"

"Le Dôme. Oh, uh, he didn't *take* me," Herb lied. Technically, he and Joel were subject to the same ethics rules as staffers: they weren't supposed to accept fancy lunches from people like Randy Craven. But no one cared very much, because they weren't in a position to exercise much influence. For the same reason, they were rarely taken to lunch.

"What did he want?"

"He didn't want anything, we were just schmoozing. The child health plan, that kind of thing."

"Oh, that. Are the drug companies still opposing it?"

"I didn't know they ever were," Herb said. "Randy seemed to be all in favor of it."

"I guess they changed."

"Why would they be against it? Everybody thinks it's a good idea to cover children."

"Right."

Some Marines ran by. One of the miracles of that neighborhood: the ceremonial platoons—from the barracks near Andrew's house, down on Eighth Street—running toward the Mall. Ten or fifteen at a time, loping by in nothing but red shorts, their brown torsos gleaming with sweat. Maybe all the congressmen who picked cute staffers weren't gay, but surely the commandant at Parris Island or wherever, who selected these matchless beauties unerringly for the honor guard . . .

Joel tore himself away from this spectacle and found that Herb was staring at him. Of course Herb knew he was gay, even used to ask sometimes how Sam was—didn't ask any more, so someone must have clued him in. What did Herb think about, as he watched Joel watch Marines? What was it like to be Herb, to sit on the wall and be presented with that sudden vista of beauty, red shorts and brown bodies flashing by like a gift from heaven, and be entirely unmoved? Like being color-blind, Joel thought, or unable to smell: going through a lifetime oblivious to a whole dimension of the world.

"Randy did mention this one thing," Herb said. "He thought

you might be doing some more work on the AIDS bill. The Harris thing."

"Uh-huh," Joel said, warily. Melanie had called him that very morning, asking if he had any numbers on how many people were having unsafe sex. Just that morning, and Randy Craven already knew about it. Sometimes Joel thought these guys were telepathic. He knew they were merely networked and not psychic; but this was in its way even more wonderful, to be so firmly and manifoldly linked to the world. At the center of a web, attuned to the tremor of every distant event. While Joel didn't even know what was happening in his own bedroom.

"What are you doing on it?" Herb said.

"Well, you know, the budget people keep telling them it doesn't save any money, because there's no way of enforcing it. There's no way of knowing who did something high-risk. So now Melanie's trying to persuade them that the rule will have a deterrent effect."

"You mean . . ."

"People won't have unsafe sex because they'll be afraid they won't get Medicare later."

"Oh. Well, I guess that makes sense."

Maybe it made sense to Herb. Joel had some trouble picturing it: two guys hopping into the sack, one of them abruptly sitting up, shaking off the trance induced by some horse tranquilizer, and saying, "Oh, we better be careful. Remember our health insurance!"

Joel went on: "So anyway, she needs some estimate of how many people are doing high-risk things now. And then she has to say that some number of them will stop doing it, and then they won't get sick, and then they won't need Medicare, and we'll save all this money."

"I see. Are you getting her what she needs?"

"I haven't . . . you know, I've been working on a couple other things. So I was going to look into it next week some time." Or next lifetime, since Joel really hadn't the slightest idea where he would get an estimate of how many demented faggots were barebacking. That was the word Melanie had used; Joel had never heard it before. He had been a little shocked to hear, over the phone, little Melanie casually tossing out this crudely self-explanatory neologism.

"Randy thought he might be able to help you," Herb said.

"What?"

"He said he thought you needed some numbers and he might have some."

"Why would a drug company want to help with the Harris bill?"

"They're supporting it," Herb said. "You didn't know that?" Herb straightened the ends of his bow tie; he was plainly delighted to know something Joel didn't. "You must have seen their ads."

"What ads?"

"The ones with that old lady who frets about losing her Medicare."

"Wait," Joel said. "Citizens for Personal Responsibility is the drug companies?"

"Who did you think they were?" As if Herb had known who they were before Randy Craven evidently blurted it out at lunch.

"Oh, I thought it was probably them," Joel said. "I just wasn't sure." He tried to imagine what possible reason they would have for pushing a bill that had no effect on them at all. Medicare didn't even cover drugs, there wasn't any reason they should have cared one way or another.

Joel couldn't figure it out. He could preen himself on his *access*: the badge that hung from a chain around his neck, that let him wander the secret hallways of the Capitol, that admitted him to closed hearing rooms while reporters and lobbyists milled around in the corridor, yearning to be inside. Like the other members of his fraternity, he wore the badge in his shirt pocket: that was how they could tell one another, the chains running around their necks and into their shirt pockets. But he was still a spectator, watching the intricate movements of the mechanical figures called members and staffers and lobbyists without, very often, getting a glimpse of the hidden clockworks that drove them.

Herb said, "You ought to call Randy this afternoon and get his numbers."

"Herb, I— You know, I guess Randy can make up numbers. But that doesn't mean I can just supply them as if they were real. I can't just take numbers from him and put OLA's name on them."

"Well, you can qualify them." Meaning Joel could send Melanie a table with a long footnote explaining why the numbers were garbage. Then she could reproduce the table without the footnote.

Joel wanted to say: you get the fancy lunch at Le Dôme, and I'm the one who has to spread his legs? He said, "I'll see what he's got."

"Good. Don't forget the staff meeting at two."

One of the astoundingly brazen squirrels from the Capitol grounds—the kind that would saunter right up to you with a gimme-your-goddamn-lunch expression—was loitering on the wall next to Joel. Joel had finished his kung pao chicken, so his salad was down to a few shreds of actual greenery. He surrendered it.

He had been thinking something important before Herb came. Oh: that he was, in fact, not at all dismayed by the picture of Michael rifling through his wallet. What was he discovering? Some sort of pathetic fifties thing, the john secretly pleased that the rough trade has robbed him, savoring the tingle of danger? No, something more elusive.

He thought back to those abortive romances he had had in the years before Sam. What is he really like, what does he think of me, when will one of us do something so profoundly uncool that it kills it, and which one of us will do it this time? You couldn't be yourself, you tried to be finer than you were—wittier, better dressed, hotter in bed than you really were—you tried not to do anything you wouldn't want the other guy to do. Even after fifteen years, years in which he and Sam had pretty much uncovered each other's most appalling traits—he couldn't ever just be, he had to try to be better than he was. Because it was a mystery why Sam was there, he didn't really think anyone could just love him. And he had been right, hadn't he? He hadn't, in the end, been good enough.

But Michael had either taken the twenty or he hadn't. If he had, then he was just hustling Joel and they would go on until Michael got tired of it or found some more promising quarry. If he hadn't taken the twenty, they would go on until Michael got tired of it or found some more promising quarry. Joel would never know which it was: a commercial transaction of necessarily limited duration, or a romance of necessarily limited duration. At the end he would not have to feel that he hadn't been good enough. He and Michael were just two people coming together for a minute, or maybe for longer: good enough wasn't part of the equation. Somehow the twenty had factored it out.

Joel felt for a second a wash of calm.

He was a person. A person having an actual experience, in the present tense. One that could not hurt him and that might—if last night was any indication—be kind of pleasant for a while.

He felt this for a second. And then—he couldn't quell it—he felt the tiniest hope that Michael hadn't taken the twenty, that they were getting together tonight because Michael actually liked him. He hoped he was good enough.

It was a special bonus day: a second platoon of Marines came running by. Chugging along in twos and threes, then one astounding guy running by himself. Not even breathing hard, just calmly loping toward Joel, his golden perfect abs glistening with sweat. Joel stared. The guy noticed; possibly Joel's tongue was hanging out. The Marine looked back at Joel with the perplexed, faintly troubled expression of the Santa Fe boy. He was proud of his body, surely—these guys didn't pick the most crowded possible route to the Mall because they didn't want anyone to watch them. He just didn't want to be watched by Joel. As if it were an incursion somehow, as if Joel were violating him simply by peering at him. When it was just that Joel was here on this planet, and the Marine was, and Joel couldn't help but look.

When he got back to the office, there was a voice mail from Bate. No information, just, "Call at your earliest convenience." A day earlier Joel would have been thrilled—not elated, maybe, but excited and anxious. Were they closer, had they hit a dead end? Today he was taken aback. Joel's life had resumed, he was having an experience in the present tense, and Bate had called to say: remember, just yesterday you were a loony embarked on a manic quest for something you know perfectly well doesn't exist.

He was too busy for the Santa Fe boy. He needed to call Randy Craven and get the numbers, and then he had a staff meeting, and then he had to hurry home and get dressed for an honest-to-God date with a three-dimensional man. His life had resumed; he was busy.

eight

Joel had the TV on, the Lehrer news hour, while he dressed. He was in the bathroom, looking over Sam's library of abandoned colognes and wondering if Michael would prefer Wall Street or Feral, when he heard Senator Harris's voice. He scurried out to look. Yes, there was Harris, on remote from somewhere in Montana, his talking head in a square box on the left side of the screen. In a box on the right side the Secretary of HHS, Charlotte Bergen.

Harris did his three minutes. Grinning—though he knew he should be somber, and modulated his voice appropriately, he couldn't help grinning because he was on the Lehrer hour. He had found a way into the spotlight, a little technical amendment had raised his head above the pack an inch. If things kept going, he could find himself chatting with Katie Couric. Then trips to New Hampshire, exploratory committees . . . Secretary Bergen listened gravely. She actually inclined her head toward the margin of her box, as if Harris were sitting next to her.

Harris wound up: he wasn't attacking responsible homosexuals, he wasn't sure if they could help the way they were or not. "Jim, this is really about a chosen, self-destructive life style. Let me read you some numbers that have really startled me, and I think will startle the American people. Last year as many as twenty-three percent of homosexual men between the ages of eighteen and thirty-four—"

Lehrer cut him off. "Senator, I'm sorry, but I did want to give the Secretary an opportunity . . ."

Amazing: Joel had given Randy Craven's spurious numbers to Melanie just that afternoon, and Harris was already spouting them on national TV. Wasn't Joel important?

Now it was the Secretary's turn. In that whiskey baritone, so surprising in such a tiny woman, she would explain how awful the Harris bill was, promise that the President would veto it as soon as it hit his desk. She began: "Jim, as you know, one of the themes of this President, this Administration, from the very beginning has been *personal responsibility.*" She uttered that phrase in the mandatory italics. "That's been the cornerstone of our welfare reform, our work in education and job training, countless policy areas. And we think it's very important to carry that concept over into health care. That people need to take an active role in maintaining their own well-being: diet, exercise, stopping smoking of course. And possibly there does come a point when people have to begin considering the consequences of their own actions."

She paused. Now she would bellow, "HOWEVER . . ."

No, she wasn't pausing, she had come to a full stop. Lehrer took a couple of seconds to realize this. Then he hurried to fill the dead time. "Madam Secretary, are you—does this mean the Administration is supporting the Harris bill?"

Bergen looked down, swallowed, looked up again, straight into the camera. "We are studying this issue closely," she said. "We think if there are safeguards to assure that the focus is on behaviors, what people *do* and not who they *are*, then there

263

may be something we can support." All this said rather wearily; it was a script she had not written. This was an argument she had lost, overruled by some White House operative or other.

"Senator Harris?" Lehrer said.

Harris was as dumbfounded as Joel was, and not much more gratified: if the Administration went along, the whole story could vanish from the papers overnight. "Well, of course I'm pleased that the Administration is willing to work with the Congress to tackle this very important issue. I'm sure if we sit down together, we can arrive at a solution that's best for the American taxpayer and the American family. I'm just happy to have been able to play some part in bringing this critical problem to the attention of the American people."

The Secretary offered the obligatory, "The Senator has filled an important role in bringing this issue to the table, and we look forward to working with him."

"Thank you, Madam Secretary," Lehrer said. "Senator Harris." The segment was over.

Joel could hear the hubbub at the Pledge before he even rounded the corner. Thursday night before Labor Day weekend, the place was packed. Everyone who hadn't gone away, to Rehoboth Beach or wherever, was here looking for someone who might last through Monday night. The crowd spilled out onto the sidewalk, a sea of men in their twenties and thirties, wearing tank tops and drinking cosmopolitans out of little plastic cups— No Stemware Outside.

Michael had insisted they meet here. Joel had thought Gentry, or even Zippers, but Michael wouldn't have it. Maybe because they would run into too many of Joel's predecessors. Joel wasn't sure if he should try to shove his way up to the bar for a drink or if he should look for Michael first. The Pledge had three floors: the street-level bar, a lounge upstairs that showed instructional videos, and a cellar bar called Initiation, whose backroom was once famous. Michael could be anywhere—except, Joel hoped, in the still-extant back-room—or, as Joel was precisely on time, probably hadn't even arrived yet.

He got his drink, after an epic struggle; what a small thing it was, a little plastic cup of brown liquid, that he should have had to clamor so hard for it. Then he wandered around—down to the cellar, out onto the sidewalk, finally up to the video bar. There was a seat! He grabbed it and watched the movie for a while, a classic from the seventies—he could tell, not just from the grainy film and the bad lighting, but because some of the men had bellies without ridges; others had body hair, or organs that didn't make Joel think of livestock. And, of course, because none of them had any protection.

The video was, in its way, a snuff movie: these men were killing one another, right in front of the camera. Yet there was a prelapsarian innocence about them. They were utterly unaware that they were—he still could not stomach the word—barebacking. As, of course, Joel had done in those years, just as innocent and unprotected. He was, as always, conscious of the injustice: that he should still be here, unpunished, while they were gone. As always, he had to suppress the thought that this wasn't unfair at all, because the men on the screen had had a good time in those years and he hadn't. Then he felt guilty watching them, as if he himself had killed them, just because sometimes he had a nasty thought he couldn't help. He didn't want to watch any more.

Halfway down the stairs he ran into Sam. Sam's mouth opened, but he didn't speak. "Hey," Joel said.

"What are you doing here?" Sam said, crossly, as if the place were an actual fraternity Joel hadn't been invited to join.

"Meeting somebody."

"Really?" Sam could at least have masked his surprise—even if Joel, too, was astonished to be meeting somebody. "Who?"

"A guy I met."

They were blocking the stairs; crowds had already massed behind each of them, guys above and below who thought true love was to be found on whichever floor they weren't on. Joel let himself be pushed downstairs. Sam turned and followed him.

"Who is this guy?" Sam said.

"I told you, just somebody I . . . you know . . ."

"Oh." Sam leered encouragingly. As if he were a tennis pro and Joel had just managed to get a ball over the net. "Well, that's good. What's he like?"

"He's . . ." Of course the very first word anyone would have used to describe Michael was "black." To withhold it would be as phony as one of those newspaper stories that reads, "The alleged assailant, Leroy X. Washington, was described as six feet tall, with black hair and brown eyes." Practically shouting what it will not say. Joel did not say it. "He's . . . I don't know, kind of young, nice-looking. He's in, um, sales."

"Kind of young. What's that exactly?"

"I don't know. A little older than Kevin."

"Uh-huh."

"You still seeing Kevin?"

"No. When's this guy coming?"

"He—" Joel was about to say, "He should be here by now." But he was afraid Sam might think what he himself, just that instant, was thinking: Michael really should be here by now. He said, "Oh, pretty soon, I guess. We left it kind of loose."

"Well, I hope I get a chance to meet him."

Joel didn't hope, not at all, that Sam and Michael got a chance to meet. He wasn't ashamed of Michael, exactly. He was just afraid of the conclusion Sam would draw, seeing Joel and Michael together. The entirely unfounded conclusion that Joel was a deluded old white guy being taken for some kind of ride by a gorgeous black guy half his age. "I hope you do, too," he said.

He wanted to know more about Kevin; that is, he wanted

to hear Sam say that Kevin had dumped him. He was trying to think how to compel this admission when Sam said abruptly, "Catch you in a minute," and was off. In pursuit of a kid with dark hair on the sides of his head and exploding strands of platinum on top, like fireworks drifting down in a night sky.

Joel found a place to lean at the bar directly across from the front door, so he would catch Michael the minute he came in. Many other people came in, not Michael, and the very first thing they saw was Joel. This was surely disappointing: they hadn't taken off early from work to groom themselves for hours, then caught the Metro or a taxi to the Pledge, in order to see Joel. Most averted their eyes and veered away from him. A few stared for an instant, with the chagrined expression of a child who has waited an eternity in line for Santa Claus and now beholds him. Joel's complementary chagrin was allayed for a while by the cheering thought that, while he might look like a loser, he was in fact a winner, who would be leaving with a beauty while most of these guys were still hunting. But he began to wonder what expression he might find on Michael's face, when Michael arrived and first caught sight of him.

Perhaps it would be better, when Michael showed up, if Joel weren't right there at the door, poised to jump on him like a starving predator. If Michael showed up. Almost an hour late already, this was tardy even by gay standards. Joel surrendered his space at the bar and wandered some more, arriving in the cellar just as Sam emerged from the backroom, his arm around the boy with the fireworks hair. Sam saw Joel and stopped short. The boy kept going, slipping free of Sam's encircling arm and skating past Joel with a beatific look that must have been chemically induced. It couldn't, in Joel's experience, have been induced by anything Sam had done.

What had Sam done? Nothing, probably. The backroom was not, as it had been so long ago, pitch dark; and the bouncers every so often patrolled it to make sure no one got much past heavy petting. The space referred to the seventies, like the disco oldies on the sound system, without allowing for a full-undress reenactment. The things that Joel imagined went on there once—he had never ventured in, not even in the old days—might be going on somewhere else; Senator Harris's statistics affirmed this. But it had been a chamber of insouciance, of the innocence Joel had seen in the video upstairs. Whatever venue had replaced it must be quite different: a party of cold deliberation, with Dr. Kevorkian as master of the revels.

It was pathetic that Sam had gone in there, with a boy so drugged he might as readily have gone in with anybody—Ron, say, or Joel. It was pathetic that Sam had groped some strange kid and had made so slight an impression that the kid had slipped away the minute they came out into the bright light.

It was pathetic that Joel was standing there alone, having boasted that he had a date.

"Hey," Sam said. "Weren't you meeting somebody?"

"I got here kind of early."

"Uh-huh. How many drinks have you had?"

"A couple."

From which Sam understood: three. "You better slow down. You know how you get."

Joel knew how he got. But it didn't matter, did it? As he had conclusively been stood up.

"Talk to you," Sam said. He hurried upstairs, probably in the hope that the kid was still there and might remember who he was.

Joel got a fourth drink. Stood up. If it had been twenty years earlier, Joel wouldn't have been surprised—on the contrary, he would have been more surprised if Michael had appeared. He hadn't kept score, but probably a majority of the repeat engagements he had made with tricks had not been kept. Until he came to see no-shows not as particular instances of rudeness directed personally at him but as emblematic of the gay sensibility: improvisatory, unfettered. To be gay was to acknowledge the primacy of impulse, so a date meant, if we both feel like it tomorrow at five . . .

Of course it never helped, telling himself this.

First thing Friday morning Joel called the only person he knew in the White House. That is, Kristen wasn't actually *in* the White House, but just up the street, close enough that her business card declared THE WHITE HOUSE and bore a little gold presidential seal. He reached her voice mail and told her he had a question about the Harris bill. Maybe she would call him back.

While he was waiting, he decided that he might as well find out what Bate had to say. That was how he put it to himself, casually. Even if the quest had seemed silly just yesterday, he had paid for Bate's time; he might as well hear whatever Bate had discovered, or failed to. But—as the phone rang twice, three times with no answer—the depth of his frustration betrayed just how deeply the hunt still mattered. This was real; it was Michael who had been the fantasy.

"Mr. Lingeman," Bate said, when he answered at last. How, in that tiny office, could it have taken him six rings to answer? "I have some amount of information." He managed to say "some amount" with no vowels at all, as if to illustrate the paucity of whatever information he had acquired.

"Great."

"Dinkeloo and Dinkeloo is, in fact, still in operation."

He paused. Joel supplied the inevitable: "However . . ."

"Needless to say, there is no record of transactions involving a minor account they stopped handling thirty years ago."

"Needless to say."

"However, my informant did suggest that in those years male models were ordinarily secured from either of two agencies, Talent International or Kennedy-Sexton."

He paused again. Joel jumped ahead. "Both of which are defunct."

"Both of which are defunct, Kennedy-Sexton only quite recently. I was able to trace one of the principals, Mr. Sexton, in fact, who is still living in New York City."

Yet another pause. Joel realized suddenly that Bate didn't do this for dramatic effect: it must have been that, given his enormous handwriting, each of these factules was on a separate page of his notes.

"Mr. Sexton recalled the model in question. I was rather surprised, actually."

Joel was not surprised: how could someone fail to recall the model in question? Still, a guy who ran a modeling agency had probably encountered his share of beauties over the years. The Santa Fe boy would have been just one of the stable: there was the cowboy for the cigarette ads, the debonair man with the eye patch for the shirt ads, the guy with the smirk who let women run their fingers through his hair goop. There was the guy with the blinding torso and the shy smile whom Mr. Sexton could recall after three decades.

"He asked me what my interest was. I didn't know what to answer. I had planned to say that I was with the Bate Agency in Washington, and that I thought the model might have the look we needed for a new campaign. But it occurred to me that he might find this . . ."

"Implausible."

"I didn't know what to say, I didn't answer at all. Finally he said, 'I don't have time for this,' and concluded the conversation."

Joel sighed. "Of course you couldn't go see him."

"New York, that would be travel."

"I'll pay for the travel."

"Mr. Lingeman, this gentleman lives at Four Fifth Avenue in New York City. I'm not going to find him out watering the lawn. I would have to go to the front desk and ask to see him, and he would say no."

"So you're just not going to do it."

"It's a wild goose chase."

"But if I'm going to pay you . . ."

"If you pay me, I'll report that I tried to see him and couldn't. And how would you know that I even tried? I just want to save you the expense."

"Thanks."

"I should have saved you the expense when we started. I almost told you: you can't trace somebody without a name. You have to start with a name."

"But look how far you got already. This guy must know the name, we're practically there." They were practically there. This time, positively, someone who knew the boy. "I'll go myself if I have to."

"Mr. Lingeman . . ."

"If I get the name, will you be able to find him?"

"If it isn't something like John Smith, there's a possibility."

"I'll get the name."

"Mr. Lingeman, I should tell you. What the gentleman said."

"Uh-huh?"

"He said, 'I'm dying. I don't have time for this.'"

As long as he was making phone calls he could make one more. Almost eleven, Michael would be at work. Ding, the phone would go, ding: a little carillon of self-abasement.

"This is Michael Greeley, how can I help you today?"

"Hi, this is Joel."

During the ensuing silence Michael was either constructing an alibi or trying to remember who Joel was.

"Joel! Oh, God, Joel, I'm so glad you called. I didn't have your number. I had to work overtime, and I couldn't meet you, and I didn't have your number, and I'm so sorry."

This was not incredible. "No problem," Joel said.

"Listen, I really want to see you again, but I can't tonight. How about tomorrow?"

"I—" Tomorrow, Saturday, Joel was going on an excursion.

He hadn't actually formed this plan, became aware of it only as an impediment appeared. An impediment? A possible date with a live human was an impediment to a silly journey in quest of someone who no longer existed?

What was it that Kevin had said to Sam? "You have to choose." The choice was obvious, he didn't have to take out a sheet of paper and make two columns headed Michael Greeley and Santa Fe. In the first column: has three dimensions.

"We could meet at . . . maybe nine-thirty or so, get a bite to eat."

"Why so late?"

"I, uh . . . I have a dinner date."

"You're going to dinner and then you're going to meet me and have dinner?"

"The President sometimes has three or four dinners."

"And he looks like it."

"I'll just have a salad or something."

"Right," Michael said. He knew Joel's pants size.

Joel first saw New York the year of the Santa Fe boy: 1964. Joel's father had a meeting, he took the family along. Joel could still remember, after the eternity of the New Jersey Turnpike, that first glimpse of the Empire State Building, the Chrysler Building. Then they plunged into the Lincoln Tunnel. Everything was magnified there: the bright tile, the echoing noise, the exhaust fumes, the heightened sense of velocity as they sped through that narrow space like blood rushing through a vein, sucked headlong toward the heart of the world.

They stayed at the Prince George, on 28th Street just off Fifth. The doorman wore livery and a powdered wig. Joel had a room of his own next to his parents'. While his father was at the meeting, his mother took him to Scribner's, that golden temple of books, then to lunch at Toffenetti's on Times Square, then to a matinee of *How to Succeed in Business Without Really Trying*. The next day they went to B. Altman's, which his mother for some reason preferred to Macy's, and then up to the Gallery of Modern Art on Columbus Circle, where Huntington Hartford had assembled a collection that only a fourteen-year-old could truly appreciate: late Dali, Magritte. In the evening, while Joel's parents dressed for dinner, Joel sat in a wing chair in the lobby of the Prince George and thought he looked grown up. One night they went to the Café Madrid and had paella. He couldn't remember where they went the other night, maybe the Stockholm for smorgasbord. Joel would surely have been dazzled if it had just been Schrafft's.

Today he was coming into New York by train: another tunnel, but pitch black, and he hardly felt that he was moving at all. He had been to the city maybe a hundred times since that first visit, and still, as the train came out of the tunnel into the patch of gray light, before it dove into the bowels of the post office, still he felt some flicker of what he had felt at fourteen. Even if he knew the Prince George wound up as the biggest welfare hotel in the city, even if every other place they visited had since disappeared, even if he had come to realize that *How to Succeed* was not the summit of the American musical theater: he still felt that he was coming into a city that was big enough for him. Big as his dreams were back then, the adult life ahead of him in the city of *man about town*: the big show, the late supper, the penthouse.

The feeling was gone by the time he came up the escalator and emerged into the cauldron of Seventh Avenue on a hot day in August. It was just a crowded, dirty city through which he needed to make his way. He walked to Four Fifth Avenue— mostly down Sixth, which had turned into a suburban mall, except not as glamorous—and he cruised the hot Hispanic boys. They were the only landmark here that aroused him now. Where were the Hispanic boys when he thought the most exciting vista in town was a billboard that blew smoke rings?

The woman at the front desk said Mr. Chambers Sexton was

out. There must have been five hundred apartments at Four Fifth, how could she possibly know who was in or out? No, Joel didn't want to leave a message, he just happened to be passing by.

He decided to wait. This was idiotic: who knew how long Chambers Sexton would be out, and how would Joel spot him if he came back? But Joel had the impression he would just know, as if someone who had once been in contact with the Santa Fe boy would give off some kind of aura. And perhaps he also supposed that a man who characterized himself as dying wouldn't venture out for very long.

Flanking the marquee out front was a pair of marble-walled boxes, each holding a bit of ivy, empty soda bottles, newspapers. Joel sat on the edge of one of them. The doorman said, "You can't sit there, mister."

Joel said, "I was supposed to meet Mr. Sexton. I guess he's running a little late."

"You can wait in the lobby."

"I just wanted to have a cigarette."

The doorman frowned, but a taxi pulled up, and he had to leave Joel to greet one of those ninety-year-old New York ladies, with the hat, the gloves—in this heat!—the designer dress with a very short hemline, to show off her astonishingly preserved gams. By the time the doorman had helped her hobble into the building and came back out, he had accepted Joel as part of the landscape.

Chambers Sexton had been in contact with the Santa Fe boy. Could this have been literally so? Joel would have liked not to think so. But there were an awful lot of pretty faces in the world, more faces than ads. He didn't suppose Mr. Sexton chose among them by playing eeny-meeny-miney-mo.

The doorman glanced at Joel now and then as he had a second cigarette, a third, watched the crowd on Fifth Avenue.

The Prince George was—what?—maybe a mile uptown. It occurred to Joel that when he and his parents got back from dinner and he went to his very own hotel room with a television set he could watch from his bed all by himself, at that very instant, Mr. Chambers Sexton was in another bed just a mile away, holding a private audition for the next vacancy in his stable: the cigarette man, the man with the eye patch. The adult life Joel would actually embark upon was already there, all around him. The hustlers loitering near Toffenetti's, the chorus boys in *How to Succeed*, maybe the waiter who brought the paella: the real city that was Joel's future was all around him, and he hadn't seen it.

The doorman was looking at Joel steadily, a little perplexed. From which Joel understood that the man just walking into the building must have been Chambers Sexton; the doorman was wondering why he didn't stop for Joel. Joel hurried inside and got to the front desk just as the receptionist was saying, "Oh, here he is now, Mr. Sexton."

Sexton turned to look at Joel. His head was hairless, his cheeks sunken. Chemotherapy or fashion, wasting or just old age? There was no way of knowing. His sweater—in all this heat—was draped over his back, the sleeves knotted in front like an enormous cravat.

Joel veered into the sitting area of the lobby and murmured, "Mr. Sexton." As he had hoped, Sexton came over to him, so that he would not have to endure his rebuff under the very nose of the receptionist. "Mr. Sexton, can I talk to you just one minute?"

"What?" Sexton said, with a mixture of curiosity and annoyance, perhaps also a hint of trepidation.

"I . . . I know you don't want to talk about this, I understand, but I've got to—"

"Oh, shit."

"Sir?"

"It's about that boy, isn't it?"

"Um . . ."

Sexton fluttered his hands in front of his eyes, as if to make

275

Joel disappear. "This all stopped years ago, you're the very last one."

Joel was too stunned to answer. The last one: there had been some procession of deranged faggots like Joel, all on the same fatuous quest. He felt like an Egyptologist who opens a tomb and finds, amid the hieroglyphs, Kilroy Was Here.

Sexton lowered his hands and looked at Joel, one eyebrow raised. "Huh. You are the very last one, aren't you?"

"I guess."

"I suppose there must be a last living member of the Rudy Vallée fan club. It must be lonesome for the poor dear, to be the only one who remembers what they all saw in that queen."

Joel chuckled with him. Hoping that he would think of Joel as a fellow queen who happened to be in an entertaining predicament. Rather than as a pathetic loser who had missed the last bus to Santa Fe thirty years ago.

Sexton stopped chuckling, shook his head. "To tell you the truth, I don't even remember his name."

Joel looked down at the floor. There could have been no more conclusive put-down than to tell Joel that the figure who haunted him was so unmemorable to someone who had actually encountered him. When Joel looked up he found that Sexton was staring into space. Trying to remember the name? No, he had the expression, not of someone searching, but of someone struck with a vision. He was remembering something other than the name.

Sexton shook his head again, brought Joel back into focus. "We could look it up."

When Joel stood behind him in the hall and he put his key in the lock, Joel had a clear vision of the apartment they were about to enter: a couple of pieces by Corb, the windows bare, on one wall a huge painting—maybe a Warhol Elizabeth Taylor, maybe a Haring.

Sexton opened the door, stood aside. Joel walked into a room that might have been decorated by his own mother. Pale green wallpaper punctuated by a few reproductions of hunting prints; the windows looking out on Fifth Avenue framed by drapes in a beige, nubby fabric; a sofa with an ill-fitting gold slip-cover; before it a coffee table that held a glass ashtray and a copy of *TV Guide*. The table had a couple of rings where Sexton or a guest had put a glass down without a coaster.

Sexton seemed to be waiting for Joel to say something. Joel walked to the window and said he liked the view, even though they were only on the seventh floor and the view was basically of the seventh floor of the building across the street. When Joel turned around Sexton was much smaller than he had seemed in the lobby: just a short, slender, bald man who looked as though he was expecting someone to punch him.

"The office is back this way," he said. He led Joel down a hallway with the same green wallpaper. Joel caught a glimpse of the bedroom, with a faux-bamboo five-piece suite from about 1960, then a bathroom with sky-blue tile. The office was the tiny second bedroom at the end of the hall. There was a steel desk with an electric typewriter and a couple of long boxes with cards in them, like the drawers of a library catalogue; one wall had shelves on which were row after row of loose-leaf binders marked with letters of the alphabet.

Sexton sat at the desk; there was nowhere for Joel to sit. "What was the name of the client again?"

"The client? Oh, Simms of Santa Fe."

"Right, right." As he thumbed through his card files, he said, "You know, I have never done this, not once, I had an absolute rule. All the years I was in business, people tried to get me to put them in touch with my boys. Friends mostly, they'd corner me and ask, 'Who is that dreamboat in the Vitalis ad?' I'd just tell them I wasn't a pimp. But this one, this one I got calls from perfect strangers. Mostly right around the time it ran, when was that?"

"Nineteen sixty-four."

"Right. But for a while after that, too. And one queen, I remember this, one queen screeched at me: 'What's it to you? If he doesn't want to see me he doesn't want to see me, but what's it to you if I call him? Can't the guy take care of himself?' And I said no. No, I didn't think he could."

He looked up at Joel. Possibly they were both framing the same question: why was he breaking his rule for Joel? Maybe because, if the guy was still alive, he must have learned how to take care of himself.

"Here we go. Peter Barry."

Peter Barry. Not exactly John Smith, but there must have been plenty of Peter Barrys in the world. How was Bate ever going to find him, and what would it cost?

Sexton got up and pulled down the first of several B binders, started thumbing through it. Page after page of head shots, interspersed with yellowing typed sheets that must have been résumés or lists of assignments. All different kinds of men, young and old, cute and distinguished and elegant and rough. His card file was the catalogue of a library of beauty. Except that the words in books didn't get older, while all of these faces had.

"Barr, Barrett, Barrow, Bartlett. Funny, he should be after Barrow."

"Maybe it's Berry. With an 'e'."

Sexton looked at Joel coolly: he didn't make mistakes. Then he started flipping backwards through the pages. At last he paused. Joel could see, over his shoulder. It was the boy. A glossy photo: the boy unsmiling, wearing a jacket and one of the absurdly skinny ties of those years, his hair in a pompadour instead of the brush cut in the ad. Joel could see, as he couldn't in the tiny photo in *man about town*, that the boy had a cleft chin. He was lit from one side, to emphasize his sculpted features, and his forehead had an even sheen that hinted at airbrushing, to hide a blemish or two.

Sexton flipped the photo over and studied the typed page

that followed it. "Oh, here's why," he said. "He wasn't really Barry, he was . . . I can't even say this."

He handed the binder to Joel.

```
7/19/63
Name:      Petras  Baranauskas
Address:   1693  Bridge  Street
           Roseville,  New  Jersey
Phone:     KL  5-9732
Born:      5/11/40
Hair:      Blond
Eyes:      Blue
Height:    6'0"
Weight:    180
Suit:      46R
Waist:     32
Shirt:     16-34
Shoes:     10  1/2-D
```

Below this, handwritten: "10/8/63. CL: Simms of Santa Fe. AG: Dink & Dink. PH: A. Markey."

"Baranauskas," Joel said.

"What kind of name is that?"

"I don't know, Greek? He doesn't look Greek."

"He looks like a Polack."

Joel turned back to the photograph. He didn't like the guy in the photograph. The guy was sleek and ordinary. A model. "Maybe it's Lithuanian or something," Joel said.

"Uh-huh."

Joel flipped through some of the other pages. Some of the models had five or six handwritten entries, some had so many they ran over to extra pages.

"It looks like you only used him once," Joel said.

"Yeah, just that one shoot, with Andy Markey. When does it say?"

"October of sixty-three. Kennedy would have been alive."

"Would he? I remember now. Peter wasn't right for most work, you know? Forty-six chest, he couldn't do suits, he wasn't rough enough for cigarette ads or smooth enough for liquor, his eyes were too sad for soft drinks or convertibles. So this swimsuit thing came up, and I sent him out on that."

"And that was it?"

"I knew that would be it. Once he'd done that ad—practically screamed, 'fairy'—I knew I wasn't going to get him any other work. I . . . I guess I sacrificed him. I threw him away on this job." He took the book away from Joel, looked at the photo. "After a while, he kind of got the picture, and he asked me if there was any more of . . . that kind of work. But the client—I think the client was already out of business."

"That's right," Joel said.

"I was beat, and guilty, and I gave him the name of GMA."

"Who?"

"The Grecian Modeling Association."

"What was that? Porn?"

"Sort of. I mean, it was as racy as things got. God, '63 or '64, they were probably still using the posing straps."

"So did he do it?"

"I don't know. I wasn't into that stuff back then." Sexton smiled. "Back then, I didn't need to look at magazines. I don't know if he did it or not."

Maybe he did? Maybe Peter Barry had become one of the oiled figures in the physique magazines, in a posing strap and possibly wearing a sailor's cap, leaning on a plaster column, behind him a clumsily draped curtain. So if Joel had gotten up the nerve in those days, if he had ever dared to walk up to a cash register and buy one of those magazines, he might have had pictures of the boy . . . not much more revealing than the one in *man about town*. Except maybe Joel would have gotten to see his butt.

"I hope not," Joel said. "I hope he went back to Roseville, New Jersey."

Sexton had been looking steadily at the picture for a while. Joel asked—he had to ask: "Did you . . . you and . . . Peter Barry, did you ever . . ."

"What? Oh." Joel expected him to be angry, but of course he wasn't. Joel had been out of circulation too long, he'd forgotten how casually one used to be able to ask that question. As one might ask, have you ever been to the Café Madrid? "I don't think so," Sexton said at last. "It wasn't, you know, part of the job description."

"No?"

"No. I don't mean that no boy ever found that the road to stardom ran through my bedroom. But I didn't force myself on them."

"Ah." Joel was still chewing on the "I don't think so." How many boys must have passed through that bedroom if the man couldn't even recall whether Peter Barry had been one of them?

"No, I'm pretty sure this one was straight."

"Uh-huh."

"So he should be especially displeased when you appear on his doorstep."

"Well . . . who said I was going to do that?"

"My dear, you've chased him down across thirty years. Are you trying to tell me you're going to stop here?"

"No."

"No, you're going all the way with this lunacy. It's funny, you don't seem especially demented."

"I'm really not."

"You really are." Sexton put the book back on the shelf and ushered Joel into the hallway. "I should be alarmed. I mean, here I've let you upstairs, I don't know what I was thinking of. You could be . . . oh, John Hinckley, or—who was that one who stalked Lennon?"

"I don't remember."

Sexton was urging Joel toward the front door; his grip on Joel's shoulder was strong for a man alleged to be dying. "You could be one of those. And I've helped you. What are you going to do when you find him?"

"I hadn't even thought that far."

"Uh-huh."

"I haven't." Joel managed to shake loose the claw on his shoulder. He wanted to acquit himself of dementia. "There isn't anything to do when I find him. I know that. Just look at him, I guess. Or maybe tell him . . ."

Sexton waited, as if there were some possibility Joel could finish that sentence. After a minute he sighed. "Before I throw you out, you might as well have a drink."

"No, thanks," Joel said, but Sexton had already drifted into the living room.

"I don't drink any more, but I think there's some kind of whiskey."

"Really, it's okay, I've got a train to catch."

"Well, sit just a second."

They sat on the sofa with the gold slipcover. Sexton produced, from his shirt pocket, a pack of cigarettes and a plastic holder. He held up the holder. "This is phase two of a stop-smoking program. I've been at phase two for ten years."

"I know how it is," Joel said, lighting a cigarette of his own.

"I won't be getting to phase three."

"I'm sorry."

"When I found out I was . . . sick, I started calling people. People I hadn't talked to in years. My college roommate. My cousins in Iowa. My first lover. 'Hi!' I'd go. 'This is Chip! Chip Sexton!' They'd go, 'Oh.' Just like that, and then there'd be this long silence, while they decided just how deeply they wished they hadn't picked up the phone. Finally, they'd say, 'Hi, Chip. Been a long time.'

"It was funny, when I asked them what they'd been doing, people didn't recap the whole last thirty or forty years or

282

whatever it had been since we'd talked. They'd say what they'd done last week: Bunny and I went to the flea market, or Suzie got admitted to Dartmouth. Then they'd ask what was new with me. I'd say, 'Nothing much. Just happened to be thinking of you.' Pretty soon we'd hang up.

"I wasn't calling to tell them I was sick. I had this notion that I ought to tell them how much they meant to me. That I shouldn't . . . go without having told them that, it was important for them to know. But it wasn't. Maybe it was important for me to know. But if I had told them, it would have been a lie. The person at the other end of the phone didn't mean anything to me. Do you understand?"

Joel nodded wearily. He recited in a monotone: "It wasn't the same person. That person didn't exist any more."

"What? Oh, no. No, that's not what I'm saying. Of course it wasn't. I mean, for God's sake, Bunny—I don't even know what gender Bunny is, how could my first lover have wound up with a Bunny? But what I'm saying is . . . how old were you when you, whatever, fell in love with that picture?"

"Fourteen."

"Fourteen, Jesus. So you must be . . ." Sexton did the arithmetic and, mercifully, didn't say: You look older than that. "If he were the very same person, you wouldn't love him any more. That's really what I mean. My roommate meant something to me when I was twenty, my first lover when I was twenty-three, but I'm not the man who loved them. If there had been a—what do you call it?—a time warp, if through some magic of the telephone switching system I had got, on the other end, the same person I loved, unchanged, no daughter at Dartmouth, no Bunny—it wouldn't have mattered."

"Then why did you make the second call?"

"I'm sorry?"

"After you called the first person and . . . made this discovery, why did you call the second one, and then the one after that, however many?"

Sexton smiled. "Good question. I don't know. I guess I was hoping it would be different. That there'd be someone I still . . . felt some connection with."

Sexton put a new cigarette in his holder, looked at it for a while without lighting it. He murmured, "That's it, I guess."

"What?"

"I was trying to call myself."

Sunday morning Joel and Michael had brunch, on the terrace at Hamilton's. Joel had never done this before: taking your trick to brunch at Hamilton's, so everybody who was there with his trick would see how much better you had done. You could tell the pairs who had just met, because they talked a lot and they looked at one another, only surreptitiously glancing at other tables. Couples who'd been together a while didn't talk much, and when they did it was about the people at other tables.

Michael said he was going to have an egg-white omelet with grilled vegetables and no cheese.

"Oh," Joel said. "Um . . . me, too, maybe."

Michael looked at Joel seriously. "You should get what you want."

"I don't want you to think I'm a piggy."

"It's too late. I already think you're a piggy." Michael grinned. "I *know* you're a piggy." Which was not about breakfast. Joel grinned back. It was wonderful to sit on this terrace and share the knowledge that they had been piggies. Or some kind of animals.

Michael went on: "If I had my way, I'd have about a dozen eggs and biscuits with sausage gravy."

This was the first identifiably ethnic remark Michael had made in their hours together. Not black, particularly, but southern. Maybe Joel was part southern himself; biscuits and sausage gravy sure sounded fine. He scanned the menu in vain. Just lots of different Benedicts: it was amazing how many different things could be interposed between a poached egg and an English muffin.

Michael wasn't very black. He didn't have any accent, not even a New Jersey one. He hadn't done anything complicated to his hair. He wasn't wearing two-hundred-dollar sneakers, or jeans whose waistband hovered at mid-thigh. Sam's Kevin acted, dressed blacker than Michael. And was possibly better hung. Really, Joel had practically forgotten that Michael even was—

Right.

Joel was perfectly conscious that, while he was brunching with the most beautiful man on the terrace at Hamilton's, everyone who saw them saw only a middle-aged white man and a young black man, the only one in the place. Michael had to be feeling the same thing. Or maybe not: he was twenty-six maybe, or twenty-seven, Joel hadn't asked because he didn't want to tell his own age. Michael had dwelt, say, twenty-six years in that skin, he couldn't spend every waking minute thinking about what it said to people. At some point, if he wasn't to go crazy, he must have said to himself: here I am, in this skin, this body, and I am just going to be. I am going to sip my mimosa and watch the people who pass by on Seventeenth Street. I am going to look out from inside here and I am not even going to think about what people see when they look back.

Which was the way he'd been in bed, really. So unselfconscious, so freely and unabashedly himself that he had freed Joel as well. They had done the things Joel could never do with Sam. Not all of them—Joel was not so limber in reality as in his dreams, and one act in particular that he had been especially fond of imagining turned out to violate several laws of physics. But they had done many things, Saturday night and into this morning. It all just seemed to happen. Joel didn't have to, impossibly, spell out his desires. Michael discerned them, from a glance, from some almost imperceptible inclination of

Joel's body. He paid attention to Joel's body, as he paid attention to his own.

Michael was still looking out at the street; neither of them had spoken for a while. Joel thought of questions he might ask. Things he actually wanted to know: Did Michael grow up poor? Had he been to college? How did he wind up at Hecht's? Did he plan to be in menswear the rest of his life? But all these questions would have been asked from across a divide, as if Joel were an anthropologist. If Michael had said yes, he grew up poor, what would Joel have done with this intelligence? Tell me in detail what it was like, living on the thrifty food plan; I'll take notes.

What did he and Sam talk about their first days, before they were able to talk about the daily business of their life together?

"Oh, look," Michael said. "A Corvette."

Joel looked. "Uh-huh."

"That's what I want. Except not red, that's a cop magnet. I want a black one. And not a convertible, the kind of Targa top they have."

"Uh-huh," Joel said. He had no idea what a Targa top was.

"What kind of car do you drive?"

"I don't have a car."

"You don't?"

Joel said slowly, as if talking to a lunatic, "We haven't been in a car."

"No, but I thought, you know, you just didn't use it to get around the city. You really don't have a car?"

Joel hadn't until now felt that this was especially eccentric. "It just isn't worth it."

"Do you even know how to drive?"

"Of course I know how to drive." He drove once a year, or had until this year. Once a year he and Sam had flown to Boston and rented a car to go to Provincetown. Sam wouldn't let Joel take the wheel until they got onto the Cape itself, to that stretch of Route 6 that was just two lanes and that a child could have navigated. Joel wondered now if he would ever drive again. "I was driving when you were in diapers."

Luckily, Michael responded to this unfortunate, and probably accurate, remark with a snap of his fingers and a haughty, "I don't do diapers."

"What—do people . . . *do* diapers?"

"Sure. There's this whole scene."

"I don't think I want to know about it."

"Me either." Michael shuddered. "But, hey, don't you have any kinks?"

Joel had thought that some of their activities last night and this morning constituted kinks. "I guess not. How about you?"

"Nah. Just this thing for old white guys."

This said lightly, as if Joel shouldn't mind. He was an old white guy, and he had stumbled on a beautiful man who had a thing for them. Or for their wallets.

Michael's zero-calorie omelet arrived, along with Joel's Piggy Benedict. Joel was ravenous: he ate everything, even the melon slice and the strawberry, and was contemplating cleaning up the remaining hollandaise sauce with a spoon, while Michael had downed one or two grilled vegetables and had taken two bites from a piece of toast with no butter. Michael ate even slower than Sam; Joel would probably be watching him nibble all afternoon.

"So," Joel said. "Are you saving up?"

"What?"

"For the car. For the Corvette with the Targa top?"

Michael put his fork down—the last thing Joel had meant him to do. "No," he said, with a rising inflection that suggested the question was crazy. Which it was. Joel understood: people didn't *save up* for things. This concept was left over from old movies where large, tumultuous families stowed spare nickels in a cookie jar so the studious daughter could go to college and then write about her tumultuous family. Michael would have a Corvette if he won the lotto or found a sugar daddy.

Meanwhile, his financial planning probably consisted of trans-
ferring his Visa balance to a new MasterCard with a low intro-
ductory interest rate. As his career planning probably consisted
of making sure he didn't call in sick so often that he got
written up.

The divide between them wasn't racial, or even generational.
There were people like Joel, who put money in accounts they
couldn't draw on until they were fifty-nine and a half, and
people like Michael, who must have thought that reaching
fifty-nine and a half was neither likely nor even especially
desirable.

Jesus, was he positive? He and Joel hadn't—that word of
Melanie's again—they hadn't barebacked. But neither of them,
not last night or in their first encounter last week, had sat up
and said, "Oh, we better be careful. Remember our health
insurance!"

If he wasn't infected, he was possibly one of those kids who
figured he would be sooner or later, that it was just a part of
being gay—eat your omelet slowly, taste every mouthful,
because you're never going to be fifty-nine and a half, or even
forty.

Could Joel ask? Did people ask this question? Maybe it was
part of contemporary dating etiquette. But if so, you were
probably supposed to ask it somewhat earlier in the proceed-
ings, not at brunch the next day. The answer couldn't matter
now. Or it could: Joel could still improve his odds by assuring
there were no further opportunities for transmission. They
would be more careful, Joel would make it plain that they
needed to—

No, he wouldn't. If Michael stayed another night—if he
didn't just finish his omelet, wait for Joel to pay the check,
and then walk away—they weren't going to shroud themselves
in Saran Wrap and talk dirty to each other from across the
room. It might be their very last time. Or, if it wasn't, then
the next time might be, or the next.

Joel and Sam had had a last time. The weekend before Sam left. Had Sam known it, that they would never be together again? What could that have been like? What would it have been like if Joel had known, too, that this was going to be it?

Michael put his fork down again. "What are you thinking?"

"Nothing."

He would have paid attention. If he had known it was the last time, he would have looked at, touched, tasted every surface of that body that was so familiar he had stopped seeing it at all.

When Joel woke up, it was seven in the evening, still daylight. Michael was in the living room, watching MTV. Joel stayed where he was. He wanted to be with Michael, but he didn't want to watch MTV. More precisely, he didn't want to watch MTV naked. Michael's clothes were on the chair in the bedroom, he was in the living room naked. Joel felt, somehow, that for him to go out into his own living room naked just now would be asking too much: too great an imposition on Michael's good will, or greed.

Once, in his tricking days, Joel had miraculously spirited home a gorgeous man—a modern dancer, the guy said, touring with some company from New York. The encounter had proceeded in the usual clunky way: the two of them seated separately in the living room, Joel at last suggesting the tour of the rest of the apartment. The clothed grappling on Joel's bed, shirts wrestled off, shoes. Then the guy said he had to pee. While he was absent Joel went ahead and finished undressing. The guy came back, looked down at Joel's body, which was arranged in whatever casual posture Joel had thought might be most fetching, and said: "That was a mistake." Joel just lay there, speechless, while the guy tied his shoes, pulled his Lacoste back on, fled. It was a wonder Joel didn't go off the next day and take holy orders.

If the guy was in fact a dancer from New York, he was

probably, in the late seventies, positive; perhaps he had unwittingly saved Joel's life.

Joel called out, "Hey."

"Oh, you're up," Michael said. He turned down the volume on MTV but didn't leave the living room. "I thought you were going to sleep till Tuesday."

"I was up half the night."

"I know, I was there."

"So how come you're not sleepy?"

Michael didn't need to answer. Because I'm not an old man.

"I guess we ought to think about getting something to eat," Joel said.

"You just had a huge dinner."

This was kind of southern, too, wasn't it? Calling the midday meal dinner, it spoke of some world anterior to Trenton, some little town somewhere from which the Greeleys had escaped.

"I'm kind of funny," Joel said. "Sometimes I have as many as two meals in one day."

Michael laughed. Joel was pleased with himself, and oddly surprised that Michael got the joke. Why shouldn't he? Probably people spoke English in Trenton.

Michael appeared in the doorway. A hundred times more beautiful than that dancer from New York. He looked down at Joel, Joel pulled the sheet up almost to his neck. Michael just stood, serenely naked, for a minute. Then he said, "I'm going to take a shower. You got any more clean towels?"

"I don't think so."

Michael clucked and headed into the bathroom. Imagine making him use the same old towel. Why was he going to take a shower anyway? They had both showered before brunch, and they hadn't done anything after, just came back and went straight to sleep.

Joel guessed he was supposed to take another shower, too. However long this lasted, they were embarked on some sort of regime. Joel's hygiene would be under continuous scrutiny, and his eating habits, and the way he dressed.

When he heard the water start, he jumped out of bed, meaning to be all dressed before Michael came out. He was gratified to unearth one pair of briefs with no holes in them. Now pants. Certainly not the Dockers Michael had scoffed at the other night. Jeans, then, and what, a polo shirt? The first two he tried on made him look like one of those little Chinese statuettes of a wise man; you were supposed to rub its belly and make a wish. The third had an enormous grease stain from some forgotten night of gluttony, the fourth had vertical stripes. When had he ever been so foolish as to buy a shirt with vertical stripes, like the longitude markings on a globe?

He lay back down on the bed, in his briefs, and despondently lit a cigarette. Impossible. Even if Michael had a thing for old white guys, there were plenty out there who did not resemble globes. Who took numerous showers, dressed impeccably. Who had cars. Corvettes, some of them, which they would cheerfully let Michael drive.

Michael came out of the bathroom, toweling himself. "That's as far as you got?"

"I don't have anything to wear."

"Just wear that. I think white briefs are hot."

Joel snorted. Suddenly Michael was on the bed, straddling him, looking down at his globular body. At his distended belly and sagging chest, so pale next to Michael's chestnut skin. Michael's brow furrowed, just for an instant, but long enough that Joel heard: What am I doing with this monster? Michael ran a finger down Joel's sternum—gently, repeatedly, stroking. He smiled and sighed. He didn't stop smiling even when his finger went lower, all but lost itself in the girdle of white fat below Joel's navel. Beads of water glistened on Michael's faceted shoulders, dripped down onto Joel.

The sun was going down. For a minute or two Michael's body was rosewood of an impossible richness. Even Joel's body was red-gold. Joel felt—not beautiful, he would never feel beautiful—he felt that perhaps he was entitled to be where he was just then. Or, more simply, he felt that he was where he was.

Michael tipped forward, his chest pressing down on Joel's, his lips nuzzling the side of Joel's neck. The weight of him, the way his hard muscles bore into Joel's softness like the prow of a ship cutting through water: so hard to breathe under the damp weight of him. Joel wanted to roll him off, but didn't want to break the moment. So he was aware that it was a moment, already past because of his awareness. Michael might have been holding him, but Joel was an actor miming holding.

What was Michael thinking? Nothing. Joel felt Michael's heart beating, heard his breathing, and imagined he was thinking nothing at all. Because Joel was a racist, because he could not attribute to Michael any human depth, just dismissed him as some sort of splendid, thoughtless animal? No, past this: because Michael was so entirely other that Joel could not see inside the way he usually saw inside people, by attributing to them his own interior life. Michael was lying on top of him, breathing into his neck, and thinking—what?

Wondering, maybe, how long to continue this tableau. Or, maybe, feeling Joel's heartbeat and wondering what Joel was thinking, or whether Joel was thinking at all. Maybe Michael was as dizzy as Joel was, spiraling into the mystery of two warm men holding one another and still strangers.

Was this it, was this all you got? Just a couple of bodies twined together, as sleeping puppies interlock in a pet shop window.

Michael giggled.

"What?" Joel said.

"I don't think you've taken a breath in the last five minutes."

"So I guess we're almost there," Joel said, when he spoke to Bate on Tuesday.

292

"Mr. Lingeman, we've only started. What you've given me now is the rudimentary information people usually bring in when they retain me."

"Oh."

"Except usually they know where the missing person was a month ago, maybe a year ago. Petras . . . how did you say it again?"

"I'm not sure how to say it."

"He's had a lifetime to hide himself."

What an odd way of putting it: as if Petras Baranauskas had actually spent his life concealing himself from Joel. While Joel, who was It, had to cover his eyes and count to a zillion before he could set off in search of the hidden one.

Being It was expensive. For what Joel had already spent on Bate, he could have gone down to Hecht's and let Michael pick him a whole new wardrobe, and Bate was only at the starting point. This was expensive and silly and Joel had almost stopped caring about it, almost hadn't called. No, of course that wasn't so. Having got the name and the birth date and the last known address, so much intelligence, he could not have kept himself from calling. But he was a little ashamed of it.

He was conscious that this game was something he couldn't tell Michael about. A deformity he would have to conceal. After a weekend that might still lead to nothing, he was already feeling: I hope Michael doesn't find out I'm crazy. He pictured himself explaining. Hey, this was just a little pastime. It doesn't have anything to do with who I really am. Just an odd thing I got into for a while.

He wondered if he should renounce the Santa Fe boy. Meet Michael tonight knowing that the Santa Fe boy was behind him, like a habit he had kicked.

Bate went on. "Do you understand? He could be anywhere. He has lived out his entire adult life since that picture was taken."

"I understand," Joel said.

"He could have died by now."

"I—"

"He could have had cancer or a heart attack or . . . for all you know he was gay and got AIDS."

"He wasn't gay," Joel said, inadvertently joining in the past tense. He could have died by now.

"He could have gone to Vietnam a few months after that picture was taken and he could have been shot in some rice paddy and he could have been dead all this time."

Dead all this time: why not? Dead while Joel went to college, got the job at OLA, dead while Joel tricked, found Sam, lost him, found Michael . . .

"Mr. Lingeman, are you there?"

"Uh-huh."

"Do you want me to continue?"

"Um . . ."

If a census-taker had canvassed the city in Joel's head he would have found, dwelling side by side in perfect concord: Joel's late parents, Sherlock Holmes, Sam, Riff from *West Side Story*, Alex Rivers, the gang from the Hill Club, Senator Harris, his boss Herb, Dorothea Casaubon, Michael, Monty Woolley, the Santa Fe boy. A democracy in which there was really no difference between the living and the dead, people he'd known and people he hadn't known, people he would never see again and people who had never existed at all. All equal in his head. How could it possibly matter which particular category Petras Baranauskas happened to fall into? Why should Joel spend one more dime to find out?

"Yes. Why don't you keep going."

Because—this was the closest he could come—there were, outside Joel's head, two possible worlds, one in which the Santa Fe boy still breathed and one in which he didn't. Joel just had to know which planet he was on.

nine

Joel and Michael met at Gentry and walked up to Adams-Morgan, to a place Michael said was good. El Elefante Blanco. Surely Michael hadn't ventured into a Thai-Cuban fusion joint on his own. Which of Joel's precursors had brought him here?

Joel wanted to taste Michael's noodles with jasmine picadillo and offered a taste of his own goat with black beans and lemongrass-plantain fritters.

"I don't share food like that," Michael said.

"It's kind of an Asian place. You're supposed to."

"I'm sorry. When I was coming up you ate from your own plate. Tried to eat off one of my sister's, you'd get a fork stuck in your hand."

We're not in Trenton, Joel thought, no one's going to starve here. Even the quaint "coming up" was somehow annoying.

"Now you're all huffy," Michael said.

"I'm not huffy."

"Food's a big thing to you. You can have a taste if you want."

"No. It didn't really sound very good," Joel said, just to show that food wasn't a big thing to him. Then he thought maybe it wasn't a crime if Michael sometimes understood him. "Just a little taste."

Michael understood Joel and Joel didn't understand Michael. He took this asymmetry to be racial: black people had to understand white people, while the reverse wasn't true. Michael could read him—could read his body, could read his mind now from across the table.

Michael dished a rather grudging sample of the noodles onto his bread and butter plate and slid it toward Joel.

"You want to try some of this?" Joel said.

"No. My church won't let me eat goat."

Joel laughed disproportionately. He was still chuckling when Michael said, "I guess you and your lover shared food a lot, huh?"

"He didn't like to either, not at first. I had to train him." Joel was about to taste the noodles when he said, "How did you know I had a lover?"

"I don't feature you buying Feral for Men."

"No."

"Or going off by your lonesome and getting a Nordic Track."

"No."

"What happened to him?"

"We broke up, a few months ago."

"How long were you together?"

"Fifteen years."

"Wow. And then you—you'd think after all that . . ."

Joel shrugged. He knew he shouldn't tell any more, the story just branded him as a loser. But not telling it seemed like more effort than telling it. Like standing in a bar the whole evening trying to suck in your stomach. "He walked out. He left for somebody younger."

"Oh."

That wasn't the story, either, or not the way Sam would have told it. It occurred to him that even the abbreviated account he had just provided didn't include a character named "Joel." It was about what Sam had done, it was Sam's story. Joel could have rephrased it: "He walked out on *me*. He left *me* for somebody younger." Turning himself into a little pronoun, the hapless object of Sam's verbs. The other way was better, after all. Sam's departure was Sam's story, while Joel's story was happening right now. One in which he was the subject of verbs. Maybe.

"Yoo-hoo," Michael said.

"Huh?"

"You went away somewhere."

"Oh. I'm sorry. You know, you get to be my age, your mind wanders."

"Okay."

"Or, in Sam's case, your body wanders."

"Sam, that was your lover? How old is this 'younger' guy?"

"Twenty-three."

"He left you for somebody twenty-three?" Michael said, as if this were bizarre.

"I would have left me for somebody twenty-three."

"Not me."

"Right, well, you have this thing for old white guys."

"Not old, I didn't really mean old."

"Whatever." Joel had to ask: "Why is that?" As though, if Michael could just supply some plausible reason for his strange predilection, Joel could stop thinking it was about money.

"You mean, why am I a snow queen?"

Joel hadn't meant that. He had been thinking about the old part; being into white guys didn't seem so peculiar. But of course it was the larger question.

"I don't know. I just am. I always have been. I mean, when I was a little kid, I'd watch TV and—you know who I used to like? On, what was it, *Happy Days*?"

"The Fonz?"

"The father."

"Tom Bosley? When you were a kid you had the hots for Tom Bosley?" This was sort of reassuring. Compared to Tom Bosley, Joel looked like Brad Pitt.

Michael was looking down at his plate, twirling noodles onto his fork, untwirling them. "I know what you're thinking," he said. Although he couldn't possibly. Joel himself didn't know what he was thinking. "You think I hate myself."

Yes, of course Joel thought that. There hung between them, as if hovering over the candle on the table, the obvious: that a little black boy who fell in love with a rotund white daddy on TV had embarked on some enterprise of self-negation. Something about magically becoming squeaky white Ron Howard and being swept away into *Happy Days* land, there to be cradled in the arms of pudgy old Tom Bosley.

"I get that all the time," Michael said. "I mean, from other black guys. That I must hate being black. It's like . . . you're into black guys, right?"

"I— I don't know if I'd say I'm *into* black guys." He didn't think he was: if pressed, he would have said he was into ambulatory guys. But he was also conscious that there was something a little disgraceful about being into black guys. "I'm into you," he said, feeling sappy.

"Whatever. So does that mean you hate being white?"

"I don't know. Maybe."

"Bullshit. It's like you just can't love somebody else, somebody outside you, it has to be about something going on inside. Like there isn't anybody else, it's just you. Some kind of show with only one actor in it."

Having delivered this frighteningly mature and concise account of Joel's life tangle, Michael plunged with uncharacteristic gusto into his noodles. He even reached over and speared a chunk of Joel's goat.

When they left the restaurant, Joel started in the direction of his place, actually took a few steps before realizing Michael wasn't with him. He turned: Michael was still at the door of the restaurant, his face striped with bars of neon from overhead. He was frowning.

Oh, Jesus, Joel thought. This is over already. He's going to thank me for dinner and kiss me on the lips and walk away. Joel went over to him, slowly. Michael said, "I need to go home."

"Okay."

"I mean, I'm still wearing my clothes from today, and I have to be in real early for inventory. I have to get stuff. You mind coming? It's not that far."

"Oh. Oh, sure."

Michael's place was near Twelfth and T. The way there took them through streets Joel would not ordinarily have traversed in an armored car. Storefront tabernacles, grocery stores whose only produce was Lotto tickets. In front of the liquor store a knot of impassive Latinos who stared at them and spat on the sidewalk, probably thinking: *maricones*. A couple blocks later— they must have crossed some boundary—a bunch of black guys who didn't even spit, just tugged on their beers and regarded Michael and Joel with a sort of listless amazement. Michael strolled on, oblivious. This was his neighborhood, he lived here.

Joel lived in a two-bedroom apartment in Dupont Circle and Michael lived in some hovel in—what did they even call this neighborhood? Ledroit Park? Not a mile distant, but about as far apart as people got in this country; it was a wonder Joel hadn't had to show a visa. Maybe this neighborhood didn't even have a name. Realtors gave neighborhoods their names. Places in areas like this showed up in the classifieds as just "NW DC," signifying that what was for sale was a worthless property in an anonymous wasteland.

To which Michael had brought Joel deliberately. He could have changed before he came out, or he could have stuffed a gym bag with fresh linen and a toothbrush and the cologne he was wearing just a little bit too much of tonight—could

Joel tell him that, were they that far along? He had planned for Joel to see where he lived. No, that was backwards. He was simply not concealing where he lived.

Michael unlocked a blank slab of a door, led Joel up a staircase whose ancient carpet bore countless stains whose origins Joel had no wish to speculate about, then down a hallway with a linoleum floor and two fluorescent lights overhead, one of them blinking as sporadically as a firefly. Michael opened no fewer than three locks on another blank door and admitted Joel to:

A room as spotless and spiritless as one in a Holiday Inn. A little white loveseat and a matching chair angled around a brass-and-glass coffee table that held an ashtray and a single copy of *Men's Health*. Beyond them a perfectly made bed, a nightstand with a clock radio. On one wall a metal wardrobe with printed oak graining, on the other a particleboard cabinet with a TV, a compact stereo, a handful of CDs, and a vase with a plastic lily. Above it, a large poster of a Corvette, a second depicting several adorable puppies, and some framed certificates Joel couldn't make out. Nothing else: no books of course, nothing on the counter of the kitchenette but a little coffee maker that looked as if it had never been used. The door over to the right must have led to the bathroom. Joel imagined that, if he went in, he would find a paper band across the toilet seat, Sanitized for Your Protection.

Except for the Corvette poster, there was no evidence that Michael had ever lived here. Or: this utter vacancy was how Michael lived. No history, nor any of those artifacts that *refer*, the scattered objects that say this place is really supposed to be in Soho, or in the hunt country, or in Provence. Zero. Just the domicile of a man who had shed everything and was poised for some kind of leap, into Joel's apartment or into some finer digs.

Michael was behind him, waiting. He turned around and said, "This is nice."

"It's not like your place."

"It's a lot cleaner."

"Yeah, you're kind of a slob," Michael said. Joel flushed—a little surge of pleasure at hearing himself characterized by Michael, at being noticed. "But I bet you could be trained."

Practically a marriage proposal. Another little wave of warmth, overtaken almost instantly by a wintry No, a refusal from somewhere deep inside.

Zero, Michael was zero. A cipher. Not the way a newborn baby is a zero, but the way you can get to zero through subtraction, effacement. Wipe away Trenton, wipe away race, fail to add in Shakespeare or Schubert, and you got this apartment.

So: he was expecting to find an open copy of *Middlemarch?* When he had first walked into Sam's apartment, he had found stacks of science fiction novels and framed copies of M.C. Escher prints. Tokens of a sensibility that was alien to his own and for which he felt—had never stopped feeling—a certain contempt. He had admired Sam, too, for his calm, his self-possession, his certainty that he was doing the right next thing. But always, also, this contempt—or rather, simple snobbery, about Sam's various pockets of ignorance, his failure to partake of the deep grounding in Western culture Joel had acquired in the freshman great books course.

This was different, scary somehow. He had never been afraid that, if he spent too much time with Sam, he would find himself one morning reading science-fiction novels. But he could imagine that, if he spent too much time in this apartment, he would slip into the vacuity it represented. A show with no actors in it at all. They would lie together on that bed, the clock radio would digitally flash out the minutes, they would feel each other's hearts beating in time with it.

Michael was waiting for him to say something. He managed, "Um. You want to stay here, or . . . ?"

Michael blinked. The words had just come out, Joel hadn't understood how cruel they were. Michael had shown him the enormous courtesy of bringing Joel to this sanctuary where he brought no one, and Joel had as much as said that he couldn't wait to get out.

Michael said, "I think I'll just change into what I'm going to wear tomorrow, and then we can go back to your place."

"No, no, why don't we stay here?"

Michael didn't answer. He opened the wardrobe, which held no fewer than five suits and, neatly aligned on hangers, dress shirts beyond reckoning. Michael stood looking at all these garments, as if overwhelmed by the difficulty of selecting just the right ensemble for tomorrow. There were advantages to having just one suit you could still fit into.

Joel ambled over to inspect Michael's CDs. Patti Labelle, Donna Summer, a scattering of gospel and, bizarrely, one disk of Sousa marches. The framed certificates above the entertainment center were Sales Associate of the Month awards from Hecht's. These made Joel sad. He turned to find Michael naked, his back to Joel, browsing through a stack of boxer shorts as if even this selection mattered.

His back, his butt, so beautiful. The serious way he pondered his underwear so heartrendingly sweet. The plaid he selected at last so exuberant. Joel watched him step into the shorts, slip them up over his butt; they were like a banner heralding coming days or months of beauty, gaiety. Life.

Joel knew this was all you got. He'd had it with Sam, all those years: contempt and boredom and frustration and, just often enough, something—a word, a pair of boxer shorts . . . Not even often enough to redeem everything. It wasn't worth it; it wasn't as though everything balanced out. It was just all you got. And if he obeyed the impulse he had right now, to bolt out of the apartment and run alone through the scary streets, then he would get nothing.

Michael's back was still turned to Joel. Was he really thinking so very hard about which shirt to wear, or was he sulking? Was Joel in for another fifteen years of sulking? Of trying to figure out what a stranger wanted, trying to give him what he wanted, if only he'd stop sulking?

Maybe he wasn't sulking, maybe he was just quiet, contentedly surveying his many fine shirts. Or maybe being with someone who cared enough even to sulk was better than being alone.

It was a couple of weeks before Kristen from the White House called Joel back. If he had multiplied out the number of, say, five-minute calls she could have completed in ten working days—fourteen-hour days, of course, that was what she paid to have the presidential seal on her business card—the product would have been Joel's exact rank on the health-policy ladder.

"I was wondering about the Harris bill," Joel said.

Kristen sighed. "What about it?"

"Why, uh . . . why the Administration is . . ." He couldn't think of any neutral way of putting the question. Even to ask it was to suggest a judgment.

He was presuming too much; he didn't really know Kristen. He had been in meetings with her a few times. Once, during the coffee break at some interminable policy forum, she had asked him something about Medicare physician fees, preventing him from running outside for a cigarette. He couldn't remember what the question was, or what he had answered, but just by approaching him she had certified that he was on her list of people who might possibly supply a credible and disinterested answer to a question. Which had raised his opinion, not only of himself, but of her. In that brief and impersonal exchange, there had passed between them the understanding that, in a city where most people were stupid or corrupt or both, they were neither. When they went back to their seats, she would occasionally catch his eye, favor him with a small, one-sided smile as a speaker said something especially fatuous and self-serving. When she herself was called on to explain the Administration's position, she seemed to aim her presentation straight at Joel, as if wanting his approval.

So he thought he was in a position to ask. Kristen said, "I suppose you don't want the official answer."

"Well, I guess I ought to hear the official answer, in case anybody asks. But I . . ."

"Okay. I hear you're likely to get involved again anyway."

"I am?"

"You'll probably be getting a call from that guy on Flanagan's staff."

"Mullan?"

"Right, Mullan." She said the name wearily, as if lately she had been seeing too much of Mullan. "Anyway, you know that break we're proposing for the pharmaceutical companies?"

"Oh, the . . . uh, tax credits for biotechnology innovation zones?"

"Right. Well, that has to be paid for. We have to find some offsetting savings."

"And the Harris bill is it?"

"If we can ever get the scoring up. That's what Mullan's working on."

"I see." He did see. It was pretty elementary: under the budget rules of the time, Congress couldn't reduce revenues without doing something to reduce spending. If they wanted to give the drug companies a tax cut, they had to find some saving in the same amount. Medicare was the biggest item in the budget; if you needed to find some money it was the obvious place to look. "I see that the credits have to be paid for, but— why is the Administration supporting the credits in the first place? Don't the pharmaceutical companies have enough?"

Kristen recited: "We feel that biotechnology innovation zones represent an important opportunity to revitalize the economies of our inner cities."

"Oh."

There was a silence—during which, perhaps, Kristen considered whether she owed Joel anything more than that official utterance. Joel was nobody. If she went on, it must have been because she didn't want even a nobody to draw the obvious inference: that someone from the drug companies had given someone in the White House a bag of money.

"We— Look, I've probably said too much already."

"I won't tell anybody," Joel said. "I'm just curious."

"Okay. You know the drug companies were opposing Kiddie Care."

"Yeah, I never understood that, either. Why do the drug companies care one way or the other about the child health insurance plan?"

"It's some complicated pricing thing. Kiddie Care is a public program, they'd have to give it some kind of discounts. And that somehow affects what they can charge other people. There are these formulas, I've never figured it all out. I just know the drug companies were against it and now they're for it."

"Because you gave them this tax break."

"That's it. You know, they've got a lot of clout, they could just have killed the kids' plan. We had to give them something."

"Okay, let me see if I've got this straight," Joel said. "You cut Medicare for people with HIV, and that pays for the tax credits, and that keeps the drug companies from killing the child health plan."

"QED."

Joel was so pleased to have been granted this little peek at the real world, like someone liberated from Plato's cave, that it took him a few seconds to work out what this clever transaction added up to. "You're taking coverage away from sick people so you can cover kids."

"What?" Kristen said. Not sharply; rather as if the simple equation hadn't occurred to her. "That's not . . ."

"It's what you're doing."

"Huh." Another silence, while she pondered this. Joel was

already sorry to have said it. Not just because it was unlikely that Kristen would ever return another of his calls. Because she was probably a decent person trying to get something done, trying to do something good in a zero-sum world, where you couldn't give anything to kids without taking away from somebody else. Robin Hood didn't have to get elected: else he would never have robbed the rich, or even the middle class, just robbed the poor to feed the poor. In the most prosperous realm the world had ever seen, the titanic budget had only one lifeboat for steerage. There fell to Kristen—who could have taught somewhere, or worked for some foundation, who had instead come to the White House to work overtime saving the world—there fell to her the dreadful daily task of deciding who could get on the boat. If she cried out, "Kids first," who was he to scorn her?

Kristen said, "You know, the Harris bill doesn't actually hurt anybody. I mean, it's prospective, it only applies to people who do unsafe things in the future. It wouldn't be such a bad thing if people changed their behavior and didn't get sick."

"I don't guess," Joel said. "It's hard for people to change their behavior." It had, for example, been impossible for a middle-aged man, just last night, to abstain from behaviors likely to be on the Secretary's list.

"They always leave us with no place to stand," Kristen said. "We try to do something for them—the military, job discrimination, whatever—and right in the middle of it they show up on TV dancing naked in the streets."

"Gay people, you mean."

"That's right." They scarcely knew one another, he thought maybe he should fill her in on this one little detail she had missed about him. He let her go on. "This is the first administration that ever even said the words 'gay people.' We've done everything we could. And the voters don't care so much, except the real nuts. The voters can live and let live as long as . . . as long as nobody reminds them just exactly what gay people do in bed. As long as nobody rubs that in their faces."

"Which the ads did."

"Which the ads did. Look, I've got a million other calls to return. Is there anything else you needed?"

"I don't guess," Joel said. "Oh, what is it Mullan's going to want?"

"Like I said, they're still working on trying to score some savings. Everybody thought you might be able to help."

He might be able to help. This was his job, as much as Kristen's. And if he didn't help, it would get done. Congress would get its work done with or without functionaries like Joel. They had managed to pass the Fugitive Slave Act with no staffers at all; they could finish the Harris amendment in their sleep. It didn't matter if he helped.

He could almost persuade himself. Congress would do whatever it did and Joel wouldn't be guilty of anything, because he was entirely dispensable. It would all have happened if he had never existed. Of course, the corollary to this splendid rationalization was that it didn't much matter if Joel was on the planet or not. Didn't matter to Mullan or Harris, didn't matter to Sam anymore. Probably didn't matter much to Michael; if he had never lived, Michael would have found some other old white guy. The planet was crawling with old white guys.

It didn't matter if he had ever lived. Lived these thirty years while Petras Baranauskas, maybe, rotted in some rice paddy. He could go down to the Mall right now and check it out, visit that black granite scar in the Mall and maybe trace with his fingers the name of Petras Baranauskas. He had been once, years before, been to the wall and cried the way everybody else cried. The way he cried at movies. The waste, the waste, all those young lives thrown away. So they couldn't, like Joel, throw their own lives away.

He had been spared. He hadn't gone to Vietnam, he had

—quite undeservedly—evaded AIDS. Evaded children or a dead lover's demented parents or any other kind of personal responsibility. Until at last he could tell himself that he wouldn't be responsible if he helped Mullan a little with the Harris amendment.

He would help because he liked having this job, so that he could afford to take Michael to dinner, could afford to keep Bate hunting for a dead man, could afford all the perks and superfluities to which he was entitled as a member of the New Class. And it wasn't his fault, was it, that society had turned out this way? That everything revolved around the needs of the drug companies and all the other companies, that there weren't any citizens any more, just shareholders and consumers and a few leftover losers who were clambering to get into the only lifeboat? He hadn't done it. He hadn't done anything ever. Just somehow drifted into the world that already favored him, it was too hard to make the other world.

Maybe Petras wasn't the one who was dead. What was this living he had done, all these years Petras had been hiding or buried? Hearing someone's heartbeat nearby, or not hearing it, that was all his life had come to. All he had to look forward to was one more night with Michael, maybe one more after that, maybe . . . Until he was dead. So he might as well have been dead already. The boy who had been, at fourteen, dumb-struck by a vision of the transcendent had been alive. The man he'd turned into, who had settled for the possible, had been dead all this time.

What had he been spared for?

Kristen was right: Mullan called a few days later. "Joel, how're you doing?"

"Okay."

Mullan waited a beat or two for Joel to ask how he was doing. Joel did not. "Listen, the senator has some interest in the Harris amendment."

"Does he?" Joel said, innocently. As if innocence would prevent him from doing whatever Mullan asked.

"Yeah, but we've got this scoring problem. Here's the deal: the budget people agreed that there would be this, whatever, deterrent effect. People would stop doing unsafe stuff."

"The budget office bought that?"

"Uh-huh." Even Mullan chuckled at this absurdity. "So they're ready to score some savings. Except only way in the future."

"How far?"

"Seven years. See, they say somebody who did something unsafe now might not get sick for five or six years. And then it would be a couple more years before they got Medicare. So they show the savings starting seven years from now; if people start acting safer right away, we'll save some money seven years from now."

"Ah." Joel's message light flashed on. Shoot, it was eleven o'clock, Michael was supposed to call from work. "Well, that kind of makes sense. That it would take some time."

"But seven years is outside the window. You know that."

"Right," Joel said. "The window." Congress dealt with the future in five-year chunks. If you did something that saved money in Year Five you could spend all the money in Year One or Year Two. If you did something that didn't save money until Year Six or Year Seven, you were outside the window: you had nothing to spend.

Mullan went on. "So if we don't save anything in the first five years, there's no point in doing it."

What a shame. "I guess not," Joel said.

"We gotta move it up somehow."

"How?"

"That's what I was hoping you'd tell me."

"I have no idea."

"Well, I hope you come up with something. We're having this meeting Wednesday."

"Wednesday?" Joel said. "Let me see if I'm free."

"With the senator."

"Oh. I'm free."

There were two messages, the first from Michael, the second from Bate. Of course he should return Michael's call first, so they could make plans for the evening.

"I've found him," Bate said.

"Jesus, where?"

"Mr. Lingeman, you have a balance due."

"Of course, sure, I'll get that off to you, whatever it is. But tell me, where—"

"Mr. Lingeman, I would prefer to tell you face to face. And I'm afraid I must ask, would you mind very much bringing a certified check?" As if he were a kidnapper, holding Petras Baranauskas for ransom.

The ransom was nearly eight thousand dollars. Joel had to close a CD prematurely. The woman at the bank mournfully recounted all the penalties that would stem from Joel's profligacy and impatience. "I'm sorry," he said, as if he had to apologize for withdrawing his own money. "I really need to get this today." She shook her head. Possibly she pictured a Mafia loan shark waiting for him in the alley.

He hesitated before knocking on Bate's door. He imagined for a moment that Petras Baranauskas would be there, that Bate was actually holding him there, ready to produce him as soon as Joel came with the money. Which wouldn't, really, have been so awfully much to expect for eight thousand dollars.

Bate opened the door before Joel could knock. He was startled; he must have been headed out somewhere. He had a raincoat on, though it was a warm, clear day—not a snappy private-eye trench coat, just a drab black raincoat such as a flasher might have worn. "Oh, Mr. Lingeman. I didn't expect you quite this soon, I was on my way to lunch. I . . . would you care to join me?"

Joel considered this for a moment. He was always happy to eat, and he would have liked to learn something about Bate, who was more a mystery than a solver of mysteries. But he expected Bate would reveal nothing—the man barely revealed information he had been paid to obtain—and that instead the conversation would turn to Joel: Joel's motives, Joel's plans. Bate would sit in his black raincoat, ignoring his little salad, and watch as Joel, mouth full, tried to explain what he could not explain to himself.

"I'm sorry," Joel said. "I hate to hold up your lunch, but I need to get back to the Hill."

"Certainly." Bate stepped aside to admit Joel, closed the door, sat behind his desk, still in his raincoat.

"I brought the check."

"Thank you."

Joel held out the envelope. Bate nodded toward a corner of the desk. Joel put the envelope there and said, "So where is he?"

"Just one minute, if you please, Mr. Lingeman. I have a document I must ask you to sign." He pulled a sheet from the typewriter—two sheets, rather, with the world's last piece of carbon paper between them. "This merely certifies that you engaged me to locate an individual, that you did not disclose to me the nature of your business with that individual, and that you have no intention of using any information I supply for the purpose of committing any—"

"A release? You want me to sign a release?"

"It seems prudent."

"Okay." Joel signed on the line next to his name, halfway down. Bate signed, filling the remainder of the page.

"Thank you," Bate said. "Roseville, New Jersey."

"What?"

"1693 Bridge Street, Roseville, New Jersey."

"You're kidding."

"He went away. He came back."

"So you didn't have to hunt very hard," Joel said, eyeing the envelope with the check in it.

"I'll describe my activities in my report. I'm sorry I haven't prepared it yet. As I said, I didn't expect you quite so . . ."

He lived in Roseville, New Jersey. Joel formed a silly picture of flowering vines trailing over one of the abandoned satanic mills that you saw from the train, pretty much all he had ever seen of New Jersey. That and, "Trenton Makes, the World Takes."

He lived. "You're sure it's the same guy?"

"I completed a visual identification."

"You . . . you mean, you went to Roseville?" Joel hadn't been sure the man even went outdoors. "Did you talk to him?"

"I didn't. I didn't, personally, have anything to say to him. I was able to take a photograph. Would you like to see?"

Bate reached into his desk drawer and extracted a manila folder. Before he could open it, Joel said, "No. Not right now."

"Very well. I'll be furnishing you a number of other exhibits. I have a credit report, a Social Security earnings history, and—"

"You're not supposed to be able to get that."

"I beg your pardon?"

"His Social Security record, no one's supposed to give you that. I mean, it's kind of an invasion."

Bate stared at him a minute.

Joel said, "Well, uh, that's it, I guess. You'll be sending me this report."

"Yes. I'll get to it right after lunch. I'll mail it to you or . . . I suppose I could messenger it, but—"

"That would be extra."

"Yes. These other materials, you might want to look through those now."

"No."

"They're really most informative. The earnings history, for

312

example: you can actually track all the gainful employment he's had since—"

"I don't want to know any of it," Joel said. He didn't care what dreary jobs Petras Baranauskas had drifted through after his one-shot modeling career. He didn't care if Petras paid his credit card balances in thirty days or sixty days or never. "I don't want any of it. Not right now."

"Not even the picture?"

"Least of all the picture." Of course part of him ached to see the picture, was ready to tear the folder from Bate's hands. But it was only a picture. Even if he had just paid more for it than he would have had to spend for a painting in one of those pricey Georgetown galleries, it merely referred, as all the other documents in the folder merely referred, attested.

"I suppose you mean to see him for yourself," Bate said.

"I guess I will."

"He . . . he isn't what you've been picturing." Bate inched the folder toward Joel, tempting him.

"I'm not sure what I've been picturing. I don't think I've been picturing anything."

"I mean he's nothing like the young man in the advertisement."

"How could he be? But enough that you're sure about him."

"Yes."

"How do you get to Roseville? Will I have to drive?"

"Oh, no, I never drive. You take the Amtrak to Newark, then a commuter train, the . . ." Bate peeked in the folder. "The New Jersey Transit Kilmer line."

"Fine." Joel stood up. "Look, don't even bother about the report. And you can, I don't know, send that other stuff. Whenever."

"I always write a report."

"All right."

"Did you want the other picture back?"

"What?"

"The advertisement you brought me, did you want it back?"

"Oh," Joel said. "Yeah, I guess."

Bate handed it over; Joel looked at it. He was stunned, as startled by the boy's beauty as if he had never seen the picture before. Well, he hadn't seen it in a couple of months: he would have thought his mental facsimile of it was faithful enough, but he must have got it mixed up somehow with the glossy Peter Barry in Chambers Sexton's binder. The boy in the picture was entirely different, rougher and at the same time more innocent. Maybe he had only existed that one instant, just long enough for a shutter to open and close.

"Mr. Lingeman." Bate stood up, in his black raincoat. Joel thought he meant to shake hands, extended his own. "No," Bate said. "I have to tell you . . . I've helped you with this, but . . . Mr. Lingeman, you have no right."

"No right to . . ."

"To just go there and—this man who doesn't even know who you are."

"I'm not going to do anything to him. I'm not sure I'm even going to talk to him."

"I've found a lot of people. People who didn't want to be found. That's what I do. But they—they knew they were missing. They'd walked out on somebody, or they'd stolen something, or . . . They knew there was someone looking for them."

"So . . . what? You're afraid I'm going to upset him?"

"He's lived his whole life not even aware of your existence, his whole life."

Joel shrugged. There were about six billion people of whom that could be said.

"For you to come to him now. Tell him that all these years you've been . . ." Bate was too fastidious to finish. All these years you've been looking at his picture and jerking off. That's what Bate thought. And that Petras Baranauskas would be disgusted, feel sullied at the very idea that someone had thought of him that way, used him that way, for so many years.

"I haven't—" Joel began. He hadn't, as it happened. When he had first possessed the picture, so long ago, he had not yet discovered the art of self-abuse. By the time he had come into possession of it again, the few weeks he had it before he turned it over to Bate, he had a drawer full of more explicit meditational aids. He didn't need to tell all this to Bate; there would be no use explaining to Bate that his feeling for the boy wasn't crudely sexual. If in fact it wasn't.

Bate shook his head. "It's like telling him he's never been anything but the boy in that picture. It's like saying he had no life."

"No, of course he did, I'm not . . ." Seconds, Petras had stood in front of a camera for seconds, and then had gone on to rack up a Social Security earnings history, a credit history, a lot of others Bate had not unearthed. Medical history, driving record, maybe an arrest or two. Maybe his name on the plaque for a winning team in the Roseville bowling league, or on the shelf that held his personal beer stein at the Roseville bar, or—so much Bate had not uncovered, so many folders he could have filled. Just one of which might have contained the single line: "10/8/63. CL: Simms of Santa Fe. AG: Dink & Dink. PH: A. Markey." The moment Joel thought of as the climax of Petras's life. The shutter opening and closing: Petras might not remember at all. Maybe he didn't even remember posing for that picture.

"I'm the one who had no life," Joel said.

"Oh, come, Mr. Lingeman. You've had a successful career, excellent academic record, you've . . ." He trailed off, having disclosed that he—and why not?—had checked Joel out. Another folder. Maybe he had six billion folders.

"I'm going to be tied up on Thursday," Joel said.

"Oh, yeah?" Michael put his fork down, waited for Joel to elaborate.

They'd been together almost every night. Possibly they had

reached the point at which it was no longer sufficient for Joel to say he was going to be tied up. "I'm going to New York. Just for the one night."

"New York? You just went."

Joel couldn't recall having told Michael this. "Yeah, but that was business. This time it's just—you know, every so often I go to New York because it's New York. I go to museums or maybe a show, whatever. I've always gone a couple times a year."

"Oh. But you don't want me to come."

"I—"

"Well, I guess I can't really afford it."

Michael went on eating, as if the topic were closed. Which was good, because of course Joel had no intention of bringing him along on this particular trip. But the topic was by no means closed. Michael must have been thinking: I'm supposed to sit alone in my little studio on T Street while my rich lover gallivants off to New York? While Joel was thinking: am I supposed to take him on trips, as if I were his sugar daddy? Or am I supposed to stay here and do only those things Michael can afford? Which didn't, so far, include paying for dinner even once.

"Where are you going to be staying?" Michael said.

"In the Village, place called the Sheridan Square Hotel."

"Is that nice?"

"It's a dump. But, you know, it's cheap, I don't care much about hotel rooms."

"Oh. I guess, if you were—I mean, if you're going anyway, then it doesn't matter much if there's one or two people in the room."

Uh-oh. "I don't guess."

"And then there'd only be the train fare. How much is that?"

"Well, I take the Metroliner. It's, I don't know, two hundred and something round trip." That would surely end the matter.

"Oh. But they have cheaper trains, too, right?"

"Yeah. Maybe half that."

Michael was quiet. Joel could offer to take the cheap train for once. He could let Michael pay for the cheap train and then he could cover the upgrade. They could travel separately and meet. Joel could say: "I have personal business in New York."

"Okay. So it's not about going to museums and shit."

"No."

"Well, you know, I don't need to know your business," Michael said. He leaned forward.

Joel took a breath. "I'm going to see . . . somebody I was in love with when I was younger."

"Oh. So you might . . . you're thinking you might get back together?"

This was too casual; it would serve him right if Joel said maybe. Then it would serve Joel right if Michael just got up and walked away. "I—actually, I never met him."

"You never—"

"He was a picture in a magazine."

Michael nodded as if this made sense, even took a bite or two of his salad before he said, slowly, "You're going to New York to see somebody you saw in a magazine."

"New Jersey, actually. He lives in New Jersey."

"How do you know?"

"I found out."

"So you fell in love with a picture in a magazine when you were . . . younger, you said, when was that?"

"Nineteen sixty-four." Michael wasn't born, of course. He must have felt as distant from Joel, hearing that date, as Joel felt when people talked about 1946. More distant, because Joel had some concept of how it was to be alive in 1946. Michael probably supposed that any picture Joel could have seen in 1964 would have shown a man wearing animal skins and carrying a club.

Michael said, "You're just going to go see what he looks like now?"

"I guess."

There was a long silence. Michael's hands were folded on the table. He looked down at them. He was trying to decide whether Joel was crazy or merely lying. Or, unable to resolve this question, perhaps he was trying to decide whether it mattered. Whether this was just a harmless oddity he could overlook or whether he should get away from this loony as fast as he could.

"Well, how long could that take?" Michael said.

"What?"

"I mean, we could go up together, and you could go . . . look at this guy while I hang out in New York, and then we could have fun."

He was going to overlook it, then. He would let Joel pursue this quixotic idiocy and treat it as no big deal. Except that it would always be between them, that Joel had done this crazy thing. Michael wouldn't even have to talk about it; it would just be something he knew. Would that be so bad, to have someone who wanted to go on seeing you even though he knew you were crazy?

Joel pictured it. They would ride up together, check in at the hotel, have lunch somewhere. Joel would push back from the table and say, "Well, I'm off to New Jersey. What are you gonna do all day?" Joel would carry out his mission, in the evening they would meet and Michael would say—polite, bewildered, indulgent— "How did it go?" Indulgent above all: Joel hated the thought of being indulged.

"Maybe I don't need to go," Joel hazarded. "Maybe it's just silly."

"Sounds like it," Michael said.

"Come if you want to."

"I don't think I want to," Michael said. The worst, the ultimate weapon, that Sam had resorted to sometimes and that made Joel want to tear his eyes out: when Joel gave in and Sam went on sulking. "You go on ahead."

"Okay."

"Maybe I'll go out myself Thursday. Who knows, maybe I'll bump into some old flame myself."

"What?"

"Just kidding. Maybe I'll rent a movie or something."

"You should go out. We're not joined at the hip." That was a line of Sam's, it just came out. Michael looked puzzled. "I mean we're not Siamese twins."

"I know what you mean."

Sam used the line all the time, and Joel had never paid attention.

While Joel was undressing, Michael went to the bathroom. Joel put his wallet on the dresser, was about to take his pants off. He stopped and looked in the wallet. Hastily, sneaking a look in his own wallet.

"New York? You just went." Joel had not told him this. The only way he could possibly have known was to have found the ticket stub, which was, yes, still in the bill compartment.

Michael was routinely inspecting the contents of Joel's wallet. Had he taken any more money? Never so blatantly again, never the only twenty left. But maybe if there were, say, seven twenties, and Joel couldn't have noticed if they became six? What did it matter, if he didn't notice? Just the occasional twenty: not enough to have made much difference in Michael's life. Maybe he bought an extra fine shirt, or a couple of CDs.

Not enough, he couldn't have kept coming just for the occasional twenty. He liked being with Joel; the twenty was just a lucky bonus. Not much different than if, when he came over, he raided Joel's icebox. Except there was nothing in Joel's icebox, and there was sometimes a little something in Joel's wallet that Joel would never miss.

"You just went." How could he be so stupid—practically telling Joel that he was going through Joel's wallet? Michael wasn't stupid. He wanted Joel to know. There: he wasn't even taking the money for itself. He was taking it so that Joel would know he was taking it. As he must have wanted Ron to know: why else would he have *put the card back*?

If this was a test, what was the correct response? If Joel called him on it, he'd deny it. If Joel didn't, just said nothing, he'd think Joel was a fool. Or maybe he'd think he had permission. Which he did, so long as he never again took the last twenty, never again left Joel standing penniless in the checkout line at the Chinese salad bar.

This was all too complicated for Joel. Sam was never this complicated; even when he was cheating, he did it in the simplest and most straightforward manner. He didn't plant little clues. Did Joel have the energy for this?

Absolutely: it might well have been the most interesting thing that had happened to him in thirty years.

Okay. (a) Michael tells Joel that he has an inexplicable passion for old white guys. (b) Michael tells Joel that the only reason they're together is so he can steal Joel's money. The latter was patently false, because he wasn't taking enough. But he wanted Joel to think it. Because otherwise Joel might think there was something pathetic about him. Might think Michael was sick or wounded, had some ugly sore for which—so pathetic—Joel was the salve.

Michael was pathetic, any way Joel worked it out. Underneath the beauty, something unhealed.

He came out of the bathroom, toweling himself. Whatever was wrong with him, underneath, the surface was certainly distracting.

"You took a shower," Joel said.

"You didn't hear me?"

"I was thinking about something."

"You're always thinking about something."

Joel shrugged. "Looks like you've been thinking about something."

Michael looked down, grinned, then grew serious again.

320

"Even then, even when we . . . I can tell you're thinking."

"I don't see—I mean, how can you help thinking? You must think something."

"Only that I'm having a good time. Just that I'm happy. Or nothing, really, I don't think anything."

Was this possible? Could a sentient being actually think I'm-happy-I'm-happy-I'm-happy, or nothing at all?

Joel tried as Michael crawled into bed with him. Having Michael in bed with him was certainly something he ought to be happy-happy-happy about. He couldn't do it, couldn't turn his mind off the way, now, he turned off the light. But if he couldn't stop thinking, it was just as well to have a man holding him while he thought.

He thought of Sam. Michael might as well have been Sam— what was the difference, in the dark? A body pressed close to his own, why should Joel care what body, or even why it was there?

Sam used to, during his periodic cleaning binges, scoop up the change from deep inside Joel's club chair and then leave it on the end table, neatly done up in a little plastic bag. Sam had never taken even what Joel would never miss.

There wasn't going to be a Sam again, dear Sam. At this stage of his life the best Joel could do was Michael. Sam had said those very words, hadn't he, that day in the park? "I was just the best you could do."

Joel chuckled. Michael or Sam or whoever was behind him murmured, "Hm?"

Joel smiled: he remembered now, as he couldn't that day in the park, when he had heard those words before. His mother, trying to get off the phone after listening to some friend's interminable recitation of her husband's deficiencies. His mother, snapping, "Well, Alice, he must have been the best you could do at the time."

By definition. If Michael was here, he was, by definition, the best Joel could do. Life reduced to one thudding tautology.

And what was wrong with Michael, why shouldn't Joel be happy-happy-happy with Michael, at the negligible price of the occasional twenty? It wasn't about Michael at all, it was about Joel. Joel wasn't good enough, by definition.

He had looked at the picture and hidden the magazine away, so long ago, looked at it again and again, so hungry to learn what it had to tell him. Shattered by what it told him; the kid who looked at it was shattered and never put back together again. You are not good enough to slip through this page and into Santa Fe. You will never be good enough.

Joel and Melanie, Senator Harris's LA, were in two of the chairs in the waiting area in Senator Flanagan's anteroom, separated by a clutch of lobbyists in pinstripe suits. So they weren't able to talk. Nobody talked; one of the lobbyists glanced now and then at his fellows, clearly wanted to tell them something, but wouldn't because Joel and Melanie were there. Joel didn't recognize any of them, they weren't the pharmaceutical guys. They must have been here for a different meeting— which, with Joel's luck, would come before the meeting on the Harris amendment. He and Melanie would have to sit here for an hour, waiting while these guys begged for whatever handout they were here to get. Whatever gift Flanagan still had it in his power to confer.

Matthew Flanagan had been a professor of economics at Rutgers who had run for the House in 1964 as a sort of lark and was swept in with the LBJ landslide. His service in the House had been undistinguished. While his capacity for Irish whiskey ingratiated him with the leadership, his tendency to lecture his colleagues on the basic principles of Econ 101 did not. He was assigned to the District of Columbia and the Fisheries and Wildlife committees, neither of which let him do very much for New Jersey. When, in his fifth term, a seat on Ways and Means came vacant, he pointed out his enormous expertise in the very subjects the committee dealt with: taxes, social security, welfare. The chairman, the omnipotent Wilbur Mills, did not desire committee members with enormous expertise. He desired committee members who would give him their proxies and shut the hell up.

Flanagan wasn't going anywhere in the House, so he decided to take a stab at the Senate. In any other year this would have been a laughable ambition, but it was 1974, the post-Watergate election; Bozo the Clown could have been elected as long as he was on the Democratic ticket. Once in the Senate, Flanagan thrived. A tendency to deliver interminable and pompous lectures is not disdained there; on the contrary, the Senate sometimes allots entire days to "morning business," during which senators take their turn in haranguing an empty chamber. And advancement in the Senate depends entirely on longevity. By 1991 Flanagan was the second-ranking Democrat on the Finance Committee—able to do so many fine things for so many people, not least the pharmaceutical companies, that he didn't have to worry about fund-raising. He was freed to write, or at least approve, innumerable op-ed pieces, which, when collected into books, earned him his reputation as the intellectual light of the Senate.

His brief tenure as chairman of Finance began two years later and was ended by the catastrophe of 1994, to which he himself had contributed by his indolent and, some said, spiteful failure to get the president's health care proposal through the committee. But he remained the ranking minority member, still able to do wonderful things for New Jersey. Such as pushing through the biotechnology innovation zones, if he could only find the savings to pay for them.

Joel was right: the receptionist collected the pinstripes and led them down the narrow hallway to Flanagan's sanctum. It was only fair, really, that their meeting should come first. They were, after all, paying for it.

"Hey," Joel said to Melanie.

"Hi."

From down the hall, Flanagan's stentorian, "Gentlemen, how very good of you—" The door closed.

"Who else is coming?" Joel said.

"I'm not sure. Leg counsel, and I'm not sure who else."

"Oh, Andrew's coming?" Joel felt himself blushing.

"I think."

He hadn't seen Andrew since their encounter in front of the Library. Hadn't thought of him, really, in all these weeks. But of course they were going to run into each other; of course sooner or later Joel would find himself in a meeting with a man he had thrown himself at. Thrown himself: as if he had gathered his pride into a ball, hurled it, it had fallen short like a missed lay-up. For the rest of his working life, maybe, he would go to meetings and there would be Andrew.

"We think we've fixed it," Melanie said.

"I'm sorry?"

"Mullan and I, we— Oh."

There was Andrew, his preposterous tan unfaded; was he touching it up? "Hey, Joel," he said, with a big smile, and he punched Joel's arm. How butch. "Melanie." He sat down between them, then turned to Melanie and whispered something. Even Joel didn't suppose it was about himself, but he was annoyed. They couldn't have any business Andrew needed to whisper about, it was just a way of making Joel feel out of the loop.

Andrew had a hickey—on the right side of his neck, toward the back, barely discernible against the field of tanning-booth mahogany. Obviously, Andrew hadn't gone and deliberately acquired a hickey as a message to Joel. Look, I'm dating someone so young he gives hickeys. But Joel wanted to say: I'm getting mine, too, you're not the only person getting any. Although possibly whoever Andrew was getting it from wasn't routinely rifling his wallet.

The door to Flanagan's sanctum opened, and Mullan appeared. "You guys ready?" The lobbyists must have left some other way; Joel pictured Flanagan's office with a dozen doors, characters popping in and out as in a French farce. But it was, when Mullan ushered everyone in, a standard-issue senator's office. The huge desk, the New Jersey and US flags, the photos of Flanagan and Kennedy-Johnson-Humphrey-Carter-Mondale, the certificates of appreciation from the Plainfield VFW and the Livingston Hadassah. The only exceptional feature was the bookcase to Flanagan's left, with stacks of Flanagan's own remaindered books and a copy of *Ulysses*.

Flanagan didn't get up. Possibly he couldn't, as it was the middle of the afternoon. He had probably had lunch with the Irish ambassador, as his staff cutely put it. Lunch with the ambassador could make him expansive or petulant or just sleepy. "Good afternoon," he said. He folded his hands on the desk, like a schoolteacher. "Thank you all so much for coming."

There was nowhere to sit. Joel and Melanie and Andrew and Mullan stood lined up before Flanagan's desk like delinquent pupils, and Flanagan didn't even seem to notice. "Mr. Mullan has suggested that we might at last come to some resolution of the matter of Medicare and the human immunodeficiency virus." The last phrase uttered as if he himself had discovered the damn thing.

"Sir," Mullan said, his voice half an octave above its normal register. "Maybe I need to find some seats."

"Oh, yes, do." While Mullan and Andrew moved furniture, Joel stayed where he was. Flanagan stared at him for a moment, expressionless, then swiveled around and looked out the window, with its view of the Capitol grounds. "Isn't it the most lovely autumn afternoon?" he said.

"Just beautiful," Melanie said. "Have you been outdoors?"

Flanagan swiveled around, looked querulously at Melanie. What would he have done outdoors, toted the Irish ambassador around in a paper bag?

When everyone was seated, Mullan began, "This is Joel Lingeman from OLA and Andrew Crawford from leg counsel.

325

And I think you've met Melanie, from Senator Harris's office." Flanagan nodded benevolently. "Melanie and I think we might have the answer."

"To wit," Flanagan said.

"That is, we kind of rejected this early on, but there really doesn't seem to be any other choice. We just have to make it apply to anybody diagnosed after the date of enactment."

"I thought it did that."

"No, sir, right now it applies to somebody's who's *infected* after the date of enactment. That's why we have to wait all these years for the . . . consequences. The deterrent thing. But if you just say anybody diagnosed after enactment, then you get savings right away. You can just start denying claims right away."

"I see."

Joel put in—sweetly, trying to sound helpful, though he really just wanted to embarrass Mullan: "I thought the budget people said you can't really score anything for that, because the medical claims never say they're for AIDS. I thought the deterrent was the only thing they'd score."

"Yeah, yeah, we fixed that. You don't have to go by what's on the claims. Because to get Medicare they have to have applied for disability in the first place. And to get the disability they have to show they have AIDS. So it's already in the record."

"Oh," Joel said.

It was real, the Harris amendment was real now. The Social Security offices knew who had AIDS, they could tell Medicare, real people could get a letter telling them they'd been naughty and would they please die. "But—"

Flanagan stared at Joel again, still with no particular expression.

Joel went on. "But you still—even if they're diagnosed after the effective date, they could actually have been infected years ago. You can't take away benefits for something that's already happened before you pass the bill."

"You can't?" Mullan said.

Flanagan nodded. "That is a difficulty, Mr. Mullan. I'm rather afraid we have caught you in the act of proposing an *ex post facto* law."

"What's that?" Mullan said.

Andrew piped up, "The constitution says you can't pass a law retroactively punishing things people have already done."

"That would be Article One," Flanagan said. "Section . . . ah . . ."

"Section nine," Andrew said. This was pretty impressive. He went on. "I've been looking into that, sir. The courts have been fuzzy about whether denial of a benefit is really an *ex post facto* law. For example, in Flemming versus Nestor—this was about cutting off Social Security for a guy who'd been a Communist—in that case, Justice Harlan found—"

Flanagan shook his head. "Perhaps you could summarize." A shame; Andrew had been studying so hard. "Can we do this retroactively or can we not?"

"It's hard to say."

"A very lawyerlike response. I think . . ." He shut his eyes for a moment. "I think, constitution or no, it would be *ungracious* to make the provision retroactive. No, I think we shan't do it."

During the ensuing silence Flanagan kept looking at Joel— as if Joel knew the solution to their problem but was perversely refusing to supply it. Joel wondered: if he really did know the solution, would he supply it? For some crumb of approval from Matthew A. Flanagan, or just to make the man stop looking at him, would he help perfect this guided missile aimed straight at the hapless circuit boys, or at himself? Luckily he would never know the answer to this question, as he didn't have the solution to their problem.

Andrew did. He looked down at the floor and said, "I don't know that you . . . I mean, I'm not exactly sure that anybody knows when something happens."

He didn't say any more. After a few seconds Flanagan smiled

and said, "Was that merely a phenomenological observation?"

"Sir?" Andrew said. Flanagan smiled more broadly. He loved saying things that went over people's heads. Possibly he had never drawn the connection between this pastime and the fact that he had never, in twenty years, passed a major bill. Andrew was undaunted. "I just mean that, you know, this is all about, really, the incubation period of the virus, or whatever. I mean, the budget people are using this assumption of five or six years. That somebody who shows up now must have been infected years ago. But that's a factual question. Congress can make its own findings of fact."

"Mister . . . ah . . ."

"Crawford."

"Mister Crawford, I could insert in the preamble to a piece of legislation an assertion that the world was flat, and Congress could enact it, but I should not thereby have made the world flat. Nor can I legislate the incubation period of a virus."

"I don't mean that. I mean—nobody can really know, in any particular case, just how much time goes by between somebody getting infected and when they start getting symptoms. It must vary. So what you could do is write a rebuttable presumption into the law."

"A rebuttable presumption," Flanagan repeated.

"Right. Anyone who shows up with symptoms *after* the effective date would be assumed to have been infected *after* the effective date, but they'd be allowed to rebut that."

Joel looked over at Andrew. Who was leaning forward, hands gripping the arms of his chair as if he were about to be ejected from it, he was that excited. And proud. See: he wasn't stupid.

"How would they rebut the presumption?" Flanagan said.

"By . . . I don't know, showing some evidence that they, whatever, had it before the effective date."

"Well, that isn't so burdensome, is it?"

"No, sir. They'd just have to have a positive test result or something."

Joel couldn't keep quiet any longer. "Nobody has that," he said. "People don't get a piece of paper that says 'John Smith has HIV.'"

"They don't?" Flanagan said.

"No, the way it works is you go and get tested and they just give you a number. And then you go back with your number and they tell you the result." From the way Flanagan looked at him, Joel supposed that he had betrayed an excessive familiarity with the process. He went on anyway. "They don't hand out little certificates."

"Very well, then, perhaps it will be a rather difficult presumption to rebut." Flanagan turned back to Andrew, beaming. "Just how would you propose to draft this?"

"You'd just . . . uh . . . you'd just say that anyone determined to be infected with the human immunodeficiency virus after the effective date would (a) be deemed to be infected as a result of an act performed after the effective date unless (b) they could demonstrate in a form to be prescribed by the Secretary that they were infected before the effective date."

Flanagan clapped his hands. "There we have it."

They had it. Andrew had fixed it all by himself. Did he understand this, that he had personally crafted a door that could be slammed in the face of whatever kid from the Pledge had given him his hickey? Could be slammed in Andrew's own face, unless he was being a very good boy. Maybe he was, maybe he never slipped for an instant, maybe he thought he was galaxies away from the circuit boys. Them. Or maybe he just didn't think it was real. Here in this office with its view of the dome, it was so easy to string words together, recite your (a)s and (b)s, and imagine that they didn't refer to anyone. How many times had Joel himself played this game?

"Except," Joel said. "Except you don't get Medicare until you've been on disability for two years. So the earliest you'd get any savings would be two years from now."

Mullan said, "That's still in the budget window."

"It is," Flanagan said. "Indeed it is."

"So we've got our savings. As long as it's any time in the first five years." Mullan, in his exuberance, had the temerity to pound Flanagan's desk. Andrew himself was smiling modestly at his triumph.

Joel was not smiling. Flanagan noticed. "Sir, I take it you disapprove of this proposal."

Joel stammered, "I . . . I'm not supposed to say. I mean, I'm with OLA, we're not supposed to give you our opinion."

"I'm on your oversight committee. I dispense you from that vow."

"Okay, I guess I don't much like the bill."

"And don't like working on it."

"Oh, well, you know, I don't necessarily like every proposal I help with."

"What is your concern?"

"I—" If his concern wasn't obvious, how could he possibly convey it? He wished he could somehow bring the world into the room. Or just one person, one living person determined to be infected with the human immunodeficiency virus. "I just think . . . this might hurt some people."

Flanagan nodded. "I should hate to do that. I am able to support this undeniably rather odious piece of legislation with only transitory regret because—to tell you the truth—I suspect it will have no practical consequences whatsoever. No matter what savings might be attributed to it by the budget office."

"Maybe not."

Flanagan leaned forward. "It is all paper, Mr. Lingeman." He had registered Joel's name; he had sensed something about Joel the minute they had all walked in. "You and I and the budget office, we all perform the dance of legislation on paper. We shall score a paper savings, our act will be enshrined in the volume of public laws for this year, the executive branch will, in its usual dilatory way, fail to execute it. We shall receive, some years hence, a report from the Comptroller General dolefully informing us that the expected savings did not materialize. Do you understand? No one is going to die in the streets."

Joel glanced around him. Everybody was looking at the floor, everybody was embarrassed for him. "Paper is important," he said. "It doesn't matter if nothing ever comes of it, maybe it's even worse if nothing ever comes of it. Because then it's just an insult. If you don't save any money, it's just a gratuitous insult."

"Insult to . . ."

"People had rights. The whole idea of Medicare was that everybody earned it, everybody paid in all their lives and they had a right to it when they needed it." Joel needed a job. It was absolutely time to shut up. "It's the only thing that made us one country, Medicare and Social Security. It said we were all in this together. And this bill, it . . . it says we weren't. We weren't after all."

Flanagan opened his mouth, ready to let forth some torrent of polysyllabic abuse. Or two syllables: you're fired. The man was on the goddamn joint committee that oversaw the OLA, he could make it happen just by picking up the phone. Joel sat up straight, ready to be fired, proud as he had ever been. Flanagan closed his mouth, just looked at Joel for a while. His bloodshot eyes, above the rim of his half-moon reading glasses, fixed on Joel. At last he said, "Are you of the affected persuasion?"

"The what?" Joel said, although he knew the what. He glanced over at Andrew, who was still staring at the floor, as if there might be an escape hatch in the carpet. "You mean am I gay?"

"I'm sorry, I withdraw the question."

Joel swallowed. He didn't mind saying he was gay: of all the things he'd said in the last five minutes, it was the one he *couldn't* be fired for. He minded that Flanagan would think that was the point. That Joel's objections had nothing to do with any grand vision of American solidarity, but with a selfish and parochial desire to go on indulging in high-risk behaviors without consequence. He minded that Flanagan was looking at him and picturing him engaged in an act or pattern of acts performed voluntarily by an individual and determined by the Secretary . . .

"As it happens," Joel said.

"I truly am sorry. It's of absolutely no importance to me. As you may know, I have consistently supported measures to prevent discrimination against homosexuals."

"Yes, sir." It was true, he had. "That just——"

"That just makes it harder to understand how I could support this bill. How could I be so—you may select the epithet—inconsistent? Hypocritical? Pharisaical?" He sat back, as if actually waiting for Joel to pick one. Then he took off his half-moon glasses, folded them, placed them precisely on the desk before him. Joel recognized this gesture from a hundred committee meetings. It meant Flanagan was about to give a speech.

"I was elected to the House in the year nineteen-hundred-and-sixty-four." He intoned the year as if chiseling it on a cornerstone. "The following year, President Johnson escalated—in the word current at the time—escalated our involvement in the conflict in Vietnam. A year after that, or perhaps two, there was a large manifestation in the capital by citizens opposed to the war."

"The march on the Pentagon," Joel said.

"That is correct. As it happens, I was one of the very first members of Congress to speak out against the war and to predict the inevitable outcome of our misadventure." Maybe this was so; though, even more than most senators, Flanagan tended to recall only those predictions that came true. His epitaph would probably read, "I told you so."

"Accordingly, I was asked to participate in the march. I pointed out to the organizers that they were gathered pursuant to 'the right of the people peaceably to assemble, and to petition the Congress for a redress of grievances.'" This was only

332

a slight misquotation. "I therefore regretted that I could not join them, as I would have been in the paradoxical position of petitioning myself." Flanagan raised his eyebrows, the way he always did when he turned a phrase he thought was destined for Bartlett's. Joel felt himself smiling admiringly. He had practically called the man an asshole, and the sycophancy region of his brain stem was forcing his face into an involuntary smile.

"This was not merely a witticism," Flanagan said. "Although I had made my opposition to the war plain, I was a participant in the body that continued to fund it. Indeed, I myself had voted for the defense appropriations bill that very year. You might say that this was hypocritical."

Joel did not say this. Flanagan went on. "In fact, I voted as I did under some duress. There is in my old district an installation named—you might find this rather amusing—Fort Dix."

"I've heard of it," Joel said. Under torture he would not have admitted that it was amusing.

"Fort Dix was, at the time, the Army's principal basic training facility in the northeast, and a source of not inconsiderable revenue for my constituents. That year, however, the Pentagon suggested that the temperate climate of New Jersey made Fort Dix a less than suitable venue in which to condition young men for the rigors of counterinsurgency in the jungle. They might be better acclimated, in a word, if they were to spend their initiatory weeks in, say, South Carolina. Which happened to be the home state of the chairman of the Armed Services Committee, a gentleman of stupefying seniority named Mendel Rivers.

"I was a gentleman of no seniority whatsoever. There was nothing I could do about it. As it happened, there were other members of the New Jersey delegation who were more favorably situated. The base was never actually in danger. But I didn't know that, not when the defense appropriations came up for a vote. It was intimated to me that, if I were to vote

No on the defense bill and if the base should subsequently close, the electorate might perceive, however erroneously, a causal relationship.

"I have often wondered why they troubled to intimidate me. I was an inconsequential member, the defense appropriations always passed overwhelmingly, my vote was supererogatory. I have concluded that I was presented with this dilemma—possibly at the direction of the President himself—precisely in order to impress upon me my own inconsequentiality. A junior member from New Jersey was not supposed to question the infallibility of the Commander-in-Chief.

"I voted Aye to preserve my seat. Not because I required the employment. I could have returned to Rutgers, or found tenure at any number of more august institutions. But I thought I was doing some good being in the House. My vote on the defense appropriations bill did no harm, and it allowed me to do some good.

"Do you see? Our little amendment will in all probability visit no actual harm on any living person, and the chimerical savings attributed to it will finance some tangible benefits to many persons living in New Jersey. Their gratitude will, in turn, allow me to retain this seat and go on doing what good I can. Including, perhaps, putting this aging frame in the way of some more palpable threats to the well-being of persons of your orientation."

Joel nodded. What else could he do but nod? Ask the man to list all the good things he had done? Probably there was a list, probably in thirty years on the Hill Flanagan had done any number of good things that he would be delighted to recite. And he wasn't a Fulbright, was he? He wasn't like Fulbright, nigger-baiting back in Arkansas every six years so he could return to Washington and be a statesman, Flanagan wasn't as spectacularly contemptible as that. He was just ordinarily contemptible.

"I see," Joel said.

Flanagan gave a curt nod of forgiveness, then turned back to Andrew. "Let us go on, shall we?"

Joel saw. He needed the job. He needed to keep those twenties flowing into his billfold, so that they could mysteriously disappear. He saw that he wasn't young enough to storm out of the room and into some other life, some other country.

He stayed in the room, said nothing more and looked out the window at the lovely autumn afternoon. He said nothing more, he wasn't helping. Not like Andrew, also of the affected persuasion, who was writing out his brilliant amendment on a yellow legal pad. Joel wasn't helping, it didn't matter if he stayed in the room.

ten

"When are you leaving?" Michael said.

"What?" Joel was in the kitchen, getting coffee. He was sad to hear Michael's voice. Six in the morning: usually Michael slept another hour or so. Joel could read the paper, pick his nose, just be himself for an hour before pulling together the Joel he presented to Michael.

"Isn't this the day you go to New York?"

"I can't go, we're on call."

"On call?"

"They're finishing up the budget bill. So they might need me for, you know, odds and ends."

"Oh. Well, great, that means you'll be here tonight."

Joel made Michael's coffee. Nondairy creamer, sugar substitute: he was stocking these things now. "I'll be here, but I might be working."

"At night?"

"You see, they have to pass this omnibus bill to keep the

336

government running for another year. Just this one bill. So they stick in everything they never got around to, all the other stuff they never passed. It's the last train leaving the station."

"Oh," Michael said again—curtly, to forestall any lengthy exposition of the budget process. Joel brought him his coffee. He was in Joel's widowed club chair, wearing boxer shorts with smiley faces on them.

"Anyway, I'll probably be up all night."

"All night? Shit."

"That's how it works. They do every little thing the very last night."

Joel sat down on the sofa and opened the *Times*. Michael watched him. "You want a piece?" Joel said.

"That's okay."

Joel couldn't focus on any of the headlines, he was too conscious that Michael was just sitting there. Sitting attractively, in his merry boxer shorts. Sitting quietly, contentedly, thinking not one single thing. Joel put his paper down. I'm-happy-I'm-happy-I'm-happy.

The phone rang. Joel raced for it with relief: it had to be Herb, telling him the marathon was beginning.

"Joel."

"Hey, Herb. We're starting already?"

"We're not starting at all. It's a snow day."

"What?"

"The President vetoed the CR last night and they didn't pass another one." The continuing resolution, the stopgap measure that kept the government going, twenty-four hours at a time, until the President and Congress could agree on the final budget.

"There's no CR?"

"Don't you read the paper? The government's closed. The Washington Monument's closed. Old Faithful is not allowed to erupt. And OLA will not be open for business."

"But—I mean, they must still be working on an agreement. They're probably going to need me to help with stuff."

"You're forbidden to help. You can't work. You can't go into any government building."

"Oh."

"You sound disappointed," Herb said.

"I guess I just wanted them to get it over with."

"It's going to be a while. They say they might be shut down for a few days."

"Really?"

"They're waiting to see who blinks first. The paper says it'll be the Congress."

"You think?"

"They're the ones who'll get the calls when the Social Security checks don't show up in the mailboxes. Anyway, enjoy your holiday."

When he had hung up, Joel said, "The federal government's closed."

"The whole government?" Michael said. "Schools and everything?"

"No, the federal government doesn't run the . . ." It was too much to explain. "Anyway, I get the day off."

"No kidding. Maybe I'll call in, too. It's supposed to be a beautiful day."

"Great," Joel said. Then: "No."

"What? Oh. You're going to New York."

"I don't know. Maybe I shouldn't."

Michael shrugged. "You're going to go sooner or later."

"Maybe. It'd be nice to spend the day with you."

"Right."

"What do you mean?"

"I saw you looking at me. Just now, before the phone rang. You were wishing I'd go away."

"Jesus." There wasn't any point denying it. "Just for a little while. I was just wishing you'd go back to bed for a little while so I could read my paper."

"I don't see how I keep you from reading your paper."

338

"I don't know. Look, why don't you get dressed and we'll go out for breakfast?"

"I got to get home, change for work. If you're not going to be here, I'm going to work."

"Are you mad at me?"

"No, I just might as well work." Michael stood up, decisively, but then didn't move. His body seemed to sag a little, above the expanse of smiley faces. "God, I hate work."

"I thought you liked your job."

"I hate it. Sometimes I just want to quit, go back to school or something."

"You should," Joel said, dismissively. Right: you don't even read the morning paper, and you're going back to college.

"I can't." Michael sat down. "I, you know, I owe money on my cards and I . . . I just can't."

"I could—" Joel began. He didn't know how to finish the sentence. He knew the predicate should specify some kind of assistance. I could help you out a little. I could let you have the exercise room. I could pay your tuition. I could adopt you.

It had come up so suddenly, this moment. Had Michael turned the conversation in this direction? No, he was just whining about work. Everybody whined about work, it didn't mean they were looking for a sugar daddy.

"I could help you out a little."

Joel was a GS-15, step 9. His income was close to six figures, he thought, before all the deductions. He made enough that he wasn't sure what he made, and he didn't spend it on cars or clothes or any travel except the occasional essential trip to places like Roseville, New Jersey. He could afford Michael. He could keep him openly, give him an allowance that would spare him the necessity of raiding Joel's wallet—which must have been a little unpleasant to him, he must have felt some twinge every time he did it.

There wasn't even any reason either of them should be bashful about it. From each according to his ability. Joel had money and Michael had . . . everything but money.

Michael was quiet. Weighing this, probably. How much help could Joel provide? How long would it last—a semester? Long enough to get him through to a Doctor of Apparel Science? What would it be like, being helped? What could it cost him, more than he was already giving? Giving away, or practically. At last he said, "That's okay."

If the entire exchange had occurred a few days earlier, Joel would have thought: of course, he has his dignity, he must think I'm patronizing him. This morning, though, only Joel's dignity was in question. He didn't mind being taken; he minded being taken for a fool. "I've sort of already been helping you out," he said.

"You mean, like, dinner? You pay for dinner? You're the one wants to go all these places. I wouldn't care if we went to McDonald's. Or we can stay in sometimes, I can cook." Michael grinned. "Maybe not goat."

Joel smiled back. They already had a little bit of history together, what was his rush to kill it? "I don't even know where you can buy goat."

Sometimes with Sam he had felt, as now, the utter contingency, the improbability that he should be sitting in a room with a stranger and imagining that something connected them. When they were no more connected than a couple of randomly colliding particles. They had bounced into one another, one of them could bounce away in the next instant, all it would take would be a word or two. He could kill this in a word or two, or refrain, and the same would be true five minutes from now, or five years.

He knew he should shut up. He wasn't even certain: he'd tried to keep track of his money, these last few days, but he'd kept losing count. He was an old white guy, how was he supposed to remember whether he had $137 or $157? Twenty bucks: he'd made that much staring out the window at Senator Flanagan's office. He was making that much right now. When the government reopened, he'd be paid retroactively for sitting here with a beautiful man whose boxer shorts had smiley faces.

Which told him, one smirking face after another, that he was a loser. "How did you know I'd been to New York?"

"Huh?"

"I just . . . you know, I couldn't remember telling you about it, that I'd been to New York before."

Michael made a persuasive show of astonishment: where the fuck did this come from, why are we talking about this? "I don't know. You must have."

There were supposed to be signs, some ways that people more perceptive than Joel could detect a liar: he doesn't look at you, he covers his mouth as he speaks, he blushes. How would he know if Michael blushed?

"What is this about?" Michael said.

Joel blushed. "Nothing, never mind." He scurried off toward the kitchen so that Michael wouldn't see him cry. A few months ago he hadn't been able to make himself cry, now he seemed to cry at the drop of a hat. Or of an illusion. He managed to croak out: "Did you want more coffee?"

"No, I better get dressed."

"Okay. Why don't you take your shower first, I can wait."

"Fine."

Joel took his shower second, dried himself, found his glasses, stepped out into the bedroom. Michael was gone.

Joel had meant to go to New York, check into the Sheridan Square, take a nap, go out and have drinks and dinner, and make his way to Roseville the next morning. But as the train pulled into Newark he found himself getting off. He'd only brought a change of linen stuffed into his briefcase, there wasn't any need to go to the hotel.

He had twenty minutes to wait for the next train on the Kilmer line. Not enough time for a drink, really; not to mention that the little bar in the station didn't look like the kind of place where you went in and asked for a pinot gris. He went out to the street for a cigarette.

Had he ever before set foot in New Jersey? Maybe a Howard Johnson's on the Turnpike. Past that, it was just a mythical place, the absolute inverse of Arcadia or Cockaigne. You said New Jersey and you thought of a burning rubber tire. Yet Newark, which he had casually assumed would resemble Hiroshima or Dresden, was just an ordinarily dilapidated eastern city. Except that his was, as far as he could see, the only white face in the crowd in front of the train station.

He had meant to use these minutes to think, finally, about what he might possibly say to his quarry. But he couldn't focus just now. He scanned the landscape, trying to settle on a good site for the biotechnology innovation zone. As his head swiveled around he couldn't help noticing that there were any number of hot men standing around. He didn't let his eyes rest on any of them, not for a nanosecond. Someone had warned him once: don't stare at black guys, they'll think you're dissing them and then they'll cut you.

He supposed he was safe; probably there was some little perimeter around the station that was patrolled enough to assure that Amtrak passengers weren't randomly murdered. But he didn't look. He felt a little thrill of danger as his eyes zipped past the vacant spaces where there was something he wasn't supposed to look at. Along with some indignation: I'm here, I have a right to look at anything. Who are you people to tell me what I can look at?

You people. Did Michael know that, deep inside, Joel still thought "you people?" Probably. He seemed to know every-thing else. Maybe that was what Joel couldn't tolerate, finally: that Michael knew everything about Joel, about himself, about each moment he passed through. Or knew all he cared to know, certainly an important distinction. Joel was the only one who needed to know stuff.

He ground out his cigarette and immediately lit another; it

was a long ride to Roseville. Twelve-thirty. Michael was at Hecht's, dealing with the lunch crowd. Of course he hated that job, must have hated his whole life: helping someone choose a tie or counting packets of underwear, going home to his cell on T Street to change, then hurrying to meet a dumpy, depressed old man who insisted, absolutely demanded that Michael tell him the obvious, that he was a dumpy, depressed old man. How tiresome for Michael, no wonder he had walked out. He had given Joel so much at such a bargain price. Michael had offered up his beauty and youth and life for the price of dinner and the occasional scarcely missed gratuity, and all Joel had had to do was shut up about it.

He had killed it. Sacrificed a chance—surely his last chance—for ordinary happiness, because he needed to know stuff he already knew. As he had made this trip in order to make the vital discovery that it wasn't 1964 and New Jersey was not New Mexico.

He had tried happiness. If he was only going once through this life, why shouldn't he do what he wanted, rather than what would make him happy?

Why should he have imagined that he would step off the train in some hamlet thirty miles from the city and find taxis waiting?

From the platform outside the station he saw, through a window, a ticket agent. But when he stepped inside, there was a shade pulled down over the ticket booth. On the shade, in black letters: "Ticket Agent 6 A.M.–2 P.M." It was only one-thirty. Joel bent down and called through the slot below the shade, "Hello." There was no answer. He went back outside, stood in front of the open window to the ticket office. The agent looked back at him incuriously, as if he were an image on a television screen, not a live person standing four feet away from her.

She was a large black woman, with a blue shirt and a necktie. Joel thought, sequentially, perhaps, but it was almost as if he

343

were thinking all these things at once: you are a lazy Negro who got this job through some quota, I am a despicable racist, I can't really be a racist if I recognize it, you're lazy anyway or you wouldn't have closed early, you're looking at me with hatred so you must be a racist too, I would probably look at me with hatred if I were you, I just want to ask a question, can't we just deal with each other like humans. And finally: I am enacting this national drama all by myself, she's just sitting there while a strange man stares at her through her window.

"Excuse me," Joel said. She just stared, and he went on. "I was wondering how you get a taxi here."

She sighed. "I don't know, honey." So sadly, as if she had been wondering the same thing for years. "Maybe you could call one."

"Uh-huh. Do you—" There was really no point asking the question. "Do you happen to know a number?"

She shook her head mournfully. Joel wondered if Michael's mother looked like this.

"Oh. Well, could I get some change?"

"I'm closed." Rather sternly: you can see I'm closed, do you think you're somebody special?

"Oh." It didn't matter: it wasn't as if he could call information and expect the semi-animate being at the other end to tell him how to get a taxi in Roseville, New Jersey. "Do you have any idea where Bridge Street is?"

"Bridge Street? Why, honey, that's Bridge Street right out there. Why would you want a taxi to take you to Bridge Street?" She shook her head—this was one stupid white boy—and probably went on shaking it as Joel made his way through the parking lot, packed tight with commuters' cars, and out to the street.

The bridge for which the street was named crossed the New Jersey Transit tracks. It led from the right side to the wrong side. Joel had never fully understood this expression until he saw how, to the west of the tracks, Victorian piles were scattered on a gently rising hill with oak and maple trees; in their driveways were Range Rovers and Mercedes station wagons.

To the east, Bridge Street marched straight by a couple of blocks of three-story shingled tenements, then softened into a curve as it entered a sea of ranch houses. A development from the fifties, probably, the houses bought with GI loans. Each still had an antenna on the roof, though cable must surely have got to Roseville by now. Joel guessed Petras Baranauskas had not grown up in one of the big houses on the hill. He headed east.

It was Indian summer, if that phrase was still permissible. Native American summer, then; anyway, warm enough that Joel took off his jacket before he'd gone half a block. He was right, the house numbers were ascending: 1261 when the tenements gave way to what a faded sign declared was Roseville Meadows, 1507 after a bend in Bridge Street that made Joel lose sight of the station. Probably 1693 would be past that next bend.

Joel stopped, trying to ready himself. For what was he planning to do? It wasn't just that he hadn't thought what to say, in the second or two he was likely to get before the door slammed in his face, what few words might sum up everything. He wasn't even sure whom the words would be for. Was there really something he wanted Petras Baranauskas to know, to carry away from this encounter? Or was it that he was trying to craft in advance his own memory? I stood before him and I said . . . Whichever, he was already thinking past the moment. He was walking toward Petras's house with no intention except to walk away from it, not to be there but to have been there. This calmed him, oddly. In a few minutes, he would have been there and would be walking back toward the train station. Unless Petras actually, say, shot him, nothing was going to happen in the next few minutes that he couldn't walk away from.

He heard singing behind him, or sing-songing, and turned to see a dark, Latino-looking woman holding the hand of a little boy with blond hair. She was walking briskly, the babbling kid could barely keep up with her. Joel realized that she was hurrying to get past him, because he was a stranger, a pedestrian in streets

345

not meant for them. The little boy went "Hi." Joel answered "Hi there!" in the bright voice he used with children and the occasional slower congressman. The woman glared and tugged the boy along still faster.

Joel was a stranger on a pilgrimage, like some movie star passing through a village on his way to visit a lama. Except the way to a lama was much clearer. First, you saw some guys with saffron robes and horn-rimmed glasses, they gave you yak milk while they instructed you in the appropriate way to approach the sage, you passed through this portal and that vestibule and at last came before him. Both of you were ready, the sage nodded calmly, prepared to deliver an inscrutable answer to whatever question you had come so far to ask.

Sometimes, when he was young, Joel had thought about going to see some holy man. Auden, except he died. Kerouac, except he died. He never went: maybe he was smarter when he was a kid, maybe he knew these great men would have nothing to impart to him except Scram. Perhaps it was, objectively, risible that Joel had journeyed at last only to see a man whose great achievement was that he took his clothes off once. But the guy would probably say Scram as eloquently as Auden would have done.

Joel continued up the street, rounded the bend, and saw, just a couple of houses away: in the driveway, a young man, wearing only cutoffs, hosing down a Mustang. His muscular back was turned to Joel, he was facing an uncovered front porch on which stood the dark woman and her toddler. Next to them an old man sat in an aluminum lawn chair. The woman was saying something. The young man shut off the water and listened to her. The woman pointed straight at Joel: there he is. The young man turned.

For one vertiginous instant, the split-second it took the young man to turn around, Joel thought he was going to see the Santa Fe boy. As perhaps some believers, in the moment of their death, must be giddily confident that they are about to see the

346

pearly gates—Joel was just that certain. If you flipped to page 174, you would unfailingly be presented with the smile, the golden immaculate torso. Joel had, only for that instant, the sensation that life was as sure, as fixed in its order, as the pages of a magazine.

The young man turned, his coarse, stupid face unsmiling, his torso—a good third of which was blazoned with a tattoo whose argument Joel could not decipher from so far away—tensed. Not a gift he was giving, but a threat. Joel didn't belong on this street, strangers didn't walk down streets in Roseville Meadows. On the porch, the old man stood up to get a better look. He folded his arms across his chest, a powerful chest for such an old man.

Everyone was looking at Joel, even the little boy stood quite still, looking. Joel looked back. At the Santa Fe boy, at his son in the driveway, at his grandson, who reached up now to take his hand. The hand of a patriarch: he and his generations of men looked intently at Joel, who had come into their world like some kind of virus.

Joel called out, "I was trying to get to the train station."

No one said anything for a minute. Ridiculous, obviously he wasn't near the train station, he might as well have said he was looking for the Eiffel Tower.

The Santa Fe boy stepped forward to the edge of the porch and said—so gently and seriously, in a low voice Joel could scarcely hear: "You've come the wrong way."

In Penn Station, Joel passed a newsstand that had an electronic ticker in the window:

```
... REDS 11, METS 7 ... FRIDAY: SUNNY, HIGH
78 ... PRESIDENT, CONGRESS BREAK BUDGET
IMPASSE ... NOBEL PRIZE IN MEDICINE TO ...
```

President, Congress Break Budget Impasse. They'd done the deal—suddenly, it always happened suddenly. This was the night they'd write up all the technicals, so the bill could go to the floor in the morning and all the members could fly home. This was the night, and Joel wasn't there; probably Herb had been frantically calling him all afternoon. He was in big trouble, but if he caught the five o'clock Metroliner he could be on the Hill by eight or so. People would just be buckling down, finishing off the free pizza brought in by the Lutheran Hospital Association or the National Academy of Proctology, ready to put the finishing touches on the rural hospital amendments or the Harris–Flanagan amendment on HIV. He could still get there in time.

He sprinted for the ticket counter, stopped short. There had to be fifty people in line. They all looked like the kind of people who wanted to go to Nebraska and would try to negotiate with the ticket agent in Croatian. Joel would stand behind them, watching as the digital clock flashed 4:50, 4:55, and his head would explode. He ran to the machine where you could buy a ticket with a credit card, but there was a sign: it was out of order, thank you for riding Amtrak.

A sign: he was not supposed to catch the Metroliner. He was supposed to stay in New York and tomorrow he was supposed to go back to Roseville and blurt out some inanity at Grandpa Baranauskas.

As he rode up the escalator to the street, he thought: he wouldn't lose his job, not for one truancy. Not to mention that he didn't need the job, as there would no longer be any particular reason to keep his wallet stuffed with twenties. Maybe Michael had just been in a hurry? No, he would at least have called to Joel through the bathroom door. He was gone, gone.

Eighth Avenue was one-way the wrong way. If he wanted a cab to Sheridan Square he should have gone out the other end of the station. But it was still beautiful out, and what were twenty blocks or so?

At each cross street the sun, low over New Jersey, seemed to burn a path for itself straight across the island. In between,

Joel saw fathers. A million other people, but he noticed only the fathers—this one holding a kid by the hand, this one with a kid on his shoulders, this one lecturing a dark, gawky son who was . . . almost ripe, a few years short of legal, and already a knockout. Old man, do you know that your son is beautiful, do you know that there are predators ready to jump him as soon as you let him out of your sight? Probably he did know.

If Joel had thought about it, he would have expected that Petras was a father. That if Petras had accomplished nothing else these thirty years, he would—even if just inadvertently—have managed to breed. Why should this have made Joel feel so sad, marginal, useless? So his particular complement of chromosomes would not be replicated. So he had missed all those wonderful experiences, changing diapers, paying college tuition. Hell, he could still have that experience if he wanted—if not with Michael, then with some other kid. There were plenty of guys at Gentry ready to suck an old man dry. He could adopt any one of them and have both the cardinal joys of fatherhood. Writing checks. Knowing somebody would jump your kid as soon as you let him out of your sight.

South of Twenty-third Street, he stopped looking at fathers and started looking at non-fathers. A scattering at first, then little gaggles, by Eighteenth Street whole herds of men who would have made the young Peter Barry look like the sucker who gets sand kicked in his face. They wore baseball caps and T-shirts; many had shaved their heads; nearly all had pierced themselves in multiple places. As if their own meticulously sculpted bodies were voodoo dolls: if I stick it here, Daddy will get such a migraine.

Any other day Joel might just have looked around and thought: my, all these hot boys. He might have been a little sad that he couldn't have all of them or, probably, any. Or he might have felt some little stab of regret—nothing so sharp, more the momentary surfacing of the numb regret that was always there, that he hadn't lived the *life* when he was younger. The life! Going from work to the long mandatory hours at the gym, home to an apartment the size of Joel's kitchen, stopping only to pick out just the right baseball cap, and heading out to the bars. Ending the evening in some sort of random coupling, hardbodies in collision.

If he had dared, if he had dared, if he had lived: he would be dead. He could have come here and joined the great party he always knew was going on without him, and he would be dead now, as surely as if he'd been shot down in some rice paddy. Instead he had won the lottery; he was still here. Still here, for no apparent purpose. Here: his whole vision darkened, as he scanned the pageant of Chelsea boys, by a thunderhead of despair and loss.

They were all so grim, wary, their eyes turned a little sideways, or half-inward. It looked as though they were . . . trying hard to remember something. That was the look. As sometimes you will see a walker suddenly stop, his face stricken: where was I headed? They were lost, constantly looking about for some sign, anything that might remind them of where they originally were headed. And at the same time knowing where they were headed, where everyone is headed.

What on earth was as mortal as these faggots? Young and beautiful and sterile as mules. And running headlong to death. These guys would have Medicare when they were thirty. If they were quick about it, if they hurried up and got their certificates before the budget bill passed tomorrow. They were burning themselves up, squeezing everything out of the time they had. And why shouldn't they, if the alternative was to grow old and turn into Joel? No wonder they averted their eyes as they passed him. He might as well have been striding down Eighth Avenue in a black robe, brandishing a scythe. There was nothing else ahead of them, they would live and die and leave nothing.

Because they didn't make babies, for Christ's sake? Did he

really think that Petras Baranauskas, sitting on his front porch and vacantly watching his son wash a car, had a life full of meaning and fulfillment? That he was any less bewildered about what he was here for, or any less scared of leaving, because he had seen to it that there would be a few more Baranauskases in the Roseville, New Jersey, phone book?

Maybe, when he didn't look straight at the camera, when he looked a little sideways, he was seeing what everybody else did. Maybe he trembled like everybody else.

Joel checked in at the Sheridan Square, left his briefcase in the room, had dinner at the bar in a Belgian place that served baskets of pommes frites and mayonnaise for dipping them in. He had two baskets, and then some mussels. There was no one around to call him a piggy.

When he got back to his room, the message light on the phone was blinking. Who? Herb, probably, saying they were close to agreement, Joel had better haul his ass back tonight and pitch in or said ass would be on the street. But of course it couldn't be Herb. There was only one person who knew where Joel was.

"Hey. I guess you're out whoring around. Just kidding. Just wanted to see how your . . . mission went. And . . . uh . . . tell you I miss you. Call me as soon as you get home."

Joel played it back a couple of times, went to the window and looked out into the airshaft. Michael, what you need to do is hop the train up here, become a Sales Associate, Men's Apparel, at Macy's or Bloomingdale's, and head straight to the clubs. Pierce yourself, tattoo yourself, throw yourself into this world while you're still young. Stay away from old white guys, because they are piggy and will devour you.

He played the message again. Was there some way of preserving it, could the hotel give him a copy on tape or something? No: it would just be erased when he checked out. It was a gift for this one night only; when he left this room, he would leave it behind. He played it over and over, so it would stay in his head. So he could play it in his head when he got old.

On the train the next morning, the local to Newark, he read: "President, Congress Reach Budget Compromise." They had done a million things to taxes, Medicare, welfare. A whole inside page was full of bullet points and pie charts, and then facing that another half page, labeled "NEWS ANALYSIS," about this or that new loophole—ornaments on the Christmas tree, as they said on the Hill—and which corporation had paid which member to obtain it. He read both pages through a second time and still couldn't find anything about the Harris amendment. But they did say the drug companies had gotten their tax break. So maybe the Harris amendment was in the package, or maybe they'd found some other way to pay for biotechnology innovation zones. He'd better find out by Monday. Staffers would be calling, wondering what their members had voted for.

What he should do when he got off in Newark was catch the next southbound Amtrak, get over to the office and see if anybody had the conference agreement yet. Or maybe skip it, just go straight over to Hecht's and let Michael pick him out a new pair of pants. Because he had Belgian mayonnaise on these and hadn't brought a change.

When he got off in Newark he transferred to the Kilmer line.

Petras Baranauskas was on his front porch again, reading the paper. So he didn't see Joel's approach—or rather, failure to approach: Joel stood a long time, maybe fifty yards away, looking at Petras. Not, on this second foray, nerving himself, or trying to think what to say. Just looking, at Petras and at the banal landscape that surrounded him. Trying to take it all in, consciously prolonging the moment. Trying to pay attention, to everything, for just one minute of his life.

He couldn't: there was too much to see, even here in blasted New Jersey. Houses, trash cans, parked cars. Trees, shrubs, grass. Human artifacts, inorganic, dead; vegetable life filling in every empty space with futile exuberance; a man on his front porch. No reason for the eye to be drawn to any one of these things instead of another. The figure of a man on his porch did not reward Joel's attention any more than, say, the tricycle on the sidewalk, the crabgrass on the lawn, the clouds in the sky. Except that he happened to have come all this way to see the man. This journey was about his having intended it, somehow.

He finished the journey, walked closer to Petras. Actually thinking: now I am a hundred feet away, now fifty. He could, with each stride, cover some part of the distance between them, he could never get all the way. All the way: that would have meant being inside Petras. Anything less was to be at some distance from him.

The distance just a couple of yards now. Petras lowered his paper and looked at Joel through the upper part of his bifocals. He didn't get up, just sat looking calmly.

What was he doing home, didn't he have a job? Maybe he was retired already. Or disabled. Fifty-five, he would have been, about the age when lots of working stiffs wore out. After five months they could get Social Security. Then, twenty-four months after that, Medicare.

Joel reached the porch steps, climbed the first one, stopped.

Petras said, "Hey," not in greeting, but as you might say it to a child or a pet, a gentle warning.

Joel didn't answer. He found himself looking, not at Petras, but at the newspaper. President, Congress Reach Budget Compromise. That seemed more real to him than the present moment.

"Can I help you?" Petras said.

Joel shook his head. No, you can't possibly help me.

Petras scratched his chest. "You still looking for the train station?"

"I—" Joel watched: Petras's liver-spotted hand scratching the little tangle of silver wire that showed above the V of his shirt collar. "I'm looking for Peter Barry."

Petras shivered. Joel heard Bate saying: you have no right.

"I haven't used that name in a long time."

"But you were Peter Barry?"

"I was." He didn't ask how Joel knew, or what Joel wanted from him. "For a little while."

He didn't need to ask what Joel wanted from him. He had been Peter Barry for a little while a long time ago. Whatever this stranger wanted from Peter Barry, there was no Peter Barry to give it to him.

"You were—" Joel began. He had thought he might just say, baldly, the only thing there was to say—you were beautiful—and hightail it back to the train station. But he had no right. Why? What kind of transgression was it to tell a man he was beautiful? Other than the obvious, that no one would be especially happy to hear this so emphatically in the past tense: you *were* beautiful. Still, wouldn't it be better to know that you had been beautiful even for an instant, and that there was someone who remembered? If Joel had been Peter Barry for one instant, wouldn't he want to know that someone had seen him and remembered? He finished: "You were in a picture. I saw it when I was a kid."

"When you were a kid."

"And I always remembered it. I don't know why, there was something about the picture."

"You don't know why," Petras repeated. With no particular inflection, nothing in his voice to say that he and Joel both knew damn well why. "So you come to see me because I was in this picture?"

"Yes."

Petras almost smiled. "You took your time."

"I did."

Petras let his paper drop to the porch floor, scratched his

354

chest again. He sighed. "What do you want to do, suck my dick?"

Joel was so shocked he stepped backwards. Into air—he had forgotten he'd gone up one step—then landed heavily, almost falling.

"No, Jesus," he said. Though of course he had to wonder, one last time, if that was what he really wanted, if it had always been as simple as that.

"No?" Petras said. "Cause there was guys used to want to do that."

"No kidding."

"Lots of guys. I wound up—I stopped going into the city for a long time. I'd be walking down the street and some guy would . . . look at me. I'd been in the city enough, I knew there was guys that looked at you. But I mean somebody would stand still and just look while I walked by, like I was a parade or something. So I'd know they seen that picture. I'd feel like punching them out. They seen that picture and they probably whacked off to it. And it was like they owned me, or like they took something from me."

"I never did," Joel said. He added, "Whack off." He wasn't sure about the other part, the part about taking something. "I just looked at it."

"You were a kid, you said."

"Fourteen."

"Fourteen." Petras shook his head sadly. Not sad, probably, about the time that had passed. Rather at the notion that some lonesome little faggot had looked at his picture. "I was . . . I don't know."

"You were twenty-three."

"Was I? You know all about me, huh? I got a fucking fan club."

"I guess." No point telling him he had a fucking religion.

Petras shook his head again, but he was smirking, maybe a little tickled by having a fan club. "Okay, I was twenty-three, if you say so. It was just some kind of joke, you know? Some girl said I should try modeling, I looked like a movie star or something, and somehow I got hooked up with this guy."

"Sexton."

"That was it, I met up with this Mr Sexton, and I thought, hey, I could make some change. Easy money." He snorted. "He only ever got me this one job. Under those hot lights for hours and hours. Wearing that goddamn little suit and . . . so embarrassed, and trying to smile."

"Were you embarrassed?"

"Shit, yeah. Guys didn't wear things like that. I thought of my friends back home, seeing that picture. I thought of my mother. I mean, I was proud of my built, I used to like showing off, at the beach or wherever, but not like that. And jeez, if I'd known—I mean, I was embarrassed, but if I'd known who was going to look at that picture . . ." He paused, looked away from Joel. He must just have realized what he had said: if he'd known that sick people like Joel were going to look. He didn't retract it.

"My buddies found out. I don't know how, it ain't like we all read that book—what was it?"

"*man about town*."

"Yeah. Somebody got hold of it, and they gave me shit, like it was a homo picture. So I'd say it was just a picture. I was me, and if homos looked at it, that didn't make me a homo. So, okay, they knew that. Except some asshole took it to my foreman and he didn't know that.

"I was working at Cooper-Dowd, you know, over in New Brunswick, they made airplane parts. Gone now. It was defense work, you had to have a clearance, and they started checking up on me. Like, it wasn't a crime to be in a picture, but I might have 'questionable associates.' That's what they said. And long as they were checking I couldn't work in the C building. Because I might draw a picture of a goddamn top-secret screw and give it to my homo associates.

356

"I didn't even know any homos. Except maybe Mr Sexton, you think maybe he was a homo?"

"I don't know."

"I guess he was, but he didn't try nothing. Anyway, I didn't know any homos, but they transferred me out of defense work. Which was where the good money was, I was pissed. And then they fucking wrote to my draft board."

"To tell them you were a . . . ?"

"To tell them I wasn't doing defense work. So there went my goddamn deferment. They had my ass in Fort Dix before I knew what hit me. Cause the Army didn't care if I was a homo, long as I could stand up and get shot at."

"Oh. Did you . . . did you go to . . ." He couldn't even say the name.

"Sure did. Got a Purple Heart."

"You did? I'm sorry."

"Yeah, see." He stood up, slowly unbuttoned his shirt. Spread it wide, so that Joel could see, on the belly that now sagged a little over the waistband of his trousers, the scar. Jagged and white, starting just below the navel and running down until it disappeared in the trousers. Those few inches of flesh, navel to waistband, that had been to Joel like the sun—torn, years ago, torn, disfigured, healed, the way things heal.

Petras didn't button his shirt again right away. He let Joel look for a second or two. At his chest, still powerful and firm but matted with silver hair, here or there a wart or a mole. At his white belly with its whiter scar.

Joel turned away, sat down on the porch step.

"What's the matter?" Joel couldn't answer; his eyes were filling with tears. Petras bent down and touched his shoulder. "Are you okay?"

The Santa Fe boy touched his shoulder.

"I'm sorry you got hurt."

"Shit, it wasn't no big deal. They patched me up. I'm still here."

357

"No, I——" I'm sorry you ever got hurt, that's what Joel meant to say. He was sorry about all the ways Petras must have been hurt since the day of that picture. But that was the same, wasn't it, as being sorry that Petras was still here? Because the only way he wouldn't have been hurt, scarred, the only way he could have stayed the boy in that picture would have been to die the instant after it was taken. Just as the only way Joel could have been the kid who saw that picture would have been to die right then, there in his boyhood room, the magazine slipping from his lifeless hands.

Petras stood up, backed away. Joel got up, too, turned to face him. To look at him one more time—the sleek arms and shoulders almost intact, the spare tire not too gross, just a sort of thickening all around his middle. As if it were a callus, as if he had grown it after being buffeted by all the travails of these decades.

He opened his hands, palms open in the immemorial gesture: I have nothing here. No weapon, no food, nothing in my hands. I have nothing to give you.

"You know, that picture didn't even look like me."

"What?"

"I never thought. I mean, you ever seen a picture of yourself and thought, that ain't me?"

"I guess."

"Guy must have taken a hundred pictures, I was under those lights for hours. And then he picks this one, this one shot where, just for a second, he caught me with this stupid shit-eating smile on my face."

Caught him. Froze him there forever, open to the gaze of strangers, predators. Of a baffled kid who turned the page of a magazine and felt the rush of blood to his head and maybe to his loins, maybe he could admit that now. Joel had known, the first minute he came upon that page and that image, when he snapped the magazine shut he had known that he was guilty of something. He had never thought that what he was

358

guilty of was injuring this stranger, as surely as if he himself had torn that innocent, once-perfect belly.

You have no right. There the boy was, caught with his shit-eating smile, the little crinkle about his eyes betraying, as Joel had always thought, some pain: pain at the thought that Joel would look at him.

"You let them take it," Joel said. "You let them take it, they printed it, there it was. I looked at it." He had a right to look. He had a right to be in this world and look, take from the world anything it would give him. He had a right to say, out loud, "You were beautiful."

"Is that what you come to tell me?"

"I guess you don't like that word."

"I don't care. It's kind of . . . your problem."

"Problem," Joel repeated. He shook his head. "You were put here to be beautiful, that one day, and I was put here to see it."

"That ain't what I was put here for," Petras said. If he had some other theory, he didn't supply it.

"All right," Joel said. "It's what *I* was put here for."

What else? He hadn't made babies, he hadn't cured cancer or written a novel, he hadn't even been there to write up the final agreement on the Harris amendment. He had seen the Santa Fe boy. Petras had radiated beauty one day in 1963, and in 1964 Joel had caught a glimpse of it, like a man watching from light years away the flash of a star that had died eons ago. By the time Joel saw it, it was already gone. But that's what people were here for, the only reason we were on the planet at all: so that a star that flared and died a billion years before we were born would not pass away unobserved.

Petras shivered, buttoned his shirt. "Was there anything else you wanted?"

"No. No, there isn't anything else I want. I better go catch my train." Joel started up Bridge Street. When he had gone a few steps, he turned around. Petras was already sitting, opening

359

his paper again. In another minute he would forget Joel had ever been there. Joel called out, "It was good seeing you."

Petras looked up and replied, with automatic politeness, "Good seeing you, too."

FOURTH ESTATE

The term "Fourth Estate," first coined during the French Revolution, is used to describe "the press." Thomas Carlyle, the pre-eminent historian of the Victorian era, attributed the original phrase to the British politician and political thinker Edmund Burke (1729–1797). According to Burke there were three "estates" in pre-Revolutionary France: the aristocracy, the clergy and the tiers état, or bourgeoisie. To this he added a "fourth estate": the press, who were the guardians of democracy and defenders of the public interest. Burke's model can be equally well applied to the British political system of the Lords Temporal, the Lords Spiritual and the Commons.

"Burke said there were Three Estates in Parliament; but, in the Reporters' Gallery yonder, there sat a Fourth Estate more important than they all. It is not a figure of speech, or a witty saying; it is a literal fact . . . Printing, which comes necessarily out of Writing, I say often, is equivalent to Democracy: invent Writing, Democracy is inevitable . . . Whoever can speak, speaking now to the whole nation, becomes a power, a branch of government, with inalienable weight in law-making, in all acts of authority. It matters not what rank he has, what revenues or garnitures: the requisite thing is that he have a tongue which others will listen to; this and nothing more is requisite."

Thomas Carlyle, *Heroes and Hero Worship in History* (1841)